STAR.WARS

The New Essential Guide to
Weapons and Technology

STAR WARS®
The New Essential Guide to Weapons and Technology

Written by W. Haden Blackman

Illustrated by Ian Fullwood

DEL REY
BALLANTINE BOOKS ▪ NEW YORK

LUCAS BOOKS

Author Acknowledgments

The *Star Wars* universe is constantly evolving and growing. Given countless comic books, novels, reference volumes, video games, articles, role-playing game sources, Web pages, collectibles, and now even cartoons and a persistent online game, it often seems as if the *Star Wars* galaxy doubles in size with each passing week. Therefore, I deeply value the friendship and support provided by all those *Star Wars* scholars and guides who have helped me navigate this ever-expanding universe.

I would like to thank Steve Saffel at Del Rey for patiently seeking me out whenever I was lost; Kathleen David for her sharp eye and attention to detail; and Jonathan Rinzler, Iain Morris, Sue Rostoni, Howard Roffman, and Leland Chee at Lucasfilm, who know every corner of the *Star Wars* galaxy better than Han Solo and always knew where to find me.

This galaxy is continually enriched by the work of literally thousands of other creators. I've had the pleasure of working alongside quite a few of them, including Camela McLanahan, Mike Gallo, Jim Tso, Peter Hirschmann, Brett Tosti, and Justin Lambros at LucasArts, who have made the galaxy even more fun to play in. I'd also like to thank the contributions of Dave Land and Randy Stradley at Dark Horse, who have gone beyond the borders of the known *Star Wars* universe and lived to tell about it. Special thanks must be given to Bill Smith, David Nakabayashi, and Troy Vigil, who provided the first complete treatise on the galaxy's weapons and technology. Of course, I also thank George Lucas for providing us a galaxy to expand in the first place.

And thank you to my wife, Anne-Marie, who has given up nearly every weekend for many months so that I could explore this galaxy far, far away.

Artist Acknowledgments

I would like to take this opportunity to thank my fellow illustrator and friend Paul Bates for many of the tremendous pieces of work within this book. Also thanks to artists Rob Garrard, Stuart Wagland, Nick Foreman, Phil Lunt, Tim Ball, and Sylvain Michaelis for his page and content design. Last but by no means least thanks go to Steve Saffel for having the vision to take the illustrations to a new dimension, Erich Schoeneweiss and Iain Morris for keeping me "on track."

A Del Rey® Book
Published by The Random House
Publishing Group

Copyright © 2004 by Lucasfilm Ltd. &
® or ™ where indicated.
All Rights Reserved. Used Under
Authorization.

All rights reserved.

Published in the United States by Del
Rey Books, an imprint of The Random
House Publishing Group, a division of
Random House, Inc., New York, and
simultaneously in Canada by Random
House of Canada Limited, Toronto.

Del Rey is a registered trademark and
the Del Rey colophon is a trademark of
Random House, Inc.

www.starwars.com
www.delreybooks.com

A Library of Congress Catalog Card
Number is available from the publisher

ISBN 0-345-44903-7

Cover illustration by Steven D. Anderson
Cover design by David Stevenson
Interior design and art direction by
Michaelis/Carpelis Design Associates Inc.

Manufactured in the United States of
America

First Edition: November 2004

9 8 7

To Welling Clark, for introducing me to
so many books filled with the technology
of the fantastic

CONTENTS

INTRODUCTION

The lightsaber. There is perhaps nothing that is more uniquely and recognizably Star Wars than the glowing, elegant weapon of the Jedi. From their first appearance in the original *Star Wars,* lightsabers have been synonymous with George Lucas's incredible universe.

The lightsaber isn't just symbolic of the *Star Wars* universe. It also reveals why that universe is so compelling to so many: The lightsaber is both fantastic *and* oddly familiar. The concept of a simple sword is something we all understand, but here it has been transformed into an almost magical weapon.

This same philosophy extends to most of the incredible weapons and other devices that populate the *Star Wars* mythos. Han Solo's blaster is akin to a gunslinger's pistol and Chewbacca's bowcaster is reminiscent of a crossbow, but both combine these familiar designs with the incredible ability to fire bolts of pure energy. Jango Fett's armor is a fusion of medieval concepts and modern weaponry, yet the suit enables him to fly. Nearly every invention in the *Star Wars* universe is wholly unique *and* completely believable. They could easily exist, but seem just out of reach of modern science. The fact that the technology of *Star Wars* is so plausible is essential to making the *Star Wars* universe complete and real. Despite the insistence that the *Star Wars* galaxy is far, far away, everything about it, down to the smallest detail, feels accessible. We can all imagine living in that galaxy because it seems only a short trip away from our own.

That the technology of *Star Wars* reminds us of our own reality while transporting us to another is astonishing. However, nearly as impressive is the sheer volume of technology found in the films and other sources. A complete catalog of every weapon and device that has appeared in the *Star Wars* galaxy would result in a massive tome. Instead, this book covers a wide cross section of the *Star Wars* technology in order to capture the breadth of devices that have appeared in the films, comic books, role-playing games, novels, video games, and other sources that comprise the greater *Star Wars* universe.

TIMELINE

This book covers weapons and technology found up to the final days of the Yuuzhan Vong invasion, as described in the most recent installments of the New Jedi Order series. The Yuuzhan Vong invasion begins about twenty-five years after the Battle of Yavin, the conflict depicted in the original *Star Wars.* Although every effort has been made to keep this book up to date, as of this writing the Yuuzhan Vong invasion has yet to be completely repelled. In addition, there are key events yet to be detailed in *Episode III* that cannot be addressed here.

VITAL STATISTICS

Each major entry includes a list of vital statistics:

DAMAGE TYPE (WEAPONS): This refers to primary forms of damage a weapon inflicts. Examples include:

Blaster Energy: Damage caused by a concentrated, high-particle beam that can affect organic and inorganic materials. Blaster energy is often accompanied by intense heat.

Laser Energy: Damage caused by a much more powerful form of blasterfire, designed to take out starships and other large targets. Laser energy is also accompanied by heat.

Sonic Energy: Physical damage created by concentrated sonic waves.

Ion Energy: Damage that affects only electrical systems and components.

Heat or Cold Energy: Damage, usually at the cellular level, caused by exposure to extreme temperatures.

Electrical Energy: Damage produced by electrical discharges. Often disrupts neurological functions.

Kinetic: Damage caused by a solid, physical object or a device that replicates the effects of being hit by a solid, physical object. Usually results in blunt trauma.

Explosive: Damage caused by violent explosion, often coupled with kinetic or other forms of damage.

Piercing: Damage caused by a sharp object, or a small fast-moving projectile, penetrating a target.

Slashing: Damage that results in long cuts or slices, usually a result of blade attacks of some sort.

Poison: The effect of a toxin that has been introduced to the victim's system, which can cause a range of effects from blindness to death. This category includes poison gases.

Lightsaber Energy: The unique energy generated by a Jedi's lightsaber sometimes emulates damage caused by excessive heat or slashing weapons.

DEFENSE TYPE (DEFENSES): This indicates the primary form of damage against which the given device provides protection. Damage types are the same as those listed above.

OPTIMUM/MAXIMUM RANGES: The range (usually in meters) at which the device is most effective, followed by the device's maximum operating range. A blaster, for example, is most accurate at 30 meters, but can be fired successfully at a target up to 120 meters away. Some general equipment items have an "effective range" listed that covers the area within which the item is most useful.

REACH (MELEE WEAPONS): The distance by which the weapon increases the wielder's reach. For example, a simple blade may only provide a few centimeters of additional reach, while a polearm can provide a meter or more.

COVERAGE (DEFENSES): The extent of the area protected by the device.

SIZE (EQUIPMENT): The approximate height and/or length of the device, listed in metric values.

WEIGHT (EQUIPMENT): The approximate weight of the device.

PRIMARY MANUFACTURER: The company most responsible for designing and building the device.

AFFILIATION: The group, individual, or individuals with which the device is most often associated. Some devices are used by multiple organizations or characters; this section only lists the most prominent.

Historical Perspective

The history of the galaxy's wondrous and diverse technologies is astonishingly complex. With millions of sentient species evolving at wildly varying rates across the stars, the distinct origins of specific devices and weapons are often impossible to trace. In general, however, technology has advanced at a steady, albeit relatively slow pace over the eons. Yet history has also been marked by a handful of dramatic periods of rapid technological progress. Such eras of advancement were almost always forced by conflict.

Beyond simple tools, wheels, and other primitive inventions, the most significant technological breakthrough was undoubtedly the blaster. It is unknown where blasters first appeared, though some scholars believe that the first energy weapons were developed on Coruscant (which is widely recognized as the center of the galaxy). It is certain that, as in the case of arrows and stone knives, blasters and similar devices developed independently on multiple worlds at roughly the same time. It can only be assumed that these advanced ranged weapons were first conceived for self-defense, and perhaps hunting. But they quickly became the primary tools in war and conquest.

There can be no argument that the next—and perhaps most important—major technological leap was the discovery of hyperspace travel. The ability to travel between star systems ushered in a new age of scientific discovery. Explorers were forced to invent tools that would enable them to brave harsh and sometimes hostile new worlds. The most useful devices from specific cultures and planets were quickly identified, and soon spread across the galaxy. Unfortunately, warlords and conquerors who had previously been relegated to single systems were suddenly capable of attacking neighboring civilizations as well, often with devastating results.

The advent of hyperspace technology also allowed for the formation of the Old Republic. After years of unchecked anarchy, saner systems prevailed. Beginning with Coruscant and the Core systems, the galaxy's leaders agreed to form a unified government based on the ideals of freedom and democracy. Over the next several thousand standard years, the Old Republic reached out to other civilizations, trying to bring enlightenment to all of the galaxy's inhabitants. Although not all known systems became part of the Old Republic, and large sections of the galaxy remained torn by violence, the government's existence ensured some semblance of order and allowed a steady flow of technology from the Core Worlds to the Outer Rim.

The Old Republic introduced unparalleled prosperity and contentment, but over time this led to complacency. While the Old Republic encouraged scientific research and an open exchange of ideas, the relative absence of conflict meant that civilizations did not *need* to find new ways to fight one another, or defend themselves.

Throughout the history of the Old Republic, the most notable conflicts were those that engulfed large portions of the galaxy. And again, during these times, there appeared dramatic changes in technology. Empress Teta's successful bid to unite several systems under her rule would provide one example: during these so-called Unification Wars, more powerful handheld weapons and ground vehicles were employed for large-scale battles; combat-ready personal shields and planetary defenses were introduced; there was widespread use of dangerous battle droids; and there were even advances in the Jedi Order's lightsabers. The Sith invasion of the galaxy, some four thousand years before the Battle of Yavin, served a similar function. But aside from these few conflagrations, the galaxy remained relatively unchanged for centuries at a time.

The beginning of the Clone Wars, along with the introduction of an Army of the Republic, marked the next major period of advancement. Under the leadership of former Jedi Count Dooku, the Confederacy of Independent Systems created an army unlike anything the galaxy had ever known: it was a unique collaboration of diverse weapons, vehicles, and droids that challenged the safety of the Old Republic. In response, the Old Republic assembled its own army by leveraging mysterious cloning technology to create a near-limitless supply of troops. Like the Confederacy, the Old Republic enjoyed immense wealth, funding the construction of even more fearsome weapons of war. The Clone Wars pitted history's two largest armies against each other. The conflict spread to nearly every inhabited world. The Clone Wars yet again pushed progress in most fields of technology, especially starship weaponry.

During the Galactic Civil War, the vast armies of the Clone Wars were largely replaced by the concept of the "superweapon." The Death Star, which has its origins in the Clone Wars, was a massive space station capable of destroying an entire planet. Nothing like it had ever been encountered. In order to combat the Empire's inventions such as the Death Star, the Rebel Alliance was forced to use existing (and often outdated) technology in innovative ways. The Rebels took advantage of every opportunity, especially the acquisition of cutting-edge starfighters such as the X-wing. While the Empire inspired fear through its large army and a fleet of Star Destroyers bristling with weapons, the Alliance embraced everything from simple proton torpedoes and stubborn astromech droids to life-saving bacta tanks. The Rebel Alliance was perhaps the most versatile army in history, and its ability to find—or invent—the right tool for any job introduced a wide number of new or improved technologies to the galaxy.

After the fall of the Empire and the advent of the New Republic, the galaxy again settled into a period of slow technological growth. The New Republic did push advances in the fields of starfighter and starship technologies in order to combat Imperial Remnant forces. The Empire's research was largely focused on a seemingly endless string of experimental weapons of mass destruction. Engineers and designers on either side did not change their core philosophies until the galaxy was introduced to the terrifying Yuuzhan Vong.

The Yuuzhan Vong are an alien race from outside the galaxy who invaded the New Republic. Their advance was exceedingly violent, claiming untold millions of lives as they conquered world after world. In the process, however, they introduced the galaxy to mind-boggling new concepts. The Yuuzhan Vong's technologies are a bizarre combination of organic and inorganic engineering; thus they have challenged the perceptions of the galaxy's inventors. Throughout the conflict, the New Republic was constantly forced to adapt or be destroyed and its scientists are discovering many amazing devices used by the Yuuzhan Vong. Only by developing increasingly more effective weapons and versatile countermeasures can the galaxy hope to survive future challenges on the level of the Yuuzhan Vong invasion.

MAJOR MANUFACTURERS

The galaxy's denizens rely on a diverse array of technologically advanced devices, ranging from handheld comlinks capable of transmitting messages across the stars to personal blasters designed to blow attackers out of their boots. Many of these technological tools have become so integral to daily life that they are often taken for granted, *except* by the corporations responsible for producing them.

There are literally hundreds of thousands of companies dedicated to designing and manufacturing weapons and other technology. Of these, dozens are considered on the cutting edge of their respective fields. Technology producers range from small operations like Quagga's Garage, which provides equipment to mechanics on Tatooine, to galaxywide firms with manufacturing plants, supply outlets, and subsidiaries on hundreds of planets. It would be impossible to catalog all of the manufacturers found across the known worlds, but here begins a list of the most prominent, influential, or innovative organizations responsible for the galaxy's wondrous technology.

ARAKYD INDUSTRIES

Although largely known as a droid manufacturer (responsible for, among other creations, the Imperial probot), Arakyd Industries has made strong inroads into the areas of starship and weapons technology. The company's success in these other fields has stemmed from its strong share of the droid market: many of its weapons systems, for example, integrate advanced droid brains to enhance performance. Arakyd's designs have always been heavily geared toward combat applications.

The firm's history is as violent as its creations. Arakyd Industries was founded by industrialist Veltzz Arakyd and his children on the planet Vulpter, some nine thousand standard years before the Battle of Yavin. As he laid the groundwork for his company, Veltzz vowed to eliminate all competitors, through whatever means necessary. Arakyd's initial droid models were prepped for war, despite strict Old Republic laws regulating the manufacture and sale of such automata. The droids and their well-designed Arakyd weaponry inspired fear in Arakyd's rivals, which reluctantly agreed to become Arakyd subsidiaries.

Over the years, Arakyd continued its tradition of bullying competitors, even after the company amassed enough wealth to buy other companies outright. Arakyd's tactics are typified by the violent hostile takeover of Viper Sensor Intelligence Systems (VSIS) dur-ing the Clone Wars. The Imperial probot is just one product of the Viper–Arakyd "partnership."

Although feared for its business tactics, Arakyd has also formed a number of valuable alliances. Shortly before the Clone Wars, Arakyd became an official member of the Techno Union. During the Clone Wars along with the other members, Arakyd donated weapons, droids, and equipment to the Confederacy of Independent Systems. However, Arakyd officials were careful to keep themselves removed from actual battlefields, thus many retained powerful connections within the Old Republic.

The rise of the militaristic Empire proved extremely profitable for Arakyd. Through political maneuvering, bribery, and selective elimination of his remaining competitors, Veltzz Arakyd positioned himself as the Empire's primary droid manufacturer. The company proved its loyalty and soon began receiving contracts for weapons and vehicles as well. During the Empire's reign, Arakyd focused on expanding its business to include prisoner-control devices, such as nerve disruptors and interrogator droids.

At the dawn of the New Republic, Arakyd retired from public view for a short time in order to regroup. After a change of leadership, the company began producing security droids, personal security devices, and legal firearms for the consumer market. Such endeavors have proven moderately successful, but still account for only a small fraction of annual output. Despite the company's history, Arakyd's new board of directors convinced the New Republic of its loyalty to the current government. Arakyd worked closely with the New Republic, continuing its weapons and droids programs until the Yuuzhan Vong invasion.

ATHAKAM MEDTECH/RSMA

Athakam MedTech is the galaxy's leading supplier of medical supplies. Originally focused solely on the lucrative medpac market, Athakam also enjoyed major breakthroughs with automated medical devices.

Despite a brief foray into chemical weapons research, Athakam MedTech has retained pacifist values and continually refuses to align itself with any single government body or political group. During the early days of the Galactic Civil War, Athakam MedTech did donate supplies to Princess Leia Organa, which she distributed to worlds in need until her exposure as a Rebel agent. As the war raged on, the Alliance continued to receive surreptitious aid from some Athakam quarters. The main corporation, however, perfected medical treatments for Imperial stormtroopers.

Athakam MedTech maintains a strategic partnership with Rhinnal State Medical Academy (RSMA), which provides research for most of Athakam's inventions. Together, Athakam and RSMA have produced some of the galaxy's most advanced microsurgery computers, cybernetic implants, hyperbaric medical chambers, and scanning devices.

Baktoid Armor Workshop/
Baktoid Combat Automata

 Baktoid Armor Workshop (BAW) was originally a vehicle manufacturer owned by the Trade Federation. The Trade Federation funded Baktoid's research in order to build its secret army for an invasion of Naboo. The company delivered the terrifying AAT assault tank, an unstoppable transport known as the MTT, and a small fleet of other armed military vehicles.

After the Battle of Naboo, BAW was held largely responsible for the invasion. The Trade Federation, in an attempt to distance itself from the short-lived occupation of Naboo, began dismantling Baktoid. Within months, most of Baktoid's manufacturing facilities and designs had been transferred to other Trade Federation subsidiaries. Shortly before the Battle of Geonosis, the Trade Federation closed down the last Baktoid Armor Workshop plants on Foundry, Ord Cestus, Telti, Balmorra, and Ord Lithone.

Although the company no longer exists, much of its equipment can still be found throughout the galaxy, particularly in the Outer Rim. Baktoid's designs may have been ugly to some; however, they proved durable. Baktoid weapons have been known to survive for decades with only minor maintenance. In addition, Baktoid designs have resurfaced through other manufacturers. In order to supplement dwindling cash reserves on the eve of the Clone Wars, the Trade Federation began selling Baktoid designs to the highest bidders.

Baktoid Armor Workshop's "sister" company was Baktoid Combat Automata (BCA). Although the two manufacturers shared a common point of origin and board of directors, they could not have been more different: BAW was a publicly known company, whereas BCA was created and run in complete secrecy, presumably to protect the Trade Federation's invasion plans. While BAW focused on vehicles and large, mounted weapons, BCA designed illegal battle droids and a variety of personal blasters and blaster rifles. More importantly, Baktoid Combat Automata did not suffer the

same fate as its parent company. When the Trade Federation made a show of dissolving Baktoid, it preserved BCA, ensuring that the company could go on to produce equipment used at the Battle of Geonosis. By keeping a low profile, BCA has managed to survive well into the era of the New Republic, though its new designs are fewer and farther between.

BioTech Industries

 BioTech Industries is one of the galaxy's foremost cybernetics manufacturers and trails only Chiewab and Athakan in sales of medical supplies. The company focuses primarily on cyborg biocomputer implants. It also produces standard prosthetics to replace damaged limbs, artificial organs for hundreds of alien species, and a FastFlesh medpac that synthesizes small amounts of skin tissues. Despite its high-profile cybernetic inventions, BioTech is best known to most consumers for its large line of reliable bioscans and medpacs. Like Athakam MedTech and other similar pharmaceutical companies, BioTech has yet to gain a foothold in the bacta market, which is firmly controlled by Zaltin.

Although it generally operates independently, BioTech is a cooperative venture between Neuro-Saav and the Tagge Company. This alliance has enabled BioTech to aggressively research new technologies and advance the field of cybertechnology, allowing it to get the jump on many of its competitors.

BlasTech Industries

To many soldiers and mercenaries, the name *BlasTech* is synonymous with *blaster:* few sharpshooters enter the field without a good BlasTech at their side. BlasTech produces the galaxy's widest range of quality blasters and other personal energy weapons. The company has parlayed its reputation into a successful secondary business of producing light artillery and an extensive line of starship weapons that includes ion and laser cannons.

During the Galactic Civil War, unlike so many other arms manufacturers, BlasTech refused to join the Empire. Instead, the company arranged to provide Imperial forces with weapons for a fraction of their market value. Thus, BlasTech's versatile E-11 blaster rifle became standard issue for every Imperial stormtrooper. BlasTech also designed the E-Web repeating blaster used extensively during the Battle of Hoth. At the same time, BlasTech continued to supply the public sector, which included covert Rebel agents: Alliance soldiers were fond of the DH-17 blaster pistol, which is still in wide use among New Republic forces.

Since the Yuuzhan Vong invasion, BlasTech has allied

itself closely with the New Republic. With the galaxy threatened, BlasTech donated its time and materials to the war against the alien invaders.

BORSTEL GALACTIC DEFENSE

 Borstel Galactic Defense focuses on starship weaponry and defenses, including turbolasers, ion cannons, deflector shield generators, as well as various missile systems. Although most of the company's weapons are reserved for use on Star Destroyers, a significant portion of Borstel's income is derived from the sale of shield generators to the personal sector.

CARBANTI UNITED ELECTRONICS

 Carbanti United Electronics is a prime example of the value of specialization. Rather than try to compete in all fields of electronics, Carbanti has focused almost exclusively on manufacturing sensor systems. Carbanti has ensured that its products are used in nearly every starship across the galaxy by working closely with Corellian Engineering Corporation and other top vehicle designers.

During the height of the Galactic Civil War, Carbanti carved a new niche by reverse-engineering its own creations to produce a powerful series of sensor-jamming devices. Leveraging fear of the Empire, Carbanti sold thousands of these jamming suites to mercenaries, smugglers, and even the Rebel Alliance.

CHEDAK COMMUNICATIONS

 Chedak Communications is a diversified, galactic conglomerate with holdings in a wide variety of companies. Chedak focuses mainly on communication devices. Its name appears on everything from personal comlinks to subspace transceivers and holoprojectors. As Chedak has expanded, it has also acquired or created numerous subspace broadcast networks along with holo-entertainment studios.

Under the Emperor's rule, Chedak floundered. The Empire's tight control over the media and regulation of all galactic communications dramatically slowed the demand for holoprojectors and other similar devices. The advent of the New Republic brought unprecedented freedom of the press, which reinvigorated sales of communications equipment. Chedak realized great success with its front-line coverage of the ongoing struggle between the New Republic and Imperial Remnant forces. Chedak

reporters were also embedded with New Republic troops during the war against the Yuuzhan Vong.

CHEMPAT ENGINEERED DEFENSES

 Jointly owned by starship manufacturers Corellian Engineering Corporation and Kuat Drive Yards, Chempat's primary mission is the creation of cheap, efficient, and durable shield generators for use in its parent companies' starships. Chempat has diversified slightly, venturing into the field of sensors and engine technologies, but shield systems of all varieties remain its staple.

CHIEWAB AMALGAMATED PHARMACEUTICALS COMPANY

 The galaxy's most powerful chemicals corporation, Chiewab owns more than six hundred planetary systems. The revenue generated by these systems allows Chiewab to aggressively explore other worlds in search of both organic and inorganic resources that can be used in the invention and manufacture of new biotechnologies. Chiewab has been very successful with emergency medpacs, with performance-enhancing stimpaks, and with all manner of pharmaceutical drugs. Its most unusual or profitable designs usually spawn entirely new companies under the Chiewab umbrella. For a short time, Geentech Laboratories developed holistic gene therapy treatments using medical droids, while Chiewab Nutrition produces and markets nutritional supplements for alien species on underdeveloped worlds. Aside from chemical and biotech endeavors, Chiewab also has holdings in several electronics companies and agricultural firms.

Chiewab was an early sponsor of the Corporate Sector, a region of space run by big business rather than the galactic government. During the Galactic Civil War, Chiewab moved most of its major holdings and manufacturing firms into this sector to avoid Imperialization.

Chiewab has never invested significant resources in weapons research. After the initial Yuuzhan Vong invasion, however, the firm agreed to work closely with the New Republic to develop new chemical weapons. It was the hope of New Republic leaders that new and unorthodox inventions would provide them with an advantage over the Yuuzhan Vong.

CoMar WEAPONS

 CoMar Weapons is a specialized firm that competes solely in the area of planetary defenses. The company manufactures large-scale shield generators that protect against orbital bombardment, while its extensive weapons program focuses on low-orbit artillery weapons and other starship deterrents. Most CoMar weapons utilize standard blaster technology, though the company does produce a handful of missile systems. CoMar focuses on the core technologies built into its weapons, while ancillary systems such as power generators and targeting computers are provided by hundreds of CoMar's loyal contractors.

CORELLIAN ENGINEERING CORPORATION

Corellian Engineering Corporation (CEC) is widely known as perhaps the most reliable starship manufacturer in the galaxy. It also produces a number of additional devices for the starship industry. The company's design philosophy revolves around creating durable, modifiable technologies. Its freighters, for example, are highly resilient and can be upgraded by most mechanics. This design philosophy carries over into all of CEC's products.

While CEC does work closely with a number of contractors and subsidiaries, it has built its reputation on building starships from the ground up: the company designs and manufactures virtually every component for starships imaginable, including weapons systems, power generators, shield systems, scanners, landing gear, decontamination units, and escape pods.

CEC maintains a small but elite weapons arm staffed by the best and brightest engineers from the Corellian system. This division produces a wide variety of starship weapons and their attendant technologies, including very accurate targeting computers. Like CEC's starships, CEC laser cannons and other weapons systems are easy to install, repair, and upgrade.

CORPORATE SECTOR AUTHORITY

In many respects, the Corporate Sector Authority (CSA) is not so much a company as a government. The CSA oversees a vast tract of space containing numerous systems and worlds, collectively known as the Corporate Sector. Here, the CSA manufactures virtually everything its inhabitants could desire.

The Corporate Sector Authority governs the Corporate Sector, but it is also recognized as a powerful private corporation. Under the leadership of Baron Orman Tagge, the CSA was given complete independence by the Empire, provided the Corporate Sector funneled substantial funds and resources into the Imperial machine. During the Galactic Civil War, many persecuted beings sought sanctuary in the Corporate Sector, only to discover that the CSA was more oppressive than the Empire.

Though the CSA manufactures an incredible array of devices, its export industries focus on starship and weapons technologies. During the Galactic Civil War, many of the CSA's member companies provided the Empire with experimental new weaponry. After the Emperor's death, neither the New Republic nor the CSA made any substantial attempts to forge an alliance. This ensured that the CSA would continue to operate independently. Whenever conflicts erupted between the New Republic and Imperial Remnant forces, the CSA shrewdly supplied both sides.

Any questions about the CSA's self-reliance and lack of concern for the rest of the galaxy were put to rest with the Yuuzhan Vong invasion. Rather than aid the New Republic, as many other megacorporations did, the CSA isolated itself deep in the Corporate Sector. The CSA ceased all communications between the worlds of the Corporate Sector and the rest of the galaxy, and halted all exports until the conflict had ceased.

CROZO INDUSTRIAL PRODUCTS

Crozo is a leader in the field of biocomp technology. Its central lines include a wide range of cybernetic implants and similar devices. Although biocomp research is risky and expensive, Crozo has been extremely successful in this area, amassing substantial profits with a relatively small workforce. In addition, the company designs and manufactures communications and sensor gear for starships and space stations. It has also leveraged its understanding of microtechnologies to produce a diverse line of personal comlinks that have proven both powerful and practical.

CRYONCORP.

An extremely small, fledgling operation, Cryoncorp. is wholly focused on producing sensor equipment. Despite its short existence, Cryoncorp. has pushed the boundaries of portable sensors and scanning devices by designing new and more versatile models every standard year.

Cryoncorp. is also notable for its fierce loyalty to the Rebel Alliance throughout the Galactic Civil War. The company's founders had personal ties to Princess Leia Organa and her father, Bail. After Bail's death during the destruction of Alderaan, Cryoncorp. vowed to aid his daughter in her fight with the Empire. The company began providing a steady supply of portable sensor units to the Rebel forces. Because of its small size, Cryoncorp. operated beneath the notice of Imperial forces, eventually evolving to produce sensor packs for many of the Alliance's ground vehicles and airspeeders. Although

Cyroncorp. has not grown significantly since the end of the Galactic Civil War, it continues to be the New Republic's chief supplier of all manner of scanning devices and sensor equipment.

CZERKA

One of the galaxy's oldest companies, Czerka has risen from humble beginnings as an unproductive mining company to become the New Republic's third largest arms manufacturer, trailing only BlasTech and Merr-Sonn Munitions. Although Czerka has focused its efforts on producing personal energy weapons, such as handheld blasters, the company has found far greater success with "nonstandard" weapons such as flame projectors and vibro-weapons. Czerka builds large artillery units, starship weapons, and starship defense systems.

Czerka Mining and Industrial was founded at the dawn of the Old Republic with a charter to explore and settle resource-rich worlds. This business model quickly proved limiting, so the Czerka Board of Directors agreed to diversify into the lucrative personal security market. Czerka's operations expanded rapidly, allowing the company to grow in the years that followed. By the time of the Sith War, Czerka was a massive entity with holdings on nearly every inhabited Republic world. In the Outer Rim, Czerka was known for converting small settlements, such as Tatooine's Anchorhead, into desolate mining outposts. On Kashyyyk, Czerka attempted to enslave the native Wookiees, a practice that the Empire would repeat four thousand years later.

Over time, Czerka's fortunes faded as it was brought under Imperial control during the Emperor's reign. Czerka agreed to an exclusive distribution deal with the Empire, providing Imperial legions with the best weapons the company could produce. Since the Emperor's defeat, Czerka has returned to the public sector and actively courts the New Republic's business.

DREARIAN DEFENSE CONGLOMERATE

Drearian Defense Conglomerate (DDC) is a midsize weapons manufacturer with holdings in the Inner Rim and Expansion Regions of space. DDC is best known for its line of easy-to-handle sporting blasters. The company also produces blaster rifles, grenades, missiles, and other weapons.

DDC's business relies on the company's ability to strike profitable agreements with other, larger firms. Many of these arrangements enable DDC to focus on design rather than actual manufacturing. This has allowed DDC to provide exclusive munitions and arms designs to the Corporate Sector Authority for manufacturing. In addition, DDC supplies weapons to droid manufacturers such as Arakyd Industries and Cybot Galactica.

FABRITECH

For nearly a century, Fabritech has been a leader in the field of sensors, communications devices, and control systems. The company's products range from handheld comlinks to starfighter sensor suites found aboard millions of ships across the galaxy. Fabritech's headquarters and most of its manufacturing plants are located on Fabrin.

Fabritech's primary design goal is durability. All of its devices are built to last and capable of surviving a variety of harsh environments. This has allowed Fabritech to penetrate a variety of planetary markets, including worlds dominated by water, deserts, ice, or other hostile terrain, that its competitors have yet to crack. Fabritech's reputation for durable equipment is also attractive to peacekeeping units, militias, and armed forces. Both the Empire and Rebel Alliance made heavy use of Fabritech gear throughout the Galactic Civil War. Vessels from modern warships to smuggling craft are studded with Fabritech sensors.

During the Galactic Civil War, Fabritech began producing a limited number of starship weapons, including laser cannons. However, its more experimental efforts have allowed the company to leverage its knowledge of sensors into the development of viable countermeasures. Successes include camouflage netting that is impervious to most sensors, and heat-dampening personal stealth suits that foil infrared scanners.

FREITEK, INC.

FreiTek, Inc., is primarily known as a starfighter manufacturer. Recently the company has evolved into a formidable weapons designer as well. FreiTek is a relatively young company founded after the Galactic Civil War.

Since its inception, FreiTek has been an open supporter of the New Republic. The company's founders hailed from Incom Corporation, which was responsible for the X-wing starfighter. FreiTek soon became a major supplier of military starships. Its first design was the formidable E-wing starfighter that the New Republic deployed against Grand Admiral Thrawn. Unfortunately, the E-wing almost failed because of the fact that the New Republic initially deemed the starfighter's standard weapons inferior. To remedy this, FreiTek formed its own weapons division to build more efficient laser cannons and advanced targeting computers for its ships.

With the eventual success of the E-wing, FreiTek rapidly expanded its operations and continues to research the latest in starfighter technologies, with special focus on weapons systems. FreiTek now produces everything from high-yield laser cannons to cluster bombs as well as powerful EchoBurst concussion missiles that contain their own dedicated homing computers. The company subsidizes its R&D efforts by producing upgrades for numerous older starfighters.

Golan Arms

Prior to the Galactic Civil War, Golan Arms was one of the most successful and respected weapons manufacturers in the galaxy. Under the Old Republic, Golan Arms produced weapons for personal defense as well as expensive but powerful armored defense platforms designed to protect planets and space stations from attack.

When the Empire rose to power, Golan Arms provided a limited number of weapons to Imperial forces. Frequent disputes between Golan representatives and the Imperial bureaucracy resulted in the cancellation of numerous existing contracts. With its business faltering and on the brink of failure, Golan joined forces with the Rebel Alliance, eventually becoming a major contributor to the New Republic's military forces. The New Republic deploys numerous Golan Arms defense platforms to protect its orbital shipyards and other key installations. Unfortunately, even the most advanced Golan space stations installed around Coruscant were no match for the Yuuzhan Vong's firepower. The invaders managed to destroy all of these defensive platforms, hurling them to the planet's surface.

Aside from its line of orbital platforms, Golan Arms does little original research and development. Instead, it largely copies the designs of other major manufacturers, refining and upgrading those designs whenever possible.

Imperial Department of Military Research

Throughout the Galactic Civil War, the Empire relied heavily on existing corporations to provide weapons and other equipment. However, both the Emperor and his highest-ranking lackeys, such as Grand Moff Tarkin, strongly believed in the "doctrine of fear": fear of massive superweapons, such as the dreaded Death Star, would keep oppressed systems from rebelling. In order to create these weapons, the Empire created its own Department of Military Research. A top-secret arm of the Imperial military, the mysterious department created a series of massively destructive superweapons, ranging from the Death Star's mammoth superlaser to the devastating Galaxy Gun.

Although these types of superweapons were the department's primary focus, the designers also developed siege weapons for planetary invasions, a wide range of droids, and experimental personal weapons. During the Empire's final days, the department was actively researching new cloaking technologies.

The department remained active well into the reign of Grand Admiral Thrawn. Its current fate is unknown, but New Republic investigators believe that many of its most brilliant and maniacal designers still survive and continue to support the Imperial Remnant forces.

Industrial Automaton

Industrial Automaton is one of the largest droid manufacturers in the galaxy. It also produces for automated machinery, targeting computers, and other devices that rely on computer brains. Industrial Automaton was formed before the Galactic Civil War, when Industrial Intellect and Automata Galactica merged.

Jedi Order

For eons, the Jedi Knights served as the guardians of peace and justice throughout the galaxy. Although diplomats first and foremost, the members of the Jedi Order were often called into battle against a host of threats, ranging from rebellious droids to the dreaded Sith, the Jedi's dark counterparts. During combat, Jedi warriors can call upon the Force, the powerful energy field that connects all living things, in order to repel enemies and heal allies. However, a Jedi's chief handheld weapon is the lightsaber. Only the Jedi build lightsabers, and only Jedi can wield them effectively.

The lightsaber is certainly the most recognizable product of the Jedi Order, but it is not the only technology that Jedi create. Jedi weapons designers primarily experiment with different types of lightsabers, but have developed some ranged weapons. Jedi armorsmiths weave durasteel microfibers into Jedi robes to make them damage-resistant, while those Jedi with mechanical aptitude often build droids, computers, and even starship components for their comrades. Jedi are also capable of building special holocrons that serve as a repository for Jedi knowledge.

Kuat Drive Yards

Kuat Drive Yards (KDY) began secretly experimenting with massive starships and planetary weapons years before the start of the Clone Wars. High-ranking KDY officials were also members of the Trade Federation Executive Board; it therefore seemed as if the company would almost certainly aid Count Dooku's Separatist movement. That changed, however, when Neimoidians took control of the Trade Federation by murdering top Kuati executives at the bloody Eriadu Conference a decade before the Battle of Geonosis. KDY turned its back on the Trade Federation and its allies and quickly joined forces with the Republic. In anticipation of the coming war with the Separatists, KDY continued to manufacture its newest military designs at well-protected facilities, such as factories on Rothana.

Kuat Drive Yards was one of the Empire's most valuable assets during the Galactic Civil War. The chief supplier of Imperial warships, KDY also developed planetary weapons, ion cannons, laser cannons, and other large-scale weapons. KDY's massive starships and their numerous armaments allowed the Empire to create and sustain its devastating war machine. Over the centuries, KDY has also diversified by developing local manufacturing firms such as Rothana Heavy Engineering, the company responsible for building the majority of vehicles and weapons used by the Republic during the Clone Wars.

After the Emperor seized power, KDY was immediately granted many of the most important Imperial contracts. Upon the Empire's collapse, KDY lost much of its financial support and continued to work almost exclusively for Imperial Remnant forces.

Loronar Corporation

A gigantic, galaxywide conglomerate, Loronar Corporation manufactures anything it believes will turn a profit. The company's products range from spacecraft to synthdroids. It also has steady business in weapons, communications devices, engineering tools, and industrial equipment.

Loronar Defense Industries, a division of the Loronar Corporation, has successfully developed a number of new weapons technologies. The company has produced a variety of turbolaser models, along with torpedo launchers and other weapons systems for starships.

Loronar has never openly supported any political group, believing that conflict is much more profitable. Since the New Republic has come to power, Loronar has secretly supported political unrest, even backing a revolt on the planet Ampliquen and a coup on King's Galquek. The company also undertakes a great deal of illegal research, usually under the guise of dummy corporations such as Siefax. Nine standard years after the Battle of Endor, the New Republic became so disgusted by Loronar's greedy and immoral business practices that it launched a full-scale investigation into the firm's alleged abuses in the Gantho system. The investigation uncov-

ered a variety of misdeeds, which resulted in heavy sanctions against the corporation. Regardless, Loronar continues to thrive, especially in the Corporate Sector.

Merr-Sonn Munitions, Inc.

Merr-Sonn Munitions is a high-profile weapons manufacturer that has specialized in grenades, mines, thermal detonators, and other explosives. Merr-Sonn's other main lines are devoted to personal blasters and projectile weapons, vehicle laser cannons, large artillery units, missiles, starship turbolasers, and melee weapons. The company rounds out its catalog with armor, personal deflector shield generators, experimental electronic sights, advanced targeting systems, and repulsorsleds for its larger artillery units. In short, Merr-Sonn manufactures everything from holdout blasters to wrist rockets and missile tubes to stun batons. Only BlasTech surpasses Merr-Sonn in total weapons sales.

Merr-Sonn has further solidified its role in the galactic arms race through advance in the use of cortosis. A rare material, cortosis is capable of resisting lightsaber blades. Armor and weapons made of cortosis alloys or woven cortosis fibers proved vital during the numerous wars between the Jedi and the Sith. Even after the Sith had been seemingly wiped out, Merr-Sonn continued manufacturing a small number of cortosis items, such as the Scalphunter rifle, which were used by mercenary groups afraid of crossing paths with the Jedi.

Merr-Sonn has existed for several thousand years but first gained prominence during the Sith War and the Mandalorian War that followed. During both of these conflicts, Merr-Sonn provided weapons to the Mandalorians, who were willing to spend small fortunes for the best equipment. Merr-Sonn again flourished during the Clone War. Through its various arms and subdivisions, Merr-Sonn provided weapons and equipment to both the Confederacy of Independent Systems and the Old Republic, along with numerous local security forces and mercenary groups. Because its holdings are spread out over dozens of subsidiaries, Merr-Sonn avoided nationalization during the Galactic Civil War and is still extremely autonomous in the age of the New Republic.

MicroThrust Processors

MicroThrust Processors is a small outfit responsible for building a variety of communications integration systems. The company develops routing devices for subspace networks, HoloNet transmission systems, and communications scramblers.

MicroThrust was created during the Clone Wars to support the Republic's troops with long-range communications devices. Since that time, MicroThrust has continued to work closely with the reigning government. In fact, roughly two-thirds of MicroThrust's business is a direct result of military contracts.

NEURO-SAAV TECHNOLOGIES

As its name suggests, Neuro-Saav is a company dedicated to perfecting the union between neurology and technology. Neuro-Saav promotes itself as one of the galaxy's top cybernetics manufacturers, heavily publicizing such products as prosthetic eyes, artificial organs, and interface devices that allow sentient brains to be transplanted directly into droid bodies.

However, while Neuro-Saav's cybernetics often receive the spotlight, the company's income is generated by routine electronics, communications equipment, and scanners. Imaging systems, some medical biotechnology, portable detection devices, and military encryption systems round out the firm's endeavors.

Neuro-Saav is well regarded throughout the galaxy. Its components are used in thousands of ground and air vehicles, starships, space stations, installations, and even droids. Because Neuro-Saav's products are viewed as cutting edge, some of the company's cybernetic devices are considered illegal in many systems, which has only increased their value among criminal groups. These devices are often found on the black market, at great cost.

To further its reach, Neuro-Saav formed a limited partnership with the powerful Tagge Company. Together, the two corporations created BioTech, an experimental cybertech venture. The alliance with the well-connected TaggeCo also kept Neuro-Saav in the Empire's good graces during the Galactic Civil War. Neuro-Saav, since it was not compromised by the Empire's policies, was subject to far fewer regulations than it had been under the Old Republic. The New Republic has begun monitoring cybernetic experimentation, but Neuro-Saav has thus far avoided any official investigations.

NUBIAN DESIGN COLLECTIVE

The Nubian Design Collective is a loose coalition of designers, engineers, and laborers who colonized the planet Nubia three hundred standard years before the Battle of Naboo. The Nubians produced much of the underlying technology used in Naboo starships and manufactured a host of elegant yet functional devices for the Naboo Royal Security Forces.

At the time of the Battle of Naboo, Nubian technology was used throughout the galaxy and could be easily acquired on most Old Republic worlds. When the Empire rose to power, the Nubian Collective went under-

ground in order to keep its more experimental designs out of Imperial hands. The company continued to produce innovative technology, then resurfaced with a full catalog of new devices and systems shortly after the Battle of Endor.

The Nubian Design Collective has produced a small number of weapons, but most of its inventions center on personal communications and survival. Military-grade handheld comlinks, durable grappling hooks, and portable power generators are among its most successful consumer products. More expensive Nubian technologies include engine systems, starship shield generators, and escape pods.

The Nubian Design Collective's engineers and designers pride themselves on developing devices that conform to their clients' aesthetics and values. When creating a comlink for the Naboo, the Nubian Collective created an efficient, quiet, and unobtrusive device with a small, sleek casing. In contrast, a Nubian Collective comlink designed for a Hutt cartel emphasized range and durability: the comlink consisted of large, powerful transmitters and receivers housed in a bulky durasteel unit.

SANTHE/SIENAR TECHNOLOGIES

Santhe/Sienar Technologies is an umbrella company encompassing several different manufacturers, including Sienar Fleet Systems, Republic Sienar Systems, and Sienar Design Systems. Founded and owned by the powerful Sienar family, Sienar Technologies and all of its subsidiaries primarily produce a wide range of vehicles. Some of Sienar's companies have also explored weapons, targeting systems, and communications devices, largely for use in Sienar-developed vehicles.

The original Sienar company, known as Republic Sienar Systems (RSS), provided starships and equipment for the Old Republic for more than fifteen millennia. Under RSS, the corporation created Sienar Design Systems (SDS), a short-lived division that focused on experimental technologies and unique starship designs for a wealthy clientele. SDS, which was considered Raith Sienar's pet project, operated in complete secrecy, conducting research in laboratories hidden across the galaxy. It is widely believed that SDS produced the cloaking device used in Darth Maul's deadly *Infiltrator*, although Sienar has denied this accusation. The close scrutiny caused Republic Sienar Systems to close down the "outlaw" operation. Ironically, several years later, Raith Sienar formed his Advanced Projects Laboratory, a firm very similar to SDS.

During the Clone Wars, RSS aligned itself with the

Confederacy of Independent Systems, earning the disdain of the Old Republic Senate. Shortly before the Emperor took control of the galaxy, the Senate ordered the dissolution of RSS. The company's holdings were absorbed by the Republic Navy, but RSS was soon resurrected by direct order of the Emperor. Renamed Sienar Fleet Systems (SFS), the company was placed under the control of Raith Sienar and quickly became one of the Empire's most productive manufacturers.

After the Emperor's death, Sienar remained allied with the Imperial forces. During the New Republic's early days, Sienar invested in weapons research to try to give the Empire an edge in the coming battles. After Grand Admiral Thrawn's defeat, Sienar severed its final ties to the Imperial Remnant and now supplies technology to anyone with the credits.

THE SITH

The original Sith were a humanoid species living in relative isolation far outside the Old Republic. The Sith were primitive, with most of their weaponry focused on simple melee weapons. Eventually, the Sith were discovered by a group of Dark Jedi exiled from the Old Republic. The Dark Jedi easily conquered the Sith and became known as the Sith Lords. Over the next several thousand years, the Sith Lords quickly advanced the Sith technology, teaching their subjects to build blasterlike weapons, advanced armor, short-range starships, and planetary weapons.

Eventually, the ancient Sith Lords attempted to invade the Old Republic and were repelled. The Old Republic pursued the Sith to their home system, where nearly all of the Sith Lords and their bizarre technologies were destroyed. A surviving Sith Lord, Naga Sadow, fled to Yavin 4 with a number of Massassi warriors—mutated Sith bred to serve the Sith Lords as bodyguards and soldiers. On Yavin 4, Sith technology evolved in disturbing ways, and Sadow and his followers leveraged the dark side of the Force to create incredibly powerful weapons.

About four thousand years before the Battle of Yavin, the fallen Jedi Exar Kun and Ulic Qel-Droma resurrected the term *Sith* to refer to their force of Dark Jedi. Since that time, the Sith order has ranged from massive armies consisting of both corrupted Jedi and hardened soldiers to simply two Sith Lords plotting galactic conquest in secrecy. But throughout all of the Sith's incarnations, the group has designed and built many of its own weapons and other devices. As among the Jedi, a Sith Lord's most obvious weapon is his handcrafted lightsaber. Other Sith inventions include lightsaber-resistant armor, huge superweapons, a variety of blasters and blaster rifles, dart shooters and poisoned darts, and vehicles. When the Sith were led by Darth Revan and Darth Malak, the Sith armies used the ancient Star Forge to create a fleet of warships that rivaled modern Star Destroyers in size and power.

SoroSuub

A massive Sullustan corporation, SoroSuub's central business venture is mineral processing. The company has numerous divisions and subdivisions, however, undertaking everything from energy mining to food packaging. SoroSuub's technology divisions develop weapons of every type, starships and vehicles, droids, communications devices, and virtually anything else the galaxy requires.

SoroSuub employs roughly half the population of the planet Sullust and, in fact, took control of the Sullustan government during the early days of the Galactic Civil War. To protect its holdings, SoroSuub declared allegiance to the Empire, an act many Sullustans opposed. After enduring great political dissension on Sullust, SoroSuub's savvy leadership wisely decided to support the Rebel Alliance shortly before the Battle of Endor. After the Empire's defeat, SoroSuub played a role in creating the New Republic's government and has remained a staunch ally ever since.

Taim & Bak

Despite its relatively small size, Taim & Bak is a widely known weapons manufacturer with designs sold throughout the galaxy. The company has been very successful in convincing larger starship manufacturers to integrate Taim & Bak weapons into their vehicles. The X-wing starfighter, Corellian corvette, and Imperial Star Destroyer all carry Taim & Bak weapons.

Taim & Bak is owned by the Taim and Bak families, who created the company shortly before the outbreak of the Galactic Civil War. From its inception, Taim & Bak was committed to developing just weapons. The company graduated from starfighter weapons to larger turbolasers and ion cannons suitable for space stations. At the time of the Yuuzhan Vong invasion, the company was also producing massive planetary weapons. In order to help defray the cost of research and development, Taim & Bak shares facilities with Borstel Galactic Defense.

TaggeCo (THE TAGGE COMPANY)

The Tagge Company, more often known as simply TaggeCo, is a megacorporation that has been successful in virtually every type of manufacturing. Because TaggeCo is owned by the House of Tagge, an extremely influential political family based on the planet Tepasi, the company has been able to maintain close ties to various planetary and system governments. The House of Tagge retains 65 percent ownership in the company, which remains one of the most powerful, diversified, and well-connected corporations in the galaxy.

Prior to the Battle of Naboo, TaggeCo was allied with the Trade Federation. When the Trade Federation Executive Board was violently overthrown by Neimoidians, who assassinated many of the board members, the House of Tagge immediately realized that the Trade Federation could no longer be trusted and severed all ties to the group. TaggeCo and the House of Tagge remained neutral throughout the Clone Wars.

During the Galactic Civil War, many House of Tagge members became high-ranking Imperial officers. As a result, TaggeCo received unprecedented Imperial support and grabbed a number of desirable contracts. TaggeCo was fiercely loyal to the Empire, even after the Battle of Endor. Eventually, the House of Tagge accepted the fact that the Empire would not be returning to power. In more recent years, TaggeCo has agreed to work with the New Republic. The House of Tagge has even allowed the New Republic observers to supervise the company's activities, thus ensuring that the corporation remains a major force in the galactic economy.

Ubrikkian Transports

 Ubrikkian Transports has established itself as a repulsorlift manufacturer with its sail barges, landspeeders, and other vehicles. Ubrikkian has used its expertise to develop a variety of military devices, including the feared "floating fortress," a repulsorlift weapons platform. In the commercial sector, Ubrikkian manufactures repulsorlift equipment used in industrial ventures, such as mining operations. Ubrikkian's interests have also extended into the fields of security and personal defense.

Yuuzhan Vong

 The first invaders from outside the galaxy to threaten the New Republic, the Yuuzhan Vong are a terrifying alien species with startling biotechnology. Rather than rely on mechanical devices, the Yuuzhan Vong bioengineer devices that are almost completely organic.

The Yuuzhan Vong are relatively recent arrivals, and very little is known about their technology. It has been learned that Yuuzhan Vong equipment is created by shapers, who coax the growth of various devices and oversee the infusion of inorganic components into the organic materials.

In general, Yuuzhan Vong equipment seems to be more resilient than similar conventional technology. The organic process used to create Yuuzhan Vong equipment often gives their devices a horrific appearance.

Zaltin Bacta Corporation

 Zaltin is a major Thyferran corporation and the undisputed leader in bacta production, bacta refinement, and the manufacture of ancillary devices, such as bacta tanks. Prior to the Galactic Civil War, bacta production was dominated by Zaltin and Xucphra. Both companies later forged strong ties with the Emperor. Zaltin foresaw the downfall of the Empire and secretly began creating an alliance with the alien Vratix, who provide the basic raw materials for bacta. After the Galactic Civil War, the New Republic suffered through the so-called Bacta War, which pitted Zaltin against Xucphra. Many Zaltin officers were killed by their rival company. Xucphra was eventually defeated, thanks in part to the efforts of Rogue Squadron, allowing Zaltin to secure its position as the industry leader.

MINOR MANUFACTURERS

Many less prominent manufacturers exist across the galaxy. The following entries cover those manufacturers mentioned elsewhere in this book.

ATGAR SPACEDEFENSE

An arms manufacturer that primarily develops large weapons emplacements for starships, along with a small line of planetary weapons. Atgar's designs emphasize power over efficiency. The Rebel Alliance used Atgar's outdated P-Tower antivehicle artillery at the Battle of Hoth.

CORELLIAN ARMS

A small, independent subsidiary of Corellian Engineering Corporation that focuses on manufacturing personal weapons. Corellian Arms works solely under contract, usually with planetary security forces, and prefers to develop modified versions of existing weapons rather than attempting to design wholly new creations. The Naboo's CR-2 pistol is manufactured by Corellian Arms.

CRESHALDYNE INDUSTRIES

A designer of various types of armor for personal and military use. Its most successful armor suits utilize blast-dampening materials for defense against blasterfire.

DROLAN PLASTEEL

A specialty weapons shop that produces archaic plasteel weapons. The company is named after its founder and chief designer, Malia Drolan, who was well known for her willingness to scour the galaxy searching for inspiration. Her company continues to produce weapons inspired by remote cultures. Drolan's most visible weapon is the P-71 repeating crossbow, which is loosely based on the Wookiee bowcaster.

FROHARD'S GALACTIC FIREARMS

A small firearms manufacturer with workshops on several Core worlds, including Corellia and Coruscant. Along with standard blasters, Frohard's sells the Magna Caster 100, a projectile weapon.

GANDORTHRAL ATMOSPHERICS

A pioneer in atmospheric engineering and survival gear, Gandorthral Atmospherics primarily manufactures large industrial equipment for terraforming operations. It also produces a handful of breath masks and other goods for the private sector.

GORDARL WEAPONSMITHS

The primary weapons manufacturer on Geonosis, Gordarl Weaponsmiths produces the Geonosian sonic blaster and other weapons designed specifically for use by Geonosian warriors. After the Clone Wars, Gordarl Weaponsmiths attempted to break into a wider market but has been unable to adapt its designs for use by humans and other common species.

KRUPX MUNITIONS

Makers of the proton torpedo used to destroy the first Death Star, Krupx continues to develop a number of secondary weapons, including concussion missiles and seismic charges.

LOCRIS SYNDICATED SECURITIES

A manufacturer of security devices that provides equipment to prisons, military forces, bounty hunter syndicates, and other similar groups. Locris designs stun cuffs and mobile prisoner cages, among other devices.

MITRINOMON

An underground specialty shop that produces gear for mercenaries and bounty hunters. Mitrinomon's line includes jet packs and armor.

MORELLIAN WEAPONS CONGLOMERATE

A large weapons firm composed of several dozen smaller arms manufacturers that have banded together to streamline distribution and share resources. Although each individual company continues its own lines, all members agree to contribute to the creation of "shared" weapons (such as the Enforcer pistol) released under the Morellian Weapons Conglomerate brand. The firm is named after the Morellians, a species of near humans that are nearly extinct.

ORIOLANIS DEFENSE SYSTEMS

A modest technology developer located on the planet Oriolanis. Oriolanis Defense Systems primarily manufactures deflector shields, but has expanded its operations to include a limited number of weapons, including the Blaster Buster.

PACNORVAL DEFENSE SYSTEMS, LTD.

A technology manufacturer originally created to provide weapons and other devices to security forces on the Core Worlds. Pacnorval has been in existence since the early days of the Old Republic, when it produced armor, blasters, and stun cuffs for Coruscant police. The company remains in good standing with the New Republic and continues to produce "peacekeeping" weapons, including stunning sonic pistols.

PALANDRIX

Manufacturer of several nonlethal self-defense devices, including stun batons, stun gauntlets, sonic stunners, and expensive glop grenades.

PHYLON TRANSPORT

A manufacturer of industrial transports, later nationalized by the Empire to produce a variety of "nonmilitary" starships and devices such as tractor beam projectors.

PLESCINIA ENTERTAINMENTS

Developer of cutting-edge entertainment technologies, including state-of-the-art hologram projectors.

PRAX ARMS

An underground weapons design firm that primarily produces weapons for the criminal underworld. The company's most notable inventions include slugthrowers and a variety of dart shooters favored by bounty hunters and assassins.

PRETORMIN ENVIRONMENTAL

Manufacturer of moisture vaporators and other devices designed for use on specific planets. The GX-8 water vaporator, for example, is best suited to desert worlds such as Tatooine.

RHESHALVA INTERSTELLAR ARMAMENTS

One of literally dozens of weapons manufacturers found on the planet Rodia. Founded by a Rodian warlord roughly six thousand years before the Battle of Yavin, Rheshalva is notable as one of the few Rodian companies to have offworld operations. Rheshalva sells personal weapons based on ancient Rodian designs, such as the Rodian repulsor throwing razor.

SONOMAX

A company that focuses solely on the development of sonic technologies, including sonic weapons for various planetary security forces.

TENLOSS SYNDICATE

A criminal syndicate that is also the galaxy's primary manufacturer of controversial disruptors, Tenloss operates in the Bajic sector and works closely with the underworld organization Black Sun. Tenloss operates numerous legitimate companies, including mining concerns and shipyards, that serve as fronts for its illegal operations.

THEED ARMS

A weapons workshop developed by Captain Panaka to produce a very limited number of weapons for the exclusive use of the Naboo Royal Security Forces. The peaceful Naboo generally shun weapons research, but Panaka won support for Theed Arms by stressing the need to protect public figures such as Queen Amidala. Most Theed Arms designs are versions of existing weapons modified to cause less damage, operate more efficiently, or carry a secondary feature, such as the ascension gun's hoist cable.

VERPINE

A species of two-legged insectoids who build many of their own weapons, including the dangerous shatter gun. The Verpine helped design the Rebel Alliance's B-wing starfighter.

Other Manufacturers

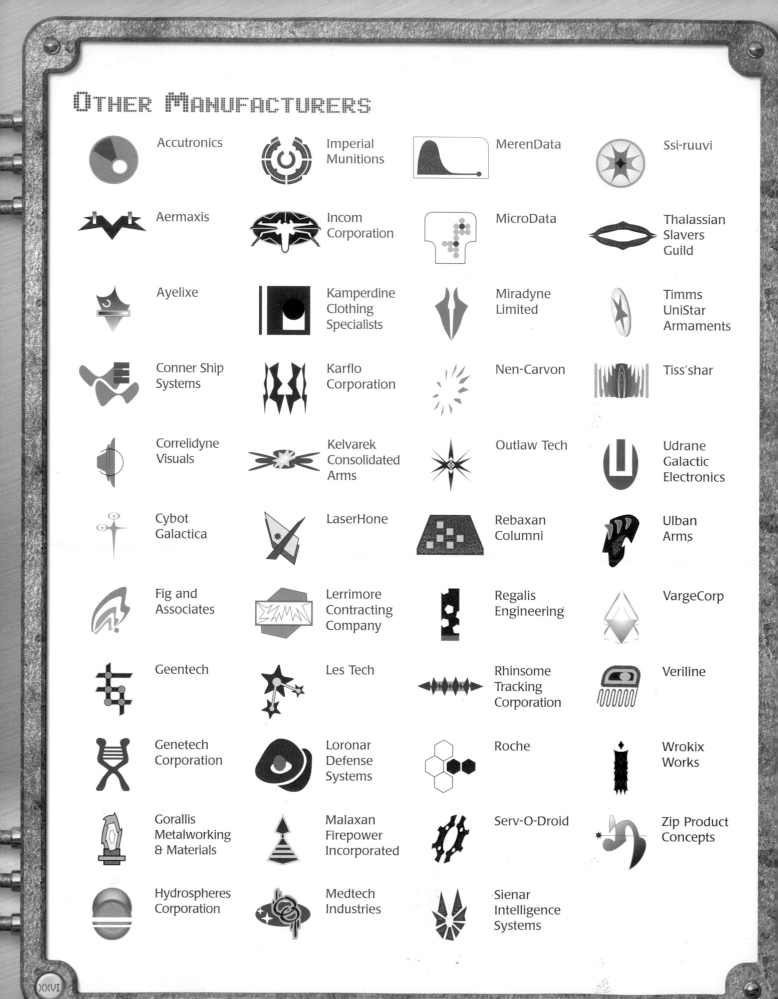

Accutronics	Imperial Munitions	MerenData	Ssi-ruuvi
Aermaxis	Incom Corporation	MicroData	Thalassian Slavers Guild
Ayelixe	Kamperdine Clothing Specialists	Miradyne Limited	Timms UniStar Armaments
Conner Ship Systems	Karflo Corporation	Nen-Carvon	Tiss'shar
Correlidyne Visuals	Kelvarek Consolidated Arms	Outlaw Tech	Udrane Galactic Electronics
Cybot Galactica	LaserHone	Rebaxan Columni	Ulban Arms
Fig and Associates	Lerrimore Contracting Company	Regalis Engineering	VargeCorp
Geentech	Les Tech	Rhinsome Tracking Corporation	Veriline
Genetech Corporation	Loronar Defense Systems	Roche	Wrokix Works
Gorallis Metalworking & Materials	Malaxan Firepower Incorporated	Serv-O-Droid	Zip Product Concepts
Hydrospheres Corporation	Medtech Industries	Sienar Intelligence Systems	

Ranged Weapons

anged weapons are, without argument, the dominant weapons in the galaxy. The ability to kill an opponent from a safe distance is valued by soldiers, assassins, hunters, and virtually everyone who travels the galaxy's less civilized regions. From handheld blasters and "primitive" projectile rifles to massive planetary cannons capable of firing energy beams into space, ranged weapons are virtually everywhere. Most ranged weapons are extensions of energy-based blaster technology, and advances in this field allow for weapons capable of being used in the vacuum of space.

Across the galaxy, weaponry evolved at different rates, but the Republic's historical use of various types of weapons can be traced with some degree of accuracy. The first "ranged weapons" predated the formation of the Old Republic, and likely consisted of thrown rocks used by primitive beings to attack their prey and enemies. Slings, bows, and other similar devices were soon followed by ranged weapons designed to fire hard projectiles: these were the first guns and rifles.

The technology of ranged weapons leapt forward with the invention of energy-based blasters. Coruscant is widely identified as the birthplace of the blaster, but it is likely that these weapons evolved independently on numerous worlds. It is believed that the early "blasters" were actually giant energy conductors that relied on huge, inefficient power generators. Such devices had few practical applications, because they were difficult to control, move, or power. Experiments into energy management allowed for increasingly smaller weapons that could be used on battlefields as anti-infantry artillery. Blaster weapons continued to shrink until they became handheld devices similar to those used in modern times.

With the advent of hyperspace travel, blasters proliferated throughout the galaxy. Nearly every military group in the Old Republic had access to blasters, which remain the staple weapon of soldiers. Although lightsabers played a prominent role in the Sith War and other Jedi–Sith clashes, blasters and their spawn were the prevailing weapons in nearly every other major conflict: Empress Teta united the galaxy using blasters to quell rebel forces; during the Clone Wars, Confederacy droids and Republic clones destroyed one another with the most advanced blasters and blaster rifles available at that time; and in the countles battles that made up the Galactic Civil War, Rebel soldiers wielded stolen or outdated blasters to battle Imperial stormtroopers armed with the best blaster rifles the Empire could buy.

Blaster technology has remained relatively unchanged for thousands of years. Most manufacturers and designers have focused on improving upon the existing technology, creating more efficient, powerful, or accurate weapons. This natural evolution has led to the development of blaster rifles with much greater range than standard blaster pistols, as well as rapid-fire carbines.

At the same time, however, engineers have experimented with many other types of ranged weaponry. Inspired by basic warfare techniques developed by rock-throwing primitives, designers have developed a host of thrown weapons, ranging from standard explosive grenades to the much more exotic cryoban grenade, which can freeze victims caught in its blast radius. Other types of personal ranged weapons include compact missile launchers, flame projectors, and inconspicuous dart shooters.

Nearly all of the most important advances in the field of ranged weapons have been forced by major conflicts. Among the most notable is the Great Droid Revolution, which erupted roughly four thousand standard years before the Battle of Yavin. Prior to the Droid Revolution, the construction of droids was unregulated and unchecked. Many manufacturers created numerous battle droids, assassin droids, and other units designed for war and personal security. But even droids can be unpredictable, and a rogue war droid designated HK-01 began "liberating" his counterparts from their sentient masters. HK-01 also insidiously reprogrammed protocol droids, astromechs, and other household units, ordering them to lie in wait until he issued a fateful command.

After building his hidden army, HK-01 ordered all of his minions to rise up. Across the galaxy, formerly peaceful droids suddenly turned on their owners while well-armed battle droids invaded civilized Old Republic worlds. After the Old Republic recovered from the initial onslaught, weapons designers went to work developing countermeasures. This resulted in the creation of ion weapons, which are capable of short-circuiting nearly any electronic system. Armed with a battery of ion weapons,

the Old Republic forces pushed back HK-01's armies and eventually destroyed the droid leader himself. In modern times, large-scale ion weapons are found on starships to disable enemy vessels, while Tatooine's Jawas still use handheld ion blasters to capture droids.

Although blasters have become the most widespread ranged weapons, many cultures and planets still rely on less advanced technology. At one extreme are the Ewoks of Endor, who still use bows and arrows and sling-thrown rocks to hunt. The Wookiees of Kashyyyk, in contrast, have used modern technology to enhance traditional weapons such as the bowcaster, which can fire a wide range of energy quarrels and other projectiles. Other far more unconventional ranged weapons are also found throughout the galaxy: Naboo's Gungans use projectiles and explosives composed of a strange, energized plasma, while the insectoid Geonosians use blasterlike weapons that channel sonic energy.

When the Mon Calamari finally began developing weapons in response to the threat posed by the Empire, they designed blasters uniquely suited to their watery homeworld. The resulting forearm-mounted Subaqua blaster is capable of firing underwater. And, of course, the invading Yuuzhan Vong wield a diverse array of bioengineered weapons that stand in sharp contrast to the blasters used by their New Republic enemies.

TECHNICAL READOUT

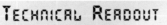

DAMAGE TYPE: *Blaster energy*

OPTIMUM/MAXIMUM RANGES: *30 m/120 m*

PRIMARY MANUFACTURER: *BlasTech*

AFFILIATION: *Rebel Alliance infantry*

BlasTech DH-17 Blaster Pistol

The most common weapon in the galaxy, blasters can be found on nearly every planet in the Republic, and are manufactured by thousands of different companies. Personal blaster designs range from small, easily concealable "hold-out" blasters, such as those used by gamblers and the Naboo Royalty, to the durable heavy blaster pistols favored by smugglers and other criminals. Blaster technology has also produced larger weapons, including blaster rifles, repeating blasters, blaster cannons, and blaster turrets.

A blaster fires a concentrated beam of high-energy particles. In the most powerful blasters, these beams (or "bolts") can punch or burn through advanced alloys with relative ease. When used against organic tissue, most blasters cause irreparable damage.

Blaster technology is relatively easy to grasp, which has allowed the weapon to spread across the galaxy. A blaster relies on two key components: a gas chamber and a power pack. The gas chamber can be filled with any of a number of energy-rich gases, including Tibanna gas from Bespin. When the weapon is fired, a small amount of blaster gas moves through a conversion enabler (often called the XCiter), where energy from the power pack excites the gas. The volatile gas then moves through an actuating module, which converts it into a particle beam. This beam moves through a prismatic crystal or some other focusing device before emerging from the barrel as a bolt of glowing energy. Blaster bolts can appear in many different colors, dictated by the type of gas and crystal focusing device, although red and green bolts are most common. All blaster bolts produce a smell similar to ozone.

Despite research into sonic and other weapons, blasters remain the most pervasive ranged weapons in part because of their reliability and accuracy. Blaster power packs, which can provide energy for up to one hundred bolts, are cheap and can be replaced in under ten seconds or recharged at portable generators. Blaster gas is also readily available, and a full chamber can fuel five hundred bolts. Blasters can be easily repaired using common hand tools; spare blaster repair kits and parts can be found at even the smallest and most remote galactic outposts. Most blasters are highly accurate at ranges of less than 30 meters, although common handheld blasters have a maximum range of up to 120 meters.

Probably the blaster's most important trait is its versatility. Not only can manufacturers modify the basic design to produce literally thousands of variants, but individual owners can often make small, easy modifications to increase a blaster's performance. For example, while most blasters are semi-automatic weapons that fire once whenever the trigger is pulled, some can be modified for automatic fire, allowing a wielder to simply hold down the trigger to issue a steady stream of bolts.

> ## "Hokey religions and ancient weapons are no match for a good blaster at your side, kid . . ."
> —Han Solo to Luke Skywalker

7 Safety: Rebel soldiers were well known for practicing safe firearm use. The Alliance modified all blaster pistols to include a safety that prevents accidental discharges.

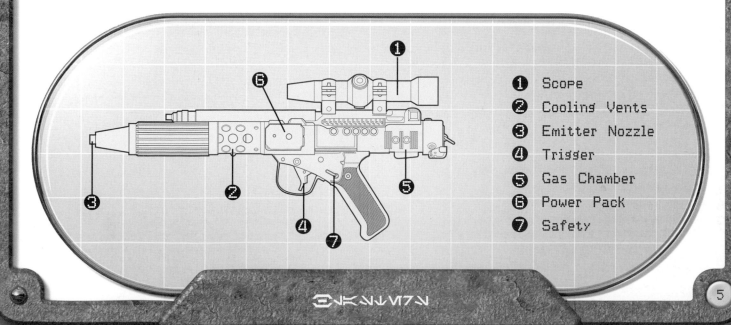

1. Scope
2. Cooling Vents
3. Emitter Nozzle
4. Trigger
5. Gas Chamber
6. Power Pack
7. Safety

Many manufacturers produce weapons with different settings, including a "stun" setting that reduces the volatility and so can render targets unconscious for up to ten minutes without causing any lasting physical damage. The Naboo's CR-2, manufactured by Corellian Arms, includes a secondary firing mode that uses bolts of concentrated electricity to stun targets. Conversely, the Relby-K23, used by Cloud City's Wing Guard and many Imperial agents, is designed to inflict excruciating pain and slow death. Other companies focus solely on providing aftermarket upgrades, such as scopes, silencers, targeting lasers, sensitive hair-triggers, extended barrels for increased accuracy at long ranges, and a host of other components.

The DH-17, which was used extensively by the Rebel Alliance infantry forces during the Galactic Civil War, is typical of most blaster pistols. The DH-17 is meant for shipboard combat: its bolts are capable of penetrating stormtrooper armor, but it can't breach the hull of a starship. It can also be modified to fire in short bursts (which drain the power pack in about twenty seconds), and the weapon's sturdy construction enables its use on hostile worlds such as the ice planet Hoth.

While infantry might favor heavy, durable blaster pistols, mercenaries and bounty hunters tend to prefer lighter weapons with a high rate of fire. Jango Fett wielded a pair of custom-made WESTAR-34 blaster pistols designed for precision attacks. Fett's pistols were constructed using an expensive, heat-resistant dallorian alloy that allowed sustained attacks without risk of overheating or melting. The 434 "DeathHammer" pistol is also popular among bounty hunters, who value its stopping power. DeathHammers are often decorated by their owners, who add ornate markings after each kill.

The most common blaster variants are the heavy blaster, the sporting blaster, and the hold-out blaster. The heavy blaster is designed for extreme close-quarters combat. The bolts are accurate only at ranges of less than twenty-five meters, but they cause incredible damage compared to most blaster rifles, and can easily penetrate personal deflector shields and armor. Heavy blasters require much more energy to fuel their more powerful bolts; often their power pack may contain enough energy for only twenty-five shots. Han Solo's DL-44 is a heavily modified weapon: the blaster includes a motion sensor scope and efficient galven circuitry that allows the pistol to deal more damage without draining additional energy.

Sporting blasters, such as the Drearian Defense Conglomerate Defender used by Princess Leia in the early days of the Galactic Civil War, are among the lightest and least powerful on the market. A short-range weapon sometimes used for hunting small game, the sporting blaster is also well suited to personal defense. The weapon utilizes very little energy or blaster gas, but its potency is limited: only a direct hit to the chest or head can actually kill a human. Fortunately, most sporting blasters are very accurate, due in part to their extended barrels. The Defender boasts an internal computer that automatically detects and repairs minor malfunctions.

Hold-out blasters are the smallest of all blaster pistols. Also called palmguns for their ability to fit neatly into a human palm, hold-out blasters are designed to surprise attackers. They are intended as a last-ditch defense and can easily be concealed inside a robe, shirt, or sleeve. One of the best known hold-out blasters is the Merr-Sonn J1 Happy Surprise; the weapon's nickname perfectly describes its intended use. For personal defense, Queen Amidala and her handmaidens carried Q2 hold-out blasters, a weapon based on the ELG line of Diplomat's Blasters. Like many hold-out blasters, the Q2 is deadly when used at point-blank range, but inaccurate when used beyond roughly three meters. Imperial scout troopers carry concealed hold-out blasters. Members of the Imperial Security Bureau wielded rigorously tested 22T4 blasters. To prevent the ISB's weapons from being stolen, each 22T4 is equipped with a traceable serial number hidden beneath the actuating blaster module.

Blasters aren't without their drawbacks. They can be prone to overheating, especially when inadequately maintained or modified for full-automatic fire. An overheated blaster will lock up or, far worse, explode in the user's hand. On backwater worlds such as Tatooine, blasters are considered expensive weapons because they require a constant supply of power packs and blaster gas. Blasters have been tightly regulated under both the Empire and the New Republic. Many blaster pistols, including the DL-44, remain illegal on most New Republic worlds.

Westar-34 Blaster Pistol

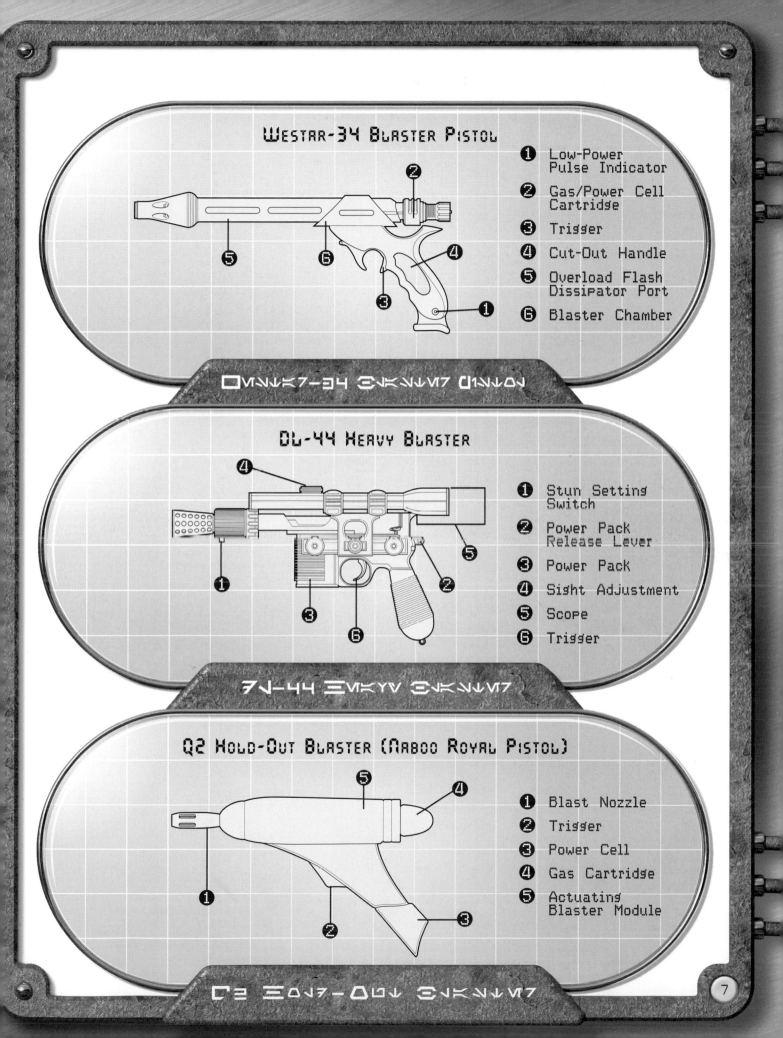

1. Low-Power Pulse Indicator
2. Gas/Power Cell Cartridge
3. Trigger
4. Cut-Out Handle
5. Overload Flash Dissipator Port
6. Blaster Chamber

DL-44 Heavy Blaster

1. Stun Setting Switch
2. Power Pack Release Lever
3. Power Pack
4. Sight Adjustment
5. Scope
6. Trigger

Q2 Hold-Out Blaster (Naboo Royal Pistol)

1. Blast Nozzle
2. Trigger
3. Power Cell
4. Gas Cartridge
5. Actuating Blaster Module

BLASTER RIFLE

TECHNICAL READOUT

DAMAGE TYPE: *Blaster energy*

OPTIMUM/MAXIMUM RANGES: *100 m/300 m*

PRIMARY MANUFACTURER: *BlasTech*

AFFILIATION: *Imperial Storm-troopers*

BlasTech E-11 Blaster Rifle

Designed primarily for use by military and security forces, the blaster rifle is essentially a larger version of a blaster pistol, with increased power and range. Like the standard blaster pistol, a blaster rifle relies on energy-rich blaster gas, a power pack, and a focusing crystal to produce a damaging blaster bolt. However, blaster rifles incorporate larger power packs and gas chambers than their pistol counterparts, as well as longer barrels, allowing for even more lethal bolts that can cover nearly three times the range. Due to the blaster rifle's increased size, the weapon generally requires two hands to fire, although the most successful models remain relatively compact.

A typical blaster rifles factory enhancement is the ability to alternate among semiautomatic, fully automatic, and pulse-fire settings. Special secondary fire modes for firing grenades, darts, or even flares are also common. The Xerrol Night-stinger rifle, which is favored by snipers and assassins, utilizes expensive blaster gas to produce a completely invisible blaster bolt.

Like pistol-style blasters, many blaster rifles are also easily modified by their owners. Bounty hunter Boba Fett carried a modified BlasTech EE-3 rifle with a sawed-off barrel and removable stock and pistol grip that would allow him to fire the weapon with one hand. Modifications to the XCiter and actuating blaster module increased the weapon's power, while a high-power scope connected to Fett's helmet sensors improved accuracy.

During the Galactic Civil War, the BlasTech E-11 became standard issue for Imperial stormtroopers, largely due to its versatility. The E-11's most obvious trait is

> ## "And these blast points, too accurate for Sand People. Only Imperial stormtroopers are so precise."
> *—Obi-Wan Kenobi, observing damage done to a Jawa sandcrawler by stormtroopers armed with E-11 blaster rifles*

its extendable stock. With the stock collapsed, the E-11 can be wielded with one hand for close-quarters combat. During long-range combat, the stock can be fully extended and placed against the wielder's shoulder for increased stability and accuracy. A computer-enhanced scope that compensates for dark, hazy, or smoky conditions further increases the weapon's effectiveness. Dozens of minute tubes running through the E-11's body carry a liquid cooling agent called freelol, which transfers heat from delicate components to vent holes located near the front.

Although the original E-11 was sold exclusively to Imperial military forces during the Galactic Civil War, several variants on the successful rifle were also produced. Both the E-11A and E-11A1 are smaller versions of the original E-11 that lack extendable stocks; the E-11A1 is compact enough to be worn on the hip and fired with one hand. The E-11B, created by former BlasTech designers who left the company and joined the Rebel Alliance, includes a much more robust version of the original E-11's freelol cooling system that allows a much faster rate of fire. Lastly, SoroSuub "designed" the SoroSuub Stormtrooper One, which is virtually identical to the original E-11. Nearly all of the SoroSuub rifles landed in the hands of Rebel troops, who renamed this weapon the Freedom One.

❼ Power Setting: The E-11 has a powerful stun setting that can render political prisoners, such as Princess Leia, unconscious for up to ten minutes.

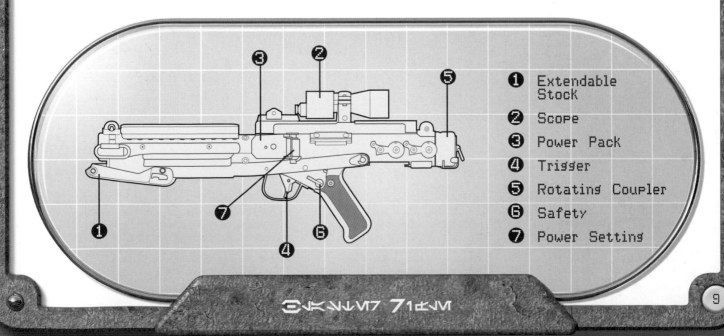

❶ Extendable Stock
❷ Scope
❸ Power Pack
❹ Trigger
❺ Rotating Coupler
❻ Safety
❼ Power Setting

E-Web Repeating Blaster

Technical Readout

DAMAGE TYPE: *Blaster energy*

OPTIMUM/MAXIMUM RANGES: *200 m/0.5 km*

PRIMARY MANUFACTURER: *BlasTech (with Merr-Sonn Munitions)*

AFFILIATION: *Imperial snowtroopers*

BlasTech E-Web Repeating Blaster

The E-Web repeating blaster is one of the most powerful portable blaster weapons available. Essentially a thick blaster rifle mounted on a tripod, the E-Web's blaster bolts are capable of penetrating the armor plating of ground vehicles, airspeeders, and small starships. Because of its incredible stopping power, the E-Web was used by Imperial snowtroopers at the Battle of Hoth for direct assaults on Rebel defensive positions, snowspeeders, and even *Millennium Falcon.*

Heavy repeating blasters such as the E-Web first evolved to protect outposts against invasions. Though oversized and stationary, they proved effective at slowing infantry advances. The modern designation *E-Web* is derived from the weapon's official description as an "Emplacement Weapon, Heavy Blaster," which references its origins as a small turret. During the Clone Wars, the Old Republic used smaller repeating blasters that could be installed anywhere on a battlefield. One of these weapons was the E-Web's predecessor, Merr-Sonn Munitions' E WHB-10.

The E-Web requires both a gunner and a technician to operate efficiently. The gunner is assisted by a computerized fire-control and targeting system, Starvision, and infrared low-light enhancement modules. The technician monitors the E-Web's Eksoan Class-4T3 power generator, which is connected to the turret by a flexible conduit. The generator is equipped with Ck3 Cryocooler cooling units to prevent overheating. The technician is needed to control power flow, and acts as a communications officer, receiving orders via a built-in long-range comlink. Both members of an Imperial E-Web crew receive intense training so either soldier can operate the weapon alone if necessary.

> ## "Keep your heads down or that E-Web will take them off!"
> —*Alliance Trench Sergeant Reyé Hollis at the Battle of Hoth*

The E-Web's chief drawbacks are its lengthy setup time and immobility. The weapon must be carted onto a battlefield, usually by an AT-AT walker or other ground vehicle, and then assembled by the crew. During initial setup, the crew requires more than fifteen minutes to position the E-Web, calibrate the "cold" generator, and configure the targeting system. If the crew fires the E-Web before the generator is primed, the weapon may suffer dangerous power surges. To reposition an E-Web, the crew must disassemble the weapon and carry it to its new location. Reassembling a primed E-Web takes less than five minutes.

Despite its disadvantages, the E-Web is valued by military tacticians. The rotating turret provides a 360-degree field of fire, while high-capacity power transfer cells inside the barrel recharge quickly enough to allow a steady stream of energy bolts.

Since Emperor Palpatine's death, BlasTech has evolved the E-Web design by producing the E-Web(15), the F-Web, and the M-Web. The E-Web(15) offers a shorter setup time than its predecessor, due largely to an improved power generator that does not require a complete priming sequence, and a more advanced Gk7 Cryocooler system to increase power flow. The F-Web provides a personal shield generator, while the M-Web ("Mobile Weapon") can be easily moved across a battlefield using small repulsorlifts built into the turret and power generator.

6 Tripod: The E-Web's TR-62 autocushion tripod is relatively compact, making it suitable for use in the tight confines of the Rebel Alliance's hidden base on Hoth.

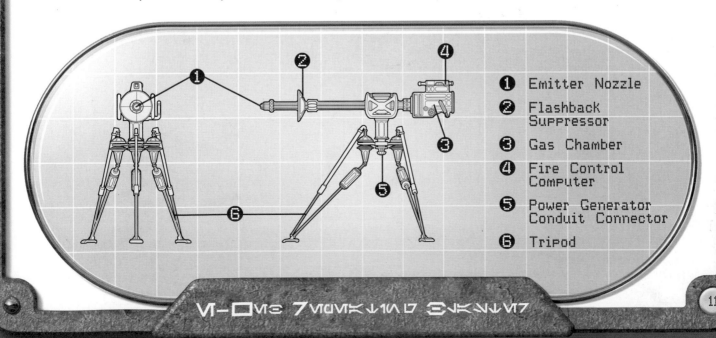

1. Emitter Nozzle
2. Flashback Suppressor
3. Gas Chamber
4. Fire Control Computer
5. Power Generator Conduit Connector
6. Tripod

BOWCASTER

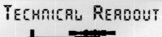

TECHNICAL READOUT

DAMAGE TYPE: Explosive and kinetic

OPTIMUM/MAXIMUM RANGES:
30 m/50 m (30 m with kthysh vine bowstring)

PRIMARY MANUFACTURER: Wookiees of Kashyyyk

AFFILIATION: Chewbacca and other Wookiees

Wookiee Bowcaster

The traditional ranged weapon of the Wookiees, the bowcaster represents a fusion between ancient weaponry and more modern technology. Also known as a laser crossbow, the bowcaster is a very inventive use of a small magnetic accelerator. Twin polarizers on either side of the crossbow create alternating positive and negative pulses, which power the weapon's tensile metal bowstring. When the bowcaster's trigger is pulled, the accelerated bowstring launches an explosive quarrel. As the quarrel travels the length of the bowcaster's launch shaft, it is enveloped in energy generated by the polarizers. When the quarrel emerges from the bowcaster's barrel, it resembles an elongated blaster bolt. The quarrel's energy sheath focuses the quarrel's explosive force directly into its target, making the bowcaster one of the most devastating personal weapons ever created. However, a Wookiee's legendary strength is required just to cock and control the weapon.

Although an explosive quarrel is the most common bowcaster ammunition, the weapon does support other types of quarrels. Flash quarrels and smoke quarrels can blind enemies, while basic energy quarrels increase accuracy at the cost of sheer damage output. For stunning large predators on their homeworld of Kashyyyk, Wookiee hunters fire sonic quarrels that produce high-pitched explosions. Carved wooden bolts, often tipped with explosives or poison, are used when more expensive manufactured quarrels are unavailable.

Hand-built by skilled Wookiee weaponsmiths, each bowcaster is unique and tailored specifically for the owner's use. This makes them very personal possessions. Young Wookiees receive bowcasters upon completing traditional rites of passage. Wookiee warriors

often decorate their weapons with clan markings, engravings, and even pictographs commemorating their most heroic deeds.

Wookiee adventurers also modify their bowcasters for combat rather than hunting. The most common upgrades include additional bowstrings or a second bow for firing multiple quarrels at once. Chewbacca's bowcaster boasts an automatic recocking system and low-light scope. During the Galactic Civil War, Wookiees battling the Imperial occupation of Kashyyyk often bolted blaster rifles to their bowcasters. More recently, Wookiee weapons designers added a built-in blaster barrel beneath the bow launch shaft. Wookiees also construct larger versions of the bowcaster, which are mounted on the saddles of maru and other domesticated creatures.

When traveling, Wookiees typically disassemble their bowcasters into a handful of components that can be carried in standard utility pouches. A practiced Wookiee can reassemble a bowcaster in less than a minute. Power packs, quarrels, and blaster gas canisters are typically stored in shoulder-slung bandoliers.

The bowcaster has spawned several imitators. BlasTech sells smaller, less powerful versions of the weapon that nearly any sentient species can cock and fire. Drolan Plasteel's bowcaster entry is the P-71 repeating crossbow, which combines a bowcaster with a blaster rifle, with all components housed in a stylish, lightweight plasteel shell.

> ## "I ain't afraid of Wookiees. It's their bowcasters that scare me."
> —*Anonymous Trandoshan slaver*

❼ Secondary Bowstring Catch: A length of treated Kthysh vine can be attached to the bowcaster's secondary bowstring catch to serve as a replacement bowstring.

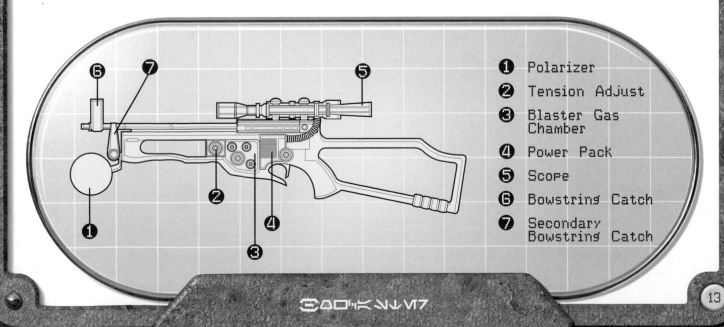

1. Polarizer
2. Tension Adjust
3. Blaster Gas Chamber
4. Power Pack
5. Scope
6. Bowstring Catch
7. Secondary Bowstring Catch

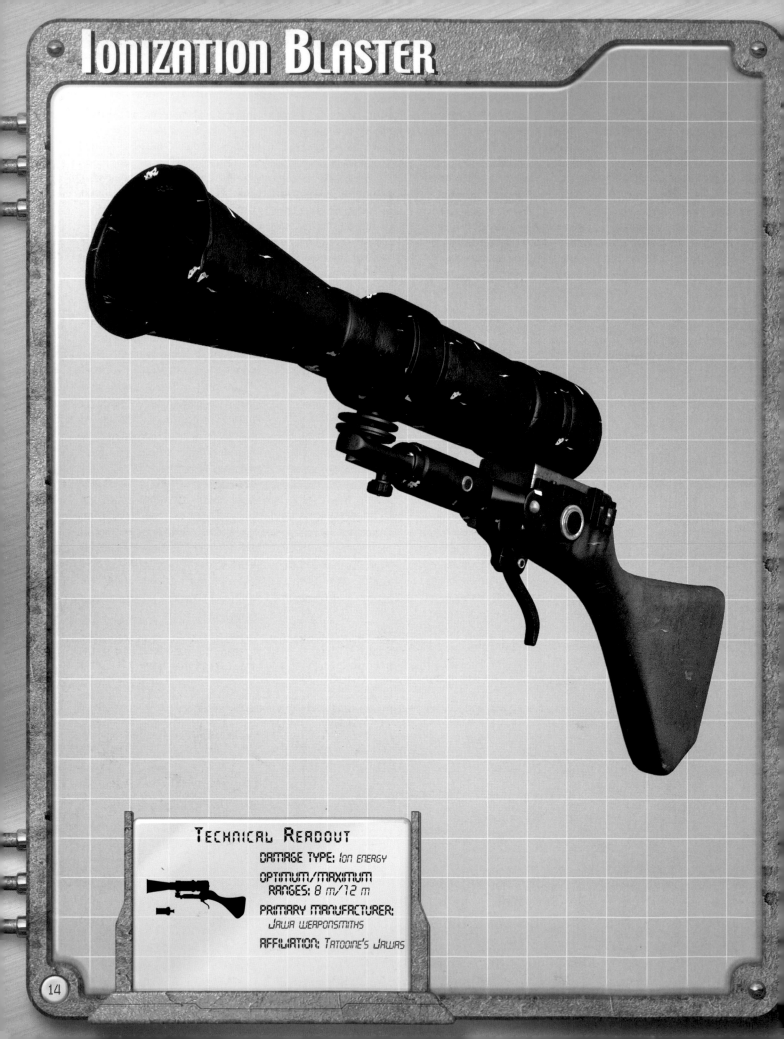

Ionization Blaster

TECHNICAL READOUT

DAMAGE TYPE: Ion Energy

OPTIMUM/MAXIMUM RANGES: 8 m/12 m

PRIMARY MANUFACTURER: Jawa Weaponsmiths

AFFILIATION: Tatooine's Jawas

Scavenged Jawa Ionization Blaster

Developed in response to a droid rebellion eons before the Galactic Civil War, ion weapons are designed to short-circuit electrical systems, rendering droids and many other forms of technology completely inert. Over the years, ion weaponry has been perfected, although the technology remains expensive, often illegal, and relatively rare throughout the galaxy. On Tatooine, however, the native Jawas frequently cobble together their own versions of ion blasters, which they use to capture droids found wandering the desert. Like its predecessors, the Jawa ionization blaster overloads the circuitry of droids, completely disabling the automata. The Jawas sell these droids to local moisture farmers, making the ionization blaster vital to the Jawas' livelihood.

Jawa ionization blasters are constructed from a variety of components scavenged from crashed starships found in Tatooine's desert. The ion blaster is actually built around a blaster rifle that has been stripped of all internal components except its power pack housing. The Jawa weaponsmith adds a restraining bolt, a device typically used to control droid behaviors and movement. in an ionization blaster, the restraining bolt is modified to release an ion stream configured to broadcast the bolt's *halt* command over a short distance. As it moves through the blaster's barrel, the energy passes through a series of ion accelerators, which amplify the beam. A droid enveloped by this beam is immediately disabled and remains inert for up to twenty minutes, but is otherwise unharmed. The blaster's range is limited to twelve meters. However, most droids are slow-moving targets, and the weapon's wide cone of fire serves to increase the wielder's accuracy. Jawa ionization blasters are virtually useless against organic targets, causing little more than a painful sting, even when used at close range.

Like many Jawa "inventions," Jawa ionization blasters are fragile and unreliable. Even if properly maintained, an ion blaster can easily malfunction. Explosive overloads are common, and an ion blaster can be broken if dropped, handled roughly, or overexposed to the elements.

Although the Jawa ionization blaster may be one of the most innovative ion weapons, it is not unique in the galaxy. In the four thousand standard years following the Great Droid Revolution, ion weapons drifted in and out of the Republic arsenal, based largely on the nature of current threats. When the Old Republic faced the technology-reliant Mandalorians in the Mandalorian Wars, handheld ion weapons were issued to many Republic soldiers for use against their armored foes. After the war ended, a number of these military-grade weapons eventually found their way onto black markets across the galaxy. During the Clone Wars, ion weapons were popular among Republic clone troopers because the Confederacy's forces were composed primarily of battle droids. Republic weapons designers even combined ion technology with traditional blasters to create weapons that could damage both battle droids and organic assailants. Ion blasters were rare during the Galactic Civil War, and are virtually useless in the New Republic's fight against the Yuuzhan Vong, whose biotechnology has few inorganic electrical components.

> ## "We're doomed!"
> —*Preprogrammed protocol droid response to seeing an ionization blaster*

5 Accu-Accelerator: A device recovered from the ion drive of a crashed capital starship, the accu-accelerator amplifies the ionization blaster's ion beam.

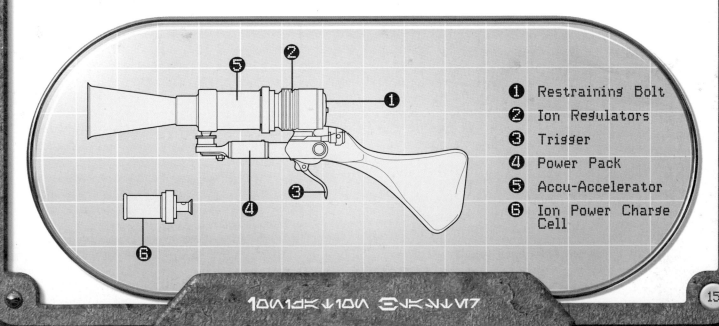

1. Restraining Bolt
2. Ion Regulators
3. Trigger
4. Power Pack
5. Accu-Accelerator
6. Ion Power Charge Cell

SONIC BLASTER

TECHNICAL READOUT

DAMAGE TYPE: Sonic energy

OPTIMUM/MAXIMUM RANGES: 15 m/40 m

PRIMARY MANUFACTURER: Gordarl Weaponsmiths

AFFILIATION: Geonosian warriors

Geonosian Sonic Blaster

Since the appearance of the original blaster weapons, most weapons designers have focused on exploiting the technology to its fullest. This was especially true in the heart of the Old Republic, where exploration of alternate weaponry was often considered too expensive. In the Outer Rim, isolated cultures developed alternate forms of ranged weapons that stand in sharp contrast to the energy blaster. On the rocky world of Geonosis, for example, the native Geonosians channeled their innate understanding of sonics into an entire suite of weapons that would later kill countless Republic clone troopers and Jedi.

Long before the rise of the Empire, Geonosians explored sonic wave theory. Eventually, Geonosian inventors built basic generators that converted sonic vibrations into other forms of energy. This gave rise to such wondrous inventions as sonic lamps, which could literally convert noise into light. The next evolution of Geonosian sonic technology involved projecting various frequencies and intensities of sonic waves. The first sonic emitters were simple navigational beacons. Soon Geonosian miners developed sonic hammers that generated far more intense sonic waves capable of blasting away rock and stone.

A natural extension of the sonic hammer, the handheld sonic blaster is now one of the Geonosians' staple weapons. The large sidearm, which is just over a meter long, is generally wielded by members of the warrior caste, who function as soldiers, guards, and security personnel. The weapon's sonic waves are generated by a series of high-energy oscillators located near the rear of the blaster. A reduction chamber collects and collapses

the waves into a powerful "sonic ball," which serves as the weapon's ammunition. When the blaster is fired, a small plasma containment charge is inserted into the sonic ball. This charge stabilizes the sonic ball until it impacts a target, exploding violently. A direct hit from a sonic blaster can cause instant death as internal organs rupture under the concussive sound waves.

Other groups manufacture similar arms. The Nagai use the versatile Kob sonic blaster, an elegant weapon designed by a cunning tactician named General Kob. It emits sonic waves of varying power, ranging from a basic sonic pulse capable of stunning most organic life to a narrow sonic beam that tears through flesh on a molecular level.

Both SonoMax and Pacnorval Defense Systems manufacture sonic pistols and rifles with effective stun settings releasing a high-pitched wail. This disrupts a target's equilibrium, and a concentrated burst can render a victim unconscious. These sonic weapons are excellent for crowd control. Wielders usually wear sonic-dampening helmets to protect against accidental exposure. During the Galactic Civil War, sonic weapons were seldom issued to Rebel or Imperial troops. However, since nearly all blasters are useless underwater, Imperial aquatic assault troopers were armed exclusively with sonic weapons. Imperial forces also mounted large sonic weapons on amphibious assault skimmers and various submersibles.

> **"Let the Jedi come. Our weapons will melt their eardrums and make their hearts explode."**
> —*Geonosian Archduke Poggle the Lesser*

❼ Trigger: The Geonosian sonic blaster is designed to be gripped by clawlike Geonosian hands. The trigger is oddly placed, making it very difficult for non-Geonosians to wield the weapon.

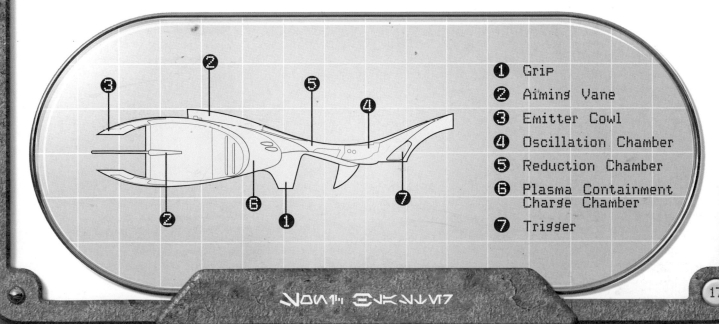

1. Grip
2. Aiming Vane
3. Emitter Cowl
4. Oscillation Chamber
5. Reduction Chamber
6. Plasma Containment Charge Chamber
7. Trigger

DISRUPTOR

TECHNICAL READOUT

DAMAGE TYPE: Blaster energy (concentrated to cause disintegration)

OPTIMUM/MAXIMUM RANGES: 10 m/20 m

PRIMARY MANUFACTURER: Tenloss Syndicate

AFFILIATION: Black Sun

Tenloss DXR-6 Disruptor Rifle

By their very nature, weapons are designed to maim and kill. Even among the many deadly weapons in the galaxy, the disruptor is infamous for its ability to disintegrate victims in the most painful and heinous manner imaginable. The disruptor's powerful beam affects an object on the molecular level, breaking it down until it is reduced to a pile of ash. Even a glancing blast can cause horrible injury and disfigurement. A direct hit results in nearly instant death. Disruptors are made even more effective by the fact that they can penetrate force fields, nearly all forms of armor, and even thick armor plating.

Illegal in most parts of the New Republic, disruptors are similar in design to blasters. However, a disruptor's oversize XCiter and actuating module is capable of processing a huge volume of blaster gas when the weapon's trigger is pulled, resulting in a much more powerful energy beam than a blaster. The weapon's galven cylinders tightly focus this high-energy particle beam into a destructive force that can disintegrate durasteel plates.

A disruptor has daunting power requirements. Most disruptors are fitted with paired power packs, which are usually drained after only five shots. A recycle time of more than five seconds is necessary to prevent damage to internal components and prepare for the next shot. Because of their extreme power needs, disruptors are seldom used by military forces, although Imperial inquisitors and interrogators did carry miniaturized disruptors for various unscrupulous purposes during the Galactic Civil War.

The Tenloss Syndicate is the galaxy's foremost manufacturer of disruptor pistols and rifles, most of which are sold to criminal organizations such as Black Sun or leaked onto the black market where they are purchased by bounty hunters, assassins, and slavers. Tenloss produces both disruptor pistols and rifles, and its most popular model is the DXR-6 rifle. The DXR-6 is relatively inexpensive when compared to other similar weapons, and its lightweight frame allows it to be fired while on the run.

Although the Tenloss Syndicate is the most prolific disruptor designer, other more prominent companies also surreptitiously release disruptor models. In fact, Merr-Sonn's MSD-32 pistol is perhaps the most advanced disruptor on the market. The MSD-32 is much more efficient than previous disruptors due to a rapid-pulse energy module. The energy pulses created by this module further increase the weapon's firepower, reducing the recycle time to three seconds and doubling the number of shots the disruptor can fire before its power packs are depleted.

> **"You are free to use any methods necessary, but I want them alive. No disintegrations."**
>
> *—Darth Vader, instructing bounty hunters on capturing Luke Skywalker's allies*

7 Cooling Vent: Most disruptors require a lengthy recycling time to cool internal components. At the Stars' End prison facility, Han Solo was cornered by the assassin Uul-Rha-Shan, who was armed with a disruptor. Solo exploited the disruptor's primary weakness, gunning down the Tiss'shar killer while his weapon recycled.

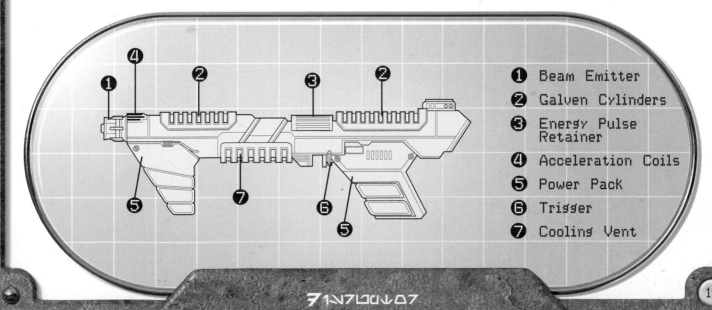

1. Beam Emitter
2. Galven Cylinders
3. Energy Pulse Retainer
4. Acceleration Coils
5. Power Pack
6. Trigger
7. Cooling Vent

TECHNICAL READOUT

DAMAGE TYPE: *Kinetic and piercing*
OPTIMUM/MAXIMUM RANGES: *150 m/300 m*
PRIMARY MANUFACTURER: *Czerka*
AFFILIATION: *Luke Skywalker*

Czerka 6-2Aug2 Hunting Rifle

Tatooine's moisture farmers endure a subsistence existence, hovering on the edge of poverty. In addition to the harsh atmospheric conditions, the farmers must brave violent Tusken Raiders, voracious krayt dragons, and brutal thugs. Unable to obtain traditional blasters because the Hutts control the gun running, these moisture farmers must often resort to outdated and "primitive" projectile weapons to defend themselves.

Among the first ranged weapons developed, projectile pistols and rifles remain in limited use throughout the galaxy, especially on backwater worlds where blasters are too expensive or difficult to acquire. Literally thousands of different projectile weapons exist, but nearly all use an explosive chemical reaction to fire some form of solid bullet or slug. These can be fashioned out of metal, hardened plastics, ceramics, or even clear transparisteel. More advanced projectile weapons may fire specialty rounds carrying toxic gases, acids, or explosive heads.

As a youth, Luke Skywalker owned a very simple Czerka 6-2Aug2 hunting rifle. Although it lacked a laser targeting sight or scope, the long barrel and Luke's keen eyesight were more than sufficient to target womp rats from a great distance. Like many other slugthrowers, Luke's rifle was easy to repair and maintain.

Czerka also manufactures the Adventurer, a slugthrower rifle used by the bounty hunter Aurra Sing. Slightly more advanced, the Adventurer includes an oxidizer release module. When the weapon fires, the slug chamber is filled with a rich oxidizer that increases the bullet's velocity. The Adventurer is also designed to

> **"We always know when the Tusken Raiders are on a killing spree. We can hear their rifles cracking across the desert like lightning strikes."**
> —*Huff Darklighter*

collapse for concealed transport. Bounty hunters and assassins often use projectile weapons for night missions because they do not produce the bright bolts common to blaster weapons.

Tatooine's Tusken Raiders favor hand-built projectile rifles, similar in design to other slugthrowers but reinforced with rare tracti wood found only in hidden Tusken oases. Sand People often lurk on high mesas or cliffs, attempting to pick off their prey at extreme range. They will target unsuspecting travelers, Jawas, and moisture farmers. Tusken Raiders have also been known to attack Podracer and swoop jockeys traveling through the Jundland Wastes. Because of the rifle's sturdy construction, it can also be used as a melee weapon in close quarters if necessary.

Some companies have endeavored to create more advanced slugthrowers, many of which rival modern blasters. The Morellian Weapons Conglomerate produces the Enforcer pistol, a weapon that fires extremely large rounds to achieve roughly the same damage output as a standard heavy blaster pistol. The Blaster Buster slugthrower, manufactured by Oriolanis Defense Systems, fires projectiles that can actually home in on recently fired weapons. Meanwhile, Frohard's Galactic Firearms has advanced projectile weaponry by integrating magnetic acceleration technology into the company's Magna Caster 100.

④ Sturdy Stock: Luke's rifle was constructed to endure the rigors of desert life, but it was no match for a Tusken Raider's gaffi stick.

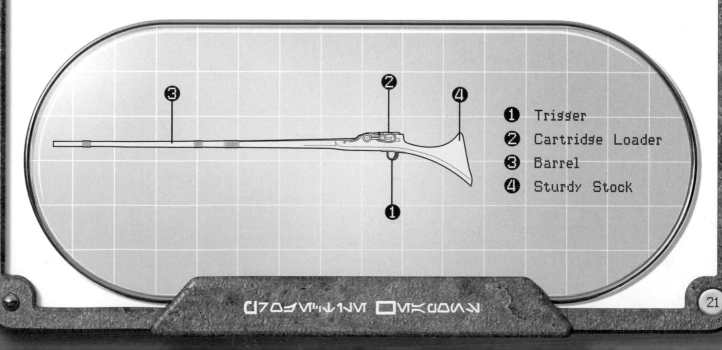

❶ Trigger
❷ Cartridge Loader
❸ Barrel
❹ Sturdy Stock

DART SHOOTER

TECHNICAL READOUT

DAMAGE TYPE: Piercing (often coupled with poison)

OPTIMUM/MAXIMUM RANGES: 10 m/100 m

PRIMARY MANUFACTURER: Prax Arms

AFFILIATION: Jango Fett

Prax Arms Velocity-7 Dart Shooter

The pinnacle of stealth weaponry, dart shooters are compact devices that fire small, metal projectiles. One of several weapons commonly found in an assassin's arsenal, dart shooters are relatively silent when fired, are easily concealed when carried, and can fool most weapons detectors. Most important, dart shooters can be calibrated to fire a number of different types of darts, ranging from razor-sharp projectiles that can puncture a victim's throat to toxic darts that kill, stun, or paralyze their prey.

Most dart shooters are basic, spring-powered weapons. Darts are loaded into a chamber. When the trigger is depressed, the high-tension springs launch the darts. The Prax Arms Stealth-2VS palm shooter is the smallest of such spring-loaded dart shooters, and can easily fit in the palm of a human hand. The Stealth-2VS is so small, in fact, that it can even be concealed within a false comlink or droid caller. Prax Arms also manufactures the Protector PRP-502, a hold-out dart shooter. The incredibly light Protector can be broken into four separate pieces to allow it to be easily hidden in luggage. Spring-loaded darts such as those fired from the Stealth-2VS or the Protector rarely have a maximum range greater than twenty-five meters.

More powerful dart shooters, such as the Velocity-7 unit integrated into Jango Fett's gauntlets, fire the darts using compressed air. Darts propelled in this manner have a much greater range and are capable of hitting targets at well over one hundred meters, although they are still most accurate within about ten. While other Prax Arms models fire very small microdarts, the Velocity-7 is designed to shoot much larger projectiles, such as the forked Kamino saberdart. The saberdart, one of Fett's favorite assassination tools, can be filled with a number of different poisons. When fired, the saberdart's two embedding prongs burrow into the target's flesh, while a long injector needle delivers the toxin.

Poison darts such as the saberdart are common throughout the underworld. The list of toxins available for these weapons is virtually endless. Malkite themfar, developed by the infamous Malkite Poisoners, is a fast-acting nerve toxin that causes death in less than ten seconds. Fex-M3 causes gray matter to release its stored energy, literally boiling the target's brain, while Bavo Six serves as a disorienting truth serum. Concentrated doses of a contact painkiller called symoxin knock victims unconscious within fifteen seconds. The poison Jango Fett used to kill Zam Wesell was a fast-acting toxin called Sennari; years later, bounty hunter and Boba Fett imitator Jodo Kast would use the same poison in his concealed dart launchers.

Aside from poisons, many darts can be modified to carry much more exotic payloads. Microscopic homing beacons can be injected into a victim's bloodstream via microdarts. Darts can also carry molecular acid, bacteria or other germs, explosive heads, and sonic emitters.

> **"I ain't seen one of these since I was prospecting on Subterrel, beyond the Outer Rim! This baby belongs to them cloners. What you got here is a Kamino saberdart . . ."**
> —*Dexter Jettster*

❼ Distinctive Cuts: The strange cuts on the saberdart allowed Dexter Jettster to identify the weapon's Kaminoan origins for Obi-Wan Kenobi.

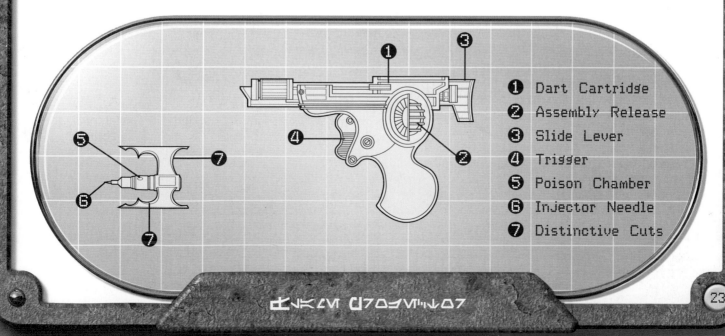

❶ Dart Cartridge
❷ Assembly Release
❸ Slide Lever
❹ Trigger
❺ Poison Chamber
❻ Injector Needle
❼ Distinctive Cuts

Flame Projector

Technical Readout

DAMAGE TYPE: *Fire/heat energy*

OPTIMUM/MAXIMUM RANGES: *5 m/10 m*

PRIMARY MANUFACTURER: *Merr-Sonn Munitions*

AFFILIATION: *Corporate Sector Authority Security Police*

Merr-Sonn CR-24 Flame Rifle

In ancient times, Trandoshan invaders assaulting enemy towers on Jabiim were likely to find themselves doused in burning oil. Primitive pictographs found on Rodia depict warriors with flaming swords. Iktotchi armies used controlled burns to drive their foes into ambushes. With the advance of technology, engineers found new and innovative ways to harness fire to produce an array of weapons, the most common of which are known as flame projectors.

A flame projector is any weapon that emits a cone or jet of flame. Most flame projectors are fueled by high-energy flammable liquid stored in a pressurized fuel chamber. When the projector is fired, the liquid is funneled through a stubby barrel, where it is ignited by special heating elements. The resulting cone or spray is capable of damaging many forms of armor and can melt flesh with ease.

The Merr-Sonn CR-24 flame rifle is a standard flame projector. The weapon resembles a bulbous blaster rifle connected to a small refueling canister that can be carried or clipped to the wielder's belt. It has surprisingly short range of only ten meters, but a wide field of fire that makes the weapon useful in close quarters. Corporate Sector Authority security police find the CR-24 useful because its dramatic flame gouts intimidate most sentient beings. Merr-Sonn also manufactures the C-22, a smaller flame carbine, as well as a much larger CR-28 flamer that can be mounted on vehicles. Czerka has consistently copied all of Merr-Sonn's flame projector designs, releasing the CZ-24 Flamemaster rifle, CZ-22 Flametongue pistol, and CZ-28 Flamestrike heavy weapon.

Because of their relative simplicity, flame projectors can be integrated into droids and armor. The HK series of combat droids prominent during the Sith Wars used flame projectors much more offensively and seemed to take perverse delight in setting enemies on fire. Mandalorian armor, including the suit worn by bounty hunters Jango and Boba Fett, often incorporates miniaturized flame projectors concealed within wrist gauntlets. During the Clone Wars, the Trade Federation used small squads of flame battle droids to terrorize innocent civilians. Recognized by their red shoulders, flame battle droids sported flame projectors fueled by large, backpack tanks. The flame droid's primary programming involved burning homes, crops, and municipal buildings on conquered worlds.

The invading Yuuzhan Vong also understood the significance of fire as a weapon. The Yuuzhan Vong's analog to the flame projector was an organism called the fire spitter. The creature is capable of expelling a thick jet of flaming biomatter and can be implanted into a warrior's arm, completely replacing the Yuuzhan Vong's forearm from elbow to wrist.

The Yuuzhan Vong also unleashed much larger monstrosities called fire breathers on the unsuspecting New Republic forces. These thirty-meter-tall creatures have several flexible proboscises that issue streams of liquid flame. The Yuuzhan Vong used a number of the bladderlike fire breathers in their invasion of Coruscant.

> ## "Fill your enemies with primal fear, then fill their lungs with fire!"
> *—Ancient Gand proverb*

❼ Refueling Canister Valve: Most flame projectors must be connected to a canister filled with flammable liquid or gas. This canister can be ruptured by a well-placed bolt from a blaster rifle, resulting in a violent explosion.

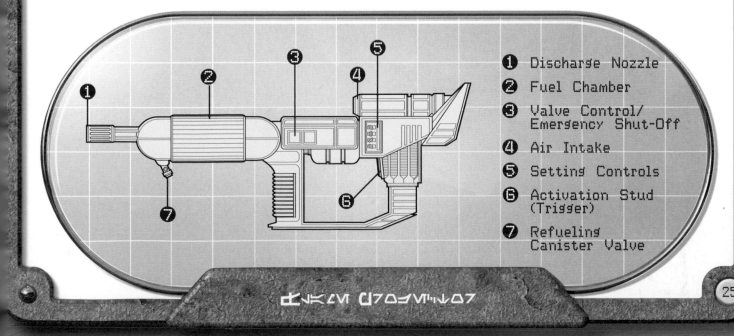

1. Discharge Nozzle
2. Fuel Chamber
3. Valve Control/ Emergency Shut-Off
4. Air Intake
5. Setting Controls
6. Activation Stud (Trigger)
7. Refueling Canister Valve

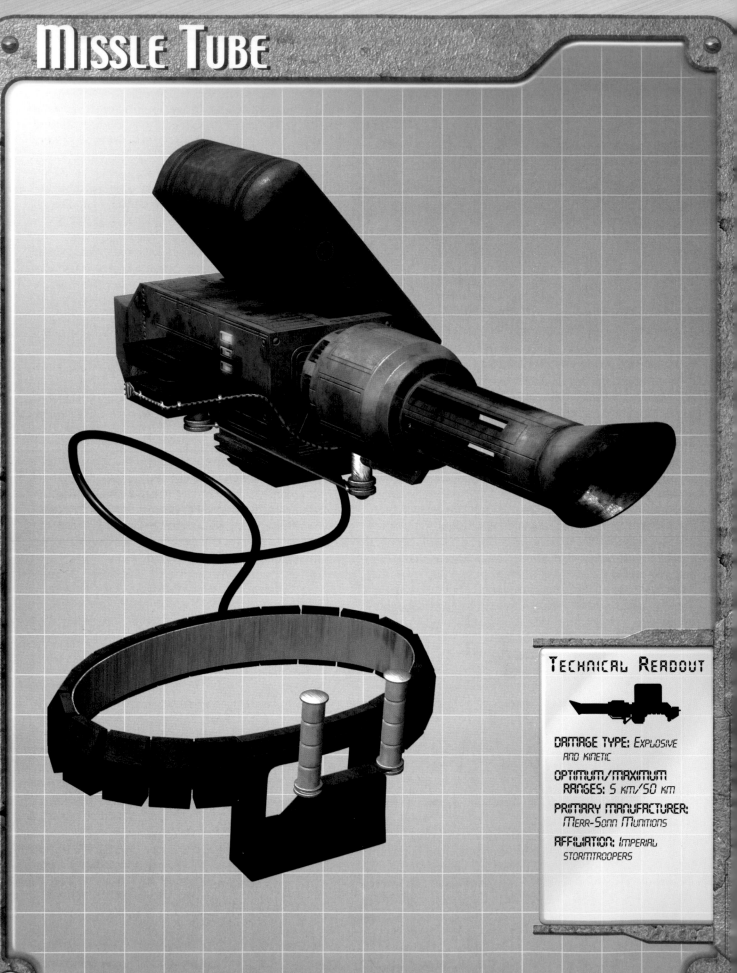

Technical Readout

DAMAGE TYPE: *Explosive and kinetic*

OPTIMUM/MAXIMUM RANGES: *5 km/50 km*

PRIMARY MANUFACTURER: *Merr-Sonn Munitions*

AFFILIATION: *Imperial Stormtroopers*

Merr-Sonn Munitions PLX-2M

Missile tube is the common name for portable missile launchers, weapons well suited to destroying airspeeders, small ground vehicles, and even starfighters flying low in an atmosphere. Most missile tubes are shoulder-mounted devices that can carry a limited number of rocket-propelled explosives.

The Merr-Sonn PLX-2M, also known as the Plex-Twoem, is one of the most common missile tubes. Originally designed for the Empire at the start of the Galactic Civil War, the PLX-2M is a durable weapon that can be easily transported by Imperial stormtroopers or other soldiers over nearly any type of terrain. The PLX-2M's missile cartridge is usually loaded with six Arakyd 3t3 missiles, each armed with miniature proton warheads capable of destroying Rebel snowspeeders, for example, with a direct hit.

The PLX-2M includes a host of advanced features. Although the weapon weighs close to fifty kilograms, a built-in microrepulsorlift unit provides support and allows the launcher to be mounted comfortably on a soldier's shoulder. The repulsorlifts and a large support collar help cushion the weapon's recoil when it is fired. A computerized tracking system with heads-up tracking and hologram displays provide the operator with a wealth of data, including a target's range, speed, and defensive energy signatures. A conventional scope is also supplied for use in extreme conditions or in the event the other systems malfunction. Despite its apparent complexity, the PLX-2M can be assembled and readied for battle in less than a minute.

Many missile tubes have only a single firing mode, but the PLX-2M incorporates an advanced homing system with two "smart" attack options. When in EPR mode, the tube's homing missiles will track intense infrared sources, such as the target vessel's exhaust. A secondary gravity-activated mode (GAM) homes in on the gravity waves generated by vehicle repulsorlifts. The missile tube can also be "dumb-fired," relying solely on line-of-sight targeting. Dumb firing is useful when a missile is launched in proximity to friendly craft that might be accidentally targeted by the EPR or GAM homing systems.

Like many other specialized weapon types, missile tubes have drifted in and out of military use dozens of times over the past several centuries. During the Clone Wars, the Old Republic found missile launchers useful for wiping out legions of battle droids with a single shot. However, the explosive weapons were seldom used on populated worlds for fear of causing collateral damage. Even prior to the Clone Wars, missile tubes were often used as antiaircraft weapons or for destroying troop transports. By the advent of the Galactic Civil War, however, most aircraft and even many ground vehicles utilized advanced countermeasures that could confuse a missile's homing systems. This increased the importance of specialized training for all missile tube operators—only a direct hit fired at exactly the right moment could hope to destroy an enemy target.

> ## "If the Rebels won't surrender, we'll bury them in their bunkers."
> —*Imperial General Veers before ordering the use of missile tubes at the Battle of Ghorman*

7 Missile Cartridge: Missile tubes can carry a variety of missiles, including armor-piercing antivehicle shells, explosive "bunker busters," and even caustic gas delivery systems.

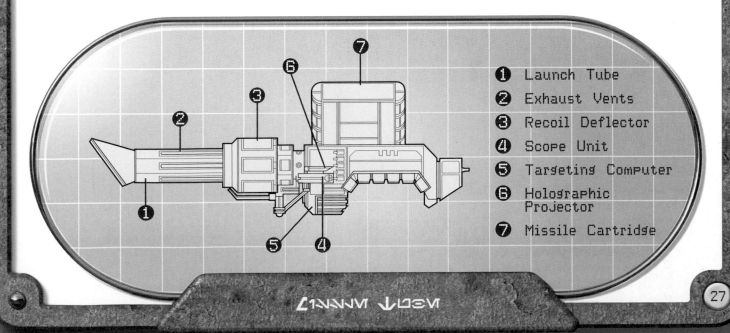

1. Launch Tube
2. Exhaust Vents
3. Recoil Deflector
4. Scope Unit
5. Targeting Computer
6. Holographic Projector
7. Missile Cartridge

TECHNICAL READOUT

DAMAGE TYPE: Explosive and disintegration

BLAST RADIUS: 20 m

PRIMARY MANUFACTURER: Merr-Sonn Munitions

AFFILIATION: Boushh (Princess Leia in disguise)

Merr-Sonn Munitions Class-A Thermal Detonator

The ability to cause sudden, disruptive chaos on a battlefield can easily mean the difference between a devastating loss and a surprising victory. One of the most effective means for achieving total bedlam is through the use of explosives, especially hand-size thermal detonators and grenades. Such weapons not only cause massive death and destruction, but also generate disorienting noise, smoke, fire, or flashes of light upon detonation. Since they are easy to carry and use, can intimidate enemies, and take down multiple targets with a single explosion, grenades are extremely attractive to mercenary groups and bounty hunters.

Most grenades are basically high-yield explosives that are designed to detonate within a few seconds of activation. An attacker merely needs to activate the grenade by depressing a trigger switch before throwing the device into the heart of enemy ranks. When the preset timer expires, the grenade will explode. Timing is often critical: if the attacker throws the weapon too early, the intended victims might be able to flee or return the grenade before it explodes. Thrown too late, the grenade will explode harmlessly in midair.

Explosive grenades, like Merr-Sonn's C-22 fragmentation grenade, consist of a small detonite charge wrapped in a chrome shell. When the device detonates, everything within a ten-meter diameter is ripped apart by metal shrapnel and burned by intense heat. The C-22 has a timer of up to two minutes, which allows the weapon to be used as a land mine in ambushes. It also has a magnetic grapple for precision placement during demolitions work.

> ### "This bounty hunter is my kind of scum. Fearless and inventive."
> *—Jabba the Hutt, after the bounty hunter Boushh used a thermal detonator to renegotiate a bounty on Chewbacca's head*

Perhaps the most powerful (and infamous) explosive is the thermal detonator. The small, metallic sphere resembles a standard grenade, but is far more destructive. The thermal detonator's volatile baradium core is encased in a thin shell of thermite. Upon detonation, the baradium fusion reaction generates an expanding particle field that disintegrates everything in the blast radius. Most thermal detonators consume everything within a twenty-meter radius, although many less potent models also exist. Stormtroopers carry thermal detonators with much smaller baradium cores, resulting in explosive blasts of no more than five meters. Conversely, some custom-built thermal detonators can generate one-hundred-meter blast spheres.

Unfortunately, baradium is notoriously unstable, and a thermal detonator can accidentally explode if the weapon is dropped, jarred, or exposed to excessive heat. Due to thermal detonators' unpredictability, they are illegal throughout the galaxy for civilians to. They can only be acquired through military sources or the black market. Since they are so difficult to acquire, thermal detonators are used almost exclusively by military forces, which employ the weapon for large-scale combat or demolitions.

4 **Pressure-Sensitive Trigger:** The sliding thumb trigger activates a six-second timer, but can also be configured to explode if the trigger is released. Princess Leia used this setting while negotiating with Jabba to prevent foolish attacks by the Hutt's cronies.

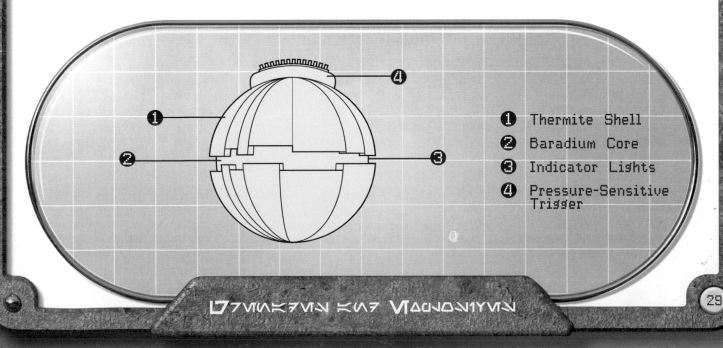

1. Thermite Shell
2. Baradium Core
3. Indicator Lights
4. Pressure-Sensitive Trigger

Grenades and Explosives (continued)

Standard explosives are the most common grenades, but Merr-Sonn and other companies also manufacture a number of specialty grenades. Merr-Sonn's G-20 glop grenade is filled with an adhesive liquid that is released via high-pressure jets when the weapon is thrown. The adhesive becomes a sticky foam that traps anyone within a ten-meter diameter of the target area. Like many other grenades, the glop grenade can be set to activate on contact or when the weapon's timer expires. Police forces, especially those in the Corporate Sector, use the glop grenade to subdue criminals without causing injury. The G-20 is reusable, although it must be refilled with adhesive between each use.

Cryoban grenades utilize a special chemical agent capable of absorbing heat. When the grenade detonates, the resulting explosion absorbs all heat in the area, creating a field of intense cold. Originally developed as a fire suppressant, cryoban grenades are excellent for damaging any electronics, droids, or even vehicles that have not been thoroughly adapted for cold-weather use. The sudden drop in temperature not only stuns organic targets, but can also cause severe nerve and cellular damage to exposed flesh.

Czerka's Spore/B stun grenade releases Bothan stun spores to render targets unconscious. Geonosian sonic grenades can disorient and destroy a victim's equilibrium. Luma grenades are effectively flares, but can be used to blind victims when detonated at close range. Both dye grenades and smoke grenades release billowing clouds for making landing zones or obstructing the vision of enemy forces.

Chemical load grenades, perhaps the most versatile grenades, are designed to carry a variety of chemical payloads. For killing enemy troops without damaging structures, military units employ chemical load grenades with the deadly, yellow nerve toxin Fex-M3. Agent T-248, which induces debilitating nausea, is well suited for crowd control or riot duty, while plank gas is a corrosive chemical that can destroy defensive structures.

Grenades have numerous military applications, but they can be used for industrial purposes as well. Proton grenades are small concussion weapons designed for large-scale demolition. While usually reserved for use at construction sights, the Rebel Alliance "acquired" hundreds of proton grenades throughout the Galactic Civil War. Han Solo and his squad used these to destroy the Endor shield generator. Companies with mining interests, such as Czerka, frequently deploy biotic grenades. These grenades release tightly focused explosions to speed the efforts of mining crews.

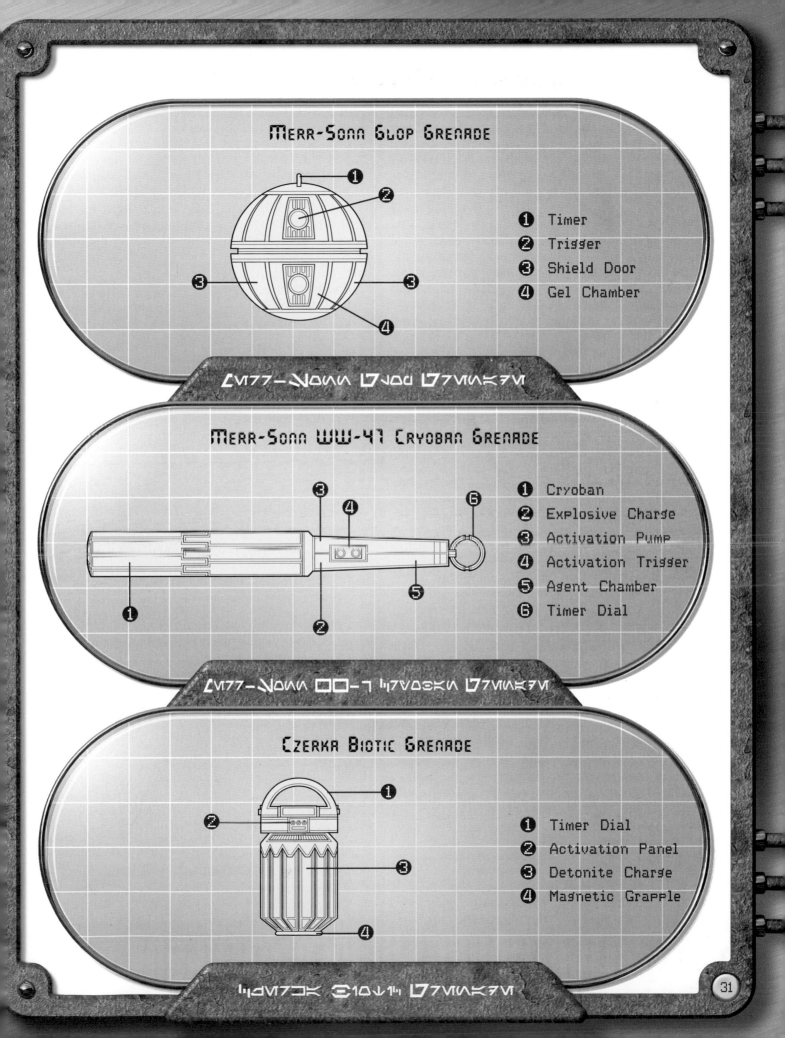

MERR-SONN GLOP GRENADE

1. Timer
2. Trigger
3. Shield Door
4. Gel Chamber

MERR-SONN GLOP GRENADE

MERR-SONN WW-41 CRYOBAN GRENADE

1. Cryoban
2. Explosive Charge
3. Activation Pump
4. Activation Trigger
5. Agent Chamber
6. Timer Dial

MERR-SONN WW-41 CRYOBAN GRENADE

CZERKA BIOTIC GRENADE

1. Timer Dial
2. Activation Panel
3. Detonite Charge
4. Magnetic Grapple

CZERKA BIOTIC GRENADE

TECHNICAL READOUT

DAMAGE TYPE: Plasma (electrical) energy/kinetic (when used as melee weapon)

OPTIMUM/MAXIMUM RANGES: 30 m/100 m

PRIMARY MANUFACTURER: Otoh Gunga Defense League

AFFILIATION: Gungan Grand Army

Gungan Atlatl and Cesta

For centuries, Naboo's native Gungans have harvested a bizarre, energized plasma from their homeworld's core. This "energy goo" helps to power Gungan vehicles and devices and, when the need arises, can be used as a weapon. The Gungans have fashioned the plasma into spheres of varying size that can be hurled like grenades. Each of these "energy balls" consists of unstable plasmic energy encased in a thin super-charged organic membrane. Upon impact with the ground or enemy forces, the goo explodes. The energized plasma causes massive external injury to organic targets. It is also capable of shorting out electrical systems, making the energy balls especially effective against droids and vehicles.

In order to throw their bizarre energy balls over greater distances, the Gungans have developed both the atlatl and the cesta. The atlatl is a short throwing stick with a cradle at one end. A single energy ball can be placed in the cradle, and then flung over short distances. The atlatl is extremely accurate at close range. Its compact size allows a Gungan warrior to wield the atlatl with one hand while holding an energy shield in the other. When traveling, the atlatl is attached to the soldier's backpack or belt. Like other Gungan weapons, an atlatl is carved out of native woods. The handmade weapons are generally fashioned by their owners, making each one slightly different. If cornered, Gungans have been known to use the small throwing sticks as clubs.

The cesta is essentially a larger version of the atlatl.

> ### "It looks like a giant skipper squid exploded on the battlefield, sir . . . I can't take two steps without putting my boot into blue slime."
> —*RSF Lieutenant Gavyn Sykes reporting from the Great Plains battlefield near Theed*

The hand-carved cesta looks like a long staff with a small cup at one end. Like the atlatl, the cesta's primary purpose is throwing energy balls at approaching enemies. The cesta is less accurate than the atlatl and requires greater skill to wield effectively, but it can propel larger energy balls over much greater distances. The cesta is strictly a two-handed weapon. When an enemy closes, however, a Gungan warrior is trained to use the solid wooden cesta as a quarterstaff. Cestas deliver powerful, stunning blows with surprising speed. The dense wood used to craft a cesta is strong enough to smash a battle droid's head without splintering or cracking.

To keep militiagungs in top form, General Ceel has established a training center for atlatl, cesta, and arbalest practice. The "shooting range" is a broad and shallow arm of Lake Paonga known as the Scrumma Jawbone. The targeting system in the Scrumma is ingenious, featuring floating bull's eyes, targets that bob above or below the water on command, and hovering methane-filled gasbags. Swamp creatures of Naboo know to give the area a wide berth when class is in session.

④ **Gungan Carvings:** Gungan warriors often carve their own cestas, decorating them with symbols and icons that hold personal significance. Survivors of the Battle of Naboo memorialized the dead by carving the names of fallen friends onto the handles of their cestas.

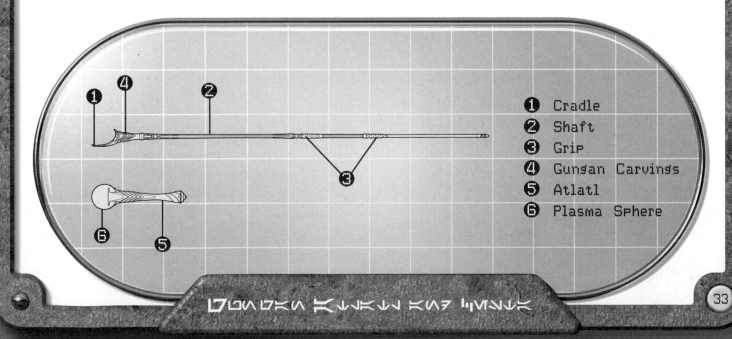

① Cradle
② Shaft
③ Grip
④ Gungan Carvings
⑤ Atlatl
⑥ Plasma Sphere

LANVAROK

TECHNICAL READOUT

DAMAGE TYPE: Slashing
(often coupled with poison)

OPTIMUM/MAXIMUM RANGES: 20 m/130 m

PRIMARY MANUFACTURER: Sith

AFFILIATION: Sith Lords

Sith Lanvarok

Long before the ancient peoples known as the Sith were conquered by Dark Jedi, they lived a primitive existence as simple hunters. They relied heavily on the use of spears, bows and arrows, and hatchets to kill their quarry. One of their most inventive weapons, however, was a "ranged polearm" known as the lanvarok.

The ancient lanvarok is a long pole topped with a compact ax head. Hidden inside the head is a spring-loaded disk launcher that can fire thin, deadly disks over short distances. A warrior can fire a single disk by swinging the lanvarok forward and then whipping it back again. A longer swing results in a wider spray of several disks. The lanvarok disks, which were often carved of bone, are capable of cutting through scaly hide and dense flesh. Using a lanvarok effectively does require great skill: the most successful attacks are those that target a victim's throat or face. The Sith sometimes applied poisons to the disks to ensure that even a glancing blow could be deadly.

The ancient lanvarok was originally designed for melee attacks on prey animals. The shape of the lanvarok's forward blade results in wide, deep cuts. The size of the front of the ax, coupled with the force of the polearm swing, can decapitate large beasts or easily hack limbs from human-size victims. The rear edge is thin, sharp, and narrow for piercing, finishing blows. A spearhead atop the lanvarok can be used defensively to ward off enemies. The earliest lanvaroks were constructed of wood or bone, but these were quickly replaced by lanvaroks made from metal alloys when the Sith discovered metallurgy.

Under the rule of the Sith Lords, the mutated Massassi

> ## "If it has blood, you can make it bleed. If it has eyes, you can blind it. If it has a mouth, you can make it scream . . ."
> —*Text found carved on an ancient Sith lanvarok*

warriors were trained to use the lanvarok as their primary weapon. The mutants' brute strength allowed the Massassi to hurl the disks much farther and with more force than normal Sith hunters. The Sith Lords themselves also carried ceremonial lanvaroks, but they relied on the Force to launch the disks.

Thousands of years after the Massassi fled to Yavin 4, the reborn Sith developed a modern version of the disk shooter. Rather than an archaic polearm, the modern lanvarok is a forearm-mounted ranged weapon that fires a volley of metal disks, usually in a small but unpredictable spray pattern, which makes dodging or blocking the deadly projectiles very difficult. Most are constructed of durasteel, although rare versions do have a thin layer of cortosis armor to protect them from lightsaber attacks.

Because the weapon is worn on the forearm, the wielder's hands are free to clutch a lightsaber or other melee weapon. For assassination and stealth missions, the lanvarok's disks are virtually silent when fired. The trigger mechanism on the lanvarok can easily be activated by a subtle manipulation of the Force; skilled Force-users can actually control the trajectory of the disks to ensure far more lethal attacks.

⑥ Force Release: This "secondary trigger" is a small nub that can be manipulated using the Force to allow the wielder to fire the weapon without actually pulling on the traditional trigger located toward the front of the lanvarok.

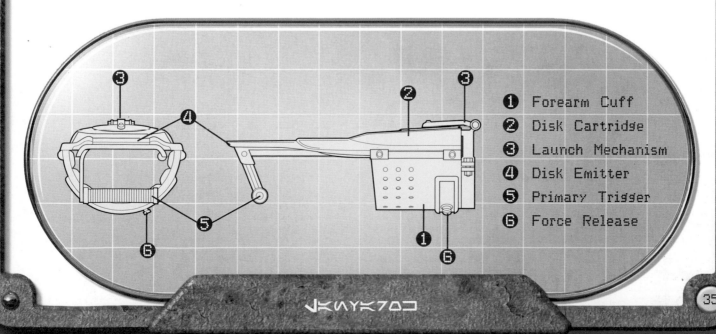

1. Forearm Cuff
2. Disk Cartridge
3. Launch Mechanism
4. Disk Emitter
5. Primary Trigger
6. Force Release

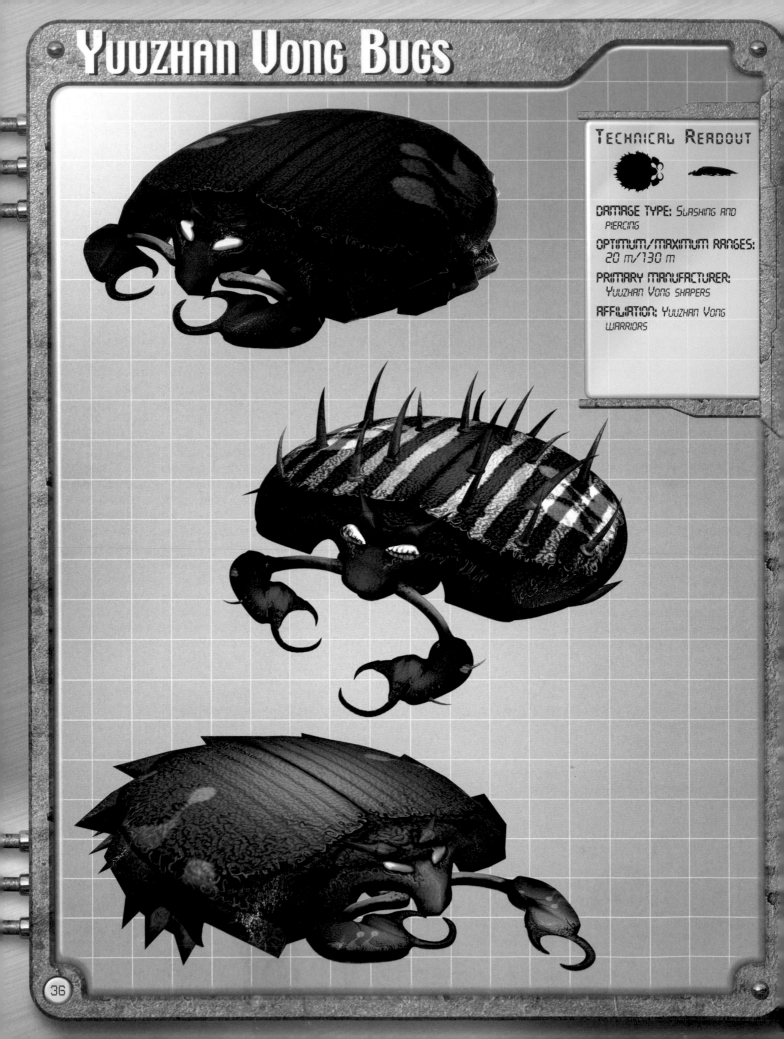

Technical Readout

DAMAGE TYPE: Slashing and piercing

OPTIMUM/MAXIMUM RANGES: 20 m/130 m

PRIMARY MANUFACTURER: Yuuzhan Vong shapers

AFFILIATION: Yuuzhan Vong warriors

Yuuzhan Vong Razor Bug

While blasters evolved as the primary ranged weapon in the Old Republic, outside the galaxy, the Yuuzhan Vong developed their own, bizarre analogs to the blaster. The Yuuzhan Vong's bioengineered ranged weapons are commonly called "bugs" throughout the galaxy, in reference to their similarity to large insects. Dozens of different types of bugs exist, but all are thrown or fired by Yuuzhan Vong warriors to attack a target at range and inflict terrible damage.

Among the most common bugs are thud bugs. Called nang hul in the Yuuzhan Vong tongue, a thud bug is essentially a bioengineered missile. The fist-size thud bugs are silver creatures small enough to be attached on a bandolier worn across the chest. When thrown by a Yuuzhan Vong warrior, the thud bug streaks toward its target with surprising agility.

> ## "One razor bug is a nuisance. Three might leave you scarred. Five will flay you alive."
> —*Jedi Knight Jaina Solo*

Thud bugs track their prey, following nearly all evasive maneuvers, even turning corners or slipping through defensive structures. A thud bug's velocity, which can exceed 150 kilometers per hour, results in an extremely painful collision when the bug hits its intended target. Depending upon the point of impact, a thud bug can knock an opponent to the ground or break limbs. If it crashes into a target's head, the result can be death. Smaller, slower thud bugs are used to stun and disorient targets, especially those whom the Yuuzhan Vong plan to capture.

Blast bugs are very similar to thud bugs, but are designed to explode when they near a target. The explosion can knock enemies flat on their backs, cause severe burns, even breach armor. A handful of blast bugs sparking simultaneously will rip through thin plate metal; a human victim caught in such an explosion has little

hope of survival. Both blast bugs and thud bugs are shaped from an organic creature known as a sparkbee.

A less destructive version of the blast bug is the snap bug. Upon detonation, the snap bug causes a bright flash of light and a sonic shock wave. This combination attack can blind, deafen, and stun victims within the snap bug's field of effect. Yuuzhan Vong, who are largely immune to the snap bug, sometimes use the creatures to provide momentary light useful for identifying enemies in the darkness.

Perhaps the most vicious Yuuzhan Vong bug is the razor bug, which functions much like a thrown knife or dagger. The insect-like weapon is covered in a thick carapace with extremely sharp edges capable of shredding flesh. When thrown, the razor bug extends a pair of wings to home in on a target. The razor bug will then flash past the victim, slicing any exposed flesh before using its wings to return to its wielder. Yuuzhan Vong typically throw several razor bugs at once, engulfing their enemies in small swarms of the slashing bioengineered insects.

Like many other Yuuzhan Vong weapons, bugs can be integrated into a Yuuzhan Vong's body. When Leia Organa Solo was attacked by a Yuuzhan Vong assassin on Gyndine, thud bugs literally burst from her assailant's chest.

5 Legs: A razor bug has visible legs that allow the living weapon to grasp a target long enough to make multiple cuts or even burrow into a victim's body.

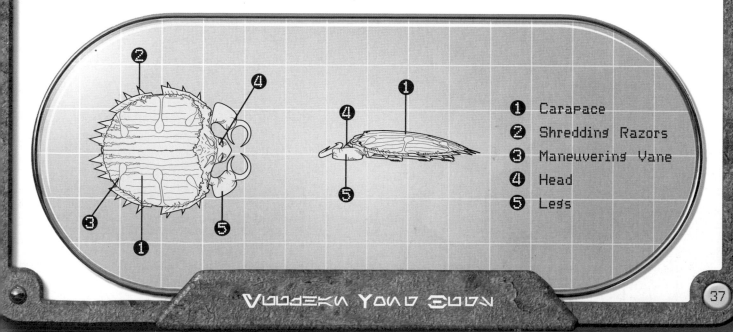

1. Carapace
2. Shredding Razors
3. Maneuvering Vane
4. Head
5. Legs

Additional Ranged Weapons

There are literally millions of different ranged weapons in the galaxy, ranging from simple slings to exotic sniper rifles. Following is a brief list of additional ranged weapons, designed to showcase some of the most important, prominent, or unusual of these devices.

Ammonia Bomb

An explosive that creates a cloud of ammonia when thrown or detonated. Ammonia bombs are lethal to most oxygen breathers and are therefore rarely used by most sentient species. Ammonia-breathing Gands, such as the bounty hunter Zuckuss, are not above using the weapons when necessary.

Ascension Gun

A modified Naboo Security S-5 blaster that supports a small grappling hook and liquid-cable launcher. The gun's cable can lift up to five hundred kilograms and was used by the Royal Security Forces to infiltrate the Theed Palace after Naboo was invaded by the Trade Federation. The Security S-5 can also fire blaster bolts, sting charges, and anesthetic microdarts.

Beam Tube

An ancient handheld weapon first developed more than twenty thousand standard years before the Battle of Yavin. The beam tube uses a backpack generator to produce an energy-particle beam. The beam can travel up to fifty meters and is capable of penetrating the simple armor worn by most soldiers long before the rise of the Old Republic. Beam-tube technology was a precursor of modern blaster technology.

Bryar Pistol

Bryar Pistol

A modified rifle that has been reduced to the size of a pistol for ease of use. Bryar pistols are very accurate, but cause little damage. The pistol does have a secondary firing mode that allows for more powerful blasts at the expense of additional charging time. The Bryar pistol remains the weapon of choice for Rebel agent and Jedi Knight Kyle Katarn.

Charric

A Chiss rifle, the charric fires a potent maser beam that causes both kinetic and thermal damage. The maser beam can penetrate ceramic or polymer-based armor.

Flechette Launcher

Any of a number of weapons designed to fire shards of metal or similar projectiles. The FC11 flechette launcher used by the Corporate Sector Authority's police forces can fire canisters of microdarts or ricocheting mines. The FC11 and other similar models are shoulder-fired weapons that can prove difficult to carry and wield. Smaller flechette launchers include the DF-D1, which is akin to a rifle, and the FWG-5 smart pistol. The smallest of these weapons, the Braceman Armor mini flechette gun, fires a spray of needles coated in paralytic toxin.

Grenade Mortar

A long-range grenade launcher designed for infantry support. Larger models, such as the Merr-Sonn MobileMortar-3, include a repulsorlift platform for ease of movement.

Ion Stunner

A small weapon that fires brief ion flashes designed to temporarily disable electronic devices, including security doors and droids, or frighten off would-be attackers.

Ascension Gun

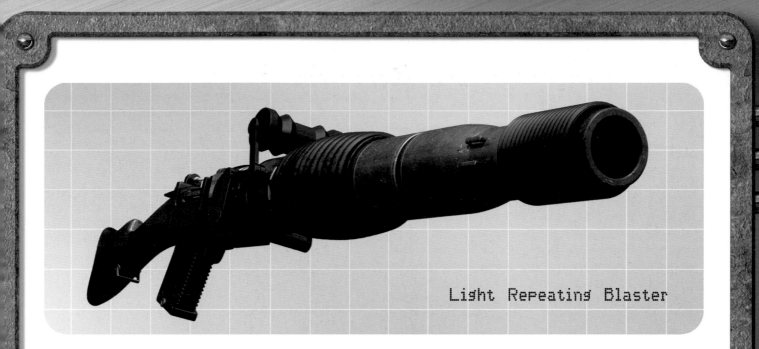

Light Repeating Blaster

Often carried by thugs living in the underlevels of Coruscant, ion stunners can also be used to disorient organic victims during robberies. An ion stunner is easily identified by the large focusing dish on its barrel.

LIGHT REPEATING BLASTER

A medium-range blaster rifle with rapid-fire capabilities. Imperial stormtroopers stationed on Tatooine used BlasTech T-21 light repeating blasters as their primary support weapons. The T-21 carries enough energy for only twenty-five shots, but it can be connected to a power generator for unlimited firing capability.

PLASMA EEL

Bioengineered grenades used by the Yuuzhan Vong. When being carried, plasma eels are pliable and can be coiled around a warrior's armor, wrist, or belt. When readied for use, however, they become rigid and can be thrown like a spear. Plasma eels explode upon impact.

PULSE CANNON

A rapid-fire weapon that fires concentrated plasma bursts ideal for encounters with multiple, fast-moving targets. Pulse cannons are shunned by military forces because they cause a great deal of collateral damage. The droid bounty hunter IG-88 carried a modified pulse cannon.

PULSE-WAVE BLASTER

The predecessor of the modern blaster pistol. Pulse-wave blasters fire small packets of coherent energy. Less powerful than blaster bolts, pulse-wave packets are nevertheless deadly when inflicted at close range.

RAIL DETONATOR

A small missile launcher that fires compact explosives that either detonate on contact with a target or attach to a target and will explode only when the detonator's trigger is pulled a second time. This latter option is extremely useful for taking hostages or ambushing large groups of enemies.

REPEATER

A blaster rifle with three barrels, which fire in succession to create a rapid volley of blaster bolts. Most repeaters fire tracers as well. All three barrels can be fired simultaneously for a single, destructive blast, but at a great loss of power.

RIOT GUN

Any of a number of ranged weapons that fire blaster stun blasts, waves of concussive force, or other attacks meant to render organic beings unconscious. Intended mainly for crowd control, most riot guns have short barrels capable of hitting multiple targets, although bounty hunters such as Dengar often modify these weapons to focus on a single enemy. The R-88 Suppressor used by Imperial forces on Coruscant during the early days of the Empire utilizes Brix-C stun fluid, which is released as a stunning aerosol rain that affects anyone within eight meters of the initial target. The Corporate Sector Security Division also makes heavy use of riot guns.

RODIAN REPULSOR THROWING RAZOR

A small, sharp blade that can be hurled at enemies with deadly effect. Designed for gladiatorial combat on Rodia, the Rheshalva Interstellar Armaments Rodian repulsor throwing razor is equipped with a microrepulsorlift motor to increase its range and accuracy. A homing beacon linked to the owner allows the razor to return automatically to its master's hand. Rodian repulsor throwing razors are most common on Rodia, but have been carried offworld by Rodian bounty hunters. They are generally sold in pairs.

SENTRY GUN

A generic term for any small, automated turret programmed to attack nearby enemy targets. Sentry guns are most often found in detention areas, command centers, or other high-security locations. They are typically mounted in corners, above security doors, or at other positions offering wide, clear fields of fire. Sentry guns are linked directly to a facility's security systems, but remain inactive until an alarm is triggered; they will then activate sensor bubbles to identify potential threats based on preprogrammed criteria. Once a threat is located, the guns open fire. Sentry guns were used extensively by the Empire during the Galactic Civil War.

SSI-RUUVI ION PADDLE BEAMER

A device that fires a thin, silver energy beam designed to disable an organic target's nervous system. The ion paddle beamer was originally used as a medical tool, but can also be employed as a very effective short-range weapon.

STOKHLI SPRAY STICK

A weapon that releases a fine mist capable of stunning targets up to two hundred meters away. Originally developed by the Stokhli for hunting, the spray stick has

Rodian Repulsor
Throwing Razor

been adopted by numerous other species for use as a personal weapon. Unfortunately, the Yuuzhan Vong are immune to the spray stick's stunning mist.

VERPINE SHATTER GUN

A small projectile weapon that utilizes advanced magnetic coils to accelerate a small, alloy projectile toward a target. The Verpine shatter gun is virtually silent when fired, but inflicts tremendous kinetic damage upon impact.

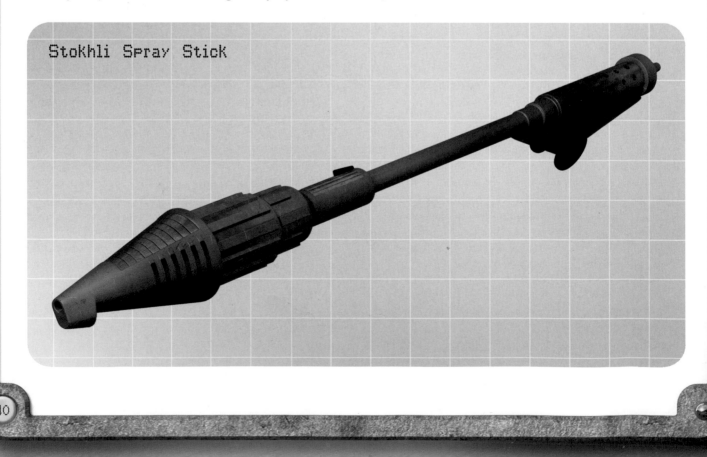

Stokhli Spray Stick

MELEE WEAPONS

Melee weapons were among the first tools developed for combat by humans and other sentient species. The realization that an attacker could cause significantly more lethal wounds by using a rock or tree branch instead of a bare fist forced dramatic evolutions in combat. Long before the advent of ranged weapons, warriors began wielding clubs, swords, axes, and other weapons that would both extend their reach and increase the amount of damage delivered by a single blow.

Early melee weapons were constructed of wood and stone. The discovery of metallurgy led to more durable weapons; however, melee weapons have improved radically since the formation of the Old Republic. By infusing traditional designs with modern technology, manufacturers now produce numerous personal weapons that are far deadlier and more resilient than their ancient counterparts. Advancements in metallurgy have resulted in a number of ultrastrong compounds, including durasteel and the more valuable cortosis. Cortosis can resist blasterfire and even lightsaber blades. Melee weapons can also be manufactured using composite ceramics, reinforced plastics, and glasslike transparisteel. All of these materials can produce weapons that are light and therefore very easy to wield. Nonmetal weapons are also easier to conceal and slip past most weapons scanners.

As power cells and other similar devices have become smaller, designers have found ways to integrate more advanced components into melee weapons. A vibrosword, for example, carries a compact power cell in its hilt, which provides energy to vibration generators that run the length of the blade. The vibrating blade can cause severe wounds with just the slightest contact. Other offensive enhancements include shock generators, which sheathe a melee weapon in an electrified field that can stun (and, in some cases, even kill) victims, and ion field generators that disable electronic countermeasures and cause damage to droids. Small shield generators and self-sharpening diagnostic modules are frequently integrated into melee weapons in order to increase their longevity.

Early in their history, the Jedi redefined melee combat with the creation of the lightsaber. Arguably the most powerful personal weapon ever known, the lightsaber allowed Jedi to deflect blaster bolts, reducing the effectiveness of many ranged weapons. Lightsabers were the primary weapons in the many battles between the Jedi and the evil Sith. Since the decline of the Jedi after the Clone Wars, lightsabers have become exceedingly rare; only members of the new Jedi Order currently build and maintain lightsabers.

Melee weapons still play an important role in personal defense across the galaxy. Nearly anyone can afford a small vibroblade, which is easy to carry and conceal. On many worlds, the sale and possession of blasters and other weapons is heavily regulated, giving melee weapons yet another advantage. Assassins and spies generally prefer quiet melee weapons to blasters, which tend to produce audible and visible energy discharges when used.

Blasters and other ranged weapons are undeniably more effective on battlefields, but melee weapons are still valuable to soldiers and mercenaries. Hand-to-hand encounters remain a reality of modern warfare, especially with the arrival of the Yuuzhan Vong, so troops continue to carry vibro-weapons. Melee weapons are also employed when planetary conditions reduce visibility, making ranged weapons impractical, or during clashes in confined spaces.

Different cultures and species rely on melee weapons to greater or lesser degrees. On worlds where blasters and other advanced weapons have not yet been discovered or introduced, melee weapons are generally the only form of weaponry available. Tatooine's Tusken Raiders have only limited access to projectile rifles and are often forced to rely on traditional gaffi sticks to kill their prey. Some species, including Wookiees, Rodians, and Noghri, place special emphsis on the use of melee weapons for hunting or combat. In fact, in some such cultures, use of melee weapons is not a necessity, but instead a point of pride and honor. On Rattatak and other worlds where violence is a way of life, melee weapons take center stage in intense gladiatorial battles or territorial disputes. In contrast, the Mon Calamari, Ithorians, and many other peaceful species never felt the need to develop melee weapons beyond those used for basic hunting.

Lightsabers

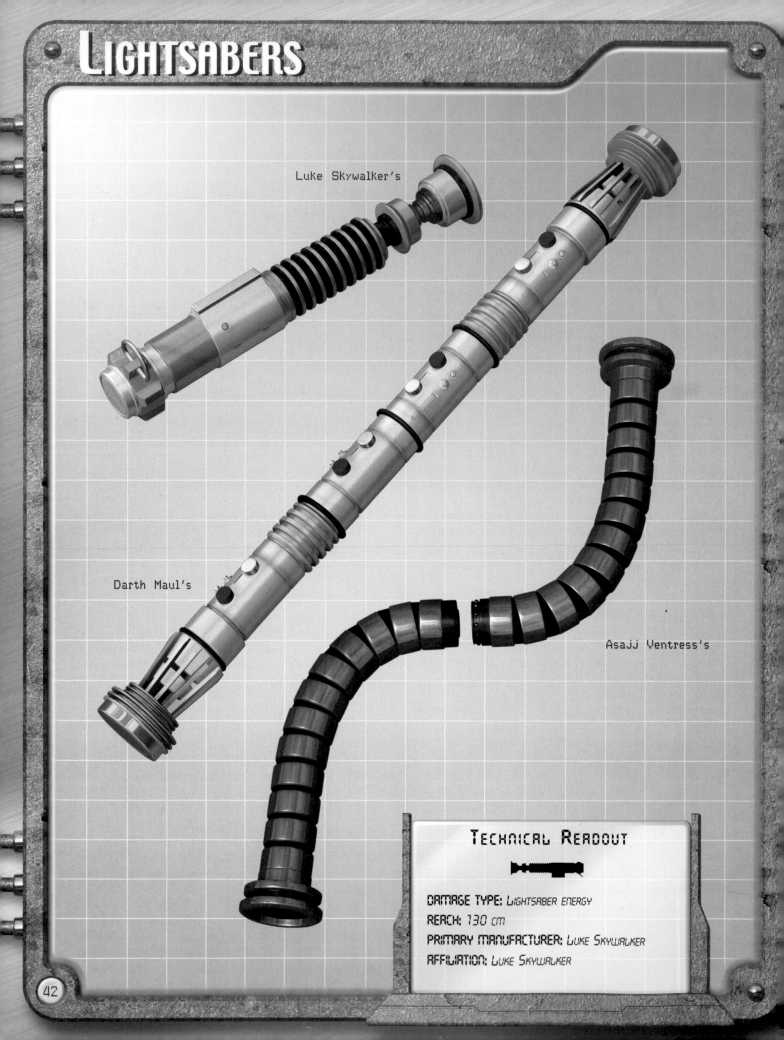

Luke Skywalker's

Darth Maul's

AsaJJ Ventress's

Technical Readout

Damage Type: Lightsaber energy

Reach: 130 cm

Primary Manufacturer: Luke Skywalker

Affiliation: Luke Skywalker

Luke Skywalker's Lightsaber

Considered by many to be the most incredible weapon ever created, the lightsaber has been the traditional weapon of the Jedi Knights since the earliest days of the Jedi Order. A blade of pure energy, the lightsaber can cut through most materials, except another lightsaber blade and a handful of special alloys such as cortosis. The lightsaber's unique design even allows it to reflect blaster bolts and melt through thick durasteel plating.

Learning to construct a lightsaber is an integral part of Jedi training, and only Force-sensitive beings are capable of building the weapon. Creating and modifying a lightsaber for the first time can take many months, although a skilled Jedi can complete a basic version of the weapon in a few days if necessary. A standard lightsaber consists of a compact handle with a diatium power cell and one to three multifaceted crystals. These crystals determine the lightsaber blade's color and focus energy from the power source through a concave disk atop the handle, resulting in a colored blade about a meter in length. Prior to the Battle of Ruusan, Jedi ignited lightsabers in every known hue, including purple, orange, and even gold. After seizing control of the Old Republic and destroying the Jedi Order, the Emperor razed or quarantined numerous planets rich with lightsaber crystals. As the last Jedi fled Darth Vader, they were forced to rely on the more common Ilum crystals, which produce only green and blue blades. When the New Republic took control of the galaxy, a number of crystal caches were regained. Luke Skywalker and his followers began using these crystals to create lightsabers in a wider array of colors. Skywalker also taught his students to imbue less powerful crystals with Force energies to enhance their properties. In contrast to traditional Jedi, Sith and Dark Jedi use bloodred lightsabers exclusively.

Mastering the lightsaber requires a lifetime of training. Before the Emperor's violent Jedi Purge, the youngest members of the Jedi Order began training in lightsaber combat as soon as they were old enough to hold the weapon. Training lightsabers use low power settings, which do little more than sting and bruise their victims.

When the Sith were at the height of their power, Jedi were able to hone their lightsaber skills on the battlefield. In later decades, although it was rare that a Jedi would face an enemy armed with a lightsaber, dueling techniques remained part of Jedi training, with Jedi Knights and Masters clashing using lightsabers set to a nonlethal "sparring mode." In the modern era, Luke Skywalker continues to emphasize lightsaber training within the ranks of his new Jedi Order.

Both Luke Skywalker and Darth Vader constructed traditional versions of the lightsaber. Luke's green-bladed lightsaber, which he built using tools discovered in Obi-Wan Kenobi's home on Tatooine, is small enough

> **"Your father's lightsaber. This is the weapon of a Jedi Knight. Not as clumsy or as random as a blaster. An elegant weapon for a more civilized age ..."**
> —*Obi-Wan "Ben" Kenobi, when presenting Anakin Skywalker's lightsaber to Luke*

❼ **Familiar Hilt:** The hilt to Luke's second lightsaber, which he built after his confrontation with Darth Vader on Bespin, closely resembles the Sith Lord's weapon.

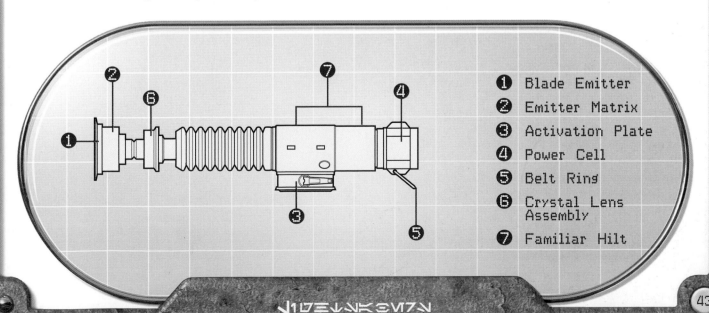

1. Blade Emitter
2. Emitter Matrix
3. Activation Plate
4. Power Cell
5. Belt Ring
6. Crystal Lens Assembly
7. Familiar Hilt

to conceal inside an astromech's dome. In combat, Luke can wield the weapon with one hand for quick attacks or two-handed for more powerful blows. Like many other lightsabers, Darth Vader's dual-phase lightsaber featured controls to adjust the length and width of his blade. Vader also mastered a deadly lightsaber throw, hurling the energy blade at his enemies and then using the Force to recall the weapon.

Far more exotic was the lightsaber built by Count Dooku. Like many Jedi, Dooku eventually retired the lightsaber he constructed as a Padawan in favor of a more powerful and refined weapon. When building this new lightsaber, Dooku scoured the Jedi archives in search of a unique design. He discovered the curved lightsaber, which is meant for sweeping, precise attacks that require an incredibly agile hand. The resulting weapon had no similarity to the lightsaber of his Master, Yoda. After joining forces with Darth Sidious, Count Dooku replaced the crystals in his lightsaber with Sith synthetic crystals, providing the weapon with a more powerful, red blade. However, these crystals have been known to exhaust their properties.

Other lightsaber variants also exist. Darth Maul's signature weapon was a double-bladed lightsaber with an oversize handle. The design for the double-bladed lightsaber originated with the fallen Jedi Exar Kun some four thousand standard years before the Battle of Naboo, and Maul selected the weapon from his Master's ancient Sith archives. A double-bladed lightsaber is wielded like a quarterstaff and is well suited to battling two enemies at once. Using a double-bladed lightsaber is dangerous and difficult, because the weapon relies on totally different maneuvers from those mastered during standard lightsaber exercises. Traditionally, such double-bladed lightsabers have been relegated to training sessions, with few Jedi or Sith actually using the weapon in

the field. Maul's lightsaber was actually two hilts fused together, with each blade possessing its own set of internal components. When his weapon was damaged during his battle with Obi-Wan Kenobi and Qui-Gon Jinn, Darth Maul was still able to use one of the blades. Darth Maul's lightsaber was also notable because it utilized synthetic crystals handcrafted by the Sith apprentice.

The misguided Dark Jedi Asajj Ventress combined unusual handle design with the double-bladed lightsaber concept to develop yet another unique lightsaber variant. Each of Ventress's two lightsabers had a curved handle. During most encounters, she battled with one lightsaber in each hand. For specific battles, however, such as her confrontation with Mace Windu, she attached the hilts. When attached, the blades emerged at slight angles, resulting in a double-bladed weapon that was extremely hard to deflect and counter.

Dark Jedi and Sith aren't the only Force-users who employ unusual lightsaber designs. Vaunted Jedi Master Yoda built an extremely small lightsaber with a hilt barely the size of a grown man's hand. Mace Windu braved the rock-encrusted natives of Hurikane to recover rare purple crystals that gave his lightsaber its distinctive violet color. In later years, Mace embellished his lightsaber with an electrum finish usually reserved for senior members of the Jedi Council. New Republic Jedi Corran Horn built a dual-phase lightsaber that alternates between a purple and a silver blade, depending upon its current length setting. Tenel Ka, the Force-sensitive daughter of a Dathomiri Witch, constructed her lightsaber using a rancor's tooth for the handle and rainbow gems as focusing crystals. The Wookiee Jedi Tyvokka, who was once a member of the Old Republic's Jedi Council, carried a lightsaber with a curved wooden handle. Clearly, lightsaber designs are as varied as the Jedi who wield them.

Darth Vader's Lightsaber

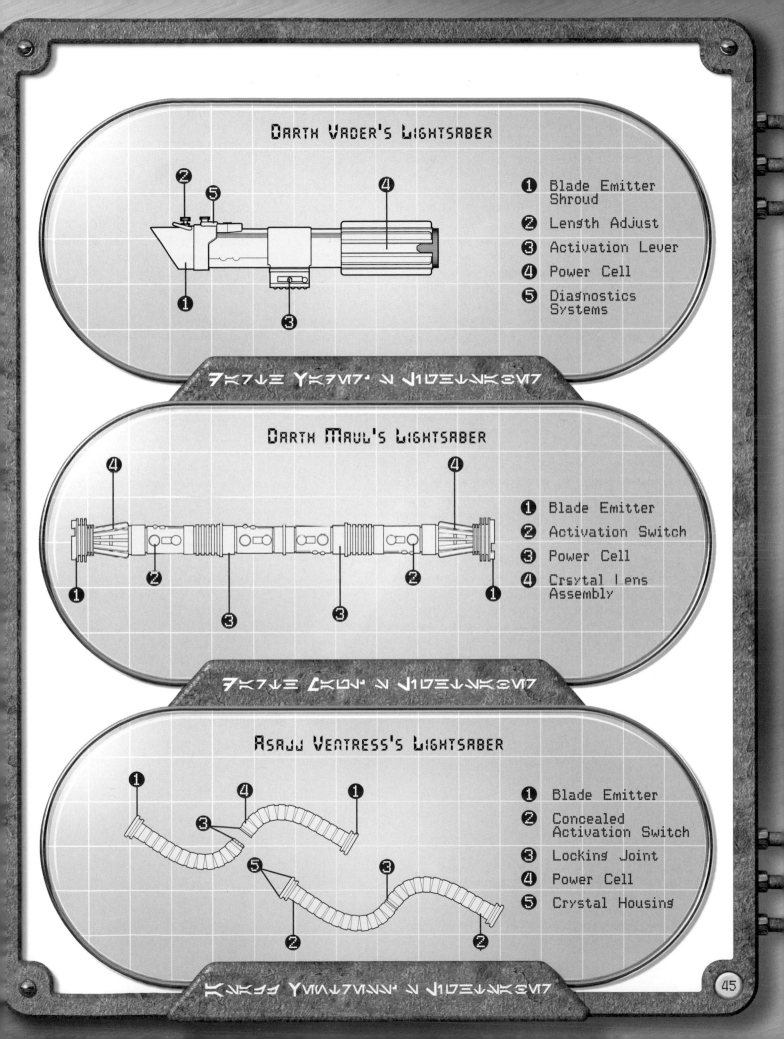

1. Blade Emitter Shroud
2. Length Adjust
3. Activation Lever
4. Power Cell
5. Diagnostics Systems

Darth Maul's Lightsaber

1. Blade Emitter
2. Activation Switch
3. Power Cell
4. Crystal Lens Assembly

Asajj Ventress's Lightsaber

1. Blade Emitter
2. Concealed Activation Switch
3. Locking Joint
4. Power Cell
5. Crystal Housing

GADERFFII

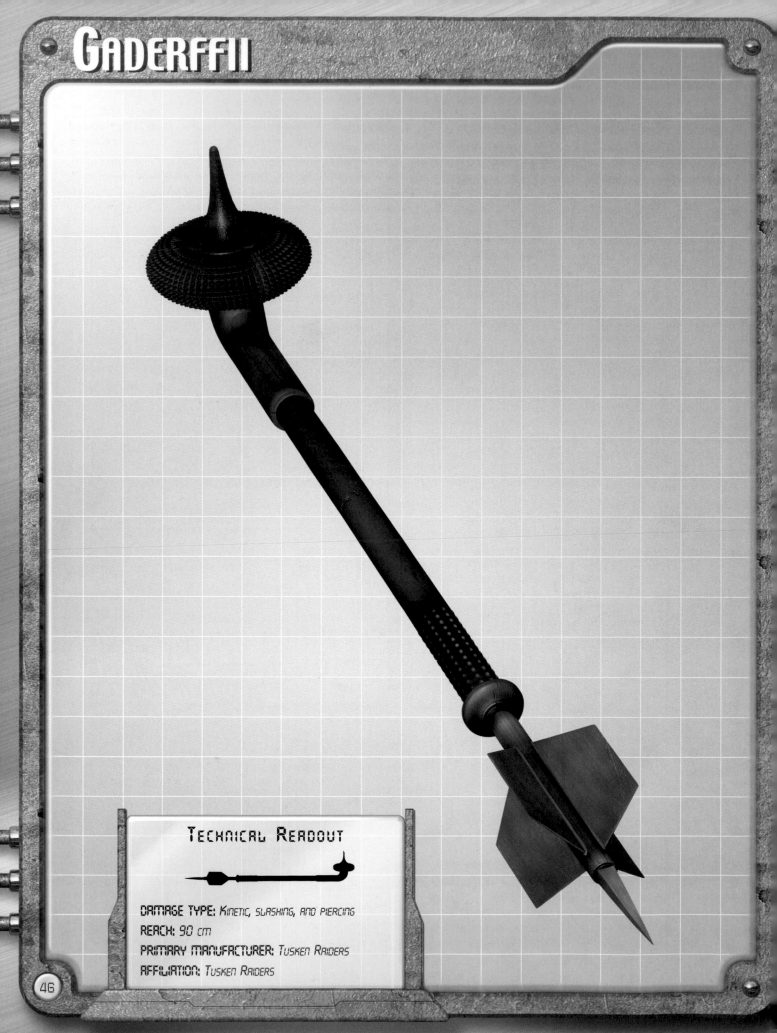

TECHNICAL READOUT

DAMAGE TYPE: Kinetic, slashing, and piercing

REACH: 90 cm

PRIMARY MANUFACTURER: Tusken Raiders

AFFILIATION: Tusken Raiders

Tusken Gaderffii

The Tusken Raiders, the violent nomads who roam the desert wastes of Tatooine, are terrifying to behold. With their gauze-covered faces, mammoth bantha mounts, and blood-chilling battle cries, the Tusken Raiders inspire fear whenever they appear on the horizon. Perhaps the most visible symbol of the Tusken Raiders' brutality is the spiked gaderffii, the traditional weapon of these notorious Sand People.

Gaderffii, or "gaffi sticks," are short polearms. One end of the gaffi stick typically sports a double-edged ax tipped with a spearing blade. The other end of the weapon is armed with a heavy, weighted club and a sharp, stabbing blade. The combination of club and blades allows the Tuskens to initiate nearly any type of attack. When fending off large predators or attacking from a bantha in full charge, Tuskens will use the spearing blade. The stabbing blade is also used to carve indications of territorial boundaries on cliff walls. The double-edged ax blade cleaves through muscle and bone; when swung in a wide arc, the ax is capable of severing limbs or causing decapitation. The club is used to stun prey, knock victims to the ground, or crush the skulls of womp rats and other animals without damaging the creatures' useful hides. The destructive Tuskens also use the club to smash droids, vehicles, moisture vaporators, and other equipment they find in the desert. The stabbing blade delivers deadly finishing blows. To increase the weapon's effectiveness, some Tusken Raiders dip the blades in deadly, fast-acting sandbat venom.

Tusken Raiders meticulously craft gaffi sticks from scavenged metal, krayt dragon horns, solid tracti wood, and other materials found in the Tatooine wastelands. Some gaderffii are built around hollow and lightweight durasteel tubes collected from crashed starships. Although crude, gaffi sticks can survive for many seasons, even in the harsh Tatooine conditions. In the Tuskens' nomadic way of life, the gaffi stick is a reliable, uncomplicated weapon perfect for the sudden ambushes that typify the Tusken Raiders' attacks.

Gaffi sticks also play an important role in Tusken culture. Aside from being the species' primary hunting weapon, gaderffii can be used as walking sticks during long, arduous treks through the desert or mountains. Tuskens frequently use the weapons as tools: gaffi sticks can crack open water-retaining hubba gourds, cut wood, and dig up roots, grubs, and other food. Perhaps most important, Tuskens wield the weapon to intimidate one another during loud displays that help determine social standing within a clan. Chieftains often carry a tribe's largest and most dangerous gaffi sticks.

> **"The Sand People are easily startled, but they will soon be back and in greater numbers."**
> —*Obi-Wan Kenobi*

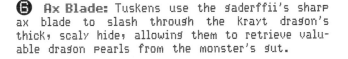

❻ Ax Blade: Tuskens use the gaderffii's sharp ax blade to slash through the krayt dragon's thick, scaly hide, allowing them to retrieve valuable dragon pearls from the monster's gut.

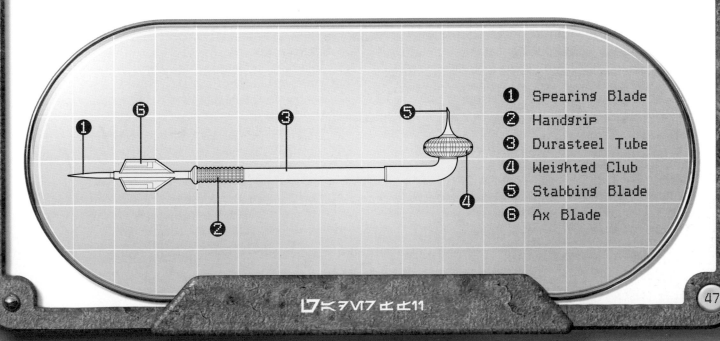

❶ Spearing Blade
❷ Handgrip
❸ Durasteel Tube
❹ Weighted Club
❺ Stabbing Blade
❻ Ax Blade

FORCE PIKE

TECHNICAL READOUT

DAMAGE TYPE: Kinetic, slashing, piercing, and electrical energy

REACH: 2 m

PRIMARY MANUFACTURER: SoroSuub

AFFILIATION: Emperor's Royal Guard

SoroSuub Controller FP

Although early melee weapons were used for warfare and murder, more civilized cultures have adopted the weapons for nonlethal applications, such as crowd control. Polearms designed to emit powerful stun charges are extremely common throughout the galaxy and can be found in the arsenals of most local and sector police forces. The weapons arm of SoroSuub combined cutting-edge stun devices with much more dangerous vibroblade technology to create the force pike (or electro-jabber), a weapon designed for both crowd control and military applications.

The SoroSuub Controller FP resembles a long spear, but the spear tip is replaced by a vibrating power tip. The ultrasonic vibration generators, housed in the weapon's butt, cause the power tip to vibrate at extreme speeds in excess of three thousand microscopic vibrations per second, exponentially increasing the amount of damage caused by a single strike. At its maximum setting, a force pike generates enough vibratory force to rip through flesh, armor, stone, and even thin durasteel plating. As with other, more traditional vibro-weapons, a grazing blow from the force pike's vibrating tip can cause terrible wounds, including dismemberment.

The Controller FP's power tip also channels a disruptive shock generator with a maximum range of four centimeters. The shock generator's lowest setting results in excruciating electrical shocks useful for dissuading attackers, herding captives or animals, interrogating suspects, or torturing enemies. The power of the electrical discharge can be increased to render even the largest rioters unconscious. The weapon was favored by Trandoshan slavers because it could knock out a full-grown Wookiee. At the higher settings, the electrical shocks overload the victim's central nervous system, resulting in paralysis and death.

Force pikes weigh less than seven kilograms, making them very easy to wield. Proper training is required to fight with the weapon effectively, but nearly anyone can master a basic jabbing technique useful for keeping enemies at bay. The two-meter shaft provides the weapon with excellent reach and creates a distance between combatants that few other melee weapons can match. In the hands of a skilled warrior, the force pike is a devastating weapon of surprising speed and precision. Although not designed as a club, most force pikes are strong enough to endure a few bludgeoning attacks. The graphite shaft gives the weapon some degree of flexibility, allowing it to bend rather than snap when it collides with an enemy.

> ### "How did I lose my arm? A stormtrooper tapped my shoulder with a force pike ..."
> —*Rebel soldier Char'Shen Larcuna*

The Emperor's Royal Guard wielded force pikes largely for ceremonial purposes, although they were occasionally for crowd control, self-defense, and even torture when necessary. Stormtroopers were also trained to use the weapons to cut open bulkheads and air locks during Imperial boarding actions. Jabba the Hutt's skiff guards carried force pikes, employing the weapons to goad the crimelord's enemies into the mighty Sarlacc. Throughout the galaxy's criminal underworld, unregulated force pikes remain in heavy use.

7 Vibration Generator: When activated, the vibration generators create a low, menacing hum.

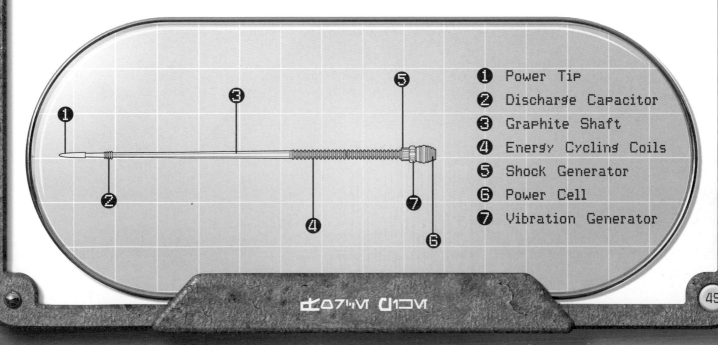

1. Power Tip
2. Discharge Capacitor
3. Graphite Shaft
4. Energy Cycling Coils
5. Shock Generator
6. Power Cell
7. Vibration Generator

Vibro-Weapons

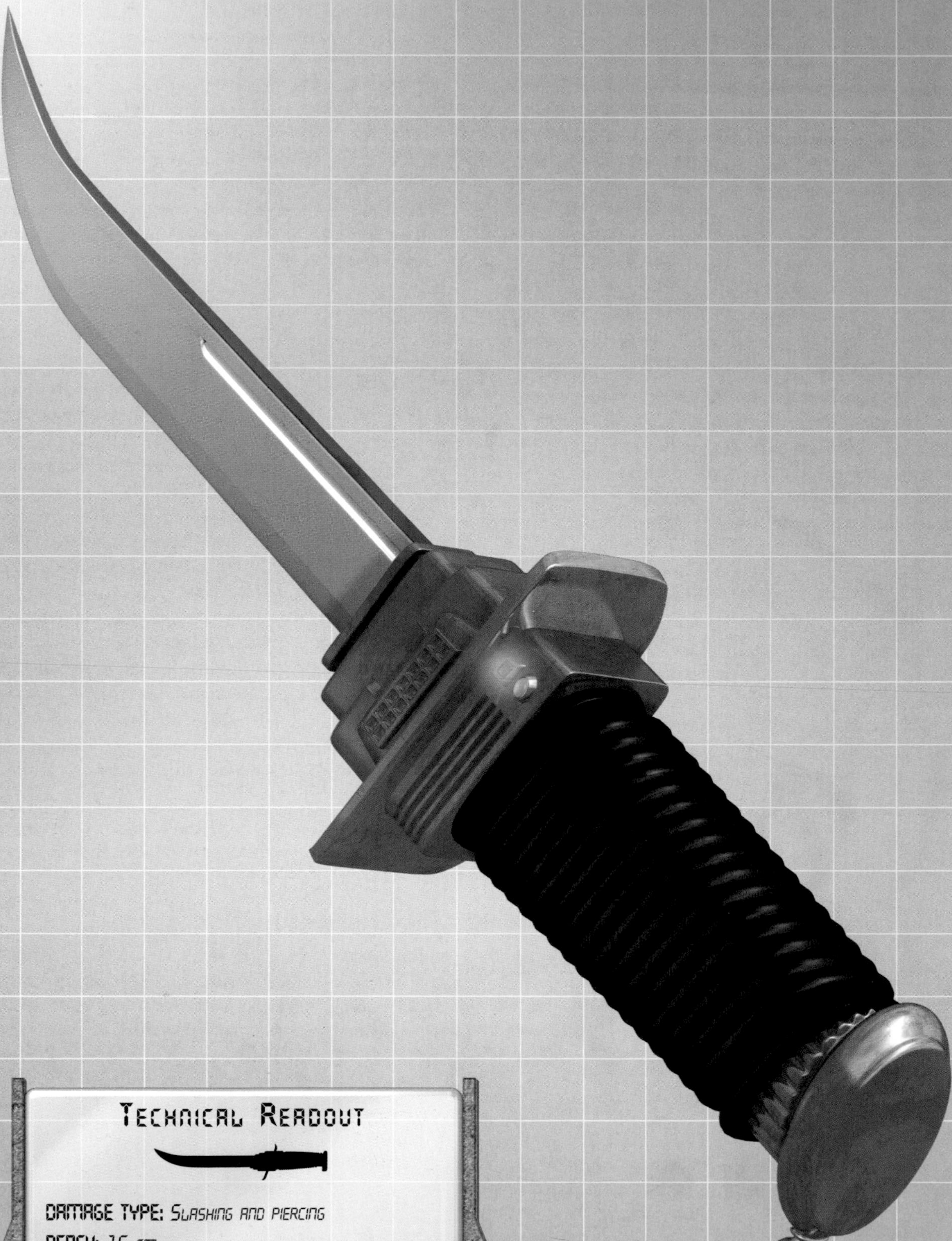

50

Technical Readout

DAMAGE TYPE: Slashing and piercing

REACH: 15 cm

PRIMARY MANUFACTURER: Merr-Sonn

AFFILIATION: Pirates, assassins, spies, mercenaries, and other miscreants

Merr-Sonn Treppus-2 Vibroblade

Vibro-weapons are hand-to-hand weapons that utilize innovative vibration technology to increase the damage they inflict. The simplest vibro-weapons rely on power cells to activate ultrasonic vibration generators at the base of the blade. The generators create rapid vibrations that travel the length of the blade at speeds between one hundred and several thousand per second. The end result is a weapon that cuts deep with just the slightest touch.

The most basic vibro-weapon is the vibroblade, a small knife or dagger with a power cell and vibration generators built into the hilt. Vibroblades are easy to conceal, inexpensive to acquire and maintain, and require little training or physical strength to use effectively. Even the simplest vibroblades can cut through duraplast, ceramic armor, and some metal alloys. The Treppus-2 features a vibration-dampening handle and is properly weighted to allow the weapon to be thrown short distances. A close cousin to the vibroblade is the vibrobayonet, designed as an attachment for most blaster rifles.

Much less subtle and far more deadly is the vibro-ax, a weapon built around a large, vibrating ax head. Numerous versions have been produced, and they vary widely in quality. Jabba's Gamorrean guards carried crude vibro-axes with wooden handles and hollow ax heads filled with rudimentary vibration generators and power cells. Vibro-axes with wooden shafts are notoriously difficult to handle because the wood conducts vibrations easily. In contrast, the longer SoroSuub BD-1 Cutter vibro-ax wielded by Jabba's Weequay skiff guards is much more sophisticated: a hollowed durasteel shaft results in a lighter weapon, while dozens of dampeners

> ## "The hum of the vibroblade gave it away. That's the only reason I still have my face."
> —*Pirate Captain Nym, after a bounty hunter attack on Lok*

installed in the staff protect the wielder from the ax head's intense vibrations. The blade itself is relatively strong. A quick-release switch allows the user to replace a damaged blade in seconds, if needed.

Many galactic denizens carry vibroknucklers, a small blade attached to knuckle rings that can be slipped over the user's fingers. The blade activates as soon as the wielder makes a fist, transforming a simple punch into a potentially lethal attack.

Perhaps the most elegant vibro-weapon is the vibrorapier, a dueling weapon developed for "civilized" combat. Vibrorapiers feature long, slender blades designed for quick, slashing attacks. The vibrorapier is also unusual among vibro-weapons because it is completely free of the low hum so often associated with other weapons in this class; this silence can give an assassin a considerable edge. However, the advanced circuitry within the weapon does consume power cells more quickly than other vibro-weapons. In order to maximize the weapon's power usage, most duelists do not activate the vibrorapier's vibration generators until seconds before an attack.

Not all vibroblades are actually used as weapons. The vibroscalpel is a small, lightweight surgical instrument. Ultrasonic vibrations activate a thin wire blade that can cut through muscle tissue and bone during operations.

❼ Adjustable Sheath: The Treppus-2's adjustable sheath extends to cover the blade when it is not being used. The sheath is equipped with simple diagnostic software and self-sharpening hardware that ensure the weapon is always honed to razor perfection.

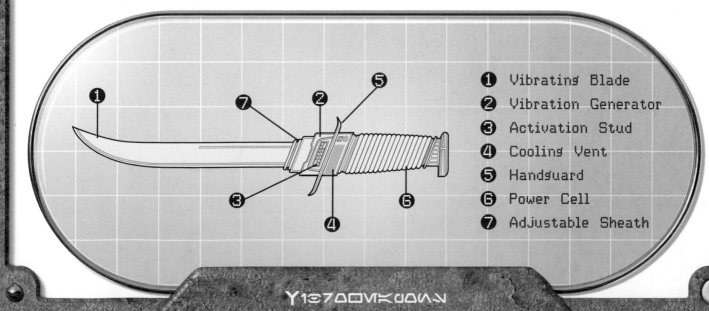

1. Vibrating Blade
2. Vibration Generator
3. Activation Stud
4. Cooling Vent
5. Handguard
6. Power Cell
7. Adjustable Sheath

RYYK BLADES

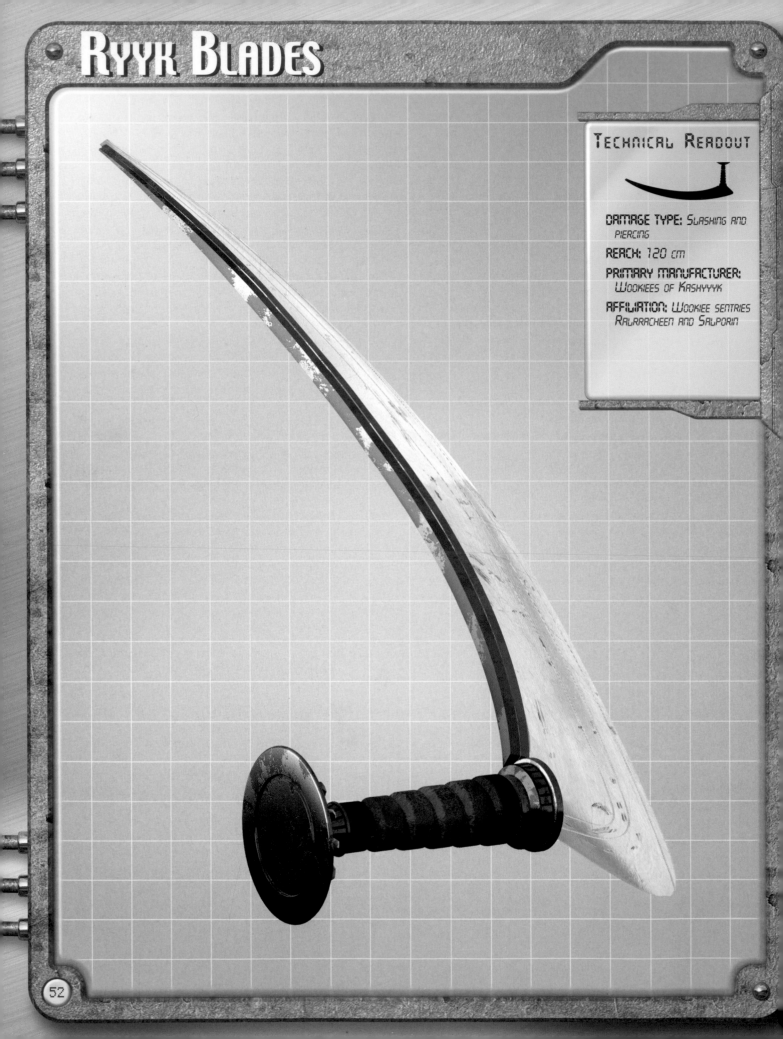

Wookiee Ryyk Blades

Of all the species that have perfected the art of hunting, perhaps none have pursued more dangerous creatures than the Wookiees of Kashyyyk. On their forested homeworld, the Wookiees descend from the treetops into the planet's lowest depths to face a number of predatory animals, from fanged katarns to poison-spitting webweavers. To aid in their hunting expeditions, the Wookiees have developed specialized weapons, including a variety of deadly melee weapons known collectively as ryyk blades.

Ryyk blades are fairly primitive weapons and were developed long before the Wookiees invented ranged weapons such as the bowcaster. A basic ryyk blade is little more than a sharp machete attached to a hide-wrapped grip. However, ryyk blade designs can differ greatly from clan to clan. The Kerarthorr blade, for example, extends from the handgrip at a ninety-degree angle, which allows Wookiees from the Kerarthorr clan to wield the weapon with a reverse grip and attack with wide, slashing motions. The Kerarthorr blade and many other ryyk blades are designed to be used in pairs, although the largest of these weapons require two massive Wookiee hands to be wielded effectively. Other clans use serpentine torch blades or vicious serrated blades, while some handgrips feature leather thongs that can be used to secure the weapon to the owner's wrist.

Like the bowcaster, a ryyk blade is a highly personal weapon. Nearly all ryyk blades are handcrafted by their owners, who decorate the weapons with markings symbolizing the wielder's strength, courage, and honor. Because of their special importance, Wookiees carry a single pair of ryyk blades their entire lives.

> **"A Wookiee warrior without a ryyk blade is a webweaver without fangs."**
> —*Traditional Wookiee maxim*

Ryyk blades are generally heavy and large, making them difficult for non-Wookiees to wield. The bounty hunter and failed Jedi Aurra Sing has been known to use the weapon, but few others have mastered its use. In the hands of a Wookiee, ryyk blades are extremely deadly. Wookiee attacks typically emphasize brute strength and ferocity, but ryyk blades allow for surprisingly precise slashes and strikes.

In modern Wookiee culture, ryyk blades are carried by Wookiee soldiers, sentries, and adventurers. They are especially useful in the species' treetop villages because they can be wielded effectively in close quarters and are unlikely to cause any collateral damage. Guards assigned to the Wookiee nurseries are never found without ryyk blades. During the conflict with Grand Admiral Thrawn, a pregnant Princess Leia Organa Solo was protected by Wookiees on Kashyyyk. Thrawn's brutal Noghri death commandos attacked Leia, but the assassins were defeated by brave Wookiee warriors wielding ryyk blades.

④ **Notches:** Wookiees sometimes cut notches into their blades to signify important kills during particularly difficult hunts.

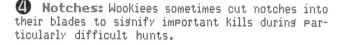

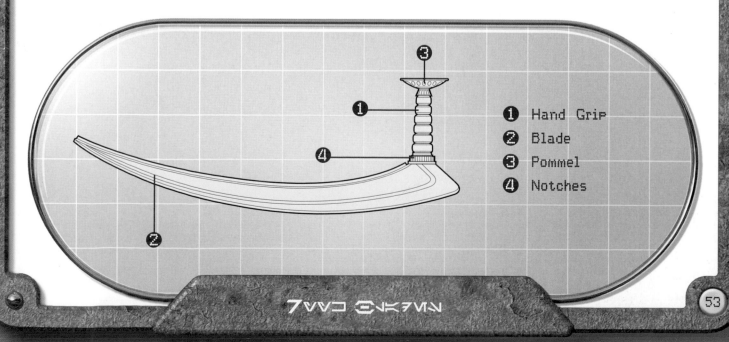

❶ Hand Grip
❷ Blade
❸ Pommel
❹ Notches

Geonosian Static Pike

Technical Readout

Damage Type: *Piercing and electrical energy*

Reach: *3.6 m*

Primary Manufacturer: *Gordarl Weaponsmiths*

Affiliation: *Geonosian warriors*

Gordarl Picador Pike

Since time immemorial, the insectoid Geonosians have gathered in giant arenas to watch a variety of brutal blood sports. Originally, this "entertainment" consisted of cruel battles pitting trained creatures against one another, often to the death. When the novelty of such animal brutality faded, the Geonosians began using the arenas for gratuitous public executions. These executions, which have continued well into the New Republic's reign, allow the Geonosian rulers to rid themselves of prisoners who would otherwise consume valuable hive resources. Most often, prisoners are eaten alive by terrifying monsters cultivated in Geonosian pens or forced to battle one another using primitive weapons. The arenas have also been used for bloody gladiatorial battles between elite members of the warrior caste.

> ## "Let the executions begin!"
> —*Archduke Poggle the Lesser*

Regardless of the exact nature of the arena events, a variety of melee weapons have been a key component of the excessively violent proceedings held in these rocky stadiums. Geonosian arena weapons range from simple swords, whips, and clubs to short-range sonic stunners and the charged static pike.

The static pike is a Geonosian invention, although it closely resembles several other similar weapons, including the force pike. The Geonosian static pike is actually an evolution of the Geonosian spear, a weapon with an extremely sharp steel point capping a short, durable pole. Since Geonosian spears were originally designed to fend off huge creatures, the spearhead can penetrate tough hide and thick fur. Geonosian warriors have mastered the spear's use, ensuring that the weapon always strikes a beast's most vulnerable area. Against the bullish reek, for example, a Geonosian warrior will shove the spear into the soft underside of the creature's neck.

The Geonosian spear eventually developed into the current static pike to suit the needs of Geonosian picadors. The picadors are assigned to controlling the creatures and prisoners released into the arena. In order to give the picadors an effective means for herding the dangerous arena animals, Geonosian weaponsmiths added a charged tip to the standard spear. The innovation quickly led to the current static pike, which is nearly twice as long as the Geonosian spear and constructed from much more advanced materials.

Unlike the traditional Geonosian spear, which is still in use among Geonosian sentries and warriors, the static pike's primary weapon is its electrically charged point. The tip can be calibrated to deliver shocks designed to disrupt the nervous system of specific creatures, or set to kill if the picadors lose control of the arena animals or prisoners. The body of the pike is an anodized staff, which prevents the picador from receiving an accidental shock. An insulated grip further protects the pike's wielder.

The Gungans of Naboo utilize a similar weapon called the electropole. Gungan guards carry these weapons to frighten away monstrous sea creatures and other large predators that threaten Gungan cities and villages.

⑥ Anodized Staff: The static pike's staff is durable, but not strong enough to withstand the claws of the mantislike acklay.

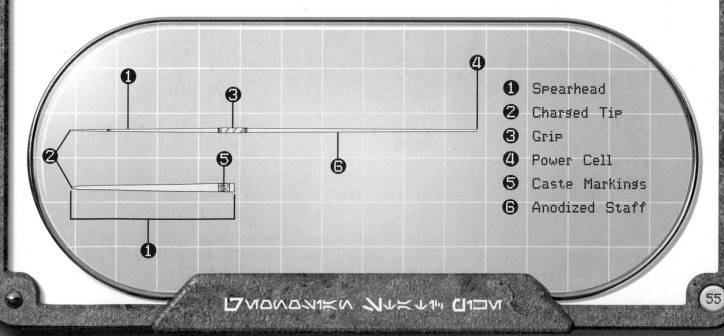

- **①** Spearhead
- **②** Charged Tip
- **③** Grip
- **④** Power Cell
- **⑤** Caste Markings
- **⑥** Anodized Staff

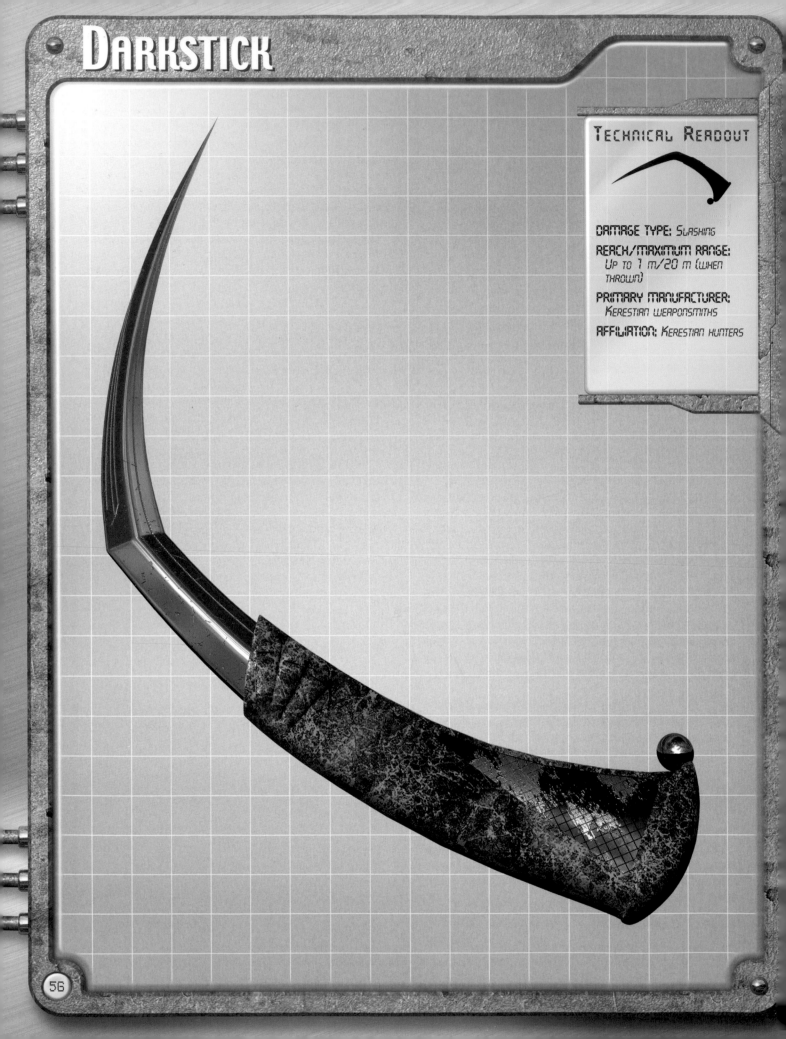

DAMAGE TYPE: *Slashing*

REACH/MAXIMUM RANGE: *Up to 1 m/20 m (when thrown)*

PRIMARY MANUFACTURER: *Kerestian weaponsmiths*

AFFILIATION: *Kerestian hunters*

Kerestian Darkstick

The planet Kerest hovers on the Outer Rim, a dying world populated by a savage and hopeless species. Kerest is on the verge of a new ice age, with thick sheets of glacial ice covering most of the planet. The Kerestians are forced to live on a small strip of land near the equator, where they struggle to survive. Only a small number of animal species have adapted to the glacial conditions, but the burly, pug-faced Kerestians manage to subsist by hunting these creatures. Although the Kerestians have discovered starship technology, which has enabled them to colonize two inhabitable moons in the system, the species still relies on oddly primitive weapons. One of the Kerestians' most effective weapons is the darkstick, a handheld melee weapon.

The traditional Kerestian darkstick is an exotic, curved blade. Modern Kerestian weaponsmiths use lightweight metals to craft the darksticks, although there is evidence that primitive Kerestians forged the weapons out of hard woods that no longer exist. Darksticks range in size from small, daggerlike weapons barely ten centimeters in length to giant, two-handed versions well over a meter in length. The most common darksticks, however, are about twenty centimeters long and can fit comfortably between a Kerestian's massive knuckles. Most Kerestian warriors wield a darkstick like a single, giant claw, attacking prey and enemies with long slashing motions. Hunters typically carry several, and often wield one in each hand.

Although the darkstick is primarily used for brutal melee assaults, the weapon's curved design and lightweight body also allow it to be thrown like a boomerang. Mastering the darkstick's ranged capability

> ## "Eventually, we all enter into the Great Darkness. For many, the darkstick serves as their only escort."
> *—Andov Syn*

is extremely difficult, and only the most skilled Kerestians attempt to throw the weapon during hunts. Those who do employ this technique can execute precise attacks at ranges of up to twenty meters. When thrown properly, a darkstick will return to its wielder's hand. Some weaponsmiths have experimented with installing basic magnetic recall units, ensuring that darksticks are always recovered by the owner.

Kerestians continue to value the darkstick because it is a completely silent weapon. To further increase stealth, Kerestians often paint their darksticks black and hunt at night.

The darkstick's unusual name is derived from Kerestian legend, which holds that, upon death, a being's spirit is resigned to eternal darkness. Thus, the traditional Kerestian weapon is designed to deliver victims into this "Great Darkness." The most recent advances in Kerestian weaponry have been inspired by the myths of old, and modern darksticks are designed to literally create darkness. Such darksticks incorporate a network of light-absorbing cells that creates a darkness field around the weapon. Kerestians can use this field to conceal themselves, and when Kerestians attack, their prey is often enveloped in the darkness field. Kerestians who carry such darksticks typically don infrared goggles. Kerestians have also been known to lace their darksticks with poison and hurl explosive darksticks during large-scale battles.

5 Hollow Tip: Some darksticks incorporate a hollow tip that can be used to hold explosives, poison, or acid.

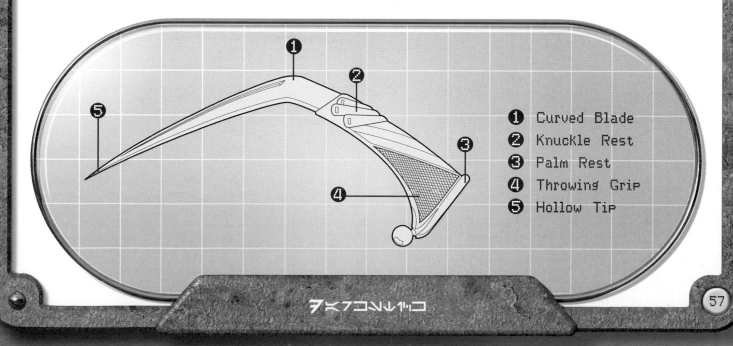

1. Curved Blade
2. Knuckle Rest
3. Palm Rest
4. Throwing Grip
5. Hollow Tip

AMPHISTAFF

Yuuzhan Vong Amphistaff

Among the Yuuzhan Vong, a weapon that can be used in any battle situation and against multiple types of foes is preferable to a standard blaster. The amphistaff typifies this philosophy.

Like other Yuuzhan Vong weapons, the amphistaff is a biotechnological device, and there is an almost telepathic link between staff and wielder. In many ways, the amphistaff is completely alien to anything the New Republic has known. It resembles a large serpent with four large fangs, and when not in use, the pliable amphistaff can be wrapped around a warrior's forearm. However, at the warrior's command, the amphistaff hardens its body to roughly the strength and consistency of stone. In its simplest configuration, the hardened amphistaff is wielded like a quarterstaff or club. The amphistaff can also narrow its neck and tail, forming razorlike edges at either end of its body designed for stabbing or slashing attacks. When the amphistaff selectively hardens portions of its body, it can serve as a whip or flail. The amphistaff's flexibility allows warriors to hide the weapon under their cloak or command the serpent to surreptitiously slither toward an enemy.

New Republic engineers have discovered that the serpents possess a chain of bizarre "power glands." When commanded to harden, an amphistaff generates an internal electrical pulse that travels through these linked glands, generating an energy field that alters the creature's semicrystalline cell structure. The field also extends about a millimeter beyond the amphistaff's surface, creating microscopic edges that can cleave through most materials.

> **"The amphistaff is not just a Vong's weapon, it is his most important ally. With an amphistaff in his arsenal, a Vong is never truly alone."**
> —*New Republic General Wedge Antilles*

Skilled Yuuzhan Vong warriors can use amphistaffs as spears, hurling them at enemies up to ten meters away. The amphistaff's most disturbing feature is its ability to spit a stream of venom, with a range of about twenty meters. The amphistaff's venom spray is exceedingly accurate and is usually directed at a victim's eyes to cause instant blindness. The blinded victim then suffers a slow, agonizing death. If the amphistaff delivers the venom through a bite, the poison causes numbness followed by total paralysis. Mara Jade Skywalker eventually developed a biotoxin drill to combat the amphistaff's venom.

The amphistaff's organic design incorporates an accelerated Force healing system that allows the weapon to regenerate from nearly any wound. The amphistaff can be killed only through a sudden blow to the head or removal of the head from the body.

Although the heroes of the New Republic have struggled to grasp Yuuzhan Vong technology, Jedi Knight Jacen Solo has formed a strong connection with amphistaffs. Jacen actually commanded seventeen wild amphistaffs to form a suit of living armor around him. Jacen also learned to fight with two amphistaffs at once, drawing replacement weapons from his armor whenever one of the serpents depleted its venom glands.

6 **Eyespots:** The amphistaff's eyespots are both infrared and motion-sensitive, allowing the serpent to seek out prey anywhere.

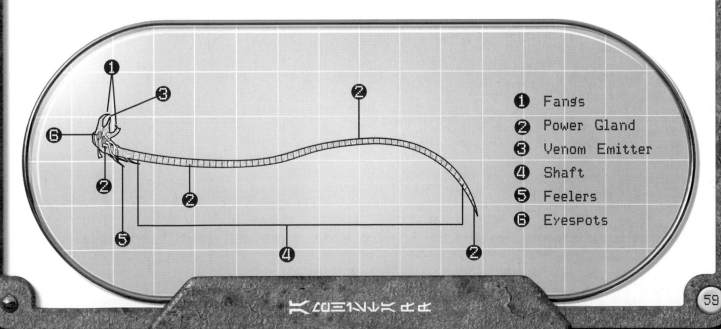

1 Fangs
2 Power Gland
3 Venom Emitter
4 Shaft
5 Feelers
6 Eyespots

ADDITIONAL MELEE WEAPONS

For every blaster or other ranged weapon that has ever been designed, the sentient species of the galaxy have created a dozen melee weapons. Although most associate melee weapons with cumbersome clubs, crude swords, or unwieldy polearms, many are as astonishing and technologically advanced as the ranged weapons that dominate the galaxy's battlefields. Following is just a brief cross section of some of the millions of known melee weapons.

COUFEE

A crude Yuuzhan Vong knife. Coufees are large, double-edged weapons carried by many Yuuzhan Vong including warriors and slaves. A coufee is typically used as a last resort.

FEAR STICK

A potent self-defense weapon developed by the Sabrashi. At first glance, the fear stick appears to be a writing stylus. However, the device is actually designed to inject a fast-acting toxin that targets a victim's central nervous system.

FIRE BLADE

A knife with a short energy blade, usually designed for use as a basic cutting tool. The lizard keepers of Dathomir use fire blades to cut the paws of their domesticated Kwi. The villain Uda-Khalid, who once fought Mace Windu, had a pair of more potent fire blades attached to his right forearm.

GEONOSIAN SPEAR

A weapon favored by Geonosian fliers. Geonosian spears are roughly half the length of the Geonosian

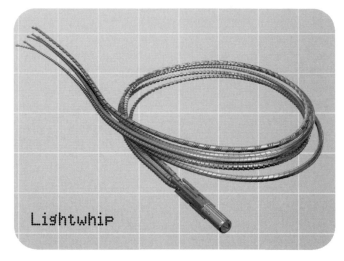

Lightwhip

static pike. They are usually constructed from hollow bone and coated with a tough, protective resin.

LIGHTWHIP (LASER WHIP)

An energy lash favored by bounty hunters and mercenaries. When activated, the length of a lightwhip is sheathed in deadly laser energy. Bounty hunter Ona Nobis used a lightwhip tipped with sharp spikes.

MORGUKAI CORTOSIS STAFF

A lightsaber-resistant melee weapon developed by the Morgukai warriors, who are a secret sect of the Nikto. Morgukai cortosis staves emit a short energy blade very similar to a stubby lightsaber. With the energy blade extended, the staff can be used as a lethal spear. It remains unknown why or how the Morgukai developed such weapons, although many historians believe that the warriors sought the destruction of the Jedi.

NEURONIC WHIP

A whip capable of disrupting neurological functions. A neuronic whip consists of a thin strand of wire attached to a black handle. When a switch on the handle is activated, a charge of electricity courses through the wire whip. Anything that comes into contact with the charged whip will suffer a debilitating neurological overload. Repeated lashings can result in permanent damage to higher brain functions, but rarely cause lasting physical harm. As a result, neuronic whips are often used by slavers.

SITH SWORD

Ancient weapons used by the Sith and, later, the Sith Lords. The menacing Sith swords were constructed of alchemically altered metals that never became dull and

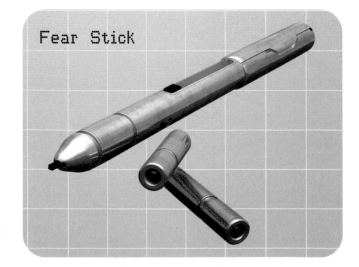

Fear Stick

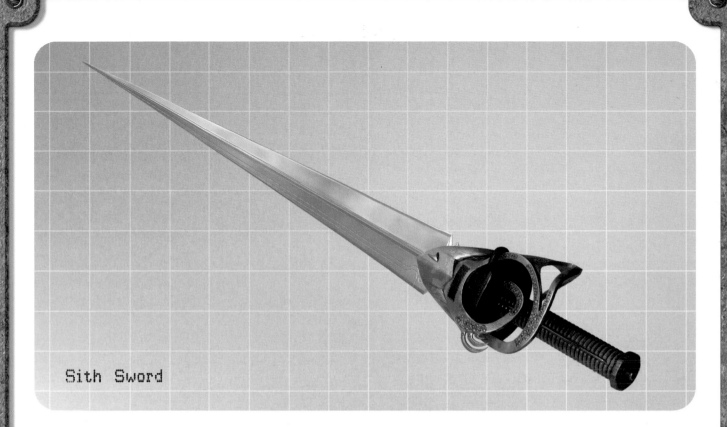

Sith Sword

could deflect both blasterfire and lightsabers. It is believed that the blade of a Sith sword was also designed to focus the Force energies of the wielder, which gave the weapon its unnaturally sharp edge. The origins of the first Sith sword are unknown, but it very well may have predated the earliest lightsabers.

Stun Baton

A nonlethal melee weapon used for crowd and riot control. Most stun batons, including the Merr-Sonn Z2, are simply weighted clubs with shock charge generators that can knock a target unconscious for several minutes.

Stun Gauntlet

A heavy gauntlet with integrated electric shock technology. Circuitry interwoven throughout the stun gauntlet's fabric allows the weapon to release an electric discharge on contact. When activated, the gauntlets glow with noticeable electrical energy. Palandrix manufactures stun gauntlets for a virtually all known sentient species.

Tehk'lka Blade

The Nagai version of the common vibroblade, featuring both vibration generators and a serrated blade, the Tehk'lka blade is used for deep stabbing attacks. When the weapon is violently withdrawn from a stab wound, the vibrating serrated blade tears at the victim's muscle and flesh, doubling the size of the original gash.

Yuuzhan Vong Claws

A Yuuzhan Vong melee weapon that resembles long claws extending from a warrior's knuckles. A set of Yuuzhan Vong claws is actually a parasite embedded deep into the warrior's bone. The claws can stretch up to four times their resting length, moving in a whiplike motion to cut through thick steel.

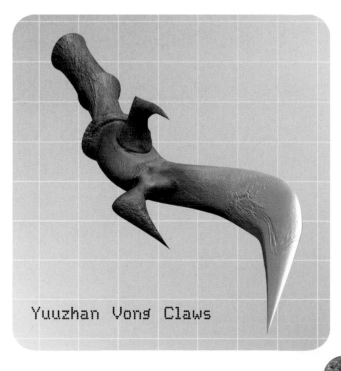

Yuuzhan Vong Claws

STARSHIP AND PLANETARY WEAPONS

The basic blaster has evolved very little over the past five to ten thousand standard years, with only minor advances in energy efficiency, range, and accuracy. However, warmongers have been able to harness blaster technology to build increasingly larger weapons, which produce devastating results on the battlefield.

The first uses of long-range blaster technology consisted of bulky, immobile emplacements that could fire beams of destructive energy. The concept of a durable weapons emplacement designed to slow enemy advances never disappeared from the lexicon of military tactics even with the event of the handheld blaster. In modern warfare, those early and crude cannons have evolved into complex, long-range antivehicle and anti-infantry turrets with sophisticated targeting systems and energy blasts strong enough to penetrate the armored hulls of most troop transports and assault vehicles. This has led to the development of increasingly resilient vehicles, such as the Imperial AT-AT walker, as well as precision bombers designed to wipe out enemy emplacements before ground troops arrive.

The technology of ranged weapons has also allowed the use of vehicles as mobile weapons platforms. Very early in the history of vehicular combat, warriors simply attached large projectile rifles, blaster rifles, or repeating blasters to their vehicles. Since the early days of the Old Republic, blaster cannons (sometimes known as flash cannons) have been found on nearly all small military and security transports, from Naboo's Flash speeder to the twin-pod cloud cars used by the Cloud City Wing Guard. When combat transcended the atmosphere and boiled into space, weapons designers quickly developed powerful laser cannons, the next step in blaster technology. All starships save diplomatic vessels boast laser cannons of some sort, which are primarily a defense against pirates and other threats but are also be used to blast space debris from a vehicle's path. The term *laser cannon* is now synonymous with the most powerful blaster cannons. With the proper power generator and support structure, large ground vehicles can also carry laser cannons; the AT-TE and AT-AT walkers, along with many military speeders, utilize the most advanced laser cannons available.

The next major evolution in large-scale weaponry occurred as a result of advances in vehicle design. The advent of atmospheric starfighters, particularly bombers, created the need for antiaircraft weapons that could hit targets in low orbit. Fear inspired by massive capital ships eventually led to the development of planetary weapons designed to dissuade invasions: gargantuan laser and ion cannons are still used to damage invading warships the moment they approach.

While large-scale combats continue to take place on planetary surfaces, starfighter battles are just as frequent. To increase the effectiveness of starships, weapons manufacturers have expanded beyond traditional laser cannons. Among the most common alternatives to laser cannons and the larger turbolasers are ion cannons, which are often integrated into designs for large warships. Even when laser cannons serve as the primary weapon on a starfighter, such attack vessels often carry secondary weapons systems to supplement the laser barrage. Usually, these secondary systems utilize destructive explosives. Short-range snub fighters such as the X-wing are often equipped with proton torpedoes. Those starfighters deployed for bombing runs on capital ships or installations can release concussion missiles and energy bombs of all types.

Perhaps the most effective "weapons," however, are nonmilitary devices that military tacticians use in innovative ways. Both tractor beams and seismic charges were originally developed for industrial use, but have been converted for both offensive and defensive use on starships and capital ships.

As ever-more-destructive weapons are produced for invading forces, potential victims will continue to develop more powerful deterrents. In the aftermath of the Yuuzhan Vong incursion, the New Republic will undoubtedly produce a host of new weapons to defend the galaxy's borders from any other potential threats.

ANTIVEHICLE ARTILLERY

TECHNICAL READOUT

DAMAGE TYPE: *Laser Energy*

OPTIMUM/MAXIMUM RANGES: *5 km/10 km*

PRIMARY MANUFACTURER: *Atgar*

AFFILIATION: *Rebel Alliance Infantry*

Atgar 1.4 FD P-Tower Laser Cannon

As vehicles took a larger role in large-scale battles, military commanders struggled to find ways to disrupt an armored advance. While primitive trenches, durasteel walls, hidden mines, and metal tank traps could be used to slow walkers and wheeled vehicles, they prove ineffective against repulsorlift craft, which can easily hover over such barriers. In truth, the most effective antivehicle weapons are simply large, powerful versions of traditional blasters, typically referred to as antivehicle artillery.

Antivehicle artillery units are generally fixed emplacements designed to fire powerful energy beams over a great range. Like many other classes of weapons, antivehicle artillery units vary greatly, ranging from small, rapid-fire turrets meant to target single-passenger speeder bikes to giant weapons that can blow the head off an Imperial AT-AT walker.

Although relatively outdated, the Atgar 1.4 FD P-Tower has all of the standard features found on most antivehicle artillery units. The weapon has a maximum range of ten kilometers. Its energy beam is strong enough to disable landspeeders, slow-moving airspeeders, and even repulsortanks. The P-Tower sits on a rotating platform that provides the weapon with a 360-degree field of fire. A layer of thin plating protects the P-Tower from blasterfire, but it is no match for an AT-AT's blaster cannons.

The P-Tower was outdated and relatively ineffective by the time of the Galactic Civil War. Its primary drawback is its dependence on a small Atgar C-6 battery, which contains enough energy for only eight shots. The power source can be quickly replaced by a skilled tech-

> **"When the P-Tower gets ready to fire, you can feel the charge, hear the hum, see the dish light up . . . It's a moment of hope. And then the blast just bounces off an AT-AT and you realize that the situation is hopeless . . ."**
>
> —*Rebel grunt Lak Sivrak*

nician, but securing an adequate supply of the batteries proved difficult for Rebel forces. Before the weapon can fire, the C-6 battery must charge sixteen micropower routers along the edge of the weapon's dish. The recharging sequence takes ten seconds, resulting in a relatively slow rate of fire. Finally, a burnout in any of the micropower routers will cause the entire weapon to fail dramatically. The battery and delicate power system necessitates a large crew to keep the P-Tower operating at peak efficiency. The crew's single gunner is supported by three engineers, who monitor and replace the batteries and continually assess the routers to prevent burnouts. Because the P-Tower is not an enclosed turret, all four crew members are exposed to enemy fire.

Against Imperial AT-AT walkers, the P-Tower is relatively useless; its blasts will just reflect off an AT-AT's thick plating. The P-Tower is equally ineffective against high-speed airspeeders, due to an outdated targeting computer and hadrium-iode tracking system.

After the Galactic Civil War, the New Republic decommissioned many of its P-Towers in favor of weapons with repulsorlift platforms. Such antivehicle artillery units can be moved across battlefields more easily, although their energy requirements are also more extensive.

❼ Power Conversion Cell: When the P-Tower is primed to fire, its eight power conversion cells activate, creating a distinctive glow around the dish. Rebel commanders always considered this a major drawback, because the glow could reveal defensive positions if used at night.

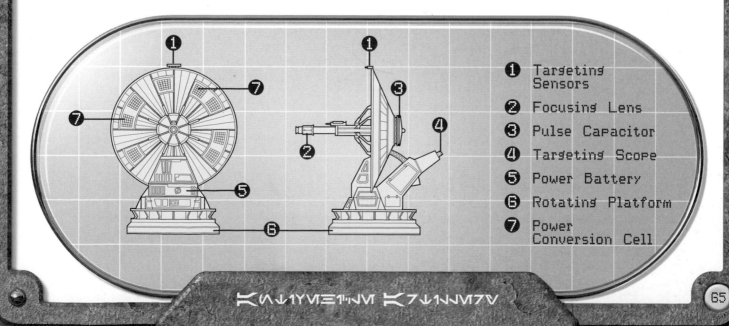

1. Targeting Sensors
2. Focusing Lens
3. Pulse Capacitor
4. Targeting Scope
5. Power Battery
6. Rotating Platform
7. Power Conversion Cell

ANTI-INFANTRY BATTERY

TECHNICAL READOUT

DAMAGE TYPE: *Blaster*
ENERGY AND EXPLOSIVE

OPTIMUM/MAXIMUM RANGES: *3 KM/16 KM*

PRIMARY MANUFACTURER: *Golan Arms*

AFFILIATION: *Rebel Alliance INFANTRY*

Golan Arms DF.9

While antivehicle artillery units are designed expressly for use against vehicles, more prevalent and perhaps more useful are anti-infantry batteries, weapons emplacements that serve as the first line of defense against ground troops. Anti-infantry units fire standard blaster beams capable of cutting down armored soldiers in droves.

Like many anti-infantry artillery weapons, the Golan Arms DF.9, which the Rebel Alliance carted onto the battlefields of Hoth, relies on advanced precision targeting computers. When coupled with the unit's 180-degree field of fire and ability to release one blast every three seconds, the DF.9 can easily sweep advancing front lines. Skilled gunners can take advantage of the DF.9's accuracy to disable an army's support equipment and even some smaller vehicles.

Early anti-infantry artillery included rotating blaster rifles similar to the modern E-Web. Larger units allow for more robust power generators, resulting in increased firepower. The DF.9 and other turrets can also support armor and proton shield generators. They can be installed in nearly any terrain and are easily modified for use in even the most hostile climates. For maximum protection, anti-infantry units are usually arranged alongside banks of antivehicle batteries, creating a defensive network that can destroy entire armies.

Anti-infantry batteries are most effective within about three kilometers, but most can hit targets up to sixteen kilometers away with less accuracy. This allows defenders to make opening salvos well before advancing troops are close enough to return fire. The DF.9 is notable because its energy beams explode upon impact

> **"For every stormtrooper you kill here today, a Rebel life is saved tomorrow."**
>
> —*General Carlist Rieekan at the Battle of Hoth*

with a target. The explosion damages everything within an eight-meter radius. During the Battle of Hoth, the limited number of DF.9 units used by the Alliance did manage to destroy a handful of stormtrooper squads before the Imperial soldiers and AT-ATs overran the Rebels.

Weapons designers have remained cognizant of the fact that anti-infantry units need to be moved quickly across battlefields. Many of the units are light enough to support repulsorsleds. Among the most mobile anti-infantry units is the SP.9, which is mounted on a self-propelled repulsorsled that can reach speeds of sixty kilometers per hour. The DF.9, however, trades mobility for power and requires a fixed emplacement for accurate use. Like other large turrets, the DF.9 can be operated by a solo gunner if necessary, but it's only truly efficient if also manned by a targeting computer specialist and a power technician who regulates the weapon's generator.

As of the Yuuzhan Vong invasion, the DF.9 was more than forty years old. Despite its age, it is still in use by pirates and various outlaws who find the weapon easy to repair. The DF.9 can also be modified to fire more devastating blaster bolts for use against lightly armored vehicles. The DF.9's core design has inspired variants, including the Twin DF.9, which has rapid-fire laser cannons and a much larger power generator that allow for one blast every second.

7 Operator's Hatch: The DF.9's gunner typically sits in a small tube atop the turret, with his or her head exposed for optimum visibility. Unfortunately, this leaves the gunner exposed to sniper attacks.

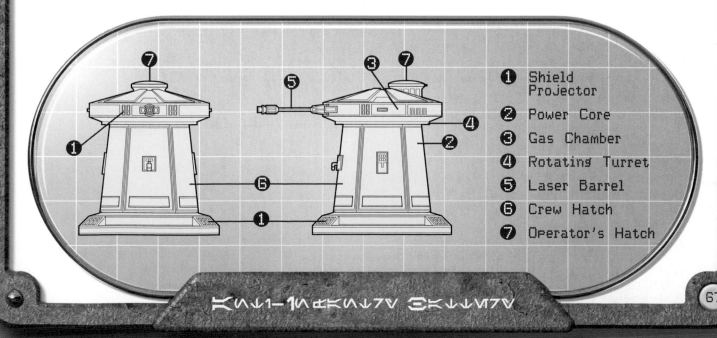

1 Shield Projector
2 Power Core
3 Gas Chamber
4 Rotating Turret
5 Laser Barrel
6 Crew Hatch
7 Operator's Hatch

Laser Cannons

Technical Readout

DAMAGE TYPE: Laser energy

OPTIMUM/MAXIMUM RANGES: 8 km/80 km

PRIMARY MANUFACTURER: Taim & Bak

AFFILIATION: Rebel Alliance X-wingstarfighters

Taim & Bak KX9 Laser Cannons

When sentient beings began traveling through space, they faced threats such as stellar debris and small asteroids. To blast such obstacles from their path, early pilots equipped their vessels with powerful laser cannons, similar to those used on military ground vehicles of the era. These first starship weapons, inaccurate and inefficient, were still more than capable of destroying the hazards encountered by the first galactic explorers. However, as with nearly all forms of technology, starship laser cannons were soon co-opted by criminals, allowing pirates to migrate from terrestrial operations to space raids, targeting transports carrying valuable goods or resources. As these villains began using laser cannons offensively, technology manufacturers focused on making the weapons more accurate and more energy-efficient without sacrificing the laser cannon's devastating power.

The current selection of laser cannons ranges from weak, low-grade weapons designed for atmospheric combat to huge emplacements that can rip through large, armored starships. Nearly every starship manufactured can support at least one laser cannon, although military starfighters generally carry two or more. The X-wing starfighter, one of the most potent starfighters deployed during the Galactic Civil War, is armed with four Taim & Bak KX9 laser cannons, two on each wing. When an X-wing enters battle, the pilot locks the starship's S-foils into attack position, allowing the wings to separate. This unique configuration gives the X-wing an unprecedented field of fire.

The most successful laser cannons are designed to fire several bursts in rapid succession. Multiple laser cannons be "fire-linked," allowing all of a ship's weapons to fire simultaneously with a single trigger pull. The X-wing's cannons can be fire-linked in pairs or as an entire group. They can also be programmed to fire in specific patterns for maximum coverage.

Laser cannons are similar to blasters in design. Volatile blaster gas, funneled from a supercooled and armored chamber, is combined with a power charge. The resulting energy is directed through a long barrel, where galven coils focus it into a damaging beam. Other circuitry in the barrel increases the beam's power, allowing laser cannons to inflict incredible damage.

The laser cannon's computerized targeting system helps the pilot track fast-moving enemies or target specific starship components, such as shield generators or power sources. Some targeting systems can be linked directly to astromech droids, allowing the automata to function as gunners. Laser cannons also require dedicated power sources and advanced cooling systems to avoid overheating.

Most laser cannons, especially those for starfighters, are designed to be compact and light. Larger starships, like *Millennium Falcon*, can carry oversize laser cannons that deliver much more destructive blasts. The *Falcon's* weapons profile includes two quad laser cannon turrets. Quad laser cannons have four tightly arranged barrels and can easily destroy an Imperial TIE fighter with a single shot.

> ## "Lock S-foils in attack position."
> *—Garven Dreis, Red Leader,*
> *at the Battle of Yavin*

❼ Flashback Suppressor: The X-wing's laser cannon is very recognizable due to its curved flashback suppressor, which prevents the cannon barrel from being damaged by overcharged laser blasts.

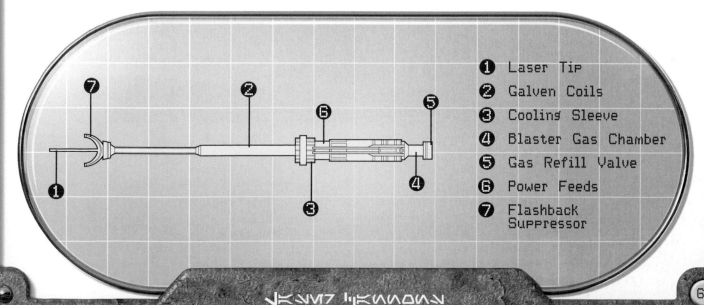

1. Laser Tip
2. Galven Coils
3. Cooling Sleeve
4. Blaster Gas Chamber
5. Gas Refill Valve
6. Power Feeds
7. Flashback Suppressor

Technical Readout

Damage Type: Laser energy

Optimum/Maximum Ranges: 15 km/100 km

Primary Manufacturer: Taim & Bak

Affiliation: Imperial Star Destroyers

Taim & Bak XX-9 Heavy Turbolasers

Turbolasers are massive weapons emplacements installed aboard space stations, orbital facilities, and capital starships. Far more powerful than standard laser cannons, turbolasers are designed to tear into enemy starships, searing through durasteel armor and hammering on deflector shields until those defenses fail. Turbolasers are almost always installed in banks, allowing gunners to generate a storm of deadly laserfire.

Unlike a standard laser cannon, a turbolaser employs a two-stage supercharging process. The first stage creates a typical laser beam, which is then guided through a stream of energized blaster gas to dramatically increase its potency. As with other laser cannons, the turbolaser's energy field is focused by galven coils in the weapon's barrel. The two-stage design creates blasts with triple the power of standard laser cannons. The Taim & Bak XX-9 turbolasers aboard an Imperial Star Destroyer can even conduct planetary bombardments.

The Imperial Star Destroyer is equipped with sixty XX-9 heavy turbolasers grouped into small banks located the length of the starship, linked to advanced computerized fire-control systems that coordinate the weapons to ensure that they fire in sustained, organized volleys. Each bank is controlled by a gunnery sergeant, safely hidden in the bowels of the Star Destroyer. Individual gunners can be deployed to each turbolaser, if needed.

Like many large weapons, turbolasers do have disadvantages in combat. If arranged poorly, the turbolasers' poor recharge rate and slow rotation speed create huge gaps in the starship's defensive screen. At the Battle of Yavin, the skilled Rebel Alliance pilots exploited this weaknesses by screaming past the Death Star's turbolasers right after each had fired.

> ## "We count thirty Rebel ships, Lord Vader. But they're so small they're evading our turbolasers!"
> —*Lieutenant Tanbris at the Battle of Yavin*

Turbolasers are very difficult to maintain. Each requires a dedicated turbine and multiple capacitor banks. Energy flow must be carefully regulated, because power surges or excess energy buildup can cause the weapon to explode. Overheating is a constant concern. Turbolasers must be protected by three separate cryosystems, and by a cooling sleeve on the barrel and a large cooling unit placed beneath the laser actuator. These cooling systems are expensive, complex, and challenging to repair.

One of the most infamous terrestrial turbolasers is the SPHA-T, or self-propelled heavy artillery turbolaser, used by the Old Republic during the Clone Wars. The SPHA-T features a large focusing array that creates a powerful laser beam that can penetrate deflector shields. This huge turbolaser is carried across battlefields atop a large, armored drive unit consisting of several all-terrain treads. Its primary weapon does not rotate, requiring the massive vehicle to turn to face targets. The turret can elevate, allowing the turbolaser to target slow-moving aircraft. The SPHA-T was vital in destroying the Confederacy's fleeing core ships at the Battle of Geonosis.

The New Republic has allowed military contractors to continue research into more powerful variants, including quick-recharge turbolasers, which provide the New Republic, the Hapes Consortium, and other forces arrayed against the Yuuzhan Vong with a small edge in large-scale space battles.

8 Quadanium Steel Hull Plating: The XX-9 turbolasers are protected by heavy armor that can fend off attacks by many starfighters, including Alliance A-wings.

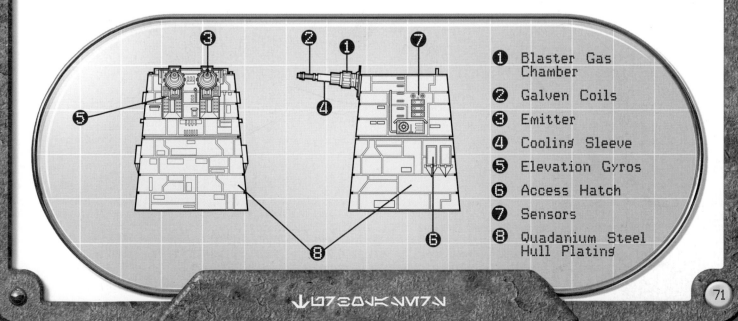

1 Blaster Gas Chamber
2 Galven Coils
3 Emitter
4 Cooling Sleeve
5 Elevation Gyros
6 Access Hatch
7 Sensors
8 Quadanium Steel Hull Plating

PLANETARY TURBOLASER

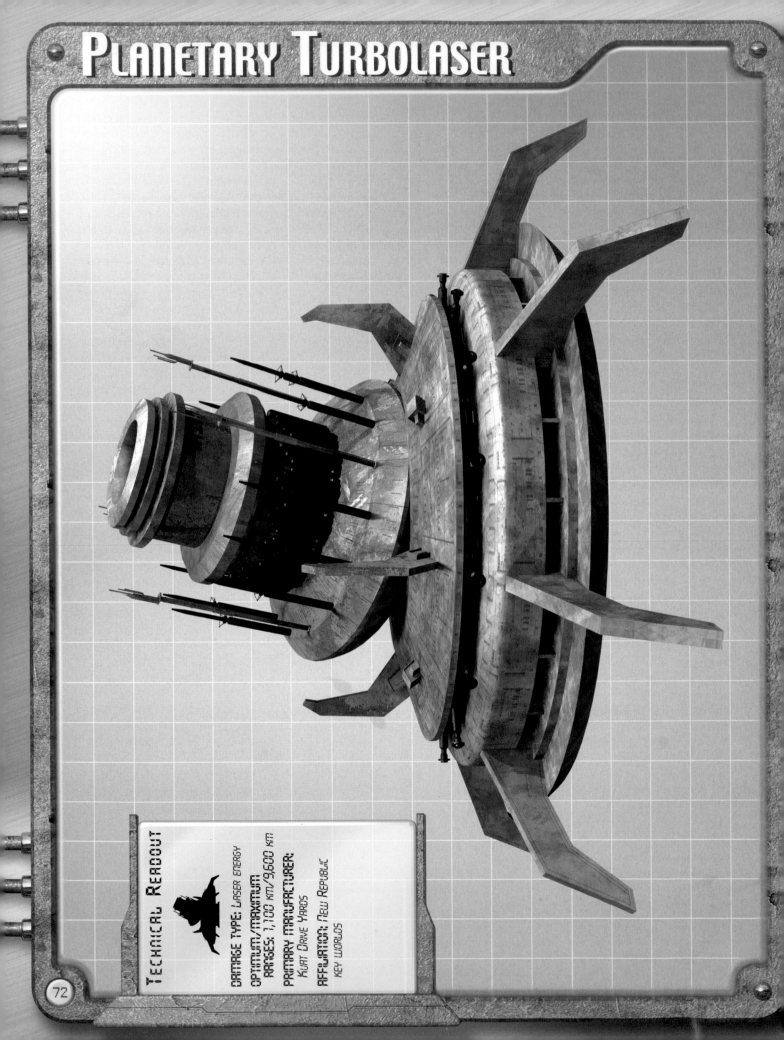

TECHNICAL READOUT

DAMAGE TYPE: LASER ENERGY

OPTIMUM/MAXIMUM RANGES: 1,100 KM/9,600 KM

PRIMARY MANUFACTURER: Kuat Drive Yards

AFFILIATION: New Republic

KEY WORLDS

KDY w-165 Planetary Turbolaser

In an age of warships capable of bombarding planets from space, planetary turbolasers are a critical part of any global defense. Among the largest of weapons, they are designed to fire a thick beam of laser energy through an atmosphere and into space, where the blast can cause catastrophic damage.

Kuat Drive Yards, a leader in large-scale weapons, manufactures the KDY w-165 planetary turbolaser. The w-165 is a massive structure that includes the turbolaser itself and a stabilizing platform nearly 150 meters in diameter. The platform can be found on more than three hundred New Republic worlds and is designed for use in any environment: its eight stabilizer legs can provide support on ice and other unstable terrain. Special aquatic turbolasers are equipped with flotation platforms and durasteel anchor cables to allow stable positioning on lakes or oceans. Although the platform is heavily armored and defended by dozens of deflector shield projectors, engineers often bury the lower portion of the base beneath rock or earth for additional protection. Protecting the platform is key, because it supports the turbolaser itself and holds the weapon's large power core with enough energy to power a small city.

The w-165 requires a large crew of fifty technicians, computer operators, engineers, and gunners. Most of the crew is safely housed in gunnery stations located along the platform's outer ring. Soldiers also patrol the platform to guard against enemy infiltration and capture.

The actual planetary turbolaser is roughly twenty-five meters in diameter, with three kilometers of galven circuitry woven throughout the barrel. As with other laser cannons, the galven circuitry focuses the weapon's energy, producing a concentrated beam.

Because of its size and energy requirements, the planetary turbolaser is susceptible to overheating and dangerous energy overloads. The w-165 combats this threat through four dozen overload dispersal tubes, which absorb and redirect excess heat. The turbolaser actuator is sheathed in a cooling sleeve programmed to keep the weapon at a safe operation temperature. All of these components must be carefully monitored especially in sustained use during an invasion.

Targeting an enemy vessel in space requires an extensive sensor system. Long-range sensors on the turbolaser's platform are supported by sensor arrays aboard orbiting satellites. The data collected by these myriad sensors are fed to a global processing network, which then delivers targeting vectors to all of a planet's turbolasers. The turbolaser is not a rapid-fire weapon, although the w-165 can unleash short volleys. The w-165 is quite capable of destroying a Star Destroyer in orbit. The weapon's field of fire is reliant on slow gears in the platform that can rotate the barrel 360 degrees and swing the turret in a complete 180-degree arc. This allows the planetary turbolaser to methodically switch targets, but the weapon still has a limited fire vector. To provide complete coverage, planets must be protected by more than a hundred planetary turbolasers, each with a cost of over ten million credits.

> ## "The first, last, and *only* line of defense your planet will ever need!"
> —*Kuat Drive Yards catalog*

7 Emitter Tip: The turbolaser's emitter produces one of the largest single laser beams in the galaxy. Only the Death Star and a handful of other superweapons can match the w-165's power and range.

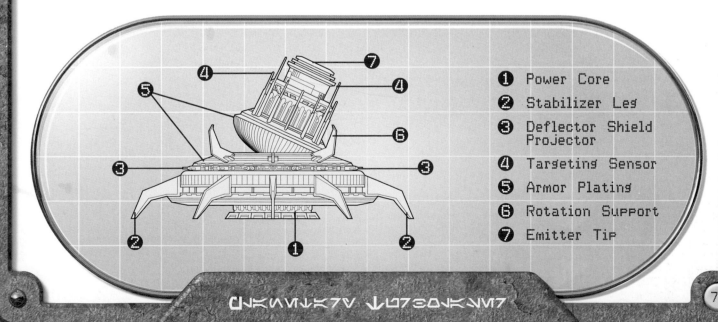

1. Power Core
2. Stabilizer Leg
3. Deflector Shield Projector
4. Targeting Sensor
5. Armor Plating
6. Rotation Support
7. Emitter Tip

Proton Torpedo Warhead

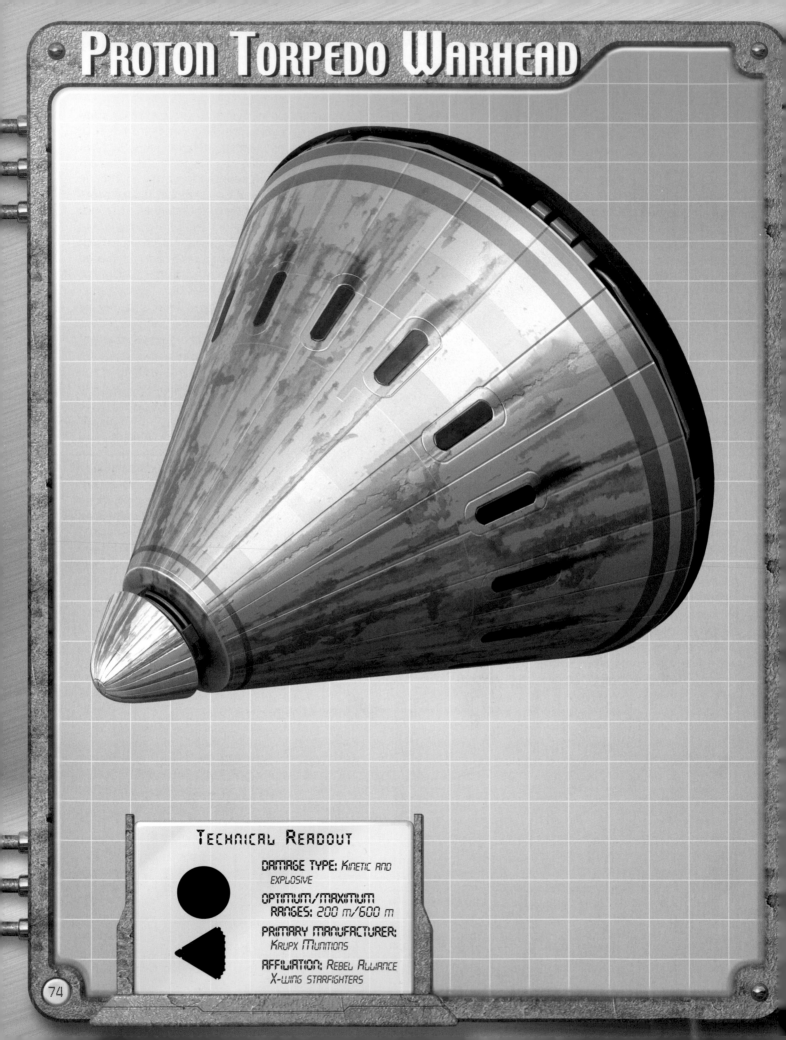

Technical Readout

DAMAGE TYPE: Kinetic and explosive

OPTIMUM/MAXIMUM RANGES: 200 m/600 m

PRIMARY MANUFACTURER: Krupx Munitions

AFFILIATION: Rebel Alliance X-wing starfighters

Krupx MG7–Proton Torpedo

The course of the Galactic Civil War was forever altered at the Battle of Yavin, which saw the destruction of the original Death Star, and emboldened numerous systems to join the fledgling Rebellion. The Empire's surprising defeat hinged on one well-placed shot from a relatively simple weapon: the proton torpedo.

Proton torpedoes are high-speed, self-propelled projectiles carried aboard a variety of starfighters and capital ships. Each torpedo employs a high-yield, proton-scattering warhead that detonates upon impact with a target. The resulting explosion can completely consume a small starfighter, such as an X-wing or A-wing. Like concussion missiles and other projectiles, proton torpedoes are extremely useful because they ignore basic energy shields designed as defense against pure energy weapons. Particle shielding will limit the effect of proton torpedoes, but few starships utilize this technology. At the Battle of Yavin, Luke Skywalker fired a pair of proton torpedoes into a small, unshielded exhaust port on the first Death Star, causing a chain reaction that destroyed the mammoth space station.

Proton torpedoes can be carried only in limited numbers. The X-wing starfighter travels with just six proton torpedoes, while the Y-wing, which often serves as a bomber, has eight. This relegates proton torpedoes to use as secondary weapons, fired to soften targets for strafing runs. Proton torpedoes are excellent for taking out key targets such as shield generators and engines.

When launched, a proton torpedo is enveloped in a weak energy shield. This envelope prevents accidental detonation from collisions with small debris. Most proton torpedoes, including the Krupx MG7-A used by X-wing starfighters, feature sophisticated guidance computers that track and home in on targets. When used against stationary targets, the MG7-A has a margin of error of less than three meters, although particularly fast vehicles can outmaneuver the warheads. Some pilots prefer to fire proton torpedoes without the aid of the weapon's targeting computer, which can become useless in especially chaotic battles and may actually lock onto the nearest ship, friend or foe.

Proton torpedo variants include smaller (and much weaker) versions of the weapon that can be fired by special shoulder launchers. Proton bombs also exist: these weapons are essentially "dumb-fire" proton torpedoes that are dropped onto targets without the benefit of onboard homing systems. Proton hydrotorpedoes are specifically designed for use during aquatic battles.

Perhaps the most important proton torpedo variant is the shadow bomb, which the Jedi order developed to combat the Yuuzhan Vong. A shadow bomb is essentially a standard proton torpedo drained of propellant. The empty propellant cavity is filled with baradium, the same volatile material used in thermal detonators. Shadow bombs lack any targeting equipment; instead, Jedi pilots use the Force to guide the explosives. Because they do not lock onto targets or create energy trails, shadow bombs are difficult to spot during space battles, allowing for stealth attacks. When a shadow bomb detonates, it causes far greater damage than an unmodified proton torpedo.

> ### "Great shot, kid! That was one in a million!"
> *Han Solo*

7 Homing Sensor: Most pilots rely on the torpedo's homing sensor, but Luke Skywalker turned to the Force instead to ensure a successful attack on the first Death Star.

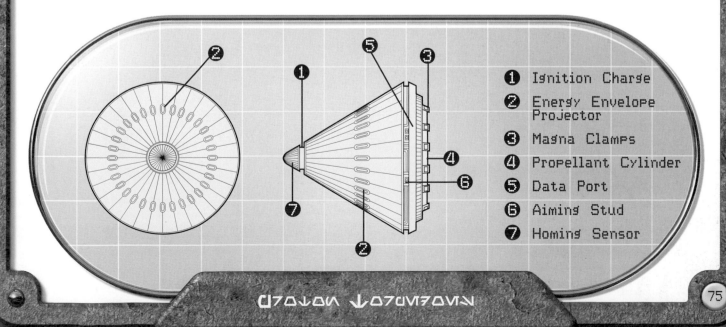

1 Ignition Charge
2 Energy Envelope Projector
3 Magna Clamps
4 Propellant Cylinder
5 Data Port
6 Aiming Stud
7 Homing Sensor

CONCUSSION MISSILES

TECHNICAL READOUT

DAMAGE TYPE: Kinetic and explosive

OPTIMUM/MAXIMUM RANGES: 300 m/700 m

PRIMARY MANUFACTURER: Arakyd Industries

AFFILIATION: Han Solo's Millennium Falcon

Arakyd ST2 Concussion Missile and Rack

Concussion missiles are among the numerous secondary starship weapons designed to complement laser cannons. Physical projectiles that travel at sublight speeds, concussion missiles generate explosive shock waves when they impact with a target. While laser cannons are useful for precision attacks, concussion missiles, which are much less predictable, cause chaos in both ground and space battles.

A concussion missile is a self-contained projectile with an explosive warhead, a guidance computer, and a rudimentary propulsion system. The body is generally constructed of reinforced armor alloy that protects the weapon's sensitive components. Missiles are carried aboard starships in automated racks, and released through tubes.

Because they are physical weapons, concussion missiles can pass through most energy shields. To take full advantage of this feature, concussion missiles are generally launched in staggered pairs less than a second apart. The first missile is meant to destroy shields, power generators, and armor plating, allowing the second missile to completely eliminate the vulnerable target. In space battles, concussion missiles are often launched to destroy shield generators on large starships. However, concussion missiles are most effective within an atmosphere, where the missile's explosion wreaks havoc. An atmospheric detonation causes a frightening sonic boom, followed by ground tremors that shake apart walls, buildings, and even vehicles, killing countless in the process.

Concussion missiles are strictly short-range weapons, with a maximum range of seven hundred meters. The guidance system and homing sensors housed in the projectile excel at locking onto targets; however, they do not adapt well to rapidly changing trajectories. Therefore, while concussion missiles are well suited to destroying stationary or slow-moving targets, they are rarely fired at agile enemy fighters.

Bombers, terrestrial weapons platforms, and tanks were among the first vehicles to utilize concussion missiles. Smugglers, pirates, and other criminals adapted the weapon for use aboard space stations and other installations, modifying the missiles to provide some defense against approaching starfighters. The Empire further evolved concussion missiles, installing small models aboard TIE bombers and larger launchers on Star Destroyers and other capital ships. The Rebel Alliance favored miniaturized missile launchers, such as the Dymex HM-6 launchers integrated into many A-wing starfighters.

> ## "The shield is down! Commence attack on the Death Star's main reactor."
> —*Admiral Ackbar at the Battle of Endor*

Arakyd Industries produces some of the most powerful concussion missiles currently available. Han Solo armed *Millennium Falcon* with two Arakyd ST2 missile launchers, each capable of carrying up to four missiles. These were vital during the Battle of Endor, when Lando Calrissian fired a pair into the second Death Star's main reactor. The missiles ripped through the reactor's armor plating, causing a chain reaction that destroyed the superweapon.

7 **Energy Envelope Projector:** When the missile is launched, projectors create an energy shroud to protect the weapon from the vacuum of space and enemy fire. This energy shroud and the missile's speed conspire to make the missile resemble a blast from a laser cannon.

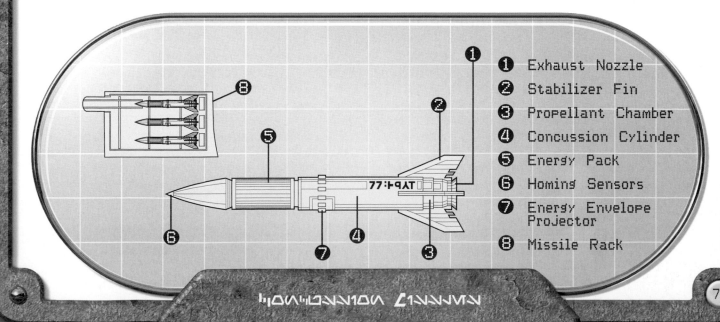

1. Exhaust Nozzle
2. Stabilizer Fin
3. Propellant Chamber
4. Concussion Cylinder
5. Energy Pack
6. Homing Sensors
7. Energy Envelope Projector
8. Missile Rack

Ion Cannons

Technical Readout

DAMAGE TYPE: Ion energy

OPTIMUM/MAXIMUM RANGES: 10 km/80 km

PRIMARY MANUFACTURER: Borstel Galactic Defense

AFFILIATION: Imperial Star Destroyers

Borstel NK-7 Ion Cannon

Few weapons are considered as significant as the ion cannon. A single, well-placed ion cannon controlled by a competent gunner can change the course of a battle, because the ion energy it discharges overloads the circuitry and electronic systems aboard enemy vessels. This effectively disables a target without causing any real damage. During the Galactic Civil War, both Imperials and Rebels used ion cannons extensively in order to capture cargo and enemy personnel. The Alliance even employed ion cannons to steal entire Imperial starships.

Ion cannons differ widely. Those designed to protect space stations are quite large, with a wide field but very slow rate of fire. Such ion cannons usually draw upon the space station's power generator, forcing the installation to shut down communications and other nonessential systems. In contrast, ion cannons stationed aboard capital ships are designed for both offensive and defensive purposes. Imperial Star Destroyers are generally equipped with sixty Borstel NK-7 ion cannon emplacements, each powered by a dedicated turbine generator. Such turrets are controlled by gunnery stations, where Imperial officers coordinate fire from multiple cannons to disable ships as quickly as possible. A typical NK-7 volley can immobilize a starship for several minutes, enough time for Imperial stormtroopers to board the vessel. Imperial forces used a Star Destroyer's battery of ion cannons to disable Princess Leia's consular ship, the *Tantive IV,* as she fled toward Tatooine.

Prior to the Mandalorian Wars, the use of ion cannons aboard personal starfighters was reserved for mer-

> ## "That's funny, the damage doesn't look as bad from out here . . ."
> *—C-3PO, observing the* Tantive IV *from space after Imperials disabled the vessel using ion cannons*

cenaries, pirates, and bounty hunters. Although the Mandalorians were eventually defeated, the weapons proved integral to nearly all of their victories.

Since that time, ion cannons have become a common secondary weapon aboard starfighters. The Rebel Alliance Y-wing is equipped with an ArMek SW-4 turret-mounted ion cannon that has an impressive field of fire and can be controlled by the starfighter's onboard astromech. The B-wing revolves around its ability to support multiple weapons of varying types, and a standard configuration includes three ion cannons. Unfortunately, ion cannons have no impact on the organic starships used by the Yuuzhan Vong.

Ion cannons are also valuable for use during ground battles. Small, stationary ion turrets are occasionally established around key military sites. Because of their power requirements, ion cannons are rarely found aboard small airspeeders or landspeeders, but during the Clone Wars, both the Commerce Guild homing spider droids and the Republic's SPHA-T artillery units carried light ion cannons for use as antiaircraft weapons. Years later, the Empire converted a small number of AT-AT walkers into mobile ion cannons, known as AT-IC (All Terrain Ion Cannon) walkers.

❼ Maintenance Hatches: Because the ion cannon's maintenance hatches are located on the exterior of the cannon, repair work requires a competent crew wearing evac suits designed to protect against the vacuum of space.

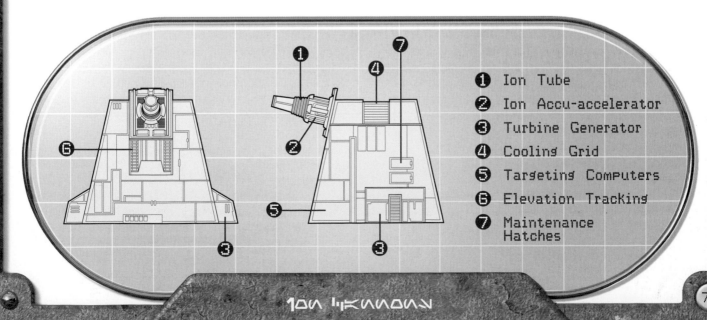

- ❶ Ion Tube
- ❷ Ion Accu-accelerator
- ❸ Turbine Generator
- ❹ Cooling Grid
- ❺ Targeting Computers
- ❻ Elevation Tracking
- ❼ Maintenance Hatches

Technical Readout

DAMAGE TYPE: Ion Energy

OPTIMUM/MAXIMUM RANGES:
4,000 km/180,000 km

PRIMARY MANUFACTURER:
Kuat Drive Yards

AFFILIATION: Echo Base

KDY v-150 Planet Defender

Like planetary turbolasers, planetary ion cannons are an integral part of an inhabited world's defense network. Planetary ion cannons can fire a beam of ion energy well into orbit, ignoring deflector shields and overloading a target vessel's electrical and computer systems, rendering the vehicle completely defenseless and immobile. Nearly all planetary ion cannons are used strictly for defense, although some pirate bands on anarchic worlds such as Lok have employed the weapons to disable passing transports, which they board for looting. The Rebel Alliance's Echo Base was protected by a huge Kuat Drive Yards v-150 Planet Defender, which ensured that at least some Rebels escaped from Imperial forces.

The Alliance favored the v-150 over other models because of its spherical permacite shell, which protected the weapon from Hoth's harsh climate. The v-150 requires an incredible amount of energy: the Hoth Planet Defender was powered by a massive reactor buried some forty meters below ground.

Ion cannons require a lengthy activation time and are difficult to position and target. The weapon's rotating base moves fairly slowly, and it can take several minutes to lock onto a stationary object in space. Planetary ion cannons are also completely immobile, making them vulnerable to enemy ground forces and aerial bombardment. To protect the weapon from such attacks, the v-150 is equipped with a retractable blast shield. Unfortunately, this shield must be opened whenever the cannon is fired.

On Hoth, the Rebels' Planet Defender was operated by twenty-seven soldiers, most native to Alderaan. Among an ion cannon's crew members are targeting specialists who process information received from long-range sensors and electrotelescopes. Like turbolasers, ion cannons can also be linked to orbital sensor stations for more accurate targeting.

Ion cannons have been designed to work in conjunction with planetary shields. Such shields consume a great deal of energy, preventing them from being raised at all times. The Hoth cannon was linked directly to the planetary shield system, allowing gunners to synchronize ion volleys with momentary shield drops.

During the Galactic Civil War, few non-Imperial worlds could afford to build the weapons. The Rebel Alliance acquired the Hoth ion cannon through theft and was forced to rely on it to protect the entirety of Echo Base. Because ion cannons have a relatively limited field of fire and a slow recharge rate of only one shot every six seconds, the Rebels installed it as close to the Rebel facility as possible. After the Emperor's defeat, the New Republic began erecting planetary ion cannons on poor but strategically important worlds. Unfortunately, the weapons did little to stall the Yuuzhan Vong invasion, because ion blasts have virtually no effect on the invaders' bizarre biotechnology.

> **"The ion cannon will fire several shots to make sure that any enemy ships will be out of your flight path."**
>
> —*Princess Leia Organa, describing evacuation plans before the Battle of Hoth*

7 Blast Shield: The ion cannon's retractable blast shield must be opened every time the cannon is fired, providing attackers with a brief opportunity to damage the weapon's delicate internal components.

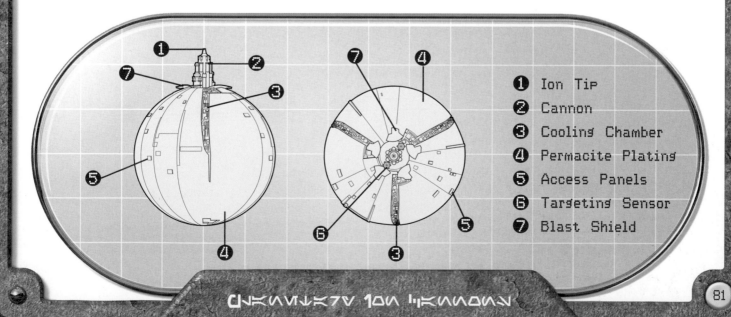

1 Ion Tip
2 Cannon
3 Cooling Chamber
4 Permacite Plating
5 Access Panels
6 Targeting Sensor
7 Blast Shield

TRACTOR BEAM PROJECTORS

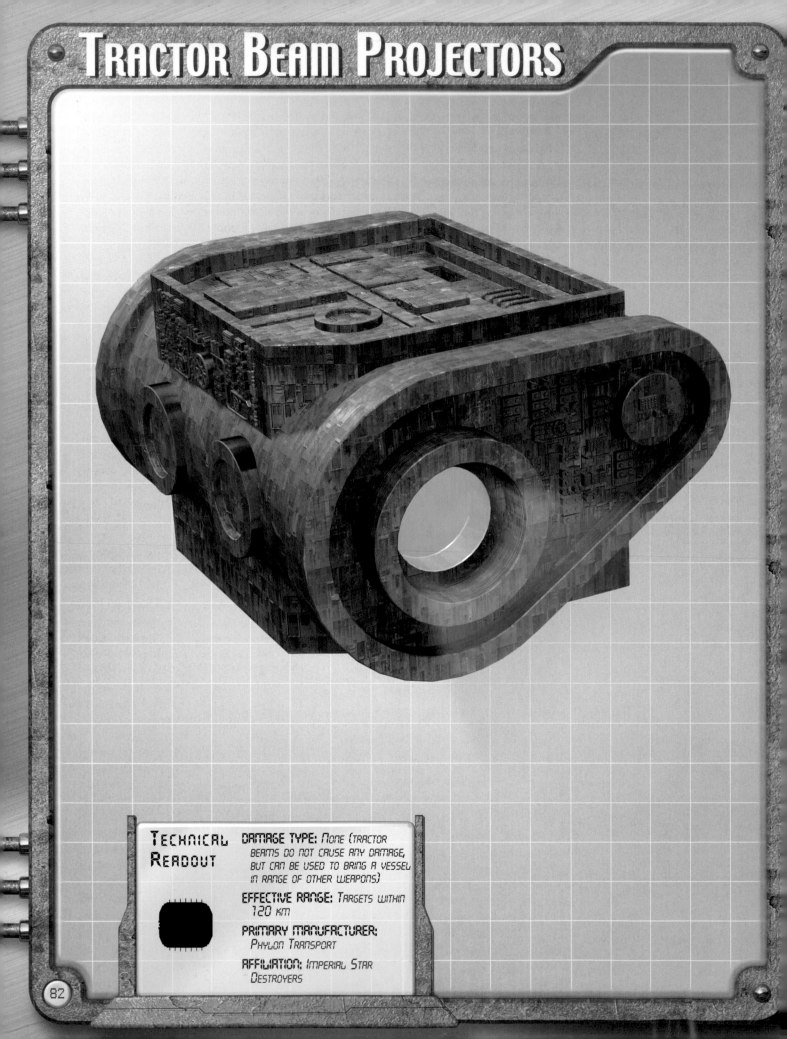

TECHNICAL READOUT

DAMAGE TYPE: None (tractor beams do not cause any damage, but can be used to bring a vessel in range of other weapons)

EFFECTIVE RANGE: Targets within 120 km

PRIMARY MANUFACTURER: Phylon Transport

AFFILIATION: Imperial Star Destroyers

Phylon Q7 Tractor Beam Projector

A tractor beam is essentially a modified force field that, when projected into space, can capture and redirect an object. Initially, tractor beams were used to guide ships into landing bays, move cargo modules, recover stranded starships or salvage, position space stations and satellites, and push debris from hyperspace lanes. However, pirate forces and later the Empire began using tractor beam projectors to immobilize starships, pulling the helpless vehicles within range for boarding or annihilation.

On large starships such as Star Destroyers, tractor beam projectors are housed in rotating turrets called emitter towers. These towers are extremely precise, although range and strength can vary depending upon the projector model. The Imperials favored the Phylon Q7, equipping each Star Destroyer with ten of the devices. A Star Destroyer's tractor beam array is capable of stalling most Rebel craft, including the Corellian corvettes notorious for slipping through Imperial blockades. The Alliance used less powerful, but far more precise tractor beams for snaring ejected pilots.

Tractor beams have difficulty targeting small, maneuverable starships. Star Destroyers generally use ion cannons to slow or disable target vessels before initiating tractor beams. The Death Star, however, proved that an excessive number of tractor beam projectors could create an irresistible force. The first Death Star was equipped with more than seven hundred of them. At any given point on the mammoth space station, twelve projectors could be brought to bear on a target. This network proved too strong for any ship, even *Millennium Falcon*.

On large space stations, tractor beams are often coupled to a main reactor to provide the device with a steady stream of energy. However, if the tractor beam's connection to the reactor is severed at any of the coupling sites, the beam becomes completely inoperative. On the first Death Star, the tractor beam that captured *Millennium Falcon* was linked to the reactor at seven separate locations. Obi-Wan Kenobi disabled the force field by simply shutting down one of those sites.

Although most starships have a limited number of tractor beam projectors near docking bays, few warships support the number of projectors necessary to use tractor beams offensively. Tractor beam emplacements consume a great deal of space, and power, and require constant maintenance. The Phylon Q2 and other similar models also need a crew of ten operators and technicians, making the projectors less desirable to the small, ragtag Rebel Alliance and similar groups.

Small vessels rarely support military-grade tractor beams, although the Empire did experiment with such weapons on both the TIE avenger and TIE defender. Geonosian starfighters also employ tractor beam arrays as weapons, although the devices are primarily used to increase the agile craft's maneuverability. The Yuuzhan Vong starships boast the strange dovin basal, which produces a black hole effect that emulates a tractor beam.

> ## "You can't win. But there are alternatives to fighting."
> —*Obi-Wan Kenobi to Han Solo*
> *after the* Millennium Falcon *is captured by the Death Star's tractor beams*

❹ **Boarding Tube:** A retractable boarding tube is often located near a series of tractor beam projectors to allow soldiers to quickly access a captured vehicle.

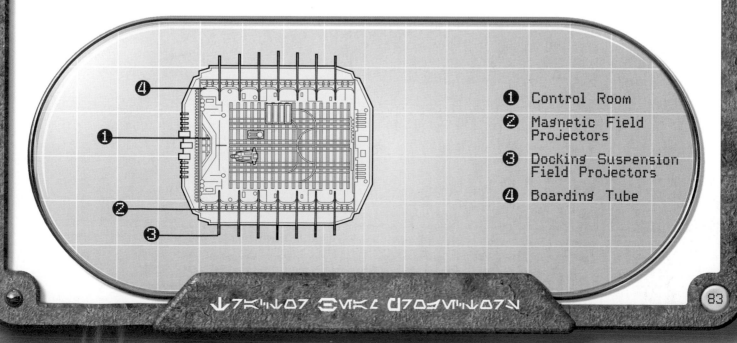

① Control Room
② Magnetic Field Projectors
③ Docking Suspension Field Projectors
④ Boarding Tube

CLUSTER BOMB

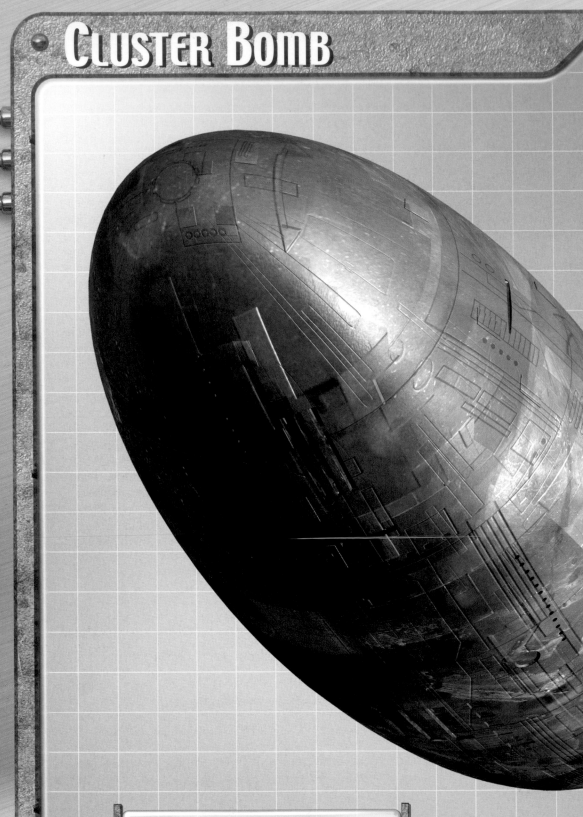

TECHNICAL READOUT

DAMAGE TYPE: Explosive

EFFECTIVE RANGE: Damages anything within 300 m radius

PRIMARY MANUFACTURER: FreiTek, Inc.

AFFILIATION: Mon Calamari Cruisers

FreiTek CL-3 Antistarfighter Cluster Bomb

The Mon Calamari are generally considered a peaceful species. While they've developed countless wondrous devices, ranging from cutting-edge bacta chambers to the galaxy's most striking starships, they have created very few weapons. Even the large Mon Cal cruisers used at the Battle of Endor carried armaments added by Rebel Alliance technicians. Under the leadership of Admiral Ackbar, however, the Mon Cal did integrate the deadly cluster bomb into the design of these cruisers.

Tactically, a cluster bomb (or cluster trap) is designed to wipe out small starfighter formations by catching these enemy ships in an explosive blast. Cluster bombs are most effective when used at close range, making the weapons highly dependent on the element of surprise. Aboard Mon Cal cruisers, cluster bombs are concealed in "blisters" or domes present on the hull of the starship. These blisters are identical to the many other ovoid shapes found across the cruiser, most of which house sensor arrays, weapons emplacements, or cargo modules. When a cluster bomb's sensor suite detects a concentration of enemy signatures, the bomb is detonated.

Upon detonation, a cluster bomb releases a cloud of magnetized proton and concussion grenades, along with shrapnel from its outer shell. The cloud measures more than a hundred meters in diameter and will destroy any small starship caught in its radius. If any of the magnetized grenades survive the initial discharge, the area will become a hazard to starships until all the grenades are detonated. While devastating to starfighter squadrons, cluster bombs have little effect on the armored hulls of capital ships. Explosive dampeners fur-

ther ensure that the Mon Cal cruisers themselves are not damaged when a cluster bomb detonates.

The grenades that compose a cluster bomb are indiscriminate when released. As a result, cluster bombs are most effective during engagements in which friendly forces are vastly outnumbered by enemy fighters. At the Battle of Endor, Rebel pilots memorized the locations of the Mon Cal cluster bombs and avoided the blisters at all costs.

Cluster bombs have also been incorporated into other Rebel and New Republic craft. Aboard Nebulon-B frigates and Corellian corvettes, cluster bombs are concealed in angular casings that resemble cargo modules, air locks, and sensor clusters. Some cluster bombs are also equipped with false signal generators that emulate emissions produced by standard sensor arrays. Enemy pilots are lured to attack these seemingly helpless targets, only to find themselves caught in the deadly explosive cloud.

During the Galactic Civil War, TIE fighter pilots were trained to be aggressive and overzealous, and attack in great numbers while in formation. Against Rebel starfighter squadrons and poorly defended capital ships, these traits proved frighteningly effective. But the TIE fighter's strengths became liabilities at the Battle of Endor, when many squadrons rushed headlong into the explosive cluster traps.

> **"Be smart! Be victorious!"**
> —*Admiral Ackbar*

5 **Blister Shell:** When a cluster bomb detonates, its blister shell is reduced to shrapnel that is quite capable of tearing through an unshielded TIE fighter even without the aid of explosives.

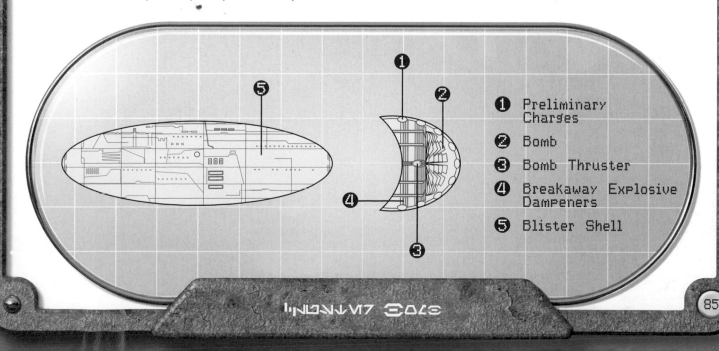

1 Preliminary Charges

2 Bomb

3 Bomb Thruster

4 Breakaway Explosive Dampeners

5 Blister Shell

SEISMIC CHARGE

TECHNICAL READOUT

DAMAGE TYPE: Explosive and kinetic

OPTIMUM/MAXIMUM RANGES: 300 m/500 m

PRIMARY MANUFACTURER: Krupx Munitions

AFFILIATION: Jango Fett's Slave 1

Krupx Void-7 Seismic Charge and Launcher

While laser cannons, concussion missiles, and proton torpedoes are designed for direct confrontations, seismic charges are among the most effective "ambush" weapons, intended to waylay pursuers and cause sudden, unpredictable devastation.

Early seismic charges were large canisters carrying raw explosives. These were often carried by basic cargo transports, starships frequently victimized by pirates. In order to dissuade such attacks, transport pilots released these explosive canisters from open docking bays. The charges would then float through space until they collided with a pursuing craft. The damage caused by primitive seismic charges varied greatly, depending upon the type and quantity of explosives packed into the weapon.

Seismic charges were eventually embraced by the pirates, who realized that, if seismic chargers were capable of wiping out pirate fleets, they would be equally effective at slowing down local security forces. Seismic charges in various forms were adopted by assassins, smugglers, spicerunners, and other criminals who could pay substantial sums for the weapons. This prompted additional research into these explosives. Manufacturers ranging from Baktoid Armor Workshop to Taim & Bak developed their own versions of the seismic charge.

The bounty hunter Jango Fett equipped his formidable starfighter, *Slave I*, with a variety of weapons for nearly every situation. For surprise encounters, such as his flight from Obi-Wan Kenobi through the asteroid field around Geonosis, Fett always carried a small number of Krupx Void-7 seismic charges, the pinnacle of seismic charge technology.

> **"Hang on, son! We'll move into the asteroid field. And we'll have a couple of surprises for him."**
>
> *—Jango Fett, before releasing seismic charges in an attempt to kill a pursuing Obi-Wan Kenobi*

A Void-7 seismic charge consists of a large, round container composed of an explosive blend of unstable liquid baradium and a volatile gas called collapsium. The core is framed by two electromagnetic exciter disks. When the charge is released into space, the electromagnetic disks infuse the core with energized impulses that excite the blended explosives. By the time the weapon collides with a hapless target, the core is supercharged. The resulting explosion creates a massive and rapidly expanding shock wave that can effortlessly slice through asteroids, enemy starships, and space stations. Deflector shields do not protect against this shock wave, and even those starships that manage to outrun the expanding concussion field can be knocked off course or pummeled by debris. The initial blast also causes a brief vacuum in space that sucks victims toward the heart of the explosion. *Slave I*'s seismic charge launcher is concealed in the heart of the starship to protect the charges from damage. The charges are locked into place by standard magnetic clamps, and then released into space through an air lock located between the starship's engines. As it spins through space, the charge's trajectory is extremely erratic, making the weapon very difficult to evade.

⑤ Fuel Door: Although the Void-7 is most often filled with a baradium-collapsium blend, the charge can be filled with less volatile fuels to prevent the excessive collateral damage caused by the weapon's signature shock wave.

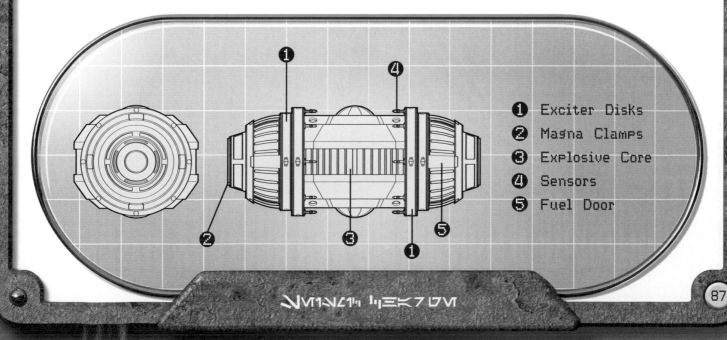

1. Exciter Disks
2. Magna Clamps
3. Explosive Core
4. Sensors
5. Fuel Door

GRUTCHIN

Yuuzhan Vong Bioengineered Grutchin

The grutchin is the Yuuzhan Vong's analog to the traditional missile or torpedo bioengineered to destroy enemy vessels quickly and efficiently.

The grutchin resembles a large, beetlelike insect with a narrow body and bulbous eyes. The weapon is launched from nearly all manner of Yuuzhan Vong craft, including the massive worldships, various frigates, and even coralskippers, the Yuuzhan Vong equivalent of the standard starfighter. Once a grutchin is released, it travels at surprising sublight speeds as it pursues any enemy craft in the area. In order to destroy a target, the grutchin latches onto the vehicle with a pair of menacing, jagged mandibles. These mandibles secrete a potent acid, allowing the grutchin to chew through almost any mineral, including the durasteel alloys used to construct many New Republic craft. Grutchins are voracious predators and will eat almost any part of a starship. However, they seem to seek out droids, ion engines, and even starfighter cockpits, perhaps because these components are constructed of "soft" metals. Grutchins have also been known to eat organic pilots.

The creature's thick carapace is highly resistant to blasterfire and conventional explosives, making the creature extraordinarily difficult to kill. At the Battle of Borleias, Jedi Master Kyp Durron did discover that a lightsaber is capable of penetrating a grutchin's outer shell and killing the creature.

Perhaps most notable is the grutchin's ability to actually enter hyperspace, survive the rigors of such travel, and even attack enemy starships while moving at lightspeed. Yuuzhan Vong tacticians often release grutchins just as their enemies are beginning to flee, knowing that

> ## "The grutchins may never come back, but neither do their victims."
> *—Yuuzhan Vong shaper*

even an escape into hyperspace can't stop the bioengineered missiles.

While many Yuuzhan Vong weapons exhibit some sentience, grutchins are completely unthinking organisms. They exist simply to destroy and consume. Once a grutchin is released into space, it can't be directed, recalled, or recaptured. After each battle, in fact, Yuuzhan Vong are often forced to destroy any surviving grutchins to prevent the creatures from turning on their masters.

The Yuuzhan Vong use grutchin queens to breed these bizarre missiles, but the creatures are easy to cultivate and and mature very quickly. As a result, the Yuuzhan Vong consider grutchins expendable. They will release the weapons in significant numbers, knowing that the grutchins are easily replaced.

Grutchins are developed in various sizes to allow their use aboard different types of starships. The grutchins launched by coralskippers tend to be smaller, but much faster, than the mammoth grutchin torpedoes fired by worldships. The Yuuzhan Vong also produce a very small grutchin known as the grutchin symbiote. These creatures are miniaturized grutchins used primarily for personal combat. Roughly half a meter long, grutchin symbiotes can be implanted into a Yuuzhan Vong's forearms. The insects retain their acid-laced mandibles, making them formidable weapons capable of cutting through flesh, bone, and most armors. Yuuzhan Vong shapers and priests frequently use the weapons for self-defense.

❼ Soft Underbelly: The grutchin has a soft underbelly that is susceptible to blasterfire, as Jacen Solo discovered at the Battle of Ylesia.

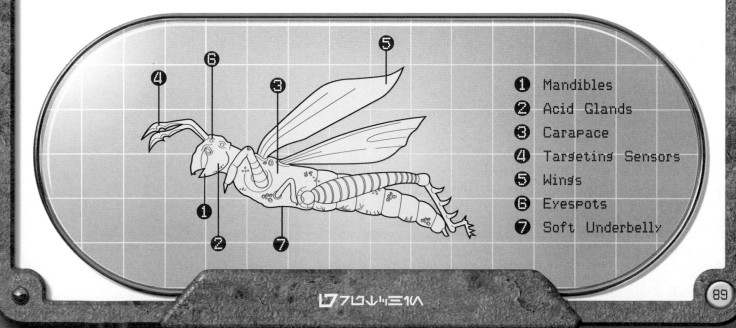

1. Mandibles
2. Acid Glands
3. Carapace
4. Targeting Sensors
5. Wings
6. Eyespots
7. Soft Underbelly

Plasma Cannon

Technical Readout

DAMAGE TYPE: Plasma energy, explosive and kinetic

OPTIMUM/MAXIMUM RANGES: 5 km/60 km

PRIMARY MANUFACTURER: Yuuzhan Vong shapers

AFFILIATION: Yuuzhan Vong starships

Yuuzhan Vong Yaret-Kor

Yuuzhan Vong weapons are not only horrific in appearance, with their strange biotech components evoking twisted experiments gone awry, they are also incredibly lethal. One of the most common and devastating Yuuzhan Vong weapons is the plasma cannon, which the Yuuzhan Vong call *yaret-kor*.

The primary weapon aboard most Yuuzhan Vong starships, the plasma cannon is a starship appendage that projects blasts of molten material. The size and composition of the plasma burst varies based on the nature of the Yuuzhan Vong vessel. A coralskipper's plasma cannon releases small, flaming rocks capable of burning through armor plating. Most plasma blasts contain some sort of solid material. These hurtling magma-covered projectiles collide with enough force to knock starfighters off their flight paths, stun enemy pilots, and rupture internal machinery.

While coralskippers possess just a single plasma-emitting appendage, the Yuuzhan Vong miid ro'ik warships have sixty magma weapons hidden in deep crags along the vessel's hull. The miid ro'ik's cannons emit steady streams of molten rock. The massive worldships carry many hundreds of plasma cannons, ranging from small openings roughly the size of a conventional blaster cannon to huge emitters that hurl gargantuan chunks of burning slag over great distances. Worldship plasma cannons tend to grow erratically along the starship's surface; they have a relatively slow rate of fire, allowing small starfighters to wind through the vehicle's defenses. Unfortunately, worldships typically carry more than five thousand coralskippers for defense.

On the coralskipper and other small Yuuzhan Vong craft, the plasma cannon serves as both a weapon and the vehicle's primary propulsion system. The opposing force created when magma is released actually pushes the starship through space.

When a coralskipper is "grown" using organic yorik coral, the Yuuzhan Vong shapers ensure that the starfighter sprouts a plasma projector. This makes it difficult for enemies to gauge the exact size of a plasma cannon or determine where the weapon ends and the rest of the ship begins. Many Yuuzhan Vong starships are grown with their plasma cannons protected by flaps of coral or other sturdy materials.

In many ways, plasma cannons are superior to standard laser cannons and other New Republic weapons. Because they are developed using the Yuuzhan Vong's biotechnology, they heal naturally over time and require very little maintenance. Most modern weaponry requires a robust power source, but plasma cannons are self-powered. And while proton torpedo launchers and concussion missiles must be restocked at a space station or spaceport, Yuuzhan Vong ships can consume rocks, small asteroids, and stellar debris in order to rearm their plasma cannons during flight. The molten rocks also ignore the deflector shields so common on New Republic vessels.

> **"During the civil war, the Imperials just chased us *into* asteroid fields. Now the enemy shoots the asteroids *at* us. And they're on fire."**
>
> —*Han Solo*

6 **Triskele Valve:** The plasma cannon's firing tube usually remains sealed by a triskele valve to protect a vessel's innards from the vacuum of space. When a plasma cannon is fired, the valve opens for a brief second to allow the plasma discharge.

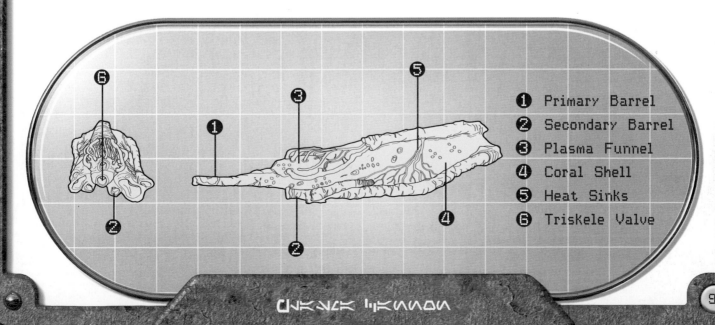

1. Primary Barrel
2. Secondary Barrel
3. Plasma Funnel
4. Coral Shell
5. Heat Sinks
6. Triskele Valve

Technical Readout

DAMAGE TYPE: Explosive and kinetic

EFFECTIVE RANGE: Damages anything within 30 m radius

PRIMARY MANUFACTURER: Arakyd Industries

AFFILIATION: Galactic Empire

Arakyd Industries Imperial Atmospheric Explosive

The land mine is one of the most insidious, yet most pervasive weapons in military warfare. A basic explosive designed to be easily concealed and triggered when an enemy comes into proximity.

There are many hundreds of variations on the classic mine design. The most common terrestrial mines are anti-infantry weapons, often placed around high-security installations. Although infantry mines typically have several settings, most are triggered by physical pressure, perhaps caused by an enemy soldier's careless footstep. Vehicle mines possess advanced microcircuitry that can distinguish between infantry and ground craft. This allows friendly troops to lure enemy vehicles into minefields. The versatile Merr-Sonn Munitions LX-4 proton mine can be set to target either foot soldiers or vehicles.

For stealth operations and ambushes inside narrow corridors, military operatives favor laser trip mines. A trip mine consists of a beam projector attached to a shaped explosive charge. When the mine is planted, an invisible beam extends from the charge to the nearest surface. If this beam is broken, the explosive will immediately detonate. Skilled soldiers install the mines in areas where they will not be readily noticed.

Timer mines use basic countdown timers as triggers, and are typically planted by mining droids for excavation. During the Battle of Naboo, the Trade Federation filled Naboo's waterways with floating proximity mines that use motion sensors to trigger an explosion. E-mag mines contain advanced scanners that can detect repulsorlift fields; when a repulsorlift craft passes over the mine, the device fires shrapnel that can cripple the vehicle's engines.

> **"These sky mines, they fill the sky with fire and death . . . I must have more."**
> —*Raith Sienar*

While mines were originally developed for terrestrial warfare, so-called sky mines are small, extremely volatile spheres that can be deposited around floating installations. Stationary sky mines are anchored in place by durasteel cables, and are fairly easy to avoid. More dangerous are drifting sky mines, such as Arakyd's atmospheric explosives. These devices drift through an atmosphere until their aggressive sensors identify an enemy craft. The mines then actually pursue target vehicles, using an advanced tracking system and agile repulsorjets to ensure an explosive collision. Before the rise of the Empire, such mines were used to great effect by Wilhuff Tarkin, who deployed hundreds of thousands of the weapons during his attack on Zonama Sekot.

In space, minelaying starships deposit orbital mines around planets or along travel routes to prevent invasions or to blockade victimized worlds. Most orbital mines are explosive proximity mines, although the Merr-Sonn Defender is equipped with ion cannons that disable passing starships. During the war against the Yuuzhan Vong, the New Republic used orbital mines to slow the alien invasion and prevent the Yuuzhan Vong from escaping key defeats. For their part, the Yuuzhan Vong established minefields filled with powerful dovin basal interdiction mines along the Corellian Run and around the entire Pyria system. When triggered, a dovin basal interdiction mine creates a miniature black hole.

7 Sensor Suite: The sky mine's sensor suite allows it to actually pursue targets, making the weapon much more dangerous than traditional mines.

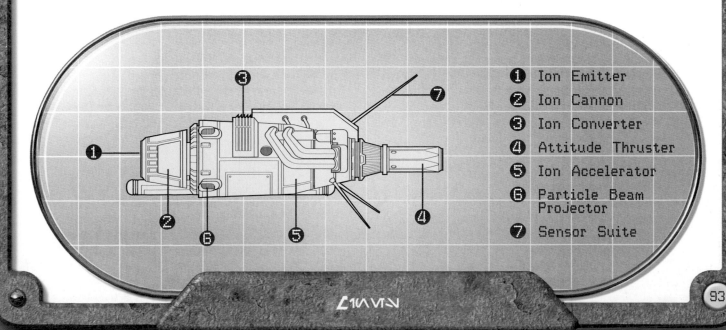

1. Ion Emitter
2. Ion Cannon
3. Ion Converter
4. Attitude Thruster
5. Ion Accelerator
6. Particle Beam Projector
7. Sensor Suite

Additional Starship and Planetary Weapons

While the laser cannon is undeniably the staple weapon of starships and even many ground vehicles, a staggering array of weapons has been invented to provide greater versatility in combat. As starships become more formidable, so, too, do the weapons that protect worlds from invading forces. Below is a short sampling of larger weapons of war.

Blaster Artillery

A generic term that covers nearly any mobile platform supporting a number of high-power blaster cannons. Blaster artillery units are terrestrial siege weapons used to destroy military installations, factories, spaceports, and other key sites. Loronar's MAS-2xB blaster artillery unit is among the most powerful ground-based siege weapons in the galaxy.

Boarding Harpoon

A projectile filled with coma gas. Boarding harpoons are fired through the hull of a target starship, at which point the gas is released and all passengers are rendered unconscious. Boarding harpoons have only recently become widespread, and most models are illegal.

Bomblet Generator

A device that generates spheres of explosive energy, which can be dropped from great heights and explode upon impact with a target. The pirate Nym has a bomblet generator installed on his starfighter, the *Havoc*.

Diamond Boron Missile

An experimental missile developed sometime during the Clone Wars, but only truly refined at the height of the Galactic Civil War. Diamond boron missiles generate a huge explosion that destroys everything within fifty meters of the blast point. A single missile is capable of taking out an entire starfighter formation. The missiles are faster than proton torpedoes and able to withstand laser cannon fire. However, they are exceedingly expensive to manufacture.

Geonosian Defense Platform

The primary heavy artillery unit used by Geonosians. A defense platform is armed with standard blaster cannons or sonic cannons, but its true strength is its incred-

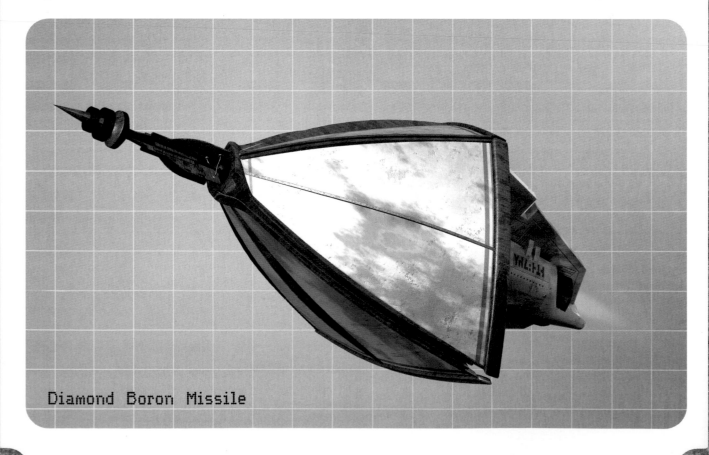

Diamond Boron Missile

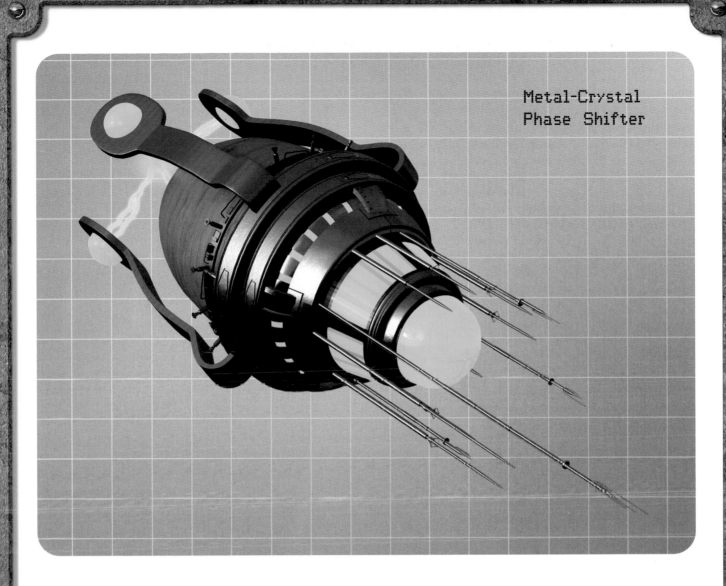

ibly precise targeting computers. The platforms are concealed in gullies and caves on Geonosis, and are typically operated by two Geonosian soldiers.

GUNGAN ENERGY CATAPULT

A primitive Gungan weapon used to hurl Gungan energy balls over great distances. Like all other catapults, the Gungan model utilizes a torsion-action arm, which lifts and throws devastating energy balls. Despite their seemingly simple design, the Gungan catapults can rapidly fire a number of energy balls with impressive accuracy. Handcrafted weapons, Gungan catapults

display the ornate style and organic appearance common to all Gungan products.

METAL-CRYSTAL PHASE SHIFTER (MCPS)

A weapon constructed by Imperials at the Maw Installation and designed to disintegrate starships. An MCPS unit emits a field that disrupts the crystalline structure of metals, including those used to construct starship hulls, thereby reducing hull plates to powder. The MCPS ignores conventional shielding.

SUPERWEAPONS

Since the appearance of the first weapons, battles have continued to increase in both size and brutality. With each evolution in modern warfare, the death toll caused by cutting-edge weaponry continues to rise. Blaster rifles allow a single soldier to gun down several enemies in seconds. Grenades, mines, and other explosives can suddenly decimate entire squadrons. In space, turbolasers are designed to destroy starfighters in droves. Planetary laser cannons can rip through even the largest capital ships, killing thousands in the process. While all weapons are terrifying and lethal, the galaxy has often been victimized by a special class of devices known as superweapons, capable of mind-numbing death and devastation.

The most infamous superweapon is undoubtedly the Imperial Death Star, a massive space station capable of vaporizing an entire planet. Like the Death Star, most superweapons are gargantuan machines designed for mass destruction or mass murder. Their size is also their greatest weakness: since superweapons are impossibly large, they are incredibly expensive to build and maintain. Superweapons generally utilize experimental technology as well. As a result of all these factors, superweapons are thankfully very rare and often unique.

Nearly all superweapons are designed for use in space. Along with a primary weapons system, superweapons require engines, life support, secondary weapons, and other ancillary systems. Mobile superweapons are often slow and difficult to maneuver. Stationary superweapons cannot be concealed, making them susceptible to enemy attack. When a superweapon is destroyed, thousands of crew members, officers, soldiers, and other key personnel are often lost.

Despite all these weaknesses, superweapons have long played a key role in military warfare. In the eyes of many tacticians, a superweapon's primary purpose is not, in fact, to cause carnage. Rather, its true strength rests in the fear that it inspires. The ancient Sith promoted this philosophy, building bizarre and disturbing superweapons such as the Sith meditation sphere, a huge starship that resembled a giant floating eye. Sith warlords used such spheres to focus their battle meditation, an application of the Force that subtly increases an ally's morale while weakening the will of enemy forces. When projected from the heart of a Sith meditation sphere, battle meditation could easily change the tide of a space battle.

Grand Moff Tarkin, one of the Empire's most ruthless "visionaries," based his vile Tarkin Doctrine on this philosophy of fear. Under Tarkin's leadership, Imperial engineers researched and built ever-more-powerful starships and weapons simply to cow rebellious systems. Ultimately, however, the Death Star and similar weapons embodied the Emperor's evil. After the Death Star destroyed Alderaan, the fear that the superweapon would attack again motivated hundreds of systems to join the Rebel Alliance.

Despite the ultimate failure of the Death Star program, superweapons remain a key component in galactic warfare. In the aftermath of the Battle of Endor, Imperial Remnant forces continued to experiment with superweapons, many based on the Death Star's core technologies. By the time of the Yuuzhan Vong invasion, most of these Imperial superweapons had been destroyed, but the alien invaders introduced new forms of destructions including massive worldships armed with thousands of plasma cannons.

DEATH STAR

TECHNICAL READOUT

DAMAGE TYPE: Laser energy

OPTIMUM/MAXIMUM RANGES: 380,000 km/ 420,000 km

PRIMARY MANUFACTURER: Imperial Department of Military Research

AFFILIATION: Galactic Empire

Imperial Death Star Battle Station

In the history of galactic warfare, the Death Star program will always hold a place as one of military technology's greatest and most terrifying achievements. Under the guidance of Grand Moff Tarkin, with others, the superweapons project spawned two battle stations of immense size and power.

The original Death Star resembled a small moon measuring 120 kilometers in diameter. One of the largest starships ever constructed, the Death Star could travel through hyperspace in search of suitable targets for the Emperor's wrath. The battle station's primary weapon was a planet-shattering superlaser, which Tarkin unleashed to destroy Princess Leia's homeworld of Alderaan.

The Death Star superlaser was powered by an immense fusion reactor located in the heart of the space station. The superlaser itself was actually produced by several individual beams, which were in turn generated by amplification crystals located around the cannon's circular well. The beams combined over a central focus lens, creating an energy blast with more firepower than half the Imperial fleet. Each amplification crystal required a separate gunnery station, where a crew of fourteen gunners adjusted and monitored the pulses.

The Empire improved on the superlaser design when constructing the second Death Star. While the first superlaser was fairly inefficient, requiring a recharge period of twenty-four standard hours, the second Death Star could fire once every few minutes. Imperial technicians added other modifications to the second Death Star, including advanced targeting systems.

> ## "Fear will keep the local systems in line. Fear of this battle station."
> *—Grand Moff Tarkin*

Even without the superlaser, both Death Stars were well armed. The original Death Star carried five thousand turbolasers and heavy turbolasers, twenty-five hundred laser cannons and ion cannon emplacements, as well as more than seven hundred long-range tractor beams. The space station's numerous docking bays carried a seemingly endless supply of TIE fighters, TIE interceptors, TIE bombers, and many other starfighters. The second Death Star was a behemoth better than 160 kilometers in diameter and boasting fifteen thousand turbolaser cannons alone. Both Death Stars required a staff of over a million officers, gunners, technicians, troopers, and support personnel.

Despite its horrifying weaponry and potential for destruction, the first Death Star had a fatal flaw: a small, unshielded thermal exhaust port. At the Battle of Yavin, Luke Skywalker managed to fire a pair of proton torpedoes into this tiny opening, causing the space station's reactor core to explode. The resulting chain reaction obliterated the Death Star and killed Tarkin, along with thousands of other critical Imperials.

④ **Trench:** An equatorial trench encircled the first Death Star. At the Battle of Yavin, Rebel forces entered the trench to avoid turbolaser attacks and launch proton torpedoes into the Death Star's exhaust port.

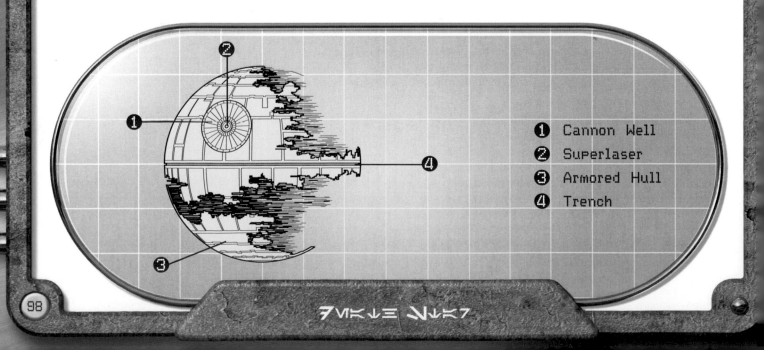

❶ Cannon Well
❷ Superlaser
❸ Armored Hull
❹ Trench

Imperial Death Star Superlaser

The second Death Star also perished as a result of a less obvious flaw: the Emperor's overconfidence. When the Rebel Alliance first learned of the Death Star II, their informants claimed that the space station's superlaser was not yet complete. During the Battle of Endor, however, the Rebels discovered that the Death Star II was part of an elaborate trap to lure them out of hiding. The superlaser was, in fact, quite operational. Fortunately, Han Solo's forces on Endor managed to lower a deflector shield protecting the Death Star II. This allowed Lando Calrissian and Wedge Antilles to fly into the space station's core and attack its reactor directly.

The origins of the Death Star program remain contested by historians. It is fairly clear that the concept of a massive space station capable of supporting a number of weapons was the brainchild of several brilliant scientists and military geniuses, including Raith Sienar and engineer Bevel Lemelisk. Sienar's version of the battle station, known as the Expeditionary Battle Planetoid, was originally designed as an exploratory starship. This nonmilitary design, however, was elaborated upon by Geonosian contractors in the employ of the Count Dooku and the Confederacy. It was Count Dooku's hope that the Geonosians could build a battle station capable of destroying Old Republic worlds. Although the Confederacy never managed to construct a complete Death Star, Tarkin acquired the designs and core technology by the end of the Clone Wars. Working with Lemelisk and his chief scientist Tol Sivron, Tarkin built a prototype of the Death Star at his secret Maw Installation: Years before the Battle of Yavin, Tarkin and his engineers began constructing the space station that would later doom billions on Alderaan.

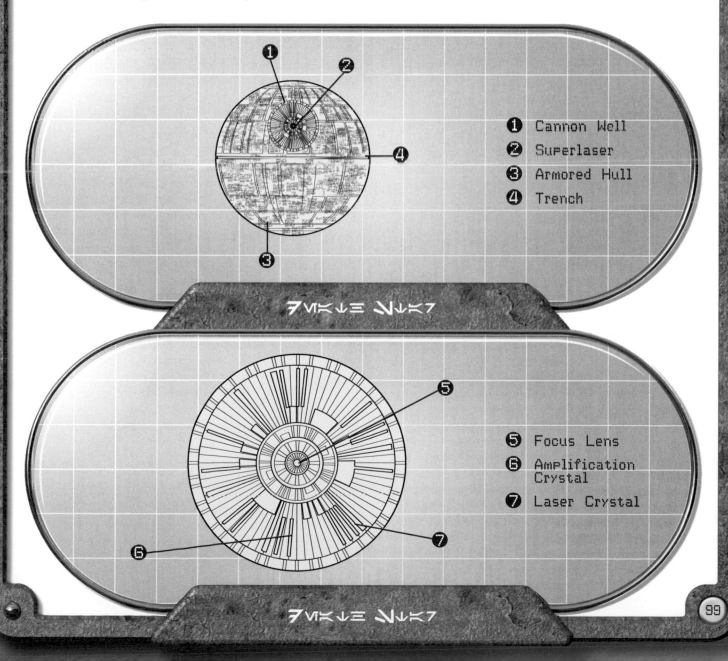

1 Cannon Well
2 Superlaser
3 Armored Hull
4 Trench

5 Focus Lens
6 Amplification Crystal
7 Laser Crystal

ORBITAL NIGHTCLOAK

TECHNICAL READOUT

DAMAGE TYPE: *Catastrophic climate change*

EFFECTIVE RANGE: *Affects entire planet when installed in low orbit*

PRIMARY MANUFACTURER: *Imperial Department of Military Research*

AFFILIATION: *Imperial Warlord Zsinj*

Imperial Department of Military Research Orbital Nightcloak

During the Galactic Civil War, the Imperial Department of Military Research (IDMR) embraced the Tarkin Doctrine. This doctrine asserted that the most effective weapons not only killed but also inspired fear and hopelessness in enemy forces. The IDMR pursued hundreds of superweapons, but few could match the demoralizing impact of the orbital nightcloak.

The orbital nightcloak is actually composed of hundreds of satellites deployed around a target planet. Each satellite is equipped with a large dish lined with electromagnetic absorption panels capable of distorting and absorbing light waves. When the nightcloak network is activated, the satellites prevent all visible, infrared, and ultraviolet light energy from reaching the world's surface. The satellites are powered by solar energy, making them completely self-sufficient. Once a nightcloak is established, it can be maintained indefinitely.

The nightcloak steals the sun's warming rays and enshrouds a planet in perpetual darkness. When used against primitive peoples, the nightcloak almost immediately secured obedience. More rebellious worlds could survive in darkness for days or even weeks, until the unrelenting darkness generated by the nightcloak caused dramatic and deadly climate changes. The lack of sunlight kills most plant life, destroying the food chain. As temperatures continue to drop, a complete deep freeze can grip the world within three weeks.

The nightcloak's satellites are also equipped with advanced jamming devices designed to block all sensors and communications. This leaves a suffering planet blind and deaf, unable to reach out to allies for help or receive intelligence data. Starships can fly through the nightcloak's darkness in an attempt to find help, but the Empire always positioned warships just outside the cloak.

The entire cloak could be disabled by destroying just a handful of the orbital stations. The satellites themselves seldom support weapons and rely on starfighters for defense. In the years after the Galactic Civil War, Imperial Remnant forces improved the original design with an advanced routing system that requires only 90 percent of the satellites to be active for the cloak to remain operational. Such nightcloak systems also utilize Mark II satellites armed with short-range laser cannons and targeting computers.

In the years after the Battle of Endor, Imperial warlord Zsinj surrounded the planet Dathomir with a nightcloak. Zsinj suspected that the Force-sensitive Witches of Dathomir had captured General Han Solo. The warlord threatened to destroy the planet unless the witches delivered Solo. Luke Skywalker disrupted the darkness field by using *Millennium Falcon*'s quad laser cannons to destroy a huge number of the nightcloak's satellites.

> **"On its brightest day, Dathomir is a shadow world. But the infernal nightcloak filled our skies with black blood and swallowed the moon we worshiped."**
>
> —*Ute Raek, Singing Mountain Clan priestess*

7 Deployment Thruster: After a nightcloak satellite is released from a starship, deployment thrusters move the device into a precise position as part of a larger network.

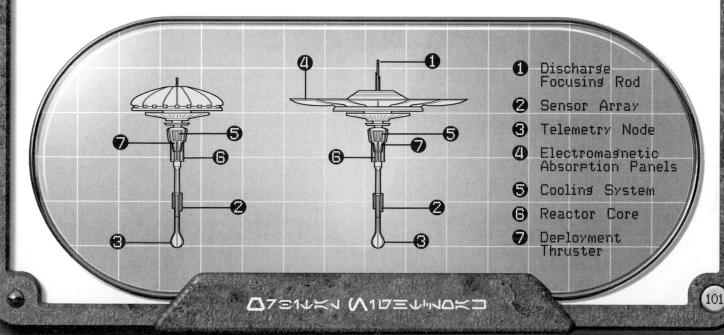

1. Discharge Focusing Rod
2. Sensor Array
3. Telemetry Node
4. Electromagnetic Absorption Panels
5. Cooling System
6. Reactor Core
7. Deployment Thruster

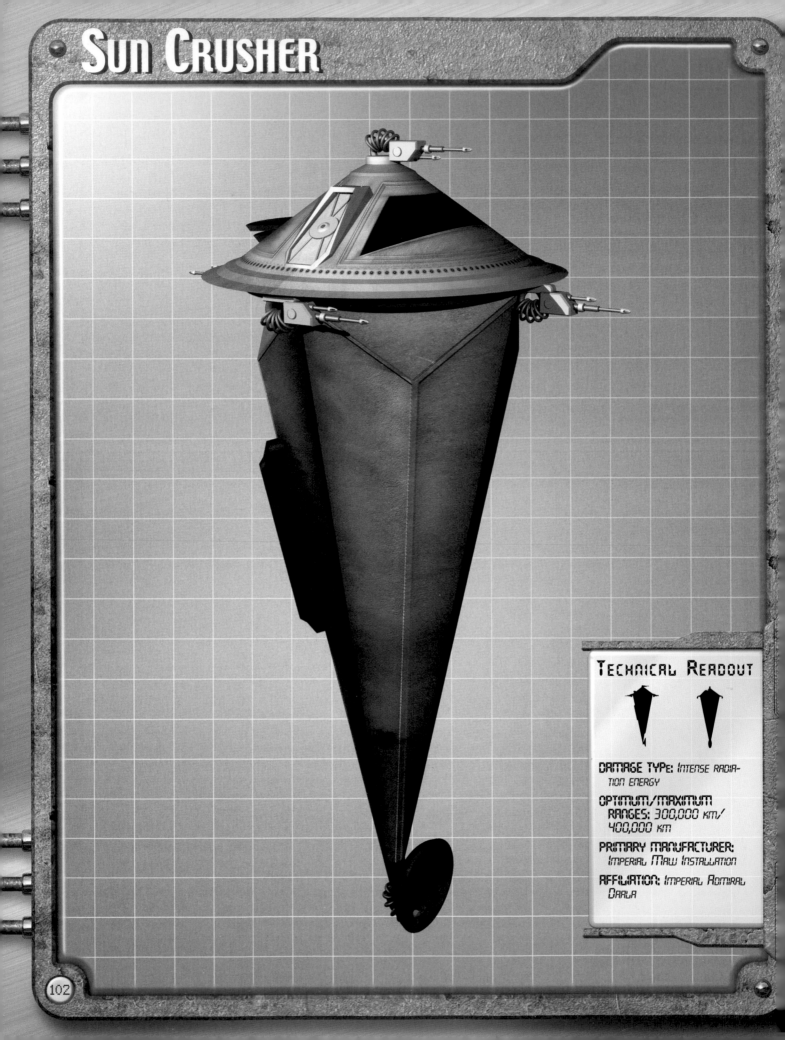

SUN CRUSHER

TECHNICAL READOUT

DAMAGE TYPE: INTENSE RADIATION ENERGY

OPTIMUM/MAXIMUM RANGES: 300,000 KM/ 400,000 KM

PRIMARY MANUFACTURER: IMPERIAL MAW INSTALLATION

AFFILIATION: IMPERIAL ADMIRAL DAALA

Custom Imperial Sun Crusher

Grand Moff Tarkin's legacy is evident in nearly every superweapon developed by the Empire. Although the Death Star remained the focus of most of Tarkin's efforts, the cunning Grand Moff secretly diverted funds from the first Death Star project to build the Maw Installation, a clandestine research outpost dedicated to designing superweapons. The Maw Installation continued to operate in secrecy long after Tarkin's death, eventually giving birth to the Sun Crusher.

Developed under the leadership of Imperial Admiral Daala and the scientist Qwi Xux, the Sun Crusher was a prototype. Its sole purpose was to attack stars, causing them to supernova and explode. When a star was destroyed in this manner, its entire system was ravaged by intense waves of energy and radiation capable of incinerating planets in seconds.

No larger than an X-wing starfighter, the Sun Crusher was a dagger-shaped craft that flew using a series of standard thruster strips. A standard hyperdrive allowed the craft to reach any corner of the galaxy. Laser turrets located around the cockpit allowed the superweapon to take offensive action against enemy starfighters. For defense, the Sun Crusher was covered in layers of quantum-crystalline armor impervious to turbolaser blasts and most other conventional attacks.

In order to attack stars, the Sun Crusher carried eleven energy resonance torpedoes in a long storage bay. Prior to being launched, each torpedo passed through a resonance energizer that activated the shell. The torpedoes were then launched from a dish-shaped torpedo projector at the bottom of the craft. When the torpedoes emerged from the Sun Crusher, they resembled ovoid plasma blasts traveling at near-lightspeed velocity. The plasma-shielded torpedoes were programmed to burrow straight into a star's core, where they released packets of concentrated energy. The torpedoes' impact created a chain reaction deep in the heart of a star, forcing the star to supernova, then explode.

If not for Han Solo, the New Republic would have remained ignorant of the Sun Crusher's existence until the Imperial Remnant decided to use the weapon against "Rebel" worlds. Fortunately, Solo was captured by Admiral Daala's forces and imprisoned in the Maw Installation. With the aid of Xux, Chewbacca, and a Force-sensitive fugitive named Kyp Durron, Solo managed to steal the Sun Crusher and flee the Maw Installation.

> **"The only thing more dangerous than a Dark Jedi is a Dark Jedi behind the controls of a Sun Crusher . . ."**
> —*Han Solo*

New Republic forces sent the Sun Crusher into the gas giant Yavin, hoping that the planet's intense atmospheric pressure would crush the superweapon. While in the grip of the dark side, Durron used his connection to the Force to rescue the Sun Crusher, intending to use the weapon to exact revenge against the Empire. Sadly, Durron instead went on a terrible rampage. He eventually destroyed an entire system by shooting a torpedo into the planet Carida's sun. Soon after, the Sun Crusher was engaged at the Battle of the Maw, where it was caught in the gravitational pull of a black hole. Durron escaped, but the Sun Crusher was finally destroyed.

7 Message Pod Launcher: Kyp Durron escaped the Sun Crusher's destruction in one of the superweapon's small message pods, designed to deliver droids and secret communiqués to Imperial forces.

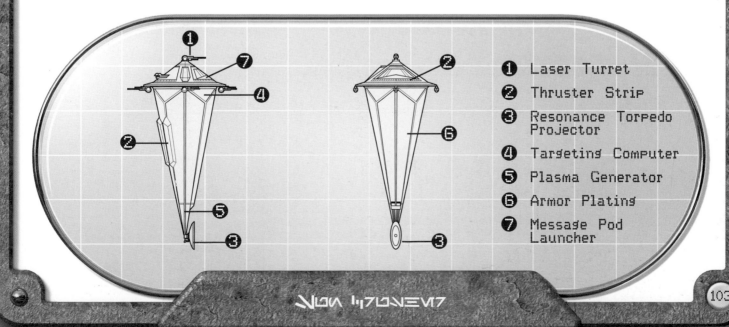

1 Laser Turret
2 Thruster Strip
3 Resonance Torpedo Projector
4 Targeting Computer
5 Plasma Generator
6 Armor Plating
7 Message Pod Launcher

GALAXY GUN

TECHNICAL READOUT

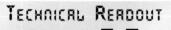

DAMAGE TYPE: Explosive and nucleonic

EFFECTIVE RANGE: Unlimited

PRIMARY MANUFACTURER: Imperial Department of Military Research

AFFILIATION: The Emperor Reborn and Imperial Remnant forces

Custom Imperial Galaxy Gun

For Emperor Palpatine, death was not the end. After his violent demise aboard the second Death Star, hidden cloning technology twice resurrected the Emperor. In each instance, the reborn Emperor made fierce attempts to topple the New Republic and reclaim the galaxy as his own. Six years after the Battle of Endor, the second clone Emperor nearly succeeded with the aid of the Galaxy Gun. Like the Death Star before it, the Galaxy Gun inspired terror in all who would oppose Palpatine's bid for power.

While the Death Star was forced to orbit a target world before firing its superlaser and annihilating the planet, the Galaxy Gun fired giant, high-yield explosive projectiles into hyperspace. These "lightspeed torpedoes" could emerge from hyperspace at precise coordinates, allowing the Galaxy Gun to target virtually any world in the galaxy.

Built in secrecy around the Emperor's throneworld of Byss, the massive space station resembled a cannon 7,250 meters long, nearly five times the length of a standard Star Destroyer. Its sole purpose was to serve as a delivery mechanism for missiles armed with particle disintegrator warheads. Each of these missiles boasted a hyperdrive that rivaled that of *Millennium Falcon*. They also carried automated laser cannon turrets programmed to attack inceptor starfighters, along with armor plating and advanced shields that defended against both turbolasers and ion cannons.

Upon impact with a planet, the Galaxy Gun's energized warhead erupted, causing unstoppable nucleonic chain reactions. These explosions instantly converted matter to energy and would spread across a planet's sur-

> **"At the time, the Galaxy Gun was the most destructive weapon we'd ever seen. But I wish we had it now. We could blast those Yuuzhan Vong worldships right out of the sky."**
> —*Luke Skywalker*

face, vaporizing everything in their path. At its highest settings, the Galaxy Gun's explosions could be maintained until the entire world was consumed. The Galaxy Gun did have less destructive settings, allowing the weapon to selectively eliminate cities or enemy bases without destroying the rest of the planet.

Although possessing its own hyperdrive system, the superweapon was permanently stationed in orbit around Byss. This allowed Imperial forces to defend it with a sizable fleet that included Star Destroyers and TIE fighter squadrons.

When Palpatine used the Galaxy Gun to destroy Pinnacle Base, which had served as the New Republic's headquarters, New Republic forces were forced to consider a full-scale assault on the new Imperial throneworld. Then the Galaxy Gun disintegrated the *Pelegria*, a troop transport carrying a hundred thousand New Republic soldiers.

Emperor Palpatine was killed, and in the aftermath Rebel forces slipped aboard his flagship, the *Eclipse II*. The droid R2-D2 managed to reprogram *Eclipse II*, sending it on a collision course with the Galaxy Gun. The Super Star Destroyer rammed into the space station. During the ensuing explosions, the Galaxy Gun misfired a torpedo onto the surface of Byss. The resulting nucleonic explosions completely destroyed Byss, killing a huge number of Imperial loyalists and vaporizing the bulk of the Empire's painfully rebuilt arsenal.

❼ Hyperdrive: Despite a Class Six hyperdrive, the Galaxy Gun remained permanently stationed near Byss, where it could be protected. Ultimately, the Galaxy Gun was used to destroy Byss.

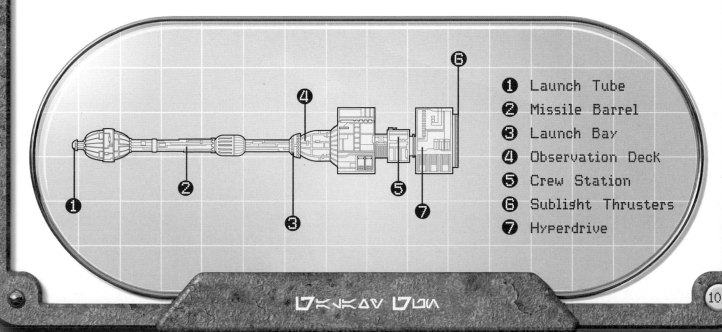

❶ Launch Tube
❷ Missile Barrel
❸ Launch Bay
❹ Observation Deck
❺ Crew Station
❻ Sublight Thrusters
❼ Hyperdrive

WORLD DEVASTATOR

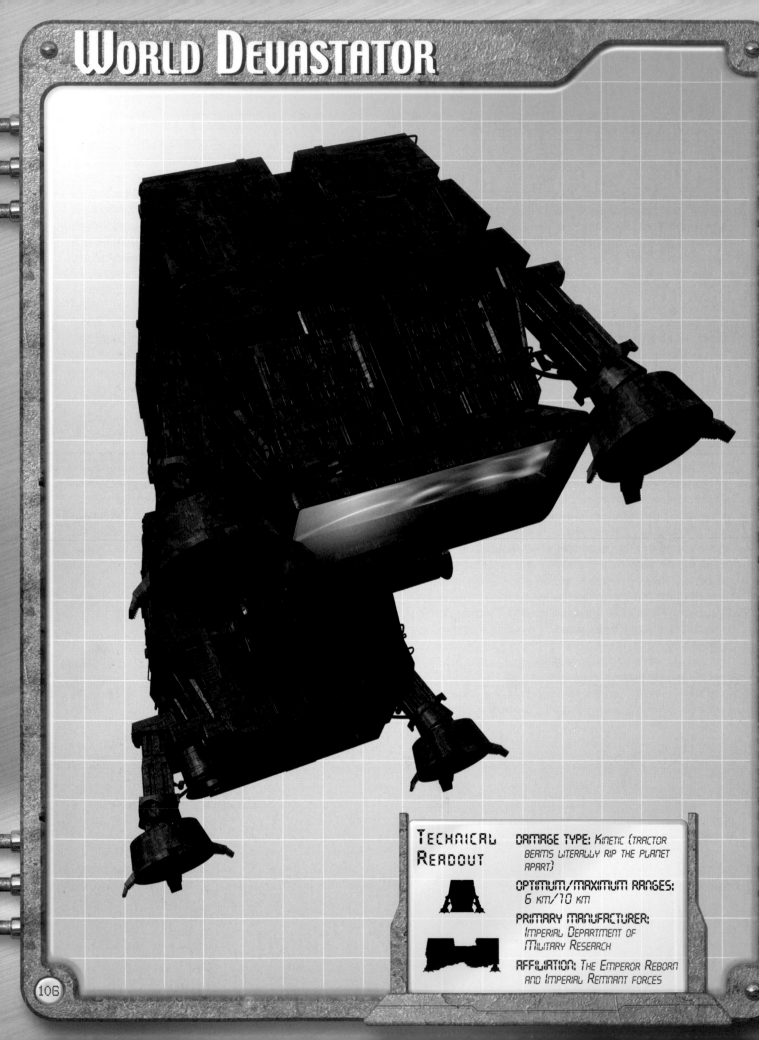

TECHNICAL READOUT

DAMAGE TYPE: *Kinetic (tractor beams literally rip the planet apart)*

OPTIMUM/MAXIMUM RANGES: *6 km/10 km*

PRIMARY MANUFACTURER: *Imperial Department of Military Research*

AFFILIATION: *The Emperor Reborn and Imperial Remnant forces*

Imperial Department of Military Research World Devastator

When the Emperor was reborn a second time, he found his forces scattered. Imperials struggled to secure weapons, starfighters, and warships. The Emperor immediately began rebuilding his Empire, reassembling the Imperial Navy around the new throneworld of Byss. And he ordered the construction of several superweapons, including the dreaded Galaxy Gun and a small fleet of World Devastators.

Among the most complex machines ever developed, a World Devastator is designed to strip a planet of its resources, which are then used to assemble weapons, starfighters, and other military supplies. The impact of a World Devastator is nothing short of horrific: the craft literally chews through a planet's surface, destroying ecosystems and eventually the entire world.

Also known as World Sweepers, World Smashers, and City Eaters, World Devastators are often deployed in small groups. They can travel across the galaxy under the power of a Class Six hyperdrive and robust ion engines. When they enter an atmosphere, World Devastators employ powerful repulsorlifts to skim across a planet's surface, seeking out targets. A dozen internal tractor beams suck up huge chunks of a planet's surface. This matter is funneled into a huge molecular furnace capable of breaking down or converting virtually any substance into useful materials. These are then routed to droid-controlled factories located throughout the World Devastator, which can be programmed to produce a variety of goods: at the Battle of Mon Calamari, World Devastators generated squadrons of automated TIE/D starfighters. In this manner, World Devastators become mobile airfields or weapons platforms.

> **"This is the greatest scourge the galaxy has ever seen . . . Far more lethal than the Death Star!"**
> —*Admiral Ackbar*

World Devastators often target cities, which are rich with useful materials. Wherever they roam, World Devastators are voracious, consuming any type of terrain they encounter. The machines continue to tear apart a planet, stripping away layer after layer until there is nothing left to consume. A small fleet of World Devastators can completely eliminate a planet in just a few months.

A World Devastator also uses pillaged resources to alter its own structure. Its droid brain is programmed to build custom modules. In this way, the World Devastator can sprout new weapons, sensors, shields, and other components. The *Silencer-7* was the largest World Devastator, measuring thirty-two hundred meters long and fifteen hundred meters tall. For defense, most World Devastators carry a number of weapons. The *Silencer-7* boasted a crew of twenty-five thousand, 125 heavy turbolasers, two hundred blaster cannons, eighty proton missile tubes, fifteen ion cannons, and fifteen tractor beam projectors.

To ensure that they would never be used against him, the Emperor equipped the superweapons with a remote command system. Using secret code signals, Palpatine could control the World Devastators from Byss. Luke Skywalker provided the signals to R2-D2, who completely disabled the Devastators on Mon Calamari and programmed them to turn on one another.

6 **Armored Hull:** The World Devastators are designed to withstand tremendous punishment. It seems that a World Devastator can only be destroyed by another World Devastator.

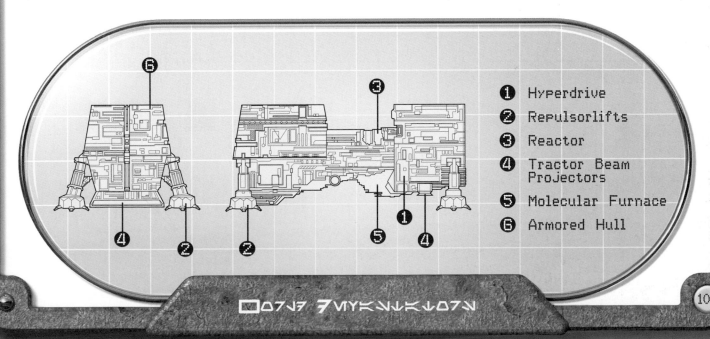

1. Hyperdrive
2. Repulsorlifts
3. Reactor
4. Tractor Beam Projectors
5. Molecular Furnace
6. Armored Hull

Defenses and Armor

Surviving in a galaxy dominated by blasters, vibroblades, and other weapons can be difficult. On Outer Rim worlds, life has always been fragile, with inhabitants constantly facing the possibility of a violent death. During times of war, aggression can easily consume entire worlds. Since the dawn of the Old Republic, blaster cannons, mines and explosives, repeating blasters, and a host of other weapons have killed billions in regional and galactic conflicts. And while struggling to survive on the surface of a war-torn or outlaw planet is tough, trying to stay alive in space often seems impossible. Aside from the dangers presented by asteroid fields, stellar debris, and voracious creatures like space slugs, starships face armed pirate ships, military vessels, and other predatory craft.

To counter the proliferation of armed assailants and their weapons, engineers have developed myriad defenses for nearly any situation. In the era before blaster technology, warriors wore basic armor constructed of bone, metal, or other materials. Such gear protected its wearer from kinetic and slashing damage caused by weapons such as swords and clubs. Since its earliest inception, the concept of armor has never lost popularity. As weapons became more advanced, so, too, did the armor that defends against various types of attacks. With the advent of blasters, engineers invented various blast-dampening materials that absorb energy. Such inventors even prevailed when faced with the seemingly unstoppable lightsaber: to combat this new threat, crafters build armors from cortosis alloys capable of deflecting the weapon.

Defenses against larger weapons, especially those used in space, proved more difficult to develop. After many centuries of research and failed experiments, engineers finally learned to manipulate specific energy signatures in order to create various types of shields. Modern starships are typically equipped with shields designed to deflect or absorb energy blasts, including those generated by laser cannons, or kinetic weapons, such as concussion missiles. These same technologies also protect ground vehicles, while miniaturized shield generators can be worn by individuals.

Although danger usually comes in the form of an aggressive and armed enemy, explorers, soldiers, and adventurers of every sort also face hostile planetary conditions. Poisonous or unbreathable atmospheres, extreme temperatures, and even the vacuum of space can all be combated through technology. A filtered breath mask allows the wearer to breathe comfortably in alien environments, while specialized armor suits protect against intense cold, heat, pressure, and other conditions. Because of its versatility, armor remains in wide use.

Despite the wealth of defenses now available, avoiding conflict completely is always the most effective method for preventing damage or death. Countless credits have been invested in the research and development of "stealth technology," such as cloaking devices that allow starships to vanish from scanners. The hyperdrive allows starships to flee from engagements after being spotted by enemy vessels, but military tacticians are still searching for a means to evade detection completely. When starships can consistently and reliably become invisible at will, the dynamic of space combat will undoubtedly change dramatically again.

Deflector Shield Generator

Technical Readout

DEFENSE TYPE: Blaster energy, laser energy, kinetic, and explosive

COVERAGE: Single starship

PRIMARY MANUFACTURER: Kuat Drive Yards

AFFILIATION: Imperial Star Destroyers

KDY ISD-72x Shield Generator Dome

The dangers presented by space travel are myriad, running the gamut from collisions with erratic meteorites to attacks from turbolasers capable of demolishing a small starship. During the early years of space exploration, starships relied on thick, armored hulls as their primary defense. Gradually, however, engineers developed energy shields for this purpose.

The first shield generators projected basic radiant shielding designed to absorb radiation and heat encountered in space and while moving through a planetary atmosphere. The development of more advanced shields took centuries. Modern shielding can also defend against laser blasts and other forms of damaging energy. Such shields permeate a starship's hull and protect the vessel through a series of energy layers that can extend up to several centimeters from the craft. Energy shields are incredibly powerful, and simply touching one can be fatal.

Particle shields were the next major development in shield technology. A particle shield can deflect solid, physical objects, including proton torpedoes and concussion missiles. Particle shields are particularly useful for exploration vessels, transports, or industrial craft because they absorb the kinetic energy caused by collisions with debris and other ships. Particle shielding also greatly enhances a ship's hull integrity by using energy charges to strengthen the molecular bonds of hull plating. Particle shields must be lowered when launching craft or firing physical weapons. With the aid of a computerized system, however, these shields can be dropped and raised again in an instant.

The standard deflector shield generator, which has become an integral part of starship design, creates a force

> ### "Sir, we just lost the main rear deflector shield! One more direct hit on the back quarter and we're done for!"
> *—C-3PO to Han Solo*

field that envelops a vessel or space station. Depending upon the configuration of the deflector shield generator, this advanced force field can be composed of ray and particle shielding. A complete deflector shield protects against both solid objects and energy attacks. Each component of the shield screen can be activated independently as well. Particle shields are usually kept powered at all times to protect against micrometeors and other small particles. Combat-grade radiant shielding consumes a great deal of energy and is only activated when combat is imminent.

Deflector shield generators are installed on all spacecraft, as well as space stations, space mining installations, and orbital platforms. Massive capital ships carry the largest deflector shield generators. A Star Destroyer carries two large KDY ISD-72x shield generator domes, which create a protective screen capable of blocking nearly any attack. The ISD-72x domes require a huge amount of energy, drawn directly from the Star Destroyer's main reactor.

While deflector shields were originally developed for use aboard starships, the technology has been refined for other applications. Although rare, some ground vehicles do have power sources capable of supporting shield generators. Many terrestrial installations have massive shield generators for protection from both the elements and unwanted visitors.

⑥ Armored Shell: The deflector shield generator's armored shell protects against many attacks, but it's not strong enough to defend against a collision with small starships. Suicide attacks can effectively disable a Star Destroyer.

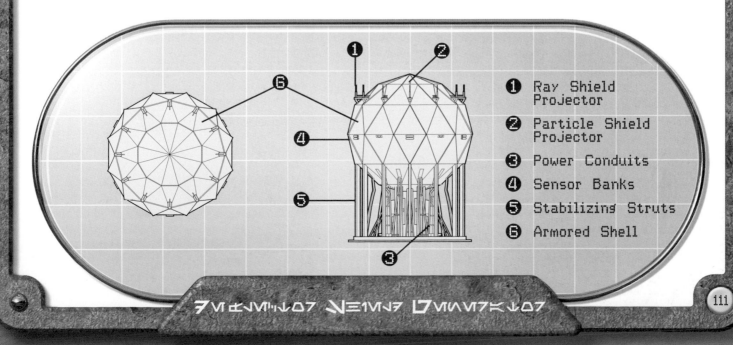

1. Ray Shield Projector
2. Particle Shield Projector
3. Power Conduits
4. Sensor Banks
5. Stabilizing Struts
6. Armored Shell

PLANETARY SHIELD

TECHNICAL READOUT

DEFENSE TYPE: Blaster energy, laser energy, kinetic, and explosive

COVERAGE: Small moon/space station

PRIMARY MANUFACTURER: CoMar Weapons

AFFILIATION: Death Star II

CoMar SLD-26 Planetary Shield Generator

The first deflector shields were developed to protect individual starships against various space hazards including attacks from other ships. The technology was later adapted for use aboard space stations, but the shields remained best suited to repelling starfighters. As enemy fleets grew in size and destructive power, galactic leaders recognized the need for global defenses. Security fleets can handle most local threats but are completely outgunned by capital ships such as Imperial Star Destroyers. Planetary shields offer a formidable line of defense against such dangers.

A planetary shield generator functions much like a standard deflector shield generator, creating a force field that nullifies both physical and energy attacks. The shield's specific energy signature can dissipate any other energy that passes through it, including turbolaser blasts and energy bombs. More impressive is the shield's effect on physical objects: any solid matter that comes into contact with it is instantly vaporized. Thus, the shield can protect against concussion missiles and other physical weapons, as well as asteroids, comet strikes, and even advancing starships. Any starship that collides with a planetary shield's energy screens will be reduced to space dust.

Most shield generators are built on planetary surfaces, where they can be easily defended by anti-infantry and antivehicle turrets. Such shields usually protect only a limited area. The Kuat Drive Yards DSS-02 planetary shield generator deployed by the Alliance on Hoth, for instance, covered an area about fifty kilometers in diameter. Like many planetary shields, the DSS-02 had to be lowered whenever the Alliance wished to fire its ion cannon or send an escaping transport into space. Such shields also require an inordinate amount of energy and take nearly half an hour to activate.

Some planetary shield generators can also project energy screens over great distances. This feature enables a planetary shield generator to protect a nearby moon or orbital space station. A CoMar SLD-26 shield generator hidden on the forest moon of Endor completely enveloped the orbiting Death Star II in a defensive screen that could only be penetrated by the blast of another superlaser. Han Solo and his commando forces managed to infiltrate and destroy the shield generator facility, causing the shield to drop—thus allowing the Rebel Alliance to attack the Death Star.

Because of their destructive power, planetary shield generators can be used offensively. The shields are virtually invisible, forcing pilots to rely on sensor readings to avoid contact with the energy screens. Unfortunately, sensors can be jammed or blocked, effectively concealing the presence of a planetary shield. This tactic nearly caused the destruction of numerous Rebel starfighters at the Battle of Endor. Unable to communicate with Han Solo, the Rebels did not realize that the battle station was still protected by its defensive screen as they began their initial attack run. Moments before the onrushing starfighters were vaporized, Lando Calrissian deduced that the Death Star's shields were operational and ordered his fleet to break off the attack.

> **"Oh, I'm afraid the deflector shield will be quite operational when your friends arrive . . ."**
> —*Emperor Palpatine to Luke Skywalker before the Battle of Endor*

7 **Power Core:** The CoMar SLD-26's efficient power core allowed the Imperials to retain a shield around the second Death Star indefinitely.

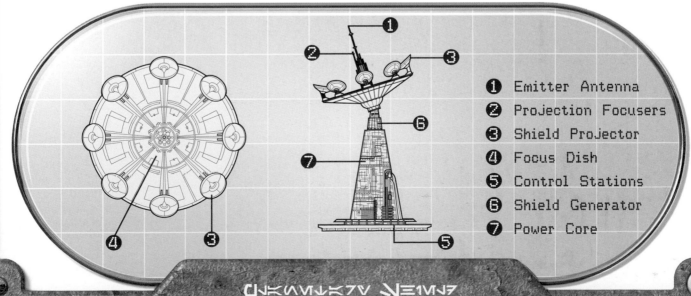

1 Emitter Antenna
2 Projection Focusers
3 Shield Projector
4 Focus Dish
5 Control Stations
6 Shield Generator
7 Power Core

Cloaking Devices

Technical Readout

DEFENSE TYPE: *None (blocks scanners and sensors but provides no defense against attacks)*

COVERAGE: *Single starship*

PRIMARY MANUFACTURER: *Sienar Design Systems (allegedly)*

AFFILIATION: *Darth Maul's Infiltrator*

114

Custom–Built Prototype Cloak Field Generator

The galaxy's most innovative designers continue to pursue a handful of elusive, fabled technologies. Chief among these is the cloaking device, an apparatus that could render starships and other vessels invisible to electronic detection systems. The value of such technology is clear: starships with cloaking devices could ambush enemies or flee authorities with ease.

Despite intense research, few cloaking devices have actually been developed. Early attempts to cloak a ship left the pilot blind. Others were too large and power-hungry. Those starship cloaking devices that do exist are relatively simple in design. All starships emit electromagnetic waves, which can be identified by a variety of sensors. A cloaking device functions by disrupting these waves, preventing the ship from appearing on scanners. But these devices do not stop simple visual contact.

Before the rise of the Empire, cloaking devices were virtually unknown. It is believed that Sienar Design Systems developed one of the first cloak field generators for the menacing *Infiltrator* piloted by Darth Maul, powered by stygium crystals. Mined only on the volatile Aeten II in the Outer Rim and prone to burnout during use, stygium crystals existed in increasingly limited numbers throughout the galaxy. By the Battle of Yavin, Aeten II's cache of crystals had been all but depleted, making the manufacture of new stygium-based cloaking devices a near impossibility.

After the Emperor took power, the development of new cloaking devices became a top priority among Imperial researchers, focused on alternatives to the stygium-based technology. Eventually, the Empire managed to produce a large prototype device that could render a vehicle invisible to both scanners and the naked eye. Starships cloaked by an Imperial cloaking device could only be detected by an expensive and rare crystal gravfield trap (CGT) scanner, which identifies gravitational fluctuations created by any large mass. However, the Imperial prototype was inefficient, expensive, and impaired the scanners and communications aboard the host ship. Because of these limitations, Imperial cloaking devices were installed only aboard the largest starships.

During the Galactic Civil War, Imperial Admiral Sarn oversaw the creation of a huge cloaking shield for use aboard Super Star Destroyers. Rebel agents discovered and thwarted this project, but they could not stop the development of similar devices. It is rumored that the Emperor's personal shuttle carried a miniaturized cloaking shield generator. The shuttle was destroyed along with the second Death Star at the Battle of Endor.

After the Battle of Endor, any surviving Imperial cloaking technology vanished. Eventually, Grand Admiral Thrawn discovered plans for nonstygium cloaking devices in one of the Emperor's hidden storehouses. He used these devices for numerous attacks against the New Republic, and even placed cloaked asteroids around Coruscant to blockade the New Republic's capital world.

> ## "They can't have disappeared. No ship that small has a cloaking device . . ."
> —*Captain Needa after the* Millennium Falcon *seemingly vanished from Imperial sensors*

6 Power Cells: Modern cloaking devices are very inefficient, burning through power cells at a surprising rate. As a result, cloaking devices are often too expensive for routine military use.

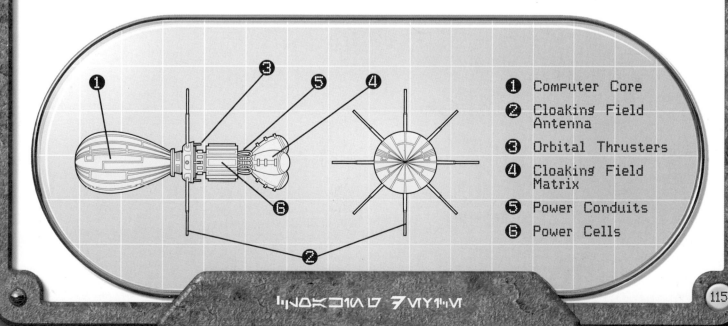

1. Computer Core
2. Cloaking Field Antenna
3. Orbital Thrusters
4. Cloaking Field Matrix
5. Power Conduits
6. Power Cells

Blast Armor

Technical Readout

Defense Type: Blaster energy, sonic energy, heat energy, cold energy, electrical energy, kinetic, piercing, and slashing

Coverage: Wearer's torso and head

Primary Manufacturer: Creshaldyne Industries

Affiliation: Naboo Palace Guard

Creshaldyne Industries Blast-Dampening Armor

Armor has been a staple on battlefields for eons. Even in primitive times, armorsmiths created armors to defend against the dominant weapons of the era. Thick leather or hide offered some protection from spears and arrows, while metal plates later deflected otherwise fatal sword blows. As weapons have evolved from basic spears and swords, so have armors adapted. Blasters are currently the most prevalent weapons in the galaxy, and nearly all armor contains some form of blast-dampening technology to help absorb blasterfire.

Armor is produced in a variety of classes, often distinguished by weight. Light armor encompasses all lightweight protective suits, usually crafted from leather, woven cloth, or strong plastics. Light armor is desirable for some adventurers because it's nonrestrictive and doesn't attract attention. Medium armor includes small plates of ceramic or metal installed inside durable cloth fabric. Some of these plates might also be visible on the exterior of the suit, especially around joints or physical soft spots. Medium armor is more restrictive than light armor, but offers much greater protection. Heavy armor represents the final class of commercially available armor. These armor suits are dominated by reinforced durasteel or ceramic plates that completely encase the wearer. While heavy armor provides a wealth of protection from both attacks and the environment, it's cumbersome and expensive. The vast majority of blast armor falls into the medium category: thick enough to carry special blast-dampening materials but light enough to allow movement for combat.

The blast-dampening jerkin manufactured by Creshaldyne Industries and worn by the Naboo Palace Guard is typical of most modern blast armor. The suit consists of protective garb that covers the chest, back, and shoulders. The exterior of the armor is composed of a rubbery material that insulates against heat, cold, electricity, and a variety of other forms of energy. This rubber shell is filled with thousands of tiny reflecting crystals suspended in a semisolid gel. The crystals both diffuse blaster energy and absorb the intense heat generated by blaster bolts. The gel also absorbs kinetic energy caused by punches, kicks, long falls, clubs, and a variety of other weapons. Finally, the combination of the rubber exterior and gel innards can slow the vibrations produced by a vibroblade, seriously diminishing the effects of such weapons.

Creshaldyne also produces the Barabel microbe armor. A light, sleeveless vest, microbe armor incorporates several sealed pockets filled with a microbe-rich saline solution. Each pocket supports a colony of millions of microorganisms that feed on radiation and energy emissions. These microbes actually absorb blasterfire as food, allowing the colonies to grow each time the vest is struck by a blaster bolt. As the number of microbes multiplies, the vest temporarily becomes more effective. Despite the microbe vest's incredible blast-dampening ability, it is not widely favored by soldiers and adventurers because it offers virtually no protection against other weapons.

> **"Before the Battle of Naboo, we wore blast armor as an indulgence. Now we consider it a necessity."**
> —*Captain Panaka*

⑥ Helmet: The Naboo blast armor comes equipped with a reinforced, open-faced helmet with sonic dampeners.

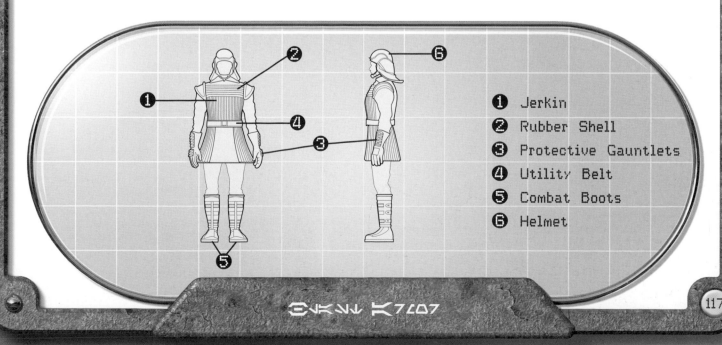

① Jerkin
② Rubber Shell
③ Protective Gauntlets
④ Utility Belt
⑤ Combat Boots
⑥ Helmet

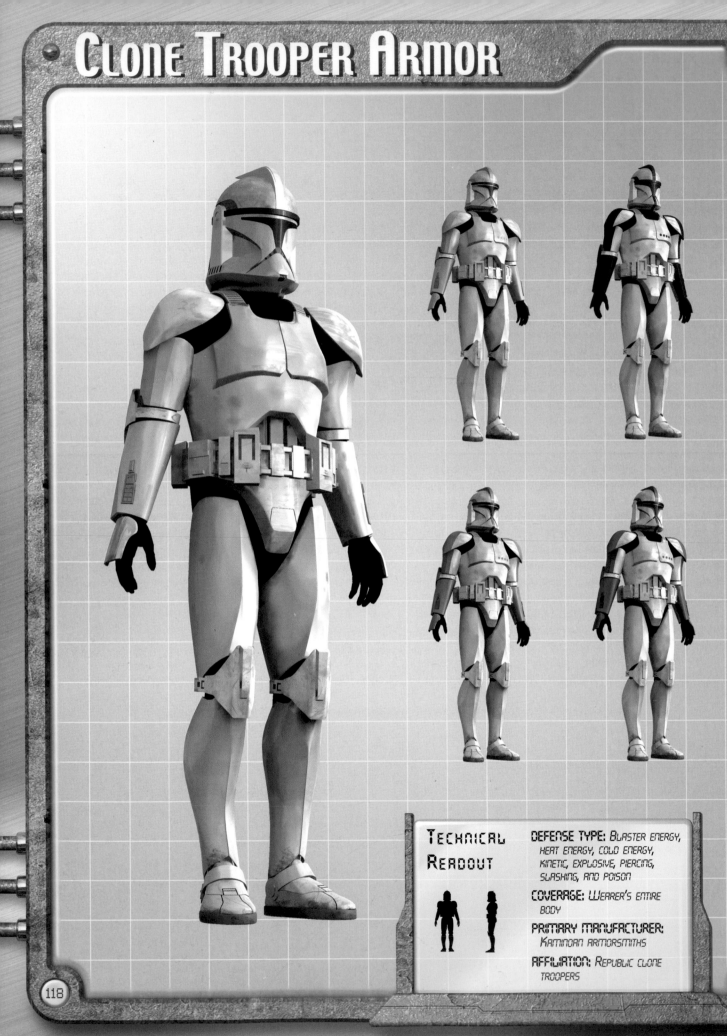

CLONE TROOPER ARMOR

TECHNICAL READOUT

DEFENSE TYPE: Blaster energy, heat energy, cold energy, kinetic, explosive, piercing, slashing, and poison

COVERAGE: Wearer's entire body

PRIMARY MANUFACTURER: Kaminoan armorsmiths

AFFILIATION: Republic clone troopers

Kaminoan Phase I Clone Trooper Armor

The cloners of Kamino were commissioned with creating the Old Republic's vast clone army, properly outfitted with the most advanced military gear available. Key to the clones' success was a suit of resilient, high-tech armor developed by Kaminoan engineers with the aid of bounty hunter Jango Fett.

Jango Fett was one of the last survivors of the Mandalorians, an order of supercommandos almost exterminated by the Jedi years before the Battle of Geonosis. Fett based the design of clone trooper armor on the versatile battle gear worn by the Mandalorians. Clone trooper armor can still be found on the black market and in secret storehouses across the galaxy.

> **"A clone army . . . And I must say, one of the finest we've ever created . . ."**
> —*Kaminoan Prime Minister Lama Su*

The first layer of "armor" is actually a pressurized black body glove that protects its wearer against acrid vapors and extreme temperatures. Twenty formfitting plates are attached to the body glove via magnatomic grip panels, which encase the trooper in a vacuum-sealed suit. Each plate is manufactured using a lightweight plastoid-alloy composite that can withstand explosions, small firearms blasts, and even blaster bolts. Knee and elbow joints are further protected by reinforced plates to prevent debilitating injuries. The molecular makeup of the plastoid armor allows clone troopers to pass through hazardous energy fields, including deflector shields. In inclement weather, clone troopers also don waterproof parkas.

Unlike Mandalorian armor, clone trooper armor is not equipped with concealed weapons. During the Clone Wars, Republic clone troopers carried standard-issue DC-15 blasters and blaster rifles. However, the clone trooper armor does boast a multifunction utility belt that carries spare blaster gas canisters and power cells, a grappling hook, explosive charges, stimpaks, and other survival gear.

The clone trooper's helmet could receive and transmit battlefield updates, orders, and coordinates using miniaturized communications equipment in the helmet. The comlink antenna is built into the distinctive fin atop the helmet.

The armor is flexible enough to allow a variety of combat movements and positions, but it is extremely uncomfortable if worn while sitting. This hampered clone trooper pilots, who eventually began using modified versions of the armor that offered far less protection.

The Kaminoans developed several variations on the standard clone trooper armor. The most sophisticated was the armor worn by the Advanced Reconnaissance Commandos (or ARC troopers). ARC trooper armor is supplemented by an advanced range finder attached to the helmet, pouches carrying grenades and electronic countermeasures, and a blast-dampening shoulder pauldron and cape. ARC trooper armor could also support specially designed modules such as jet packs, shoulder-mounted rocket launchers, concealed flamethrowers, grappling guns, and a host of other attachments. The modular concept was later expanded into the standard clone trooper armor design, allowing clones to take on well-defined roles: a clone trained as a medic might be equipped with a portable bacta module, while a grenadier could carry a miniature grenade launcher.

6 **T-Visor:** The clone trooper's signature visor plate includes an enhanced breath filter that allows for comfortable breathing in dust-filled or poisonous environments.

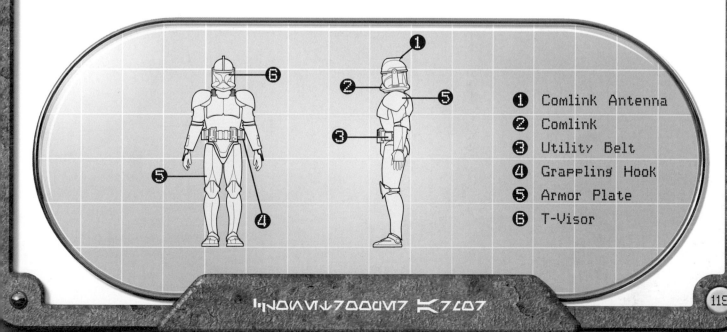

1. Comlink Antenna
2. Comlink
3. Utility Belt
4. Grappling Hook
5. Armor Plate
6. T-Visor

STORMTROOPER ARMOR

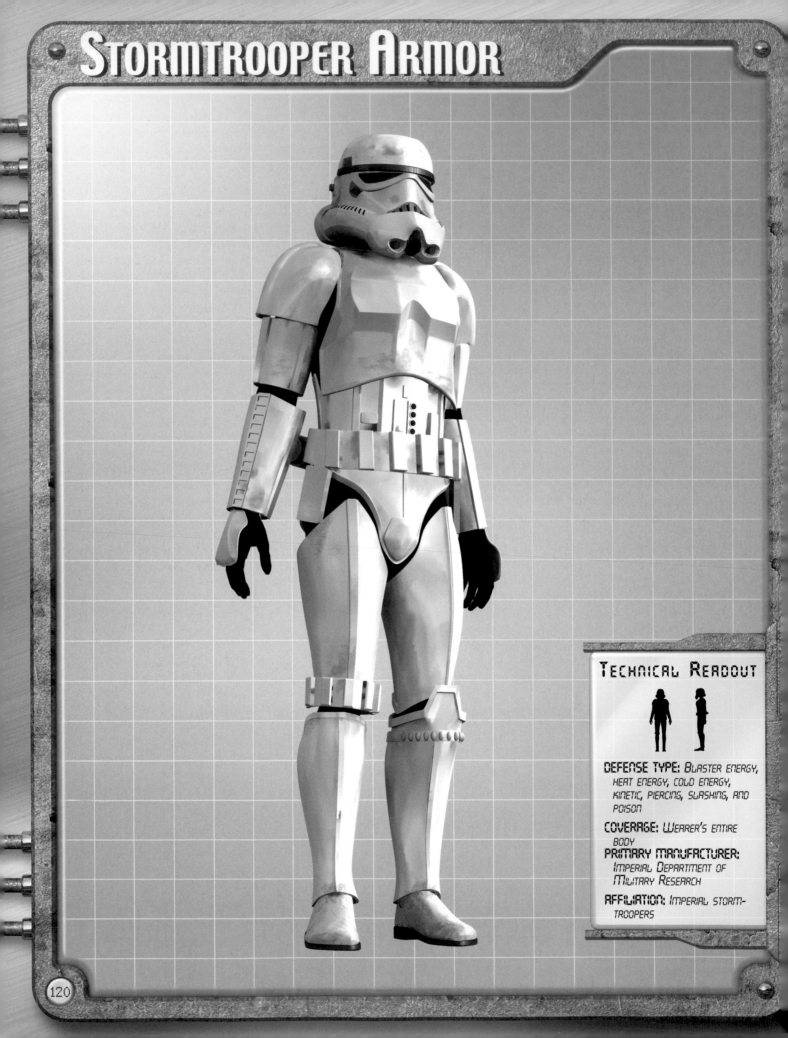

TECHNICAL READOUT

DEFENSE TYPE: Blaster energy, heat energy, cold energy, kinetic, piercing, slashing, and poison

COVERAGE: Wearer's entire body

PRIMARY MANUFACTURER: Imperial Department of Military Research

AFFILIATION: Imperial stormtroopers

Imperial Stormtrooper Armor

A natural evolution of the Old Republic's clone trooper, the imposing stormtrooper has become a symbol of Imperial tyranny across the galaxy. Well trained, heavily armed, and completely dedicated to the Emperor, stormtroopers served as the Empire's elite shock troops throughout the Galactic Civil War.

Stormtrooper armor is simultaneously more advanced and less formidable than its clone trooper predecessor. While clone trooper armor is designed to sustain significant damage, a stormtrooper's plastoid shell protects only against glancing blaster blows and physical attacks. However, the armor does serve as extremely sophisticated survival gear. Aside from the insulating black body glove, the stormtrooper's armor contains sensitive temperature controls that automatically adjust based on prevailing conditions.

A stormtrooper's helmet is replete with high-tech gear. Polarized lenses protect troopers from bright flashes, such as those caused by explosions, and allow them to see in dark or hazy conditions. A powerful transmitter allows stormtroopers to communicate over long distances, while built-in sensor arrays can pick up enemy signals and detect nearby life-forms. Other helmet features include cellular padding to prevent head injuries, a helmet computer that monitors the armor's functions, a Comtech Series IV speaker using three-phase sonic filtering for clear sound, an atmospheric recycling unit, and a complex air intake and exhaust system. A hermetic autoseal can be engaged to completely seal the armor suit, which is self-contained and has its own small oxygen supply. This feature allows stormtroopers to brave poisonous atmospheres and even the vacuum of space for short periods of time.

> ## "Aren't you a little short for a stormtrooper?"
> —*Princess Leia to a disguised Luke Skywalker*

Stormtrooper armor was adapted for use in numerous different environments by specialized squads. Snowtroopers deployed at the Battle of Hoth wore armor designed to withstand unrelenting cold. Snowtrooper helmets include warmers that protect the soldiers' lungs from chilled air. Scout troopers don the lightest armor, but their helmets are equipped with advanced navigational computers vital when piloting speeder bikes. Desert sandtroopers wear armor laced with cooling units and a helmet armed with a robust sand filter. Other variants include spacetroopers (or zero-g troopers), flying airtroopers, aquatic seatroopers, and even tunneling underminers. Although extremely rare, the Empire also commissioned magma troopers designed for combat on volcanic mining worlds and radtroopers capable of fighting in lethal radiation zones.

Perhaps the most fearsome of all stormtroopers unleashed during the Galactic Civil War were the Storm Commandos. Trained by General Crix Madine, who later defected to the Rebel Alliance, Storm Commandos wore black scout trooper armor and excelled at assassination and espionage missions. To support their mission profile, Storm Commando armor included a small generator that created a sound-dampening field, numerous concealed weapons, and a small thermal detonator that a commando could detonate if faced with capture.

5 **Utility Belt:** A stormtrooper wears a utility belt that contains a grappling hook, extra ammunition, a spare comlink, and other gear. A thermal detonator that can only be activated through a special security code is attached to the back of the belt.

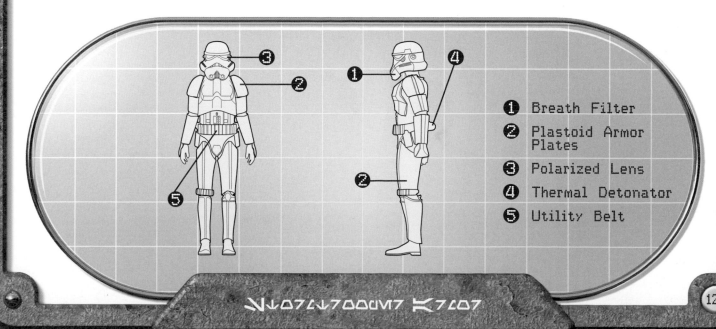

1. Breath Filter
2. Plastoid Armor Plates
3. Polarized Lens
4. Thermal Detonator
5. Utility Belt

MANDALORIAN ARMOR

TECHNICAL READOUT

DEFENSE TYPE: Blaster energy, heat energy, cold energy, explosive, piercing, slashing, poison

COVERAGE: Wearer's entire body

PRIMARY MANUFACTURER: Custom-built by Mandalorian warriors

AFFILIATION: Jango and Boba Fett

Custom–Built Mandalorian Battle Armor

andalorian. For centuries, the word has been synonymous with violence and death. In their earliest incarnation, the Mandalorians were brutal mercenaries who won wars for the highest bidder. Over time, they evolved into supercommandos capable of toppling governments, destroying criminal cartels, and even challenging the Jedi Order. Throughout all of their incarnations, the Mandalorians have relied on a host of weapons and vehicles, but it has been their armor that has made these warriors unique.

Two of the most infamous Mandalorians are Jango Fett and his son, Boba. Both men have worn Mandalorian armor while working as bounty hunters. In fact, Boba's primary suit was handed down to him from his father. Boba now maintains two full versions of his suit, along with backup weapons and items that can be added for specific missions.

Mandalorian armor is a collection of blast-resistant duraplast armor plates attached to a waterproof, armor mesh flight suit. A liner shirt with a micro energy field projector and two layers of ceramic plates greatly improve protection around the chest, back, and stomach. The careful layering of segmented armor plates ensures mobility, which is further increased by the suit's short range jet pack.

Mandalorian armor is best known for its array of weapons. Standard holsters can hold a variety of blasters and blaster rifles, but Boba relies heavily on concealed weapons. Fett's gauntlets alone hide a Czerka Zx miniature flame projector, a sonic beam weapon, a dart shooter, several blades of varying length and shape, and a twenty-meter-long fibercord whip with a grappling hook. The gloves are also reinforced to increase damage

caused by a single punch. The armor's most powerful weapon is a miniature concussion rocket launcher built into the suit's jet pack. The rocket launcher can fire antipersonnel, stun, and antivehicle rockets, and features a computer tracking system that interfaces directly with Boba's helmet. A larger jet pack can be equipped to carry more powerful warheads. Other weapons include rocket dart launchers concealed in the armor's kneepads, retractable boot spikes, and a BlasTech Dur-24 wrist laser with a range of up to fifty meters. Grenades, gas pellets, caltrops, and other small weapons can be carried in belt utility pouches.

> ### "The Mandalorians wear the finest armor blood can buy."
> —*Count Dooku*

A range finder attached to the duraplast armored helmet can track up to thirty targets, while a battle computer inside the helmet allows Boba to control the suit's weapons, sensors, and jet pack through verbal commands. The dark macrobinocular viewplate offers a variety of vision modes, including infrared. A pineal eye sensor on the helmet combines with an internal overlay display to provide tracking information within a 360-degree radius. Motion sensors, an encrypted internal comlink, and a broad-band antenna complete the helmet devices, all of which can be linked to Boba's weapons or his personal starship, *Slave I*. An environmental filter system with a two-hour reserve tank allows Boba Fett to pursue quarry onto even the most inhospitable worlds.

❼ Finish: Unmodified Mandalorian armor has a chrome finish, but Mandalorians were known to paint their armor to identify units and rank. Boba Fett resurrected this tradition with his own armor suits.

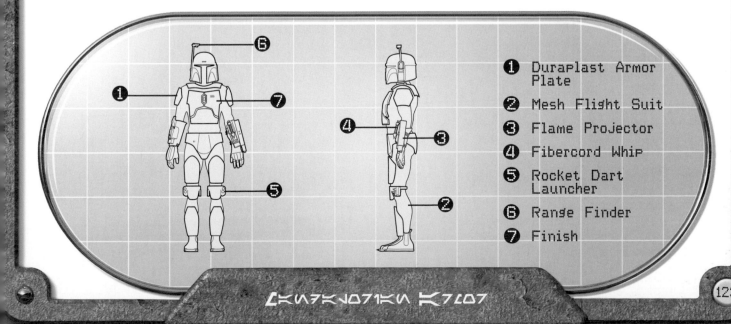

1. Duraplast Armor Plate
2. Mesh Flight Suit
3. Flame Projector
4. Fibercord Whip
5. Rocket Dart Launcher
6. Range Finder
7. Finish

Breath Mask

Technical Readout

DEFENSE TYPE: Poison

COVERAGE: Wearer's respiratory system

PRIMARY MANUFACTURER: Gandorthral Atmospherics

AFFILIATION: Han Solo and crew

Gandorthral Atmospherics Roamer-6 Breath Mask

A staple aboard nearly every starship, the breath mask is a portable life-support system designed to purify air-poisonous environments or supply oxygen in thin atmospheres. A basic breath mask, such as the Roamer-6, provides breathable air even in a near vacuum. After fleeing Imperial forces, Han Solo, Princess Leia, and Chewbacca donned breath masks to explore an asteroid cave near Hoth.

The Roamer-6 is very compact and easy to wear, even while undertaking rigorous activities. The breath mask is typically worn over the nose and mouth, held in place by a comfortable, adjustable strap. The mask's flexible air hose is connected to a purifier equipped with powerful filters. The lightweight unit can be slipped into a vest or pants pocket, clipped to a belt, or carried in a free hand.

A Roamer-6 breath mask is air purifier is equipped with six layers of versatile filters. Also known as atmospheric scrubbers, these filters trap nearly all microscopic contaminants, including poisonous gases, dust, pollen, sand, bacteria, and viral organisms. In very thin atmospheres, the scrubbers convert compound gases such as carbon dioxide into oxygen. A temperature-control unit warms or cools air to safe levels to prevent any damage to the wearer's throat or lungs. The computerized filters can be programmed and adjusted to handle the needs of any number of species: The Ubese bounty hunter Boushh wore a breath mask that provided him with vital trace gases when on oxygen-rich worlds. Unfortunately, filters on these units are usually expended after only one hour, but inexpensive replacement filters can be snapped into place in just seconds. The unit's compressed gas tank contains a ten-minute supply of air in the event the air filters

fail or atmospheric conditions suddenly suffer radical change. The tank is most often filled with oxygen, but can contain any type of gas to allow the breath mask to be used by non-oxygen breathers.

Most galactic travelers need little more than an unmodified Roamer-6. For major industrial or military operations, breath masks can be equipped with an assortment of special features. A coupler on the bottom of the gas tank can be attached to a larger, backpack air tank with several hours of breathable gas. Explorers often wear breath masks with microfine scrubbers that can detect and neutralize even the most unusual trace gases. Breath masks can also be hooked to goggles or blast helmets, equipped with voice amplifiers, and outfitted with small comlinks that can be programmed to virtually any frequency.

On their own, breath masks do not protect against a total vacuum or corrosive atmospheres. Breath masks are often built into helmets, including those worn by stormtroopers, Darth Vader, and many bounty hunters. A handful of breath masks, such as the VargeCorp Easy Breathing breath mask, are actually full face masks that cover the eyes, ears, nose, and mouth. Breath mask technology has been miniaturized to create specialized devices that provide a single type of purification. While on Naboo, Obi-Wan Kenobi and Qui-Gon Jinn used small A99 Aquata Breathers that draw oxygen from the surrounding water.

> **"Serving all worlds polluted by the Empire since the Battle of Yavin."**
> —*Excerpt from Gandorthral Atmospherics mission statement*

7 Formfitting Mask: The breath mask is essentially a one-size-fits-all device. The flexible mask can be worn by a wide range of species, including Wookiees.

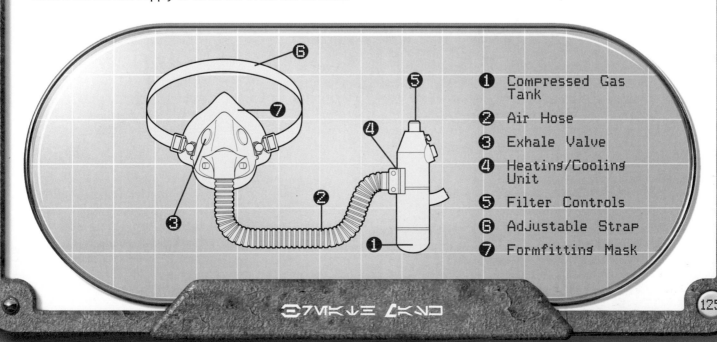

1. Compressed Gas Tank
2. Air Hose
3. Exhale Valve
4. Heating/Cooling Unit
5. Filter Controls
6. Adjustable Strap
7. Formfitting Mask

Vonduun-Crab-Shell-Plated Armor

Technical Readout

DEFENSE TYPE: *Blaster energy, kinetic, explosive, piercing, slashing, and light-saber energy*

COVERAGE: *Wearer's entire body*

PRIMARY MANUFACTURER: *Yuuzhan Vong shapers*

AFFILIATION: *Yuuzhan Vong warriors*

Yuuzhan Vong Vonduun Skerr Kyrric

Yuuzhan Vong warriors are terrifying to behold. Their tattooed and skull-like faces embody death, while their bioengineered weapons resemble nightmare creatures come to life. And when encased in vonduun armor, a Yuuzhan Vong warrior is reminiscent of a giant, bipedal insect covered in a thick black carapace.

Yuuzhan Vong armor is actually a giant bioengineered vonduun crab designed to wrap itself around a Yuuzhan Vong warrior. A vonduun crab's shell is capable of repelling blasterfire, resisting most conventional melee weapons, and even deflecting lightsaber blades. The crab's shell appears to be composed of an intricately structured crystal. The creature's unique power glands generate a protective field that covers the shell, greatly enhancing the crab's defensive properties. During desperate melee combat, the crab's spearlike legs can be used as weapons. The vonduun crab also secretes a special chemical that functions as a natural antiseptic, disinfecting wounds that the warrior or the crab might suffer.

> **"As if they weren't ugly enough already . . ."**
> —*Lando Calrissian, upon seeing Yuuzhan Vong wearing vonduun crab armor for the first time*

Vonduun crabs are grown in special nutrient-rich bogs. As a crab matures, shapers direct its growth to ensure a specific body shape. In this way, the crab's shell can later form the chestplates, gauntlets, greaves, boots, and other components of an armored suit. A crab's shell can even sprout sharp appendages, resulting in boots with long spikes or shoulder plates covered in razors. Each crab is grown and modeled for a specific Yuuzhan Vong warrior, who is continually fitted and refitted until the armor is ready for battle. Additional creatures bond with the crab to serve as communications devices, life support, and concealed weapons. Like many Yuuzhan Vong bioengineered devices, the armor itself is not necessarily sentient, acting largely on instinct. During battle, the armor will subtly shift to protect its warrior. When anyone other than a Yuuzhan Vong warrior dons the armor, the crab will repeatedly attempt to kill the wearer; the Peace Brigaders on Ylesia created laminate versions of the vonduun crab armor to avoid such attacks.

The vonduun crab may have been bred originally to help Yuuzhan Vong shapers control amphistaff populations. The vonduun crab is the juvenile amphistaff's only natural enemy. In the wild, the curved shell of a vonduun crab can withstand an amphistaff's attack.

Although the vonduun crab armor is formidable, the New Republic has discovered a handful of weaknesses possessed by the crab itself. The vonduun crab is allergic to the pollen of the intelligent, crystalline bafforr trees found on Ithor. If a crab is exposed to the pollen, it begins to swell violently. The swelling quickly kills the crab, which suffocates its Yuuzhan Vong host. Jacen Solo also learned that, beneath its shell, a vonduun crab is relatively soft. The young Jedi attacked a crab from the inside, using his lightsaber to sever the creature's field-nerve cables and rendering it useless. The crab's shell is vulnerable to flames created by enzyme-activated sparkbee honey.

6   Grip Legs: The small "grip legs" near the top of the crab armor sometimes grab hold of a Yuuzhan Vong's mouth, exposing the warrior's teeth and creating an evil, skull-like grin.

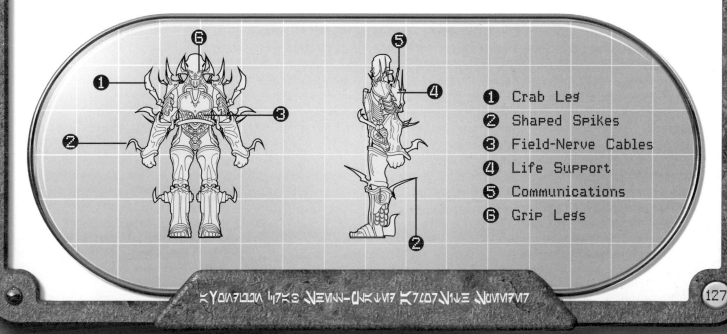

1 Crab Leg
2 Shaped Spikes
3 Field-Nerve Cables
4 Life Support
5 Communications
6 Grip Legs

TECHNICAL READOUT

DEFENSE TYPE: Blaster energy

COVERAGE: Wearer's entire body

PRIMARY MANUFACTURER: Merr-Sonn Munitions

AFFILIATION: New Republic agent Kyle Katarn

Merr-Sonn Munitions Military Mobility Shield

The creation of deflector shield technology represents one of the most important advances in military and personal defense. Not only has this technology proved invaluable to starships and space-based installations, but it is becoming increasing popular for use during ground engagements. In recent times, deflector shield generators have been miniaturized and calibrated to produce small, portable shields that protect a single individual against blasterfire and other attacks.

Commonly known as personal deflector shields, these miniaturized deflector screens are small enough to be worn on a belt. The belt-mounted device is activated with a simple flip of a switch, upon which it envelops the wearer in a glowing energy field.

Personal deflector shields are composed entirely of limited radiant shielding, a field that can absorb energy but little else. Therefore, personal deflector shields offer little protection against weapons other than blasters. They provide virtually no defense against non-energy weapons, extreme temperatures, or kinetic damage caused from falling, collisions, or the receiving end of a gloved fist.

Personal deflector shields are ablative; they will weaken as they absorb damage intended for their wearer. The shield does slowly recharge, but if subjected to a number of blaster bolts within a short period of time, the shield will fail. The Merr-Sonn Munitions Military Mobility Shield was originally designed for use on battlefields and can absorb approximately fifty full-power blaster bolts before it is rendered useless.

Like all deflector shields, personal deflector screens are notoriously inefficient. They consume huge quantities of energy, burning through power cells with frightening speed. As a result, personal deflector shields are activated only when combat is imminent. Some models, including the Merr-Sonn entry, can be recharged at power stations, while others require completely new power cells. A very few personal deflector shields are fueled by dedicated power generators, since these are bulky devices that must be worn as a heavy backpack.

Because personal deflector shields have so many limitations, they are rarely used alone. The shield generators usually bolster blast armor and blast vests worn by sentries and security personnel. Although Imperial stormtroopers shunned personal deflector shields because of their power requirements and expense, many Imperial officers did wear the devices.

> ## "The Imperials think I'm somehow immortal, but I just have a good supply of power cells."
> *—Rebel agent Kyle Katarn*

6 Side Clasp: A personal deflector shield generator can be worn on the side of a belt, where it is fairly inconspicuous. Imperial officers often wore these devices near their hip.

1. Shield Projector
2. Cooling Vents
3. Activation Panel
4. Power Indicator
5. Power Cell Housing
6. Side Clasp

DARTH VADER'S ARMOR

TECHNICAL READOUT

DEFENSE TYPE: BLASTER ENERGY, SONIC ENERGY, HEAT ENERGY, COLD ENERGY, ELECTRICAL ENERGY, KINETIC, EXPLOSIVE, PIERCING, SLASHING, POISON

COVERAGE: DARTH VADER'S ENTIRE BODY

PRIMARY MANUFACTURER: UNKNOWN

AFFILIATION: DARTH VADER

Custom–Built Imperial Life–Support and Defense System

The villainous Sith Lord known as Darth Vader was once an idealistic young Jedi Knight named Anakin Skywalker. During his tragic transformation into Vader, Skywalker was horrifically scarred. Though the extent of Vader's injuries remained concealed by his foreboding armor, it is known that he required an advanced life-support system to keep him alive.

Although terrifying to behold, Darth Vader's armor was primarily designed to provide life support. Circuitry throughout the suit monitored pulmonary, respiratory, and neural systems. Diagnostic information collected by the suit could be accessed via three slotlike dataports located on Vader's chest unit. Like stormtrooper armor, the suit was equipped with a sensitive temperature-regulation system, which could be controlled by a function box on his belt. The suit's heating unit was powerful enough to allow Vader to walk the surface of icy Hoth without any additional protection. Another belt-mounted function box housed the respiratory sensor matrix responsible for controlling Vader's breathing. Impulse generators lacing the armor provided electrical impulses to stimulate Vader's muscles, providing him with great mobility and strength despite his destroyed muscles and nerves.

Vader's helmet was the center of the life-support system. The helmet was fitted with an air pump, which was connected to a flat filter system worn on Vader's back. Together, the backpack and air pump continuously cycled purified air through Vader's ravaged lungs. A small, back-up air-processing filter was located in the helmet near Vader's mouth. The helmet also monitored and regulated Vader's body temperature, and contained radiators to diffuse heat generated by the suit's electrical systems. A pri-

> ### "He's more machine now than man. Twisted and evil."
> *—Obi-Wan Kenobi on Darth Vader*

mary environmental sensor continually evaluated Vader's surrounding for potential hazards. A nutrient feed provided Vader with all the nourishment he required.

Durasteel armor plates protected many parts of Vader's body, including his shoulders, rib cage, and shins. His gloves and the padding on his chest and arms consisted of blast-dampening armor. Various displays inside Vader's helmet supplied the Sith Lord with a steady stream of data, amplifying his already formidable connection to the Force. His helmet's eye coverings provided infrared and ultraviolet vision, allowing Vader to see clearly in complete darkness, and dampeners offered limited defense against sonic attacks. The suit was also equipped with all-terrain combat boots and an armor weave cape. Although he had access to lightsaber-resistant cortosis, Vader relied on his own skill with the weapon to protect himself from Jedi attacks.

All of the armor's functions and Vader's prosthetic limbs were powered by dozens of rechargeable energy cells located throughout the suit. These allowed Vader to travel alone for long stretches without recharging his armor. Even when the energy cells were depleted, he could maintain basic life-support functions through backup, replaceable power cells. Vader typically recharged his suit within a meditation sphere located aboard his personal Super Star Destroyer, the *Executor*, although he could access any standard fusion furnace for this purpose.

6 Electromagnetic Clasp: Darth Vader's belt buckle includes an audio-enhancement unit, small tool kit, spare energy cell, and backup comlink.

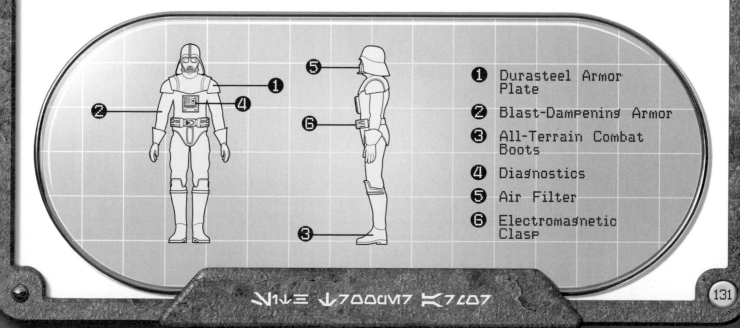

1. Durasteel Armor Plate
2. Blast-Dampening Armor
3. All-Terrain Combat Boots
4. Diagnostics
5. Air Filter
6. Electromagnetic Clasp

ADDITIONAL DEFENSES

For nearly every weapon developed, there is some form of defense. Below is a small sampling of the armor and other defenses found throughout the galaxy.

AV-1c Combat Armor

Fully enclosed power armor designed for front-line infantry attacks. The AV-1C augments the wearer's strength and can fly using repulsorlift engines. Other features include a computerized targeting system, low-light vision and dark-vision, a built-in comlink, and a powerlamp.

Chitin Armor

Bizarre, plated armor developed by a long-dead alien species and now replicated across the galaxy. Chitin armor is resistant to all forms of energy, including blasterfire. A unique visor, which resembles the wings of a prehistoric insect, enhances the wearer's vision.

Dark Armor

A generic term for any armor worn by Dark Jedi or Sith warriors. Dark armor is usually frightening in appearance and is designed to complement the wearer's Force powers and lightsaber combat style. The ancient Sith warrior Larad Noon wore a dark combat jumpsuit to enhance his mobility, while the terrifying Belia Darzu crafted heavy battle armor for maximum protection during fights with multiple Jedi.

Electromesh Armor

Lightweight and glossy black armor worn by Nagai soldiers. Electromesh armor offers some protection against physical attacks and generates an electrical field that can absorb some damage from energy weapons.

Enviro-suit

Any type of suit designed to protect the wearer on harsh or inhospitable planets. Enviro-suits are useless against blasters and other attacks, but will protect against radiation, poisonous atmospheres, intense temperatures, and other conditions.

Gungan Personal Energy Shield

A handheld energy shield used by the Gungans of Naboo for defense against physical attacks and light blasterfire. The shield is held in one hand or strapped to a forearm. When activated, it projects a thin force field roughly one and a half meters tall.

Gungan Shield Generator

A device that generates a large, domelike protective force field that can deflect blaster- and laserfire, projectiles, and other small, fast-moving objects. Gungan shield generators are typically carried by powerful creatures such as fambaas. During large battles, Gungans combine multiple shield generators to protect entire armies.

Individual Field Disruptor

A portable energy projection system emits powerful energy signatures that temporarily disable defensive energy screens. Individual field disruptors are worn on a belt or backpack. When activated, the wearer is surrounded by a disruptive energy field. The device can be used as a makeshift weapon because the field will deliver a painful energy discharge to anyone who touches its wearer.

Mimetic Suit

A camouflage suit that can change color to blend into its surroundings. Mimetic suits are used by assassins, spies, scouts, and mercenaries.

Ooglith Cloaker

An organic environment suit worn by the Yuuzhan Vong. The suit includes a gnullith, a star-shaped creature that

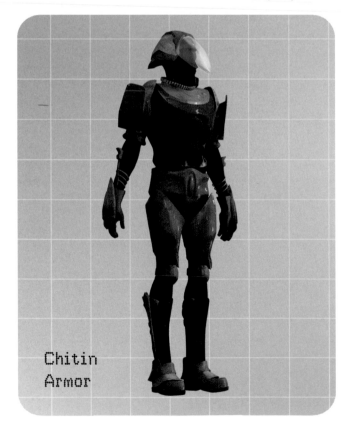

Chitin Armor

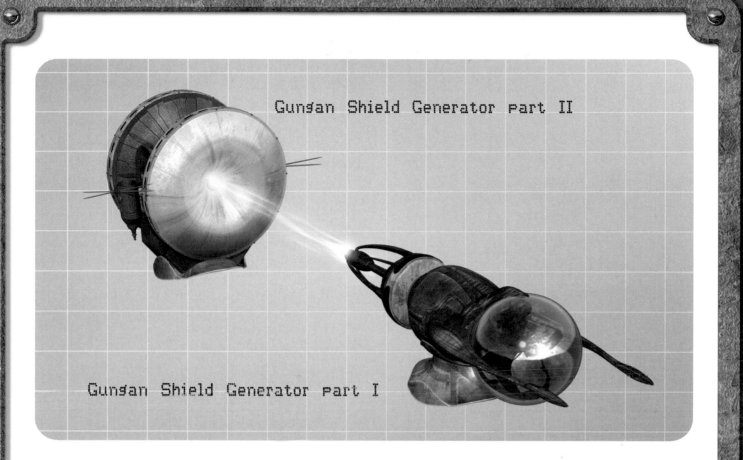

Gungan Shield Generator part II

Gungan Shield Generator part I

attaches to its host's face. The gnullith then sends a tendril down the host's throat, enabling the host to breathe in hostile environments, including the vacuum of space.

Ooglith Masquer

A Yuuzhan Vong bioengineered organic creature that serves as a disguise for Yuuzhan Vong agents. The masquer uses thousands of tiny grappling tendrils to attach itself to a Yuuzhan Vong's pores, creating a false outer skin. Yuuzhan Vong can use masquers to appear human.

Simcronic Magnaforce Security Shield

A small device worn on the wrist and capable of producing a small, localized defensive field. The security shield can resist up to medium-power blaster bolts.

Spider Silk Armor

State-of-the-art armor capable of deflecting blaster bolts. The bounty hunter Mahwi Lihnn wears spider silk armor.

Stalker Armor

Bounty hunter armor developed on Rodia. Stalker armor is durable, offers good protection against most conventional attacks, and is equipped with a small arsenal of both ranged and melee weapons.

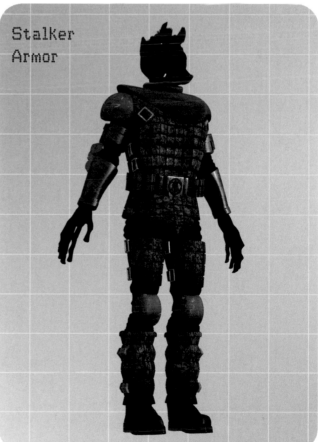

Stalker Armor

Sensor, Communications, and Security Devices

Because the galaxy is filled with so many threats, being able to gather information from one's surroundings is critical for survival. In early warfare, scouts conducted reconnaissance on foot, relying on eyesight and instinct to spot enemy troop movements. Ground vehicles allowed scouts to cover more territory; however, long-range scanners truly redefined reconnaissance. Scanners include any devices designed to search a surrounding area to collect specific data. Scanners can detect life-forms, movement, and a wide variety of energy signatures and emissions.

In space, scanners are an absolute necessity because they allow pilots to identify space debris, stellar anomalies, and enemy craft. Early space travel proved exceedingly dangerous due to everything from a lack of established travel routes, to threats posed by enemy vessels, to natural hazards. The advent of visual scanners provided little relief, because these devices had very a limited range and could not penetrate dense asteroid fields and other obstacles. The first navigation aids were equally ineffective: crude electronic telescopes required navigators to take star readings to determine a proper course. Failure to decipher star readings correctly could easily result in a starship becoming lost in the depths of space forever.

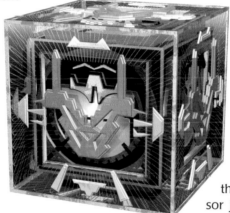

Fortunately, modern starship scanners allow for safe and reliable travel. Each starship is typically equipped with several different sensor suites, each designed to gather specific data for pilots, navigators, gunners, and other crew members. Sensors are also used to scan approaching craft, identify space lanes, and pinpoint debris even while moving at incredible sublight speeds.

Although it is undoubtedly integral to both military actions and space travel, scanner technology has also facilitated exploration of dangerous worlds, increased efficiency while surveying for valuable ore and minerals, and dramatically improved medical procedures.

Long-range communications devices were developed hand in hand with advanced scanner technologies. As scouts ventured afield, they required increasingly powerful communication tools to deliver their reports and other data. Handheld comlinks and other similar equipment were adopted by military factions, but also proved invaluable to local security forces, explorers, scientists, and industrial operations. Private citizens also began carrying such devices for use in unexpected emergencies or natural disasters.

Devices that allowed communication anywhere on a planet's surface soon evolved into equipment that could send signals across the vacuum of space. In the modern era, the most powerful communications devices transmit from the Core Worlds to the Outer Rim. All starships have at least rudimentary long-range transmitters, often built into sensor suites. Homing beacons that allow accurate tracking of individual craft, identity tags for broadcasting a ship's vital information, and transceivers capable of tapping into the galactic HoloNet are all extensions of the first, primitive communications devices.

The heavy reliance on scanners and advanced communications devices, especially aboard starships and space stations, has led to an entire industry devoted to creating countermeasures for these technologies. While the cloaking field—which completely masks a starship from scanners and sensors—may be the most infamous of these devices, engineers have devised many other countermeasures. So-called sensor stealth systems dampen or conceal energy emissions created by engines, weapons systems, and power generators. In contrast, sensor jammers operate by flooding the area around a ship with random signals and other "noise" that can confuse or blind enemy sensors. Most jamming efforts are easy to detect, although the Empire did develop relatively quiet sensor jammers used at the Battle of Endor to mask the presence of the Death Star's deflector shield. Among the most costly but effective sensor countermeasures are sensor decoys, which are small pods or shuttles that electronically duplicate a host ship's sensor signature. When a sensor decoy is released, enemy sensor operators suddenly find themselves faced with two or more versions of the target vessel. Short-range visual scanners can expose this ruse, but sensor operators must first pick a target to pursue before the visual scanners can be effective. By the time a decoy is exposed, the real starship has likely escaped.

When used by the reigning government, specialized scanners, communications devices, and scanner countermeasures are often called simply *security devices* because they protect sensitive information and personnel. Under the paranoid Empire, manufacturers that produced such security devices flourished. The technology ranges from simple magnetic cuffs to powerful scanners capable of identifying weapons and cybernetic implants. The New Republic continues to use similar devices, including encrypted comlinks and other transmitters that encode and decode data.

Comlinks

Technical Readout

WEIGHT: 0.5 KG

OPTIMUM/MAXIMUM RANGES: 100 KM/HIGH ORBIT

PRIMARY MANUFACTURER: SoroSuub

AFFILIATION: Qui-Gon Jinn

SoroSuub Hush-98 Comlink

The comlink is the standard long-range communications device found throughout the galaxy. The most basic and common comlinks share a relatively simple design, which consists of a receiver, transmitter, and small power source all contained in a small, handheld unit. Comlinks can also be worn on the wrist, mounted on headsets or in helmets, or incorporated into armor or clothing.

Like so many other common devices, comlinks are manufactured in seemingly endless variety. The least powerful comlinks can transmit only on audio signal, usually the user's voice, and cover only a few kilometers. Most comlinks, however, have a range of about fifty kilometers and, under the proper conditions, can even reach starships or space stations in low orbit. The Cirenian Communications Model SW-95 Message Transceiver relies on relay stations on populated worlds to achieve a range of two thousand kilometers.

The devices can be adjusted to operate on one of several million broadcast frequencies found throughout the galaxy. Comlinks such as the Crozo 3-MAL personal comlink carried by the Rebel Alliance on Hoth also monitor the "Standard Clear Frequencies" used to broadcast civil defense warnings and provide vital information about local laws and nearby medical and governmental facilities. The Imperial-issue SoroSuub C1 personal comlink supplements a stormtrooper's built-in helmet transmitter–receiver system with improved range and communications security. The C1 and other comlink sets can be tuned with sophisticated encryption algorithms and broadcast and receive over secured frequencies. Within or near Imperial bases, comlink signals are boosted and relayed automatically for optimum transmission.

> ## "Shut down all the garbage mashers on the detention level!"
> —*Luke Skywalker to R2-D2, via a comlink*

Aside from the most rudimentary designs, comlinks offer a host of special features. Some comlinks can be configured to transmit a wide range of data, including secret codes, holographic images, and three-dimensional schematics. The Hush-98 comlink used by Qui-Gon Jinn was even capable of transmitting complex blood sample data. Among the most expensive comlinks, the Hush-98 is also equipped with silence projectors that create a field of white noise around the comlink and its wielder. This field is difficult to penetrate, allowing the comlink's user to communicate in relative security.

Larger comlinks, such as the BCC OmniNode Communications set, are the size of small backpacks. They typically have much greater ranges; can be incorporated into vehicles, such as landspeeders; and include scrambling technology. Comlink technology can also be converted into cybernetic implants. The Traxes BioElectronics Implant Communicator consists of a series of small transceivers concealed just beneath the skin, with clusters located against the skull and next to the vocal cords. The transceivers transmit subvocalized words using a built-in comlink. Cybernetic implant comlinks are susceptible to ion energy and have short ranges, but they are excellent for completely private communication.

❼ Locator: A locator can be placed in a comlink to help the user determine his or her exact position anywhere on a planet's surface.

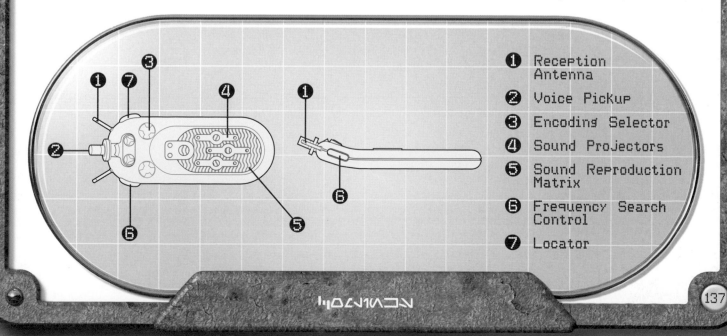

1. Reception Antenna
2. Voice Pickup
3. Encoding Selector
4. Sound Projectors
5. Sound Reproduction Matrix
6. Frequency Search Control
7. Locator

STARSHIP SENSOR ARRAY

Fabritech ANq-51 Sensor Array Computer

No device is more important to modern starship travel and combat than the sensor array. Even the most advanced weapons system and deflector shield generators are completely useless if the host starship fails to identify its enemies. Sensor arrays aid in nearly all starship duties by first gathering information using a variety of sensor types, and then using advanced computer processors to analyze this data.

A simple sensor array needs only three components to function properly: a long-range sensor device that can scan the area around the starship; a computer to evaluate the data the sensor collects; and some sort of display to present the computer's findings in text or graphics. Beyond this basic configuration, sensor arrays display surprising variety, with some starships boasting very specialized arrays.

> ## "Don't worry. With the *Falcon*'s sensors, it's like seeing the future. You'll know where each Imperial fighter is headed before the TIE pilots have made a move."
> —*Lando Calrissian to Nien Nunb before the Battle of Endor*

Large starships and transports have the luxury of carrying multiple sensors, forming arrays that can scan in several different modes. Passive-mode sensors merely gather data from the immediate area around a vessel, while scan-mode sensors (or active sensors) actually send out long-range pulses to collect information from a much wider region. Search-mode sensors can be programmed to scan in a specific direction. Finally, the very accurate focus-mode sensors scrutinize small, defined areas of space.

Full-spectrum transceivers, or "universal sensors," consist of several scanners designed to detect nearly any object, energy emission, or energy field. Short-range electrophoto receptors (EPRs) serve as visual scanners that use a combination of standard, infrared, and ultraviolet telescopes to gather data. Most targeting computers rely on EPRs. Dedicated energy receptors focus on energy emis-

sions, including those created by engines, comm transmissions, heat, and weapon discharges. Sensors can also search for organic materials (life-form indicators), gravitational anomalies (crystal gravfield traps), and hyperspace disturbances (hyperwave signal interceptors).

The *Millennium Falcon* combines many advanced devices to create one of the most formidable sensor arrays in the galaxy. The system is built around a large rectenna dish connected to a Fabritech ANq-51 computer. Along with passive- and scan-mode sensors, the rectenna's scanners include a powerful EPR and a subspace comm detector. The array is supplemented by jamming devices, short-range targeting systems, and an Imperial identification transponder.

Starfighter sensor arrays are designed to be small and light. The X-wing starfighter's Carbanti universal transceiver package fits within the vehicle's nose. The array is energy-efficient, updates rapidly in combat, and can be easily upgraded.

Imperial Star Destroyers actually utilize a variety of sensor arrays, all connected and coordinated by Txs-431 flight-control consoles. Such arrays allowed Imperials to scan fleeing vehicles for shield status and life-forms, coordinate TIE fighter attacks, and intercept Rebel transmissions.

⑥ Subspace Comm Detector: The rectenna's comm detector can identify the unique energy signatures created by communications devices, allowing Han Solo to pick up basic communications traffic, coded Imperial transmissions, and distress signals.

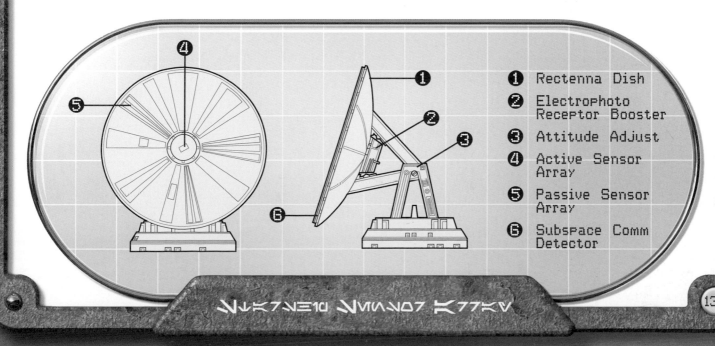

1. Rectenna Dish
2. Electrophoto Receptor Booster
3. Attitude Adjust
4. Active Sensor Array
5. Passive Sensor Array
6. Subspace Comm Detector

PORTABLE SCANNER

Cryoncorp. Enhancescan General-Purpose Scanner

Scanner technology has spread across the galaxy, appearing on nearly all settled planets in various forms. Military applications of scanner technology are endless, resulting in a number of small, portable scanners that can be installed in vehicles or issued to troops. Portable scanners are less powerful and more specialized than starship scanners, but they fulfill basic scanning needs at a fraction of the cost of larger devices.

Used for reconnaissance, scouting, exploration, surveying, and many other functions, portable scanners generally include several types of sensors. The Cyroncorp. EnhanceScan general-purpose scanner used by Rebel Alliance forces on Hoth features a motion sensor, metal scanner, comm scanner, and life-form sensors. Other portable scanners can be configured to detect droids, vehicles, mineral deposits, energy fields and emissions, power generators, and hundreds of other specific items.

> **"There isn't enough life on this ice cube to fill a space cruiser . . ."**
> —*Han Solo on Hoth, shortly before Luke Skywalker is attacked by a wampa*

Early "portable" scanners were fairly large and bulky, requiring repulsor carts. The EnhanceScan, however, is small enough to be carried on a shoulder strap or attached to a soldier's belt. On Hoth, the device was typically used to detect life forms, as well as to monitor comlink signals to help coordinate troop movements or identify potential threats. Technicians within Hoth's Echo Base frequently attached their portable scanners to datapads or droids for more thorough data analysis. Scouts linked the scanners to comlinks in order to broadcast their findings to Alliance command. On other worlds, the Rebels programmed the scanners with up to three hundred different recognition templates, allowing the device to identify specific species, vehicles, and

transmission types as necessary. The device is powered by six rechargeable power cells that allow continuous use for up to ten days.

The EnhanceScan's optimum ranges can vary depending upon planetary conditions. The life-form detector recognizes organics within about fifteen hundred meters; the comm scanner intercepts comlink transmissions within about three kilometers. The motion detector, which is often programmed to sound an alarm for use as an automated camp sentry, has a range of five hundred meters. The metal scanner, useful for locating downed starships or buried equipment, has a maximum range of one hundred meters, although it can be blocked by more than one meter of rock or metal.

The EnhanceScan's computer controls all four scanner modes simultaneously, displaying its findings on a readout screen. The scanner is highly precise, providing exact locations for metal concentrations, moving targets, life-forms, or comm transmissions.

While the EnhanceScan is a multipurpose device, single-purpose scanners also prove very popular. Geologists use specialized scanners that locate geothermal energy, precious minerals, or ore deposits. Sonic scanners amplify sounds at long range and can detect audio signals above and below the user's hearing. Medical scanners identify potential health threats.

8 Life-Form Scanner: Han Solo used the EnhanceScan's life-form scanner to search for Luke Skywalker when the fledgling Jedi was lost in the snowy wastes of Hoth.

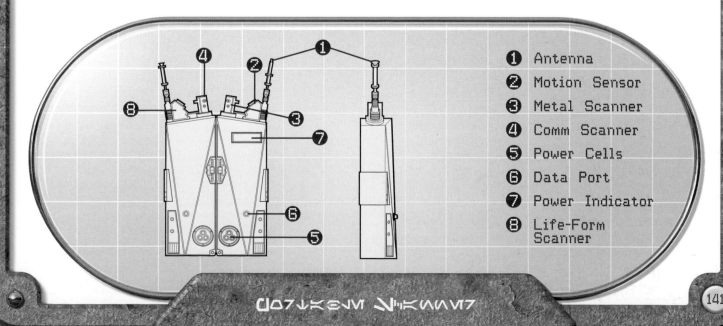

1 Antenna
2 Motion Sensor
3 Metal Scanner
4 Comm Scanner
5 Power Cells
6 Data Port
7 Power Indicator
8 Life-Form Scanner

HoloNet Transceiver

Technical Readout

SIZE: 3 m

EFFECTIVE RANGE: Entire galaxy

PRIMARY MANUFACTURER: SoroSuub

AFFILIATION: Darth Vader's Executor

SoroSuub Hologram Projection Pod

Created during the rule of the Old Republic, long before the rise of the Empire, the HoloNet is a widespread network that transmits communications in holographic and hologramic formats. Prior to the HoloNet, long-range communication was conducted using subspace transmitters, relay stations, and receivers. While such transmissions could eventually travel between the Core Worlds and the Outer Rim, they were slow and unreliable. They allowed audio data but could not transmit real-time communications. The HoloNet represents a major advance in communications technology. HoloNet transmissions comprise moving, three-dimensional images that can cross the galaxy almost instantaneously. The HoloNet was originally used by the Old Republic populace to view Senate meetings, access nearly any information stored in massive data libraries, and communicate "face to face" with loved ones located on the far end of the galaxy.

A HoloNet transmission is initially generated by a standard holorecorder, but then is broadcast via a powerful transceiver. From the transceiver, the HoloNet transmission is funneled through a network of satellites capable of relaying and boosting messages through hyperspace simutunnels. The HoloNet signals travel along very specific channels known as S-threads, designed to carry massive amounts of data. Under the New Republic, the HoloNet network consists of hundreds of thousands of satellites. Once the signal reaches its destination, it is received by another transceiver. The hologram can be decoded and projected by virtually any projection system, ranging from holoprojectors installed in astromech droids to very large projection dish systems found aboard starships. Darth Vader used a SoroSuub hologram projection pod to converse with the Emperor shortly after the Battle of Hoth.

The HoloNet has become the preferred method for long-range galactic communications because of its accessibility and security. Nearly all New Republic worlds possess at least once transceiver for public use. The devices are also installed on many capital ships, including Star Destroyers and Mon Calamari cruisers. Transceivers are typically well guarded to prevent the devices from being bugged or sabotaged, but the signals themselves are virtually impossible to intercept due to their extremely narrow bandwidth. HoloNet messages can also be scrambled through encryption devices; however, this is an unnecessary layer of security used only by the most paranoid.

The HoloNet was widely available to all citizens of the Old Republic. The Empire seized complete control of the network when it took over. By securing the HoloNet, Emperor Palpatine could stop the spread of information about his various evil actions and ensure a steady flow of propaganda through the galaxywide newsnet and other outlets. Imperial forces shut down huge sections of the public HoloNet, using the rest for strictly military purposes. This gave the Empire a significant edge over the Alliance, because Rebel forces were forced to rely on couriers, messengers, and short-range comlinks to communicate with one another. The New Republic has strived to restore the HoloNet to all.

> ### "What is thy bidding, my Master?"
> *—Darth Vader*

❽ **Central Projector:** The projection pod generates a hologram that can be several meters in height. The Emperor used this feature to intimidate his subordinates.

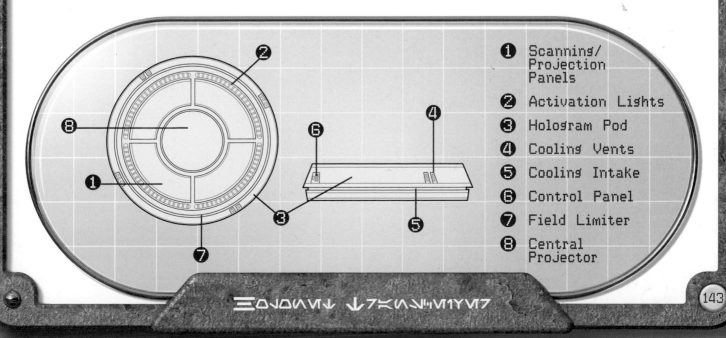

❶ Scanning/ Projection Panels
❷ Activation Lights
❸ Hologram Pod
❹ Cooling Vents
❺ Cooling Intake
❻ Control Panel
❼ Field Limiter
❽ Central Projector

STUN CUFFS

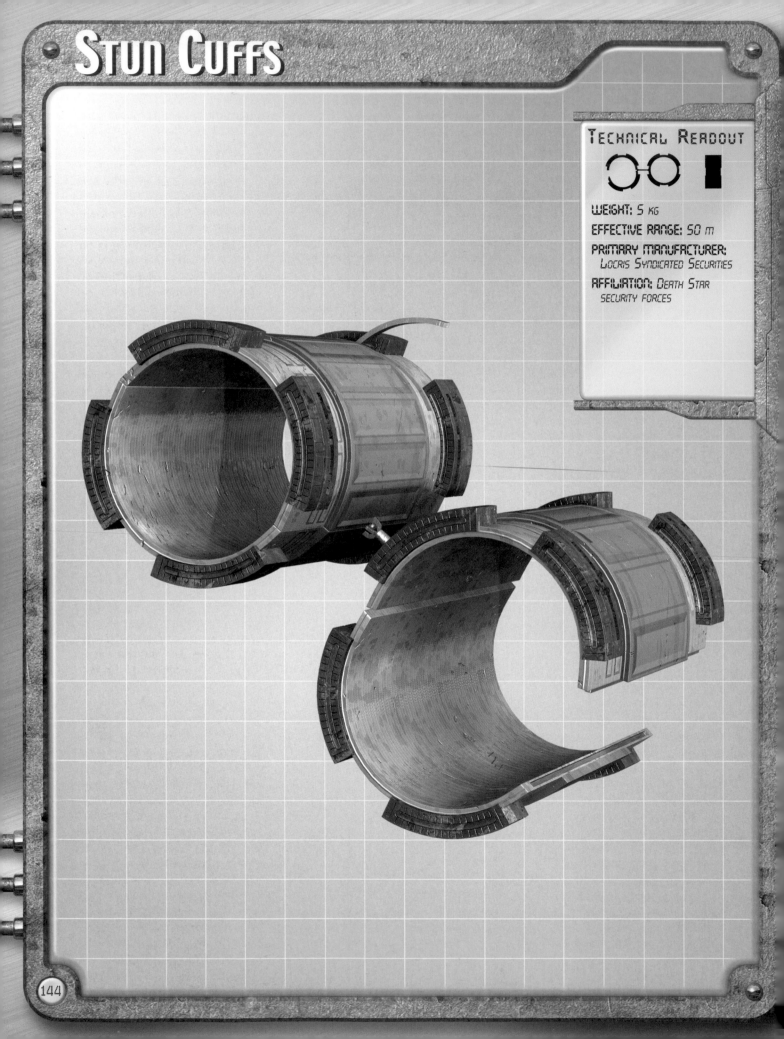

Locris Syndicated Securities SC-401 Stun Cuffs

Stun cuffs are one of several types of restraints used to control captives by binding arms or legs. Stun cuffs and similar devices, such as magnacuffs and binders, are inexpensive yet extremely effective tools found in all prisons and Imperial facilities.

Binders are among the most basic restraints available. Manufactured from extremely resilient durasteel, binders are strong enough to hold a grown Wookiee captive. Different binders have locks of varying complexity. The most primitive use a standard lock-and-key mechanism, while others rely on code inputs, key-code chip readers, or identity scanners.

Magnacuffs represent a slight evolution in binder technology. Nearly identical to binders, magnacuffs enhance their durable construction with miniature micromagnetic field generators. The magnetic field functions as a second locking mechanism, making the cuffs nearly impossible to foil and tripling the durasteel's strength. The magnetic field can be deactivated only through the use of a coded datachip or a scanner that is programmed to identify authorized fingerprints.

Stun cuffs are again one step more advanced than magnacuffs. The restraints feature the magnacuff's magnetic field generators, but also add a series of electrical stun filaments. These stun filaments can be activated by remote control and are designed to render unruly prisoners unconscious.

The Locris Syndicated Securities SC-401 stun cuffs encompass traits possessed by the most successful binders and magnacuffs. Again, durasteel is used to construct the binders, which are designed to be adjustable, allowing them to fit over the wrists of nearly any species from diminutive Ugnaughts to burly, pig-faced Gamorreans. The binders are lined with sensors that cause the wrist cuffs to automatically tighten if the prisoner strains against the device. In extreme cases, the cuffs will tighten until they cut off all circulation to the hands or crush the prisoner's wrists. A channeled magnetic field, superior to the micromagnetic field found on most magnacuffs, reinforces the entire restraint system. The stunning microfilaments include several settings, ranging from a painful jolt meant to force a prisoner back in line, to a paralyzing surge that can render the captive's arms useless, to a rush of stun energy that knocks the victim unconscious.

> ### "Where are you taking this . . . *thing*?"
> —*Imperial Lieutenant Shann Childsen to a disguised Han Solo and Luke Skywalker, upon seeing a cuffed Chewbacca*

Large groups of prisoners can be controlled by a single remote control, each of which is capable of commanding twenty to forty pairs of cuffs at a range of about fifty meters. Individual cuffs can be programmed to activate automatically under specific conditions, such as if the prisoner moves a certain distance from the remote. The remote consists of a small keypad and readout screen used to regulate the stun setting and unlock the binders through a seven-digit master code.

7 Simple Cuff: Stun cuffs look nearly identical to standard binders. Prisoners usually can't tell the difference until they receive a debilitating shock.

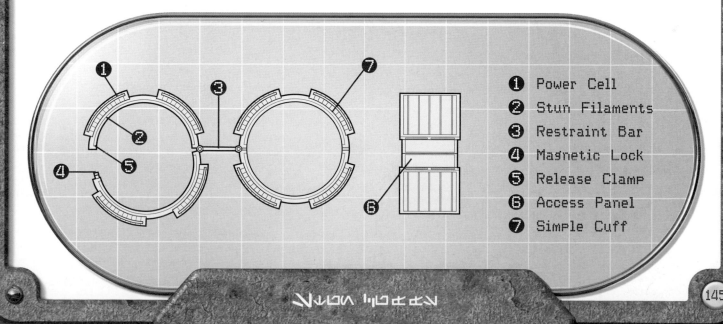

1. Power Cell
2. Stun Filaments
3. Restraint Bar
4. Magnetic Lock
5. Release Clamp
6. Access Panel
7. Simple Cuff

SECURITY SCANNERS

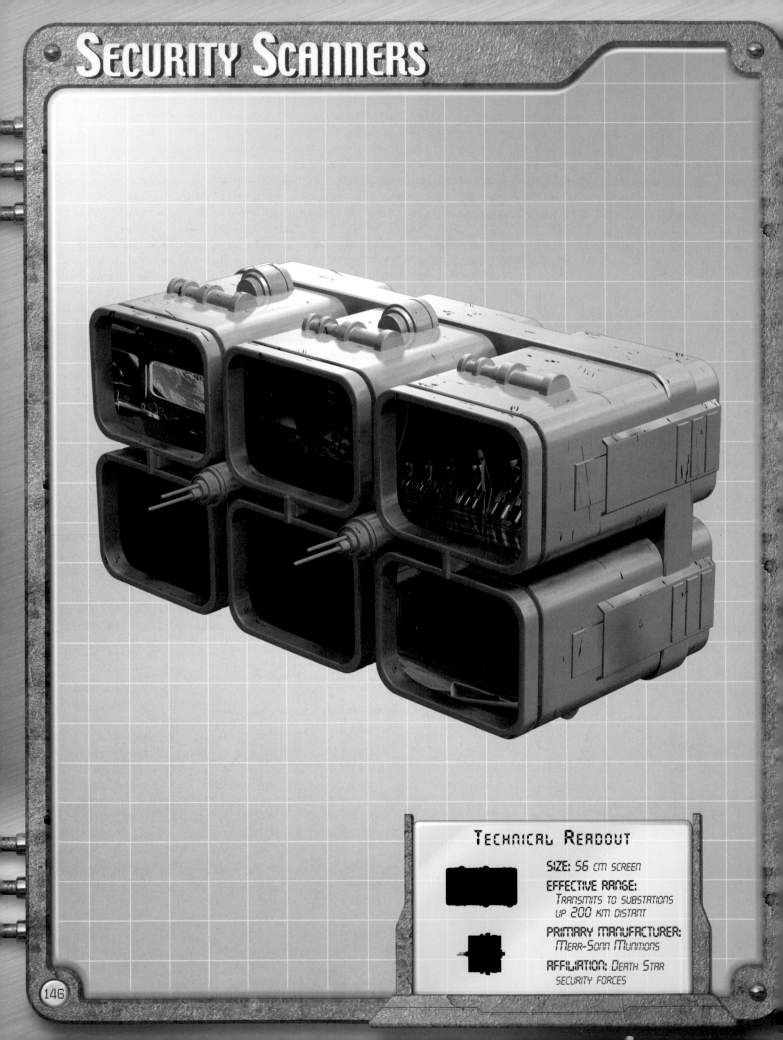

TECHNICAL READOUT

SIZE: 56 cm screen

EFFECTIVE RANGE: Transmits to substations up 200 km distant

PRIMARY MANUFACTURER: Merr-Sonn Munitions

AFFILIATION: Death Star security forces

Merr-Sonn Munitions 57C Holocam

All military bases, prisons, factories, mining operations, and other secure facilities rely heavily on constant surveillance to prevent infiltration (or escape), sabotage, and accidents. The most basic networks consist of a handful of simple visual scanners, but more formidable security webs include motion detectors, heat sensors, weapons detectors, and holographic recorders.

Two-dimensional video scanners are the most common security scanners. They are relatively inexpensive and can be easily installed aboard starships, in other vehicles, in private homes, or along the perimeter of settlements. Such scanners are housed in weatherproof units, allowing them to be used in a wide range of conditions and environments. Video scanners can record both images and sounds, storing these recordings on data disks. Units such as the Merr-Sonn 17C also feature motion tracking systems to allow the devices to follow the movements of targets. Video scanners are controlled from secure stations, where trained personnel or droids review the data feeds and authorize security measures. In many facilities, the video scanners are linked to a variety of preprogrammed security measures, including alarm systems or even automated blasters. Scramblers often encrypt all data transmitted throughout these security networks.

Holographic scanners such as the Merr-Sonn 57C holocam capture far more detail than standard video scanners. A holoscanner records an actual holographic image of its targets, allowing technicians and authorities to review subjects in far more detail. In a single, high-security area, these scanners are installed in large banks and in multiple locations to provide 360-degree coverage. Holoscanners captured every movement within the Death Star's detention center, including the brazen rescue of Princess Leia.

Security scanners vary almost as widely as the facilities that use them. Precision scanners are mounted on agile, rapid tracking systems that can rotate in wide arcs. These devices typically include magnification lenses allowing guards to zoom in. In poorly lit areas, guards employ security scanners with ultraviolet and infrared optics. Long-range exterior scanners identify enemies many kilometers away. Aboard the Death Star and in other facilities, scanners are plainly evident, perhaps to deter infiltrators. Smaller, less obvious scanners monitor the activities of one's own troops. Miniaturized scanners can be hidden within devices, such as a comlink or datapad, although such scanners have limited range.

While most scanners focus largely on collecting visual data, audio also proves important. A standard video scanner may record the audio in the area directly around the scanner, but long-range scanners contain more powerful audio sensors. These unidirectional devices can capture conversations at a great distance. Darth Vader's forces frequently employed such scanners to root out Rebel sympathizers on the planet Ralltiir.

> **"We broke into Leia's cell, and the next day, our faces were all over Imperial HoloNet channels. Those holocams don't miss anyone."**
> —*Luke Skywalker*

7 Explosive Screen: Security scanners are not designed for use in major combat, and the screens will explode violently if hit by a blaster bolt. Han Solo used this weakness to clear out many of the security scanners in Death Star Detention Block AA-23.

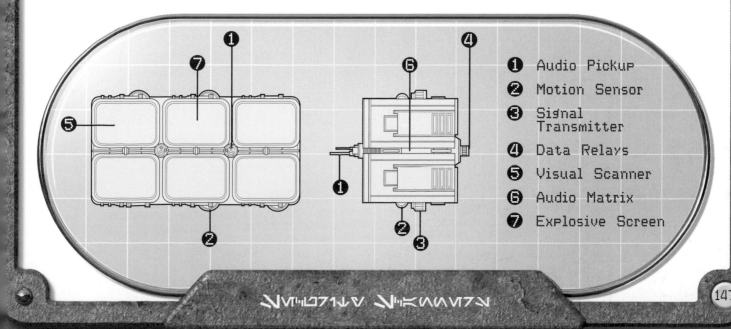

1. Audio Pickup
2. Motion Sensor
3. Signal Transmitter
4. Data Relays
5. Visual Scanner
6. Audio Matrix
7. Explosive Screen

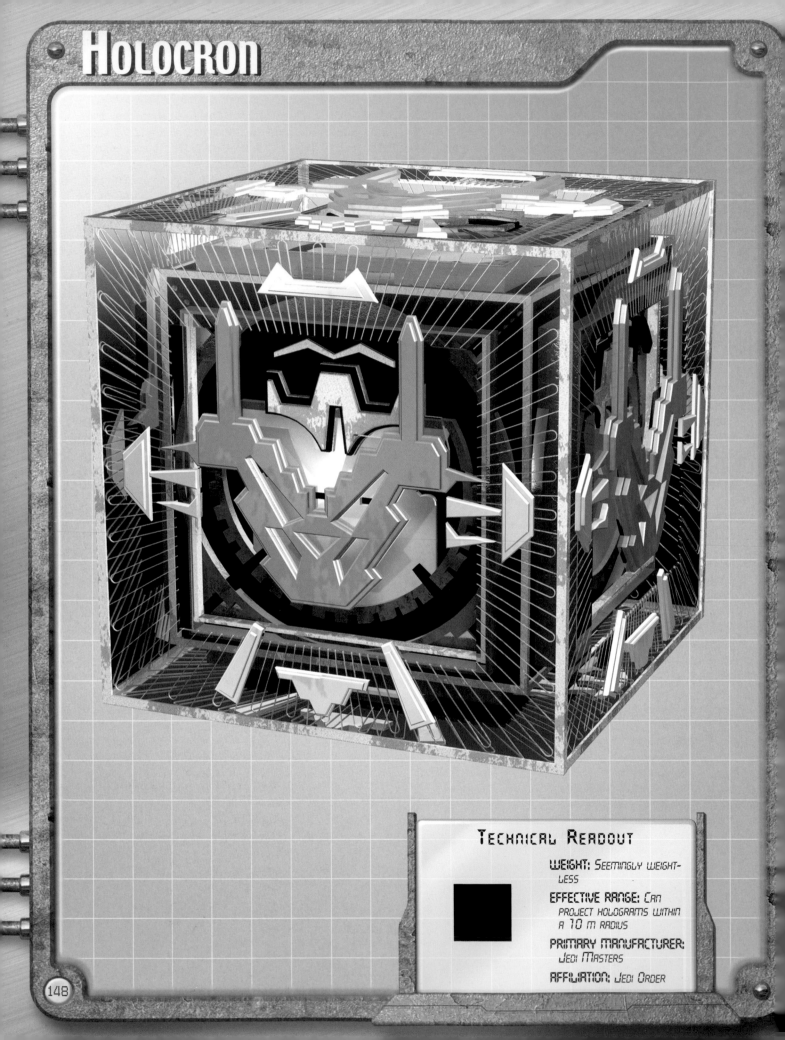

Technical Readout

WEIGHT: Seemingly weightless

EFFECTIVE RANGE: Can project holograms within a 10 m radius

PRIMARY MANUFACTURER: Jedi Masters

AFFILIATION: Jedi Order

Handcrafted Jedi Holocron

Eons before the rise of the Empire, Old Republic inventors developed a means to record and project holograms using a complex crystal latticework. This crystal technology seemed to yield an unlimited storage capacity and did not require an independent power source. However, producing these items proved incredibly difficult, and the devices themselves were challenging to use. The experimental "holocrons" were abandoned in favor of more conventional data tools, such as datapads. But the Jedi embraced the devices, which harbored their secrets for millennia.

Palm-size, glowing cubes constructed of crystal, each Jedi Holocron is infused with the teachings of a single Jedi Master. Young Jedi can use the Force to activate a Holocron, at which point a hologram of the Jedi Master appears. The hologram interacts with the student as if it were a living being, even if the particular Jedi Master has been dead for centuries. The hologram can ask questions, evaluate a student's performance, and share virtually any knowledge the Jedi possessed. Jedi Holocrons are powered by the Force.

Four thousand years before the Battle of Yavin, Jedi Master Vodo-Siosk Baas was the keeper of the powerful Tedryn Holocron, which he used to train his students. After his death, Baas's teachings were preserved in this device. Baas's Holocron eventually fell into the hands of Princess Leia and was then used by Luke Skywalker to train his students on Yavin 4. Sadly, the spirit of Dark Jedi Exar Kun destroyed this Holocron.

The most powerful of all Jedi Holocrons was the Great Holocron, which the Jedi Order kept in its archives

> **"Strike us down, and the Jedi will continue to live on. In memory moths and history books, in Holocrons and the power of the unifying Force, we will always survive."**
> —*Eeth Koth*

on Coruscant prior to the rise of the Empire. The Great Holocron was a crystal dodecahedron and allegedly held the teachings of the greatest Jedi who ever lived. Its fate remains unknown, although it is presumed that the artifact was destroyed or stolen during the Jedi Purge.

The evil Sith also developed sinister versions of the devices. Sith Holocrons are generally small pyramids that radiate a reddish glow. Nearly all Sith Holocrons contain the personalities of multiple Sith, who continue to squabble and compete long after their deaths. Freedon Nadd, Count Dooku, Darth Sidious, and Darth Bane all used Sith Holocrons to expand their powers and knowledge. Darth Maul also used secrets hidden in his Master's Sith Holocron to build his double-bladed lightsaber.

The most powerful Sith Holocron contained Sith teachings and histories that covered some hundred thousand years. Nearly five thousand years before the Emperor's reign, Jedi Master Odan-Urr recovered this "Dark Holocron" as the Sith Empire crumbled. The Dark Holocron and other Sith artifacts were secreted away in Jedi vaults on Coruscant. The Dark Holocron was taken by Jedi Lorian Nod, who maintained that he saw "true evil" when he accessed the device. Motivated by Nod's claims, Dooku later used the Sith Holocron as well, unlocking its secrets in preparation for his transformation into Darth Tyranus. The Dark Holocron's current whereabouts remains a mystery.

6 Etchings: Holocrons vary in appearance based on the Jedi who created them, but many are covered in intricate designs and etchings.

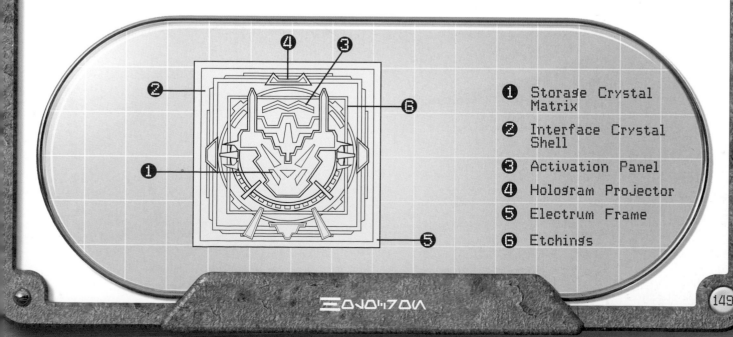

1. Storage Crystal Matrix
2. Interface Crystal Shell
3. Activation Panel
4. Hologram Projector
5. Electrum Frame
6. Etchings

TECHNICAL READOUT

SIZE: *Cone of energy about 2.5 m tall*

EFFECTIVE RANGE: *Up to 40 m (remote control)*

PRIMARY MANUFACTURER: *Gordarl Weaponsmiths*

AFFILIATION: *Geonosians*

Gordarl Weaponsmiths Containment Field Generator

Despite their role as weapons contractors and developers, the Geonosians have a reputation of being fiercely isolationist. In order to keep their planet safe from invaders, the Geonosians have conjured a number of weapons, security systems, and containment devices specifically designed for use against alien species. Among the most notable of these is the Geonosian containment field, a contraption that is well suited to restraining virtually any prisoner, including a powerful Jedi such as Obi-Wan Kenobi.

The Geonosian containment field generator consists of two glowing orbs laced with complex circuitry. One of these orbs is installed on the floor of a rocky Geonosian cell, while the other hangs from the cell's ceiling. These orbs generate magnetic energy in opposing polarity in order to create a "magnetic bottle" that can contain enemies. A victim is forced to wear unlinked, metallic cuffs on his or her wrists and ankles. When caught in the flow of magnetic energy, the cuffs cause the victim to levitate a few centimeters from the ground, effectively suspending the prisoner within the containment field. All but the strongest captives find it impossible to move their limbs against the force of the magnetic field. The cuffs serve other functions as well: they monitor life signs and can emit stun charges similar to those created by stun cuffs.

The Geonosian containment field was of special interest to Count Dooku because of its ability to restrain Jedi. Along with the magnetic field, the generators produce a random pattern of electrical impulses. These manifest as visible electrical energy signatures snaking across the field's exterior. The electrical interference has a direct impact on the victim's brain, disrupting concentration

> ## "It may be difficult to secure your release . . ."
> —*Count Dooku to Obi-Wan Kenobi*

and causing mild pain at its lowest setting. When used on normal subjects, the electrical surges can slowly strip away all willpower. As a result, the field is an excellent tool for interrogation. Prolonged exposure to the field can cause irreparable brain damage that will permanently alter the victim's short- and long-term memory, self-control, and even speech functions. When used against a Jedi, the impulses disrupt the captive's connection to the Force by preventing the intense concentration necessary for using any Force powers. Although it may require weeks, a Geonosian containment field is capable of stripping away all of a Jedi's defenses.

The Geonosian containment field generator is costly and requires its own dedicated power generator. It must also be installed in an isolated cell, because other nearby technology can disturb the delicate magnetic field. This makes it impractical for incarcerating most prisoners. Geonosian jailers use the containment field only for particularly dangerous or powerful captives.

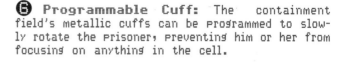

6 Programmable Cuff: The containment field's metallic cuffs can be programmed to slowly rotate the prisoner, preventing him or her from focusing on anything in the cell.

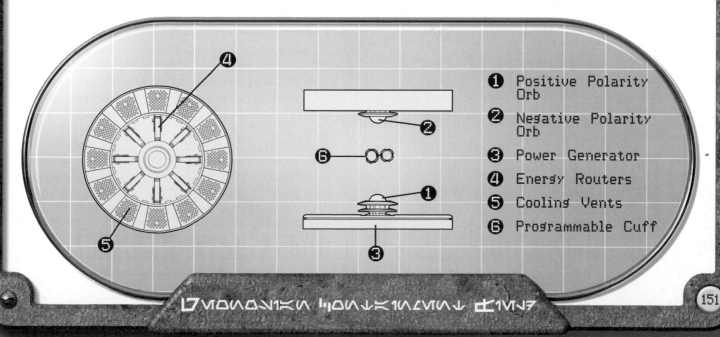

1. Positive Polarity Orb
2. Negative Polarity Orb
3. Power Generator
4. Energy Routers
5. Cooling Vents
6. Programmable Cuff

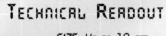

TECHNICAL READOUT

SIZE: Up to 10 cm

EFFECTIVE RANGE: Can receive signals from up to 10 km

PRIMARY MANUFACTURER: Yuuzhan Vong shapers

AFFILIATION: Yuuzhan Vong slavers

Yuuzhan Vong Yorik-Kul

The Yuuzhan Vong are well known for developing bioengineered creatures that can be implanted within the bodies of their fierce warriors. More disturbing, however, is the species' proclivity for subjecting their enemies and captives to this horrifying and destructive process. While warriors receive armor and weapons implants, prisoners must suffer under the influence of such devices as the coral restraining implant. Also known by the Yuuzhan Vong as yorik-kul, coral restraining implants are inserted into the body of a captive, who is then completely controlled by the bioengineered creature.

Like the coralskipper and several other Yuuzhan Vong inventions, the coral restraining implant is cultivated from biologically refined coral reefs. A mature yorik-kul is only a few centimeters in diameter and resembles a sharp fragment of glistening black coral. The creature can be surgically implanted (or forcibly shoved) into a victim's body, usually through the neck. Once implanted, the coral begins to reproduce within the host, generating millions of microscopic offspring. These microbes travel through the victim's bloodstream and infect every cell.

As they spread, the coral implant's offspring actually begin to mutate on a genetic level. Each coral spawn alters based on the type of cell it has infiltrated: the genetic sequence of a microbe living within a blood cell, for instance, is vastly different from the makeup of a creature that has infected a neuron. Despite these drastic mutations, the coral spawn remain intimately connected to the original coral implant. In many ways, the millions of coral spawn combine with the coral implant and the host to form a single, compound organism. After

> ### "Some say the coral implants ruin our slaves. Only the weak ones."
> —*Yuuzhan Vong slaver*

prolonged exposure to a coral implant, it becomes virtually impossible to distinguish where the Yuuzhan Vong creature begins and the host ends. The Yuuzhan Vong's victim is controlled by impulses sent from the coral restraining implant. These impulses reach infected cells instantaneously and can force the host to respond.

The coral restraining implants have wide-ranging and debilitating effects on victims. Soon after implantation, the host begins to lose any sense of reason or independent thought, becoming a mindless drone. Prolonged exposure causes physical decay as the microbes sap the victim's energy and health, destroying countless cells in the process. The implant can also sever a being's connection to the Force.

The Yuuzhan Vong eventually realized that the extreme effects of the coral implants were robbing them of valuable slave labor: prisoners too weak or stupid to work are useless. Many coral implants have been modified to simply infect pain receptors or muscle cells. This allows Yuuzhan Vong slavers to inflict excruciating pain or complete paralysis to control workers, but does not threaten a slave's efficiency.

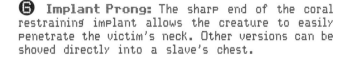

6 Implant Prong: The sharp end of the coral restraining implant allows the creature to easily penetrate the victim's neck. Other versions can be shoved directly into a slave's chest.

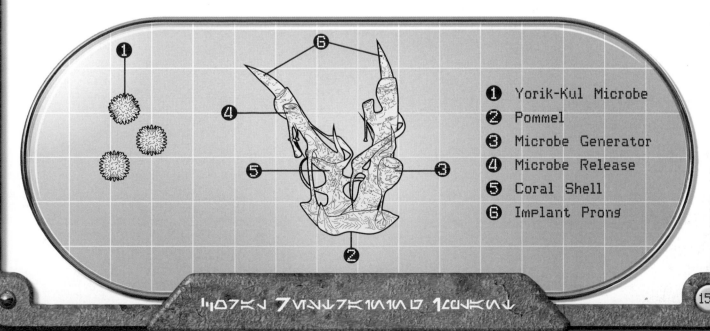

1 Yorik-Kul Microbe
2 Pommel
3 Microbe Generator
4 Microbe Release
5 Coral Shell
6 Implant Prong

VILLIP

TECHNICAL READOUT

SIZE: 20 cm tall

EFFECTIVE RANGE: Unknown, but believed to be unlimited

PRIMARY MANUFACTURER: Yuuzhan Vong shapers

AFFILIATION: Yuuzhan Vong slavers

Yuuzhan Vong Villip

The Yuuzhan Vong rely heavily on efficient and reliable communications devices to coordinate troop movements and orchestrate attacks. However, while the New Republic utilizes "hard-tech" tools for its communication needs, the Yuuzhan Vong utilize a bioengineered organic communication device known as a villip.

Yuuzhan Vong shapers cultivate villip colonies in large paddies. The villip plant is recognized by three triangular blue leaves and a long stalk growing out of the center of the organism. The stalk sprouts between two and five round berries, each roughly the size of a human head. These berries eventually mature into adult villips. On the surface, a mature villip resembles a fist-size mollusk covered in a ridged, leathery, and membranous tissue. A hole reminiscent of an empty eye socket forms a small break on the creature's back. Villips can mold their own appearance, but their true strength is their ability to join consciousness with one another. A pair of villips connected on a conscious level can communicate even across vast distances of space. This feature allows two Yuuzhan Vong to hold long-range conversations.

Villips are typically stored in private chambers, where they are displayed on yorik coral blastulae. A Yuuzhan Vong merely needs to stroke the creature to activate it, at which point the small hole on the villip's back puckers to absorb its master's voice. The villip can invert its body around this empty socket, shape-shifting to conjure the appearance and voice of the villip-joined Yuuzhan Vong with whom its master is communicating. Villips bend hyperspace in order to send transmissions to one another. Yuuzhan Vong conversations can therefore occur instantaneously and in real time, despite distance. The bizarre nature of the transmissions prevents them from being interrupted or monitored.

Because they can survive the vacuum of space, villips can be used to send messages between Yuuzhan Vong starships. Such villips record a message and are then shot into space at a target starship. A spacefaring villip collides with its target and is absorbed by the Yuuzhan Vong craft, only to reappear within the starship in order to relay its message. Master villips are exceedingly large creatures capable of communicating with smaller subordinate villips. Master villips are typically used by high-ranking Yuuzhan Vong, including priests and commanders, to communicate with subordinates. Villip choirs are similar to the master villip organism, but they use their buds to simply collect visual data. To display this data, all components of a villip choir work together to broadcast a panoramic video image. The Yuuzhan Vong have also modified villips for use over New Republic communications channels and can even implant the devices into a victim's skull in order to "steal" thoughts.

> **"When we entered the villip paddy on Belkadan, I could hear the villip buds whispering to one another. I know they were talking about us."**
> —*Luke Skywalker*

5 **Eversion Stoma:** The stoma is a break in the villip's tissue that resembles an eye socket. The stoma functions as the villip's mouth and is also the focal point for the creature's shape-shifting.

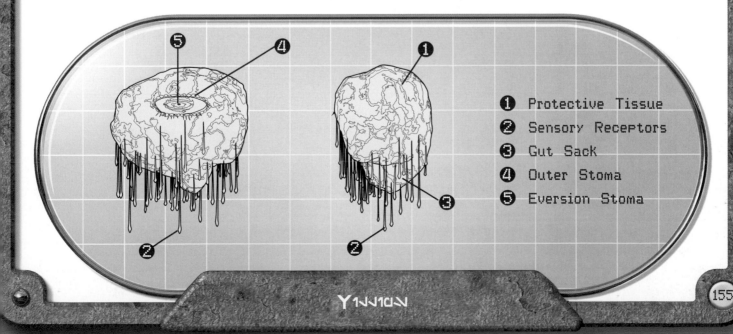

1 Protective Tissue
2 Sensory Receptors
3 Gut Sack
4 Outer Stoma
5 Eversion Stoma

Cognition Hood

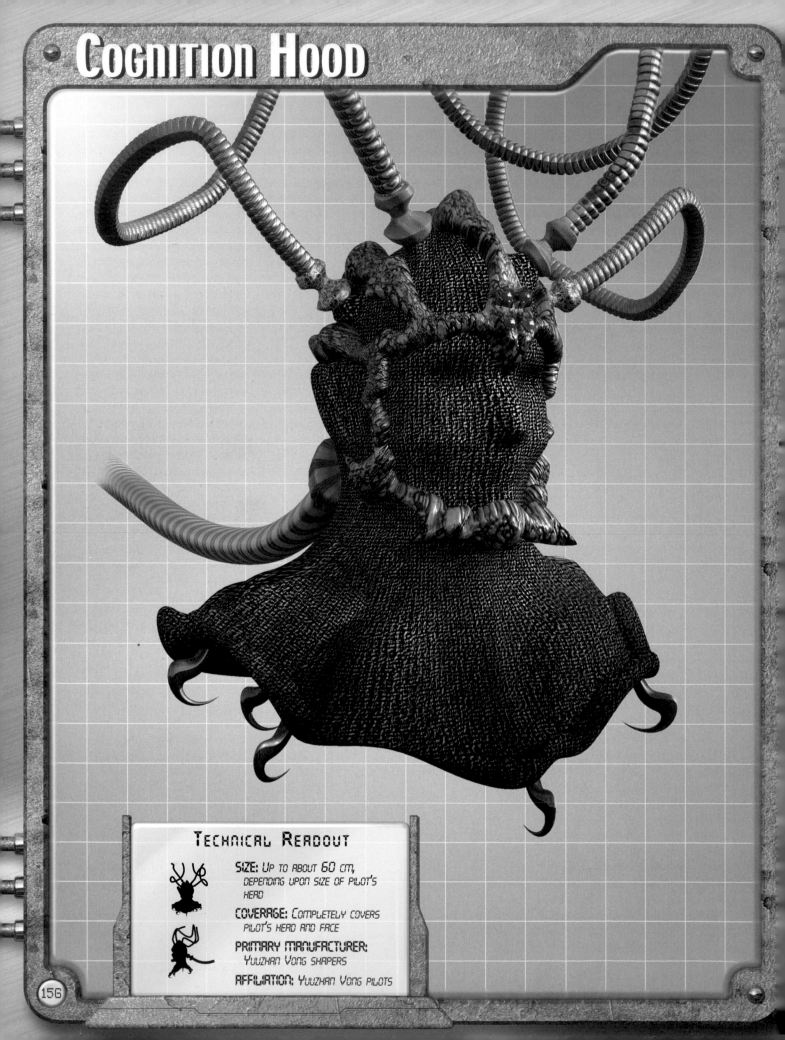

TECHNICAL READOUT

SIZE: Up to about 60 cm, depending upon size of pilot's head

COVERAGE: Completely covers pilot's head and face

PRIMARY MANUFACTURER: Yuuzhan Vong Shapers

AFFILIATION: Yuuzhan Vong Pilots

Yuuzhan Vong Tall-Yor

The Yuuzhan Vong starships are bred to carry pilots and their crews across the galaxy and into battle. In order to communicate with these organic vessels, the Yuuzhan Vong have developed a unique symbiote known as the cognition hood.

Found aboard nearly every Yuuzhan Vong starship, cognition hoods resemble loose, leather bags covered in a gelatinous ooze. Until worn, cognition hoods do not move or indicate any signs of life. When placed over a pilot's head, however, a cognition hood immediately begins to undulate and squirm. The organism adjusts its body and thin flesh, shrinking until it completely covers the Yuuzhan Vong's face and skull.

The cognition hood is not sentient and does not distinguish Yuuzhan Vong from other species. It is merely a means of communication between a pilot and a living starship. A Yuuzhan Vong wearing a cognition hood will hear the craft speaking in the Yuuzhan Vong language. A starship can relate its status, issue reports on collected data, and raise alarms through the cognition hood. The pilot, in turn, can issue orders to the vehicle by merely speaking into the hood. It is still unclear whether the bioengineered starships actually speak and understand the Yuuzhan Vong tongue, or whether the cognition hood is designed to translate a vehicle's data readouts. New Republic engineers suspect the latter.

Non–Yuuzhan Vong can don cognition hoods, although they serve very little purpose. The cognition hood only transmits in Yuuzhan Vong, a language that very few in the New Republic have managed to grasp. Anakin Solo attempted to communicate through a cog-

nition hood using a tizowyrm, a Yuuzhan Vong translation tool. Unfortunately, even with the tizowyrm firmly implanted in his ear, Anakin was unable to speak the Yuuzhan Vong language. Even with an understanding of the Yuuzhan Vong language, attempting to communicate through a cognition hood can be disconcerting. Jedi Knight Tahiri Veila eventually learned Yuuzhan Vong and was able to don a cognition hood in order to fly a Yuuzhan Vong starship. However, she began hearing several voices in her head, all of them urging her to abandon her mission. The voices distracted Tahiri, forcing her to remove the device. New Republic researchers also believe that the cognition hoods react to precise and subtle physical movements that are difficult for non–Yuuzhan Vong to emulate.

While cognition hoods are primarily designed as an interface between pilot and ship, the organisms have a handful of other features. Advanced cognition hoods can store memories captured from the pilot or the starship. These memories can be replayed later, allowing another Yuuzhan Vong to experience them. Cognition hoods can also reach out to other hoods, forming a tight network that enables precise formations and coordinated attacks. Slave transports are almost always networked to coralskipper escorts to prevent the larger vessels from straying off course.

> **"You do not understand us. We do not just *talk* to our starfighters. We *become* our starfighters."**
> —*Captured Yuuzhan Vong pilot*

6 **Umbilical:** The cognition hood is actually an organic extension of its host starship and not a separate organism. It is connected to a vehicle via a flexible umbilical that transmits communications and nutrients.

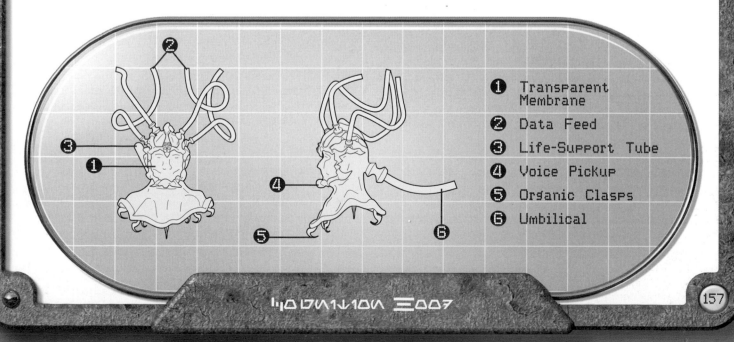

1. Transparent Membrane
2. Data Feed
3. Life-Support Tube
4. Voice Pickup
5. Organic Clasps
6. Umbilical

Additional Sensor, Communications & Security Devices

Although galactic paranoia reached its height under the Emperor's rule, denizens of the Old Republic have always been intent on protecting their privacy and security. This section contains a cross section of devices used by private citizens, local governments, and the military for scanning, spying, and security.

Anti-Register Device

A rare tool that enables the user to crack into any print-reliable security system. The only known anti-register device was destroyed during the liberation of the planet Phindar.

Bioscan

Any of a number of devices capable of scanning an object in order to determine the target's biological makeup, origin, age, and other factors. Bioscans rely on both hardware and software to detect anomalies created by cybernetic implants, energy cells, weapons, and transmitters. The devices are used by medical staff to locate any health problems and by security personnel to scan for concealed weapons and contraband.

Caller

A small, handheld transmitter used to summon droids. Callers can also activate a droid's restraining bolt.

Clone Trooper Learning Helmet

A special helmet worn by maturing clones on Kamino during their studies. The helmet included a mental receptivity enhancer to help the clones process the massive amounts of new data they received on a daily basis. The helmet's durable plastoid construction allowed it to be worn during combat exercises.

Com-scan

A standard scanner that can detect energy generated by communications signals. Com-scans allow military commanders to identify enemy communications lines and triangulate enemy positions based on these broadcasts. The Rebel Alliance used a MicroThrust Orc-19 Com-Scan console at both the Battle of Yavin and the Battle of Hoth.

Creeper

A Yuuzhan Vong bioengineered creature that is used to control slaves. The small, gray creature has six legs and carries dozens of seeds along its dorsal shell. The creeper uses feathery frondlike appendages to disrupt a victim's nervous system, causing terrible pain and disabling the target. Then the creeper implants its seeds, which begin to grow. Anyone carrying these seeds can be paralyzed by Yuuzhan Vong slavemasters.

Cybernetic Implant Comlink/Pager

A cybernetic implant that functions as a comlink. The implant consists of a vocalizer implanted in the throat and a short-range transponder located on the neck.

Data Goggles

A Neimoidian device that provides pilots with real-time holographic displays of starship system updates, sensor readings, data uplinks from ship-based droids, and other information. Data goggles include a cybernetic implant that provides direct access to the starship's central computer, allowing the pilot to activate systems with a simple thought. Neimoidians have jealously guarded schematics for data goggles, ensuring that few non-Neimoidian pilots have ever used the device.

Electronic Lock Breaker

An antisecurity slicing device that can override alarms and open all but the most sophisticated computerized locks. Jango Fett owned a lock breaker with the ability to bypass security codes based on complex algorithms. Although closely regulated, electronic lock breakers are carried by many slicers, criminals, espionage agents, bounty hunters, and thieves.

Embrace of Pain

A creature bioengineered by the Yuuzhan Vong as a teaching tool, but that could be used to both restrain and torture prisoners (though the Yuuzhan Vong did not see it as torture). The Embrace of Pain resembles a living rack, with its prisoner suspended facedown by restraint bands. When the victim is tortured, the creature's sophisticated nerve web reads the electrochemical output of the victim's nerve impulses and evaluates the victim's brain chemistry. The Embrace of Pain uses this data to keep pain at constant and optimum levels. Some Yuuzhan Vong have been known to subject themselves to the Embrace of Pain as a meditative technique.

Holocube

A small cube that contains static three-dimensional, holographic images. Holocubes are used to store maps, schematics, and personal images.

Inhibition Field

A force field used by the Yuuzhan Vong to hold prisoners. The field is maintained by dovin basals, mind-boggling Yuuzhan Vong creatures that can create miniature black holes and are found on most Yuuzhan Vong craft.

Irradiators

Round lighting devices that emit narrow bands of energy that can kill bacteria, viruses, and microscopic organisms before they can attack or infect other lifeforms. Irradiators, which often double as interior lighting, are found in nearly all spaceports and aboard many transports, including *Millennium Falcon*.

Jedi Reader

One of the Emperor's tools for exposing Force-sensitive beings across the galaxy. Also known as a Force detector, a Jedi reader consists of two silvery paddles and a small readout display. The device is powered by thaissen crystals found only on the planet Mimban. These crystals glow lightly when in close proximity to Force-sensitive individuals. When the paddles are passed over a Force-sensitive individual, the crystals activate.

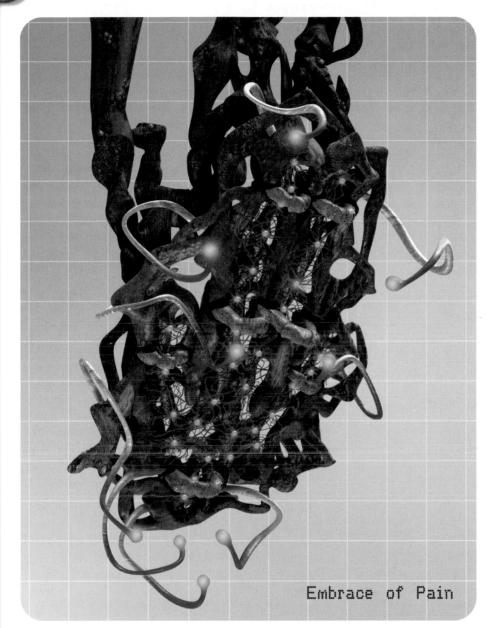

Embrace of Pain

Homing Beacon

A small device that emits an encoded signal even across hyperspace. Homing beacons are hidden aboard starships to allow constant tracking of these "bugged" vessels. The Empire used homing beacons to locate hidden Rebel bases, including the base on Yavin 4.

Identichip

A common form of identification. Also known as an ID card or identity chit, the indentichip is designed to adhere easily to a piece of clothing and can be scanned by basic countertop readers. Some organizations, such as Vannix Intelligence, use indentichips with unique seals.

Laser Gate

An energy barrier used to block entry into high-security or dangerous areas, such as the Theed power generator complex on Naboo. The energy created by a laser gate can vaporize anything that attempts to pass through the barrier.

Magna Lock

A device that harnesses and shapes micromagnetic fields. Magna locks operate on a molecular scale, essentially creating molecular bonds that hold two items (such as a door and a door frame) in place.

Man Trap

One of the most effective incarceration tools ever invented, a man trap uses a reverse repulsorlift generator to generate a gravity field that immobilizes targets but does not damage them in any way.

Nerve Disruptor

An Imperial torture and interrogation device that resembles a small, three-legged droid. The nerve disruptor is equipped with a variety of needles and microfilament injectors to deliver drugs (including truth serums) and trigger pain responses in sensitive nerve clusters. Nerve disruptors can induce spasms along with altered states of consciousness, but the device's droid brain monitors vital signs to ensure that the victim remains alive until interrogation is complete.

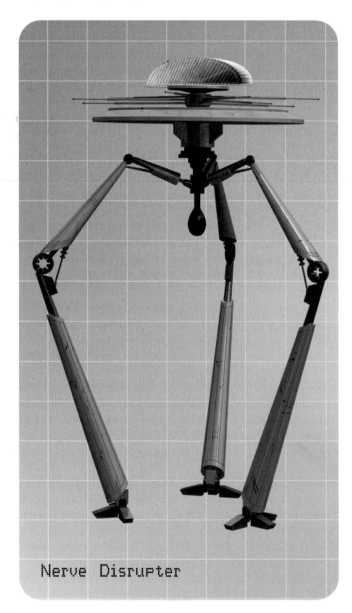

Nerve Disrupter

Rank Cylinder

A standard security access tool used to identify rank and verify security clearance. Imperial officers used rank cylinders, also known as Imperial code cylinders, to gain access to sensitive areas or information. At checkpoints, the cylinder is inserted into a scomp link access that reads the cylinder's encrypted computer codes and verifies these with the facility's central computer. Many high-ranking Imperials carried up to four cylinders.

Recording Rod

A long, clear, and cylindrical tube used to record and play back audio and visual images. Recording material appears as two-dimensional images on the recording rod's surface, and data is stored on chips or storage crystals.

Restraining Bolt

A round device that can be attached to a droid to override its motor functions and enslave the robot. The restraining bolt monitors the droid's activity and can automatically disable the droid if it strays from its programmed duties. A restraining bolt can also be keyed to a caller.

Sand-buzzer

A Tatooine security device that emits an electronic field capable of driving away small vermin. Many moisture farmers surround their homesteads with sand-buzzers.

Sensor Beacon

A standard security scanner and alarm system deployed around large tracts of land, such as farms, airfields, and shipyards. Each sensor beacon is armed with a variety of scanners, including motion sensors and visual recorders designed to watch for unwanted visitors. Sensor beacons are linked directly to a command station where collected data can be processed. A carefully placed network of sensor beacons can replace energy fences or armed patrols. The Rebel Alliance frequently surrounded its hidden bases with sensor beacons.

Sensor Tag

A tiny homing beacon that can be discreetly attached to a target's clothing or belongings.

Slaving Collar

A brutal security device used to control slaves and other prisoners. A slaving collar includes an adjustable neck brace, usually connected to heavy chains or cables. It can also be equipped with shock panels that deliver electrical charges at the slavemaster's command. Princess Leia was forced to wear a slaving collar after she was captured by Jabba the Hutt.

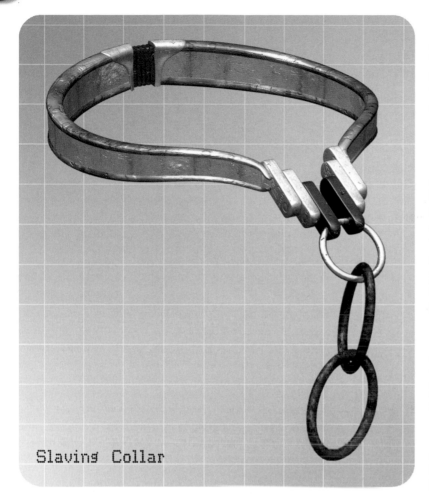
Slaving Collar

TRANSFER REGISTER

An electro-optical device that documents the sale or trade of property and merchandise. A transfer register records the thumbprints of buyers and sellers, officially documenting a transaction.

UNIVERSAL ENERGY CAGE

A floating confinement cell designed to hold powerful prisoners, including Jedi. The cage generates an energy force field that can disrupt a Jedi's connection to the Force. The force field automatically intensifies as energy is applied against it. The cage also possesses automatic stun charges activated whenever the prisoner touches the cage's bars.

UNIVERSAL JAMMER

A versatile sensor countermeasure that can foil the most common scanners. Universal jammers are extremely expensive, yet they fail to jam specialized scanning devices.

VOCAL ENHANCER

A device that can enhance vocal cords, increasing the volume of the wearer's voice. Some species with particularly bizarre voices wear specialized vocal enhancers that transform the wearer's voice into something more palatable. Other vocal enhancers are used for disguise.

WEAPONS DETECTOR

A scanner that can detect power cells and clearly identifiable weapons profiles. Weapons detectors are used in restricted facilities such as military bases, detention centers, and spaceports to scan for unauthorized weapons.

WRIST LINK

A multipurpose tool that usually incorporates a comlink with other devices, such as a chrono. The Sith Lord Darth Maul wore a programmable wrist link that enabled him to arm traps and explosives from afar, remotely detonate bombs, and receive signals from a wide range of surveillance equipment, including his Sith probe droids. He could also use it to remotely summon and direct his speeder bike.

SLICER CHIP

A miniaturized version of the electronic lock breaker, specifically modified to hack into computers, droids, and automated devices. The most powerful slicer chips can override vehicle navigation systems and controls, confuse security scanners, or strip a droid's primary programming.

SUBSTANCE ANALYZER

A common scanner that can scan and analyze various substances, usually in search of anomalies. Food analyzers search for toxins, such as poisons.

TIZOWYRM

Yuuzhan Vong bioengineered creatures originally bred to function as universal translators and decoders, allowing Yuuzhan Vong to understand and speak alien languages. Tizowyrms crawl inside a Yuuzhan Vong's ear and emit information to their host subliminally.

OTHER EQUIPMENT

For every blaster and other weapon in use in the galaxy, the worlds of the New Republic are also home to thousands of utilitarian devices. These range from simple hand tools to necessities of life, and from industrial equipment to personal luxury items.

While it's true that the technology found throughout the galaxy has expanded the scope of war and empowered military forces to engage in increasingly more destructive battles, that same technology has also dramatically improved the quality of life for many galactic citizens. Advances in medical technology have extended the life expectancy of many species. Miniaturized computers increase the efficiency and capabilities of everything from vehicles to simple binoculars. A greater understanding of environmental conditions and climate changes allow for specialized equipment to make life bearable anywhere from arid deserts to ice-encrusted arctic regions.

Prior to the advent of hyperspace travel, access to technology was extremely limited. Developed planets were forced to create a wide cross section of devices. Hyperspace travel not only allowed trading of manufactured goods but also led to an exchange of ideas, theories, equipment designs, and scientific discoveries. In the centuries that followed the first hyperspace jumps, technology evolved at a staggering pace.

Alien cultures, in particular, proved integral to the advancement of technology. The unique physiological needs and strange habitats of many species forced them to create devices that humans had never even considered. Human scientists studied and learned from alien technologies, using concepts developed on alien worlds to enhance their own inventions. Exposure to Mon Calamari technology, for example, allowed human designers to develop much more effective underwater engineering equipment.

In general, the worlds of the Old Republic supported and even encouraged the proliferation of technology. Reliable access to miraculous inventions was often touted as one of the benefits of joining the Republic. Unfortunately, corruption within the Old Republic gradually chipped away at the widespread circulation of technology. Large and greedy galactic corporations saw great value in limiting distribution of important technology, especially medical equipment. Republic Senators could be bribed into creating and ratifying complex regulations and trade rules that benefited megacorporations and effec-

tively stopped commerce to many worlds. Outer Rim worlds, including Tatooine, were hit especially hard by the Old Republic's thousands of obscure rules and regulations. The creation of the Trade Federation, the Corporate Sector Authority, and similar organizations only increased these problems. The Hutts and other criminal groups took advantage of the new technology vacuum, creating black markets to sell seemingly innocuous devices at huge markups.

Under the Empire, the situation did not improve noticeably. The Empire did Imperialize many corporations, but these companies were required to produce technology for Imperial forces rather than needy worlds. In the era of the Old Republic, many megacorporations grew wealthy beyond imagining; after the rise of the Empire only Imperial forces and their designated manufacturers profited. The Empire's efforts to contain the Rebel Alliance led to even greater restrictions. Medical supplies, common tools, and even creature comforts were all tightly controlled lest they fall into Rebel hands. Frustration over the Empire's tactics actually encouraged many neglected worlds to join forces with the Rebel Alliance.

The New Republic has once again transformed research and development. Prior to the Yuuzhan Vong invasion, most forms of technology were widely available. Entire worlds were converted into efficient manufacturing facilities, and transports used well-protected hyperspace routes to easily move goods between factories and potential consumers. The New Republic regulated very few nonlethal devices, allowing the demands of free trade and competition to drive innovation.

The Yuuzhan Vong have virtually destroyed the New Republic. Yuuzhan Vong attack craft threatened trade routes, preventing the safe transport of technology. At the height of the war, the Yuuzhan Vong also razed entire worlds once devoted to producing vital goods. Alien cultures were lost, taking their valuable knowledge with them. The New Republic was forced to expend billions of credits to wage war against the Yuuzhan Vong. In the aftermath of the invasion, the New Republic will require many decades of rebuilding before the reliable flow of technology resumes. The only positive aspect of the invasion is the fact that is has exposed the New Republic to incredible, if bizarre, new technology in the form of the Yuuzhan Vong bioengineered devices. It's highly likely that future generations will benefit from this technology in ways that have yet to be imagined.

FUSIONCUTTER

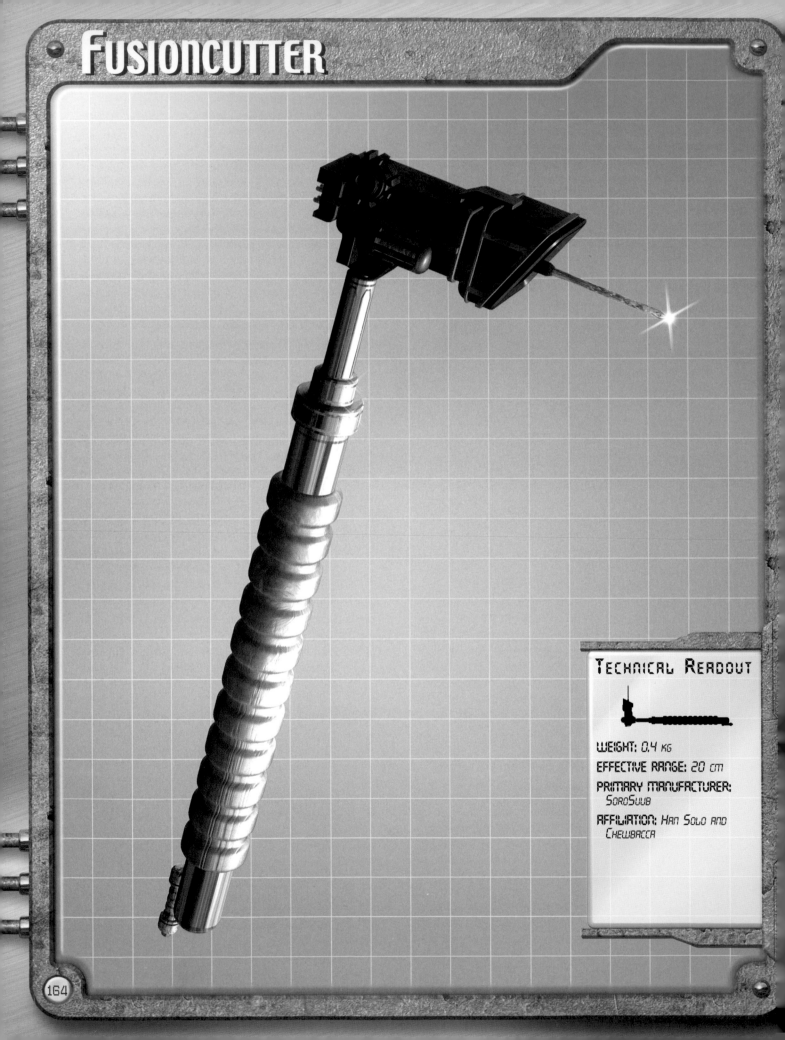

TECHNICAL READOUT

WEIGHT: 0.4 KG

EFFECTIVE RANGE: 20 CM

PRIMARY MANUFACTURER: SoroSuub

AFFILIATION: Han Solo and Chewbacca

SoroSuub F-187 Fusioncutter

Nearly every important device used throughout the New Republic, from droids to starships, relies heavily on hundreds of moving parts. These complex technological devices require constant maintenance and when a key piece of machinery breaks, mechanics or engineers require specialized hand tools to repair the device.

Fusioncutters prove vital to most starship and vehicle repairs. A fusioncutter is basically a small cutting torch that uses a high-energy plasma beam to carve through durasteel and other dense materials. The SoroSuub F-187 fusioncutter is a versatile tool with an adjustable beam. For stripping away large sections of starship hull plating, the beam can be set to create trenches up to twenty centimeters deep and six centimeters wide. During precision work, the device employs a beam only one centimeter deep and a millimeter in width. Most fusioncutters also feature a drill-bit setting that uses a concentrated plasma burst to create deep holes in any surface. Fusioncutters require a small power cell and a fuel cylinder that holds enough fuel for about an hour's worth of work, depending on the size of the beam. Larger versions of the fusioncutter are employed at mining operations, manufacturing facilities, and construction sites. For automated tasks, fusioncutters can be mounted on droid-controlled armatures.

Other significant hand tools include power calibrators and hydrospanners. Useful for evaluating the performance of equipment, especially droids and generators, power calibrators take readings on an appliance's energy output and efficiency. If an energy leak or other flaw is observed, the technician can use the power cal-

> ### "I just got this bucket back together. I'm not going to let something tear it apart."
> —*Han Solo*

ibrator's circuit tester and power flow detector to pinpoint the problem. The power calibrator can also be plugged into datapads, hologram projectors, comlinks, and other small devices, offering an energy supply that can last up to several days. The Udrane Galactic Electronics ReliaCharger power calibrator is also capable of powering a droid for up to ten hours and a landspeeder for nearly thirty minutes.

A hydrospanner is essentially a very advanced socket and bit driver. It is capable of tightening or loosening standard nuts, fuse pins found on droids, powerful fusion bolts necessary for attaching starship hulls, even microscopic molecular screws used on comlinks and other devices. Regallis Engineering produces the aptly named FastTurn-3 hydrospanner. The FastTurn incorporates a hydraulic compression cylinder that mechanically improves the tool's torque, thereby minimizing the amount of energy expended by the user. The FastTurn is equipped with a variable-size socket that can grasp fasteners as small as two millimeters in diameter. Many hydrospanners can also be fitted with special attachments to turn specific types of fasteners, such as large fusion bolts up to twenty-five centimeters in diameter. Some models, including the FastTurn-3, also incorporate a miniature fusioncutter to cut around bolts prior to their removal.

8 Plasma Drill Bit: The drill bit generates a bright beam of energy. Mechanics using a fusioncutter generally wear protective goggles to prevent the beam from causing any optical damage.

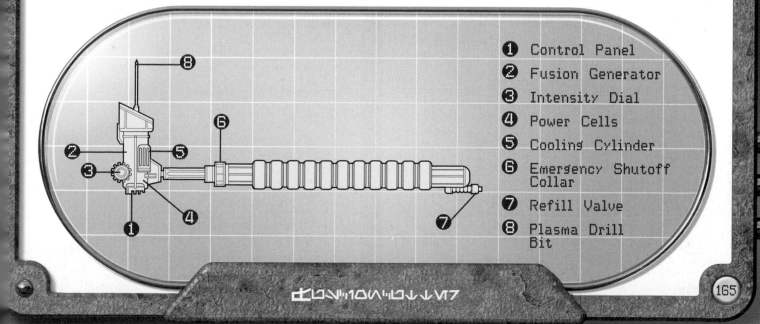

1. Control Panel
2. Fusion Generator
3. Intensity Dial
4. Power Cells
5. Cooling Cylinder
6. Emergency Shutoff Collar
7. Refill Valve
8. Plasma Drill Bit

Vaporator

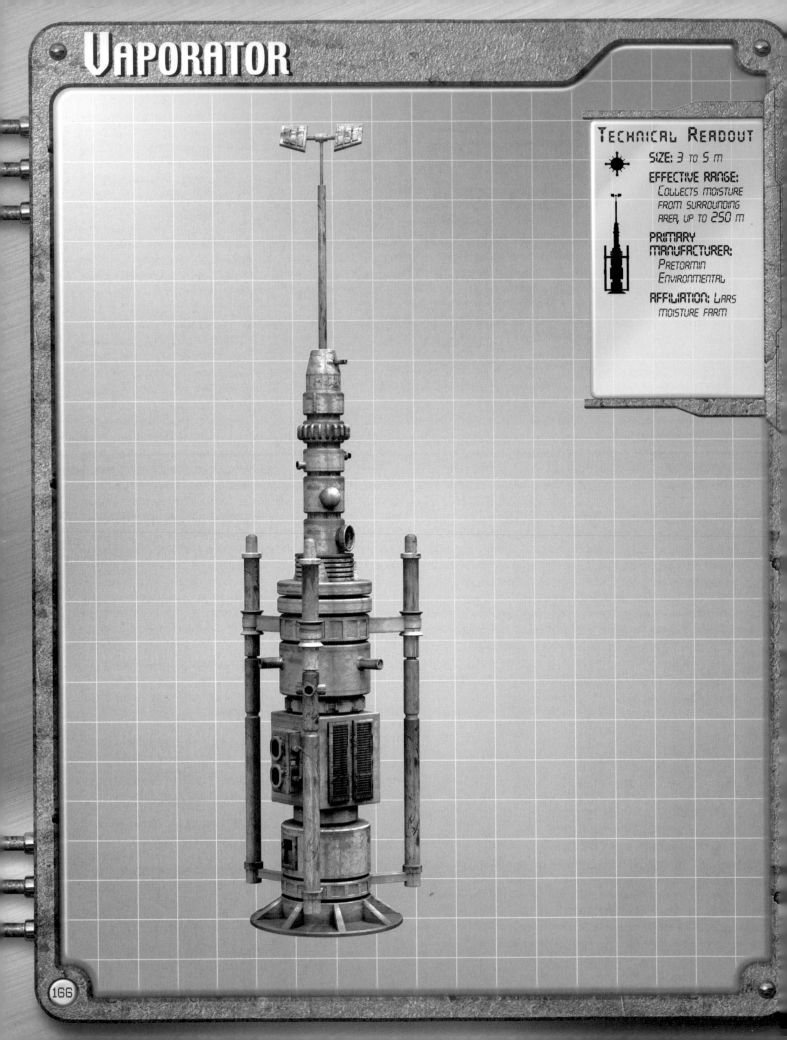

SIZE: 3 to 5 m

EFFECTIVE RANGE: Collects moisture from surrounding area, up to 250 m

PRIMARY MANUFACTURER: Pretormin Environmental

AFFILIATION: Lars moisture farm

Pretormin Environmental GX-8 Water Vaporator

Among the most important technological devices are those that allow colonization of inhospitable worlds. Frost-resistant generators enable survival on frigid planets such as Hoth, while sonic beacons frighten away predators and giant insects on jungle worlds. The moisture vaporator, meanwhile, is used by colonists on Tatooine and other hot, dry desert worlds to eke out what little water exists.

The GX-8 water vaporator is the most common moisture vaporator used on Tatooine. Each vaporator is a cylindrical installation between three and five meters tall. The apparatus relies on a low-power ion field and a series of chilling bars to cool surrounding air. The resulting condensation collects on the chilling bars and is eventually filtered into a collection chamber in the heart of the unit. The water is analyzed for impurities then pumped into a secure underground storage tank. Vaporators are placed at least 250 meters from one another, allowing each to collect about a liter and a half of water each day.

The GX-8 utilizes a series of basic sensors and a rudimentary control computer to continually adjust the vaporator's performance. Both the ion field intensity and the cooling bar temperature can be altered based on humidity, atmospheric temperature changes, and wind speed. Moisture vaporators are relatively self-sufficient, requiring only a small amount of power to fuel the cooling bars, computer system, and sensors. The energy cells used to power the vaporator are constantly recharged by retractable solar panels.

Vaporators are very difficult to disguise, making them a frequent target for Sand People, Jawas, and other scavengers in search of water. Many collection tanks are protected by security locks or voice-recognition scanners, but the fragile devices can be easily cracked open by a gaffi stick or similar weapon. However, it is Tatooine's gritty sand that proves the vaporator's greatest threat. Sand can clog a vaporator's sensors, foul the device's lubricants, and disable the refrigeration mechanisms. Like many moisture farmers, Luke Skywalker spent hours cleaning sand out of vaporators' sensitive machinery. Finally, the simple computer brain communicates only through a binary programming language, which must be translated by certain droids.

Moisture farms dot the Tatooine desert from Mos Taike to Wayfar. Each moisture farm consists of several vaporators spread out over the farmer's land. Security beacons protect the perimeter of the farm, but moisture farmers must still rigorously patrol the area. Collected water is sold in Anchorhead, Mos Eisley, and other settlements, although moisture farmers rarely collect enough to turn a sizable profit. To make the best use of gathered water, moisture farmers often build underground hydroponics labs to grow vegetables.

> ## "Well, he'd better have those units in the south range repaired by midday or there'll be hell to pay!"
> —*Owen Lars*

❼ "Mushroom Patch": Nicknamed the "mushroom patch" by Tatooine locals, the area around the base of a vaporator is often moist and dark, allowing hardy Tatooine mushrooms to grow around the apparatus. Shmi Skywalker Lars was picking mushrooms from vaporators when she was abducted by Tusken Raiders.

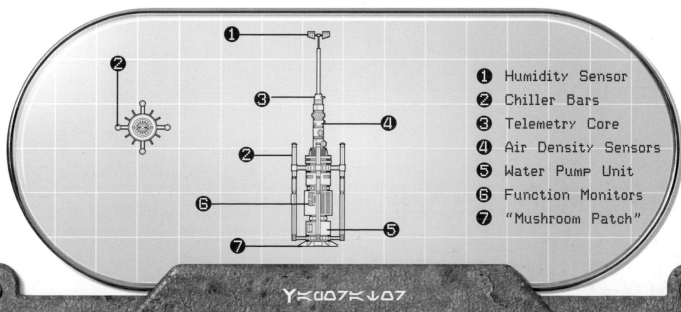

❶ Humidity Sensor
❷ Chiller Bars
❸ Telemetry Core
❹ Air Density Sensors
❺ Water Pump Unit
❻ Function Monitors
❼ "Mushroom Patch"

ELECTROBINOCULARS

TECHNICAL READOUT

WEIGHT: 0.7 KG

EFFECTIVE RANGE: Can focus on targets up to 600 KM

PRIMARY MANUFACTURER: Neuro-Saav

AFFILIATION: Luke Skywalker

Neuro–Saav Model TD2.3 Electrobinoculars

One of the most common personal devices in the galaxy, electrobinoculars are handheld viewing devices used to view objects over great distances. While living on Tatooine, Luke Skywalker always carried a pair of electrobinoculars for surveying the terrain around his uncle's moisture farm. Luke also used his electrobinoculars to observe an Imperial attack on Princess Leia's starship, the *Tantive IV*, as it approached his homeworld.

Electrobinoculars consist of stereoscopic sights and a computer-enhanced magnification system housed in a resilient, weatherproof plastic casing. Models such as the Neuro-Saav TD2.3 include imaging chips that allow clear use on the brightest days or darkest nights. Automated dampener filters shield the user from sudden flashes caused by blasterfire, flash grenades, or atmospheric anomalies.

The heart of a pair of electrobinoculars is its telescopic lenses, which provide up to five hundred times magnification. An instant-focus function automatically adjusts as the user switches between targets and ensures high-resolution images even when a target is on the move. Most important, the electrobinoculars incorporate screen readouts that relate a viewed object's range, size, elevation, and a variety of other data. All of this information is collected and analyzed by a very basic internal computer. The computer also automatically enhances and sharpens images and can employ both wide and zoom angles. The automated functions are powered by self-changing energy cells that last up to six months.

All of the electrobinoculars' functions are operated by simple controls. A user can manually adjust magnification, focus, light compensation, and other settings. On the T2.3 and several military models, the control dials are supplemented by focus studs that allow the user to adjust the telescopic magnification in precise increments. A calibration switch initiates a diagnostic review of the electronic imagers to ensure constant and clear reception. Finally, a nonelectronic secondary lens serves as a backup to the primary lens, but offers only one hundred times magnification.

Electrobinoculars are extremely useful alone, but they can become versatile reconnaissance tools when coupled with other equipment. Nearly all electrobinoculars have dataports that allow the devices to transmit captured images to datapads, recording rods, and even holorecorders. Internal recorders are not uncommon: Neuro-Saav's TT-4 includes both hologram and visual recorders that can capture and store up to three hours of images. For military use, the TD2.3 can also be linked directly to blaster rifles to increase the effectiveness of long-range attacks.

Electrobinoculars can be expensive and difficult to acquire on Outer Rim worlds. When electrobinoculars are unavailable, those who need visual-enhancement devices usually turn to macrobinoculars, which lack image-enhancement chips and light-adjustment circuitry. They are cheaper and more resilient than electrobinoculars, making them a popular choice among mercenaries.

> **"I almost forgot! There's a battle going on! Right here in our system! Come and look!"**
> —*Luke Skywalker*

8 **Carry Strap Fastener:** Electrobinoculars are usually carried on a leather shoulder strap, although the owner must be careful not to let the device strike another object as any collision can disrupt internal calibration.

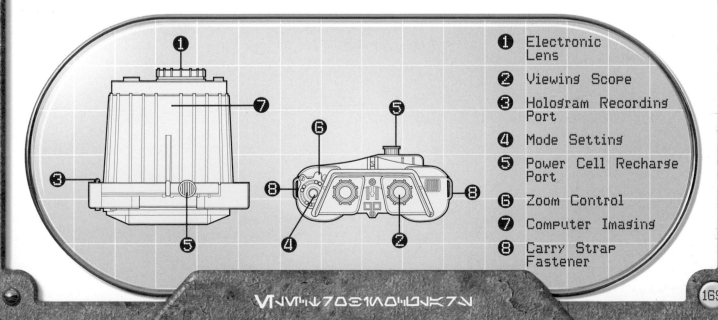

1. Electronic Lens
2. Viewing Scope
3. Hologram Recording Port
4. Mode Setting
5. Power Cell Recharge Port
6. Zoom Control
7. Computer Imaging
8. Carry Strap Fastener

HOLOGRAM PROJECTOR

TECHNICAL READOUT

SIZE: 2.8 m diameter

EFFECTIVE RANGE: Can project images up to 2 m from projector

PRIMARY MANUFACTURER: Neuro-Saav

AFFILIATION: Luke Skywalker

Plescinia Entertainments CS-Mark 12

Hologram projectors, more commonly known as holoprojectors, generate three-dimensional images for entertainment, personal or military communications, and information displays. Hologram projectors are typically connected to the widespread HoloNet via powerful transceivers, but many smaller, independent models also exist.

During the recording phase, the holoprojector uses two synchronized images to scan the subject while other devices capture audio data. An internal computer then combines these feeds to generate the hologram. The most advanced hologram recorders capture realistic colors, crystal-clear sound, and the subject's most subtle movements. The consolidated recording can be transferred to countless storage devices, including data disks, data tapes, and even crystals.

The most common playback mechanisms are miniaturized holoprojectors installed in astromech droids, datapads, map readers, and many other machines. R2-D2 used his built-in holoprojector to relay Princess Leia's urgent plea for help to Obi-Wan Kenobi. Small, handheld holoprojectors like the SoroSuub Imagecaster carried by Jedi Qui-Gon Jinn often include a standard image library that can be bolstered by uploading data. The most effective miniaturized hologram projectors are those that can project images in real time. When integrated into a comlink or other communications device, these allow for face-to-face conversations. During playback, many miniaturized holoprojectors suffer some form of degradation, such as flickers and color shifts.

Some of the most advanced and powerful holoprojectors can be found aboard starships or in military installations. The Rebel Alliance used a Plescinia

> ## "Help me Obi-Wan Kenobi, you're my only hope..."
> —*Princess Leia*

Entertainments CS-Mark 12 holoprojector to plan the assault on the second Death Star. Originally designed for public presentations, the CS-Mark 12 is a fairly large emplacement that can generate images up to five meters in diameter. Data can be received through any standard storage device or via direct feeds from droids, datapads, or computers.

During presentations, operators have full control of the images being displayed. Audio levels, aspect ratio, and playback speed can all be changed with a simple button press. The CS-Mark 12 is also preprogrammed with a full editing suite, allowing operators to edit, enhance, sharpen, and otherwise modify any holographic image. Rebel technicians used this feature to outline attack flight paths and highlight potential targets aboard the second Death Star.

Simple hologram games, such as the dejarik holochess enjoyed by Chewbacca, utilize gaming tables equipped with miniature holoprojectors. Hologramic films and broadcasts are carried on virtually all subspace networks. Coruscant and other Core worlds are home to hologramic theaters that entertain the masses with live sporting events from around the galaxy alongside a steady stream of news programming. The most advanced systems can generate completely realistic environments. Such holoprojector networks form the basis for Hologram Fun World, an amusement center once owned by Lando Calrissian.

7 Input Slots: The input slots can accept any standard storage medium, including the encrypted data disks secured by Bothan spies that contained schematics of the second Death Star.

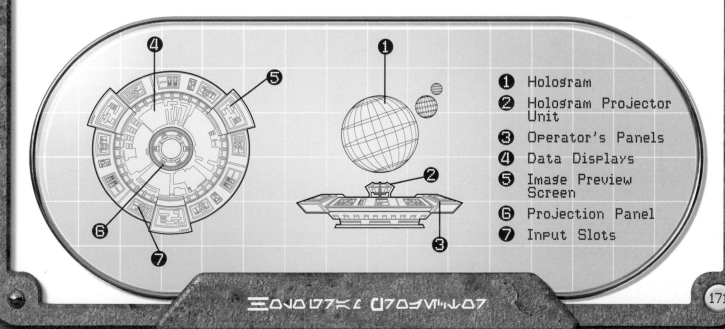

1. Hologram
2. Hologram Projector Unit
3. Operator's Panels
4. Data Displays
5. Image Preview Screen
6. Projection Panel
7. Input Slots

JETPACKS

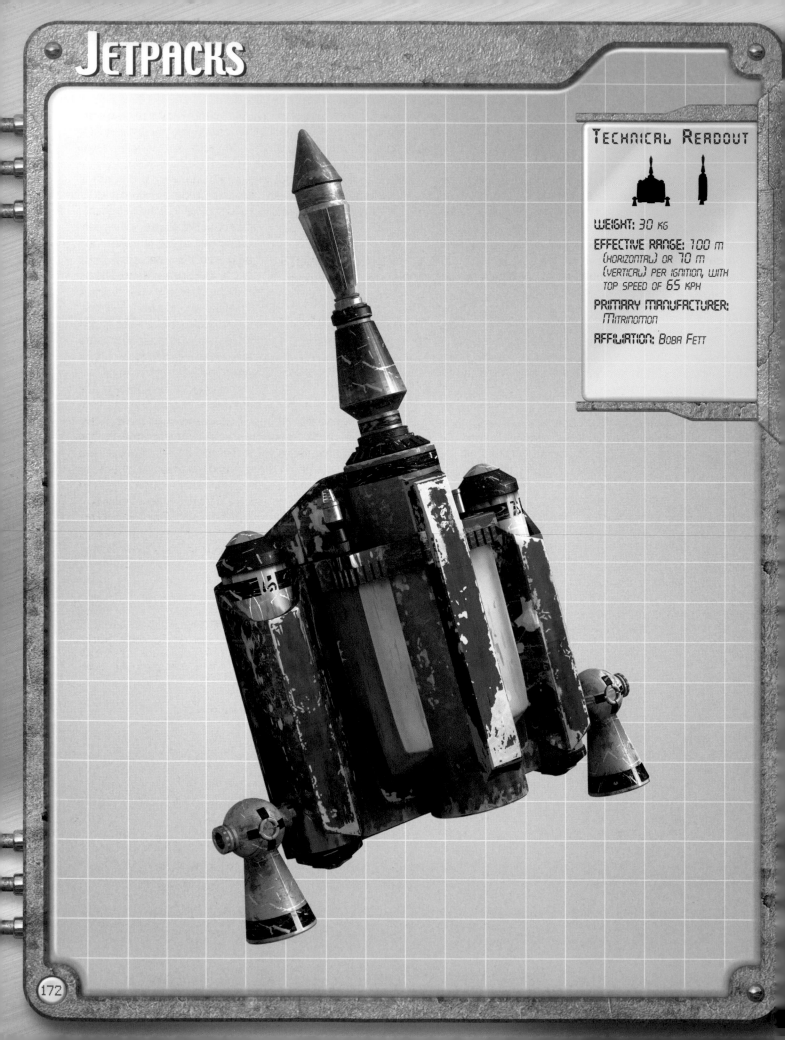

TECHNICAL READOUT

WEIGHT: 30 KG

EFFECTIVE RANGE: 100 m (HORIZONTAL) OR 70 m (VERTICAL) PER IGNITION, WITH TOP SPEED OF 65 KPH

PRIMARY MANUFACTURER: Mitrinomon

AFFILIATION: Boba Fett

Mitrinomon Z-6 Jetpack

In the era of the New Republic, nearly every citizen has access to some form of rapid personal transport. Most often, such transports consist of landspeeders or airspeeders, both of which combine high speed with some protection from collision and the elements. In contrast, the jetpack allows the user to fly only at great personal risk. Despite this down side, jetpacks remain in limited use across the galaxy, largely because they offer a great degree of mobility. Mercenaries, bounty hunters, thrill seekers, and and soldiers all make heavy use of the devices.

Personal jetpacks are typically worn on the user's back, although they can also be integrated into armor suits. Boba Fett uses a powerful Mitrinomon Z-6, which contains many features common to the most successful jetpacks. The Z-6 is activated from a wrist-worn control panel or through verbal commands routed through his helmet's onboard computer. Upon launch, the jetpack's intake system funnels both air and fuel through miniaturized turbines. Within the turbines, the air–fuel mixture is ignited, providing enough thrust to hurl Fett into the sky or rocket him toward enemies. The ignition process also generates a thick cloud of exhaust that can be useful for masking Fett's escape.

Once airborne, Fett can control his flight path through directional exhaust nozzles. Even a very short burst from one of these nozzles can radically alter Fett's course and heading. During descents, a gyrostabilizer counterbalances Fett's velocity to ensure a safe landing.

Jetpacks are generally impractical for public use. The units weigh about thirty kilograms and can carry

> **"A lot of the younger soldiers think we oughta be zipping around the battlefield on jetpacks. But one direct hit, and you're grounded, maybe forever."**
> —*Rebel Alliance Major Derlin*

enough fuel for only twenty bursts. They can also misfire if involved in a collision or struck by a stray blaster bolt or other attack. Boba Fett experienced this design flaw firsthand when Han Solo blindly struck the bounty hunter's jetpack near the Sarlacc. Fett lost control of his flight pack and spiraled into the Sarlacc's open maw.

Military forces often prefer bulkier but more reliable rocket packs. Because they rely on oxygen to fire, jetpacks can't be used underwater, in space, or in the low-oxygen atmospheres found on many alien worlds. Rocket packs, however, use premixed fuels that can be ignited anywhere. Military rocket packs are often protected by light armor plating.

Repulsorlift technology has also been miniaturized to produce alternatives to fuel-dependent jet-and rocket packs. Repulsor packs move more slowly, but offer much greater maneuverability. They also allow the wearer to hover in place. The devices rapidly burn through energy cells, enabling only about ten minutes of flight time, and they can't be used in zero-gravity environments. Currently, the most advanced personal propulsion devices actually combine fuel-powered thrusters with secondary repulsorlift systems for greater stability, especially during landings

⑥ Homing Missile: The Z-6 Jetpack is notable for its ability to support a missile launcher mechanism. Boba Fett can equip his Jetpack with one of several missile types, including accurate homing missiles.

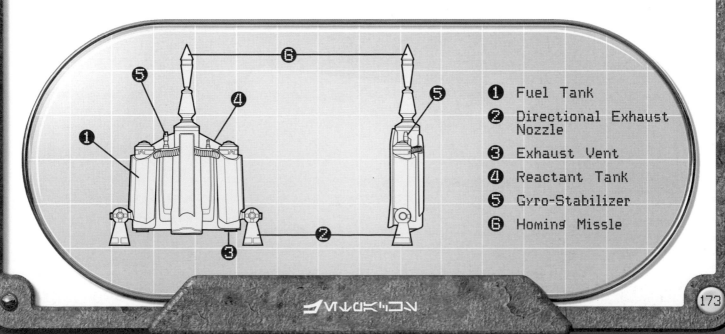

① Fuel Tank
② Directional Exhaust Nozzle
③ Exhaust Vent
④ Reactant Tank
⑤ Gyro-Stabilizer
⑥ Homing Missile

Bacta Tank

TECHNICAL READOUT

SIZE: 2.5 to 5 m tall

COVERAGE: Patient's entire body

PRIMARY MANUFACTURER: Zaltin Bacta Corporation

AFFILIATION: Rebel Alliance (Echo Base)

Zaltin Bacta Tank

For eons, researchers have pursued the secrets of long life and good health. This has led to an untold number of medical breakthroughs, but few of these have had the far-reaching impact of bacta. An exotic chemical compound, bacta can heal nearly any wound. The curative liquid has spawned an entire industry, allowing manufacturers to produce bacta tanks, bacta patches, and many other medical miracles.

The insectoid Vratix, native to the planet Thyferra, created the foundation for modern bacta. Since time immemorial, the Vratix have produced a healing lotion by combining gelatinous red alazhi with chemically created bacterial particles known as kavam. Researchers who discovered the Vratix's curative lotion later added colorless liquid ambori, which acts as a nutrient, disinfectant bath, and preservative. The resulting synthetic chemical, now known as bacta, mimics a body's vital fluids.

Bacta application methods vary depending upon the extent of the patient's wounds. Minor flesh wounds and second-degree burns can be treated using disposable patches coated in thick bacta gel. Patients suffering from multiple wounds, third-degree burns, or cellular damage resulting from frostbite must be completely submersed in bacta. For these treatments, companies like Zaltin have produced large cylindrical bacta tanks.

Patients treated in bacta tanks are fully immersed in the liquid. A breath mask provides breathable gas, while a number of sensors attached to the subject's skin monitor vital signs. This immersion therapy allows the bacterial particles to saturate wounds and seep into damaged tissue, thus encouraging regeneration in all organic tissues (including nerves, muscles, tendons, and skin) with

only minimal scarring. Zaltin's bacta tank also supports several retractable spray hypos designed to inject medicines, stim-shots, adrenaline boosters, and immunity enhancers into the patient or the healing mixture. In most cases, bacta tank patients recover from life-threatening injuries within a week. Patients can also be transported to medical centers in portable "bacta coffins."

Soon after its creation, bacta production fell under the tight control of two corporations: Zaltin and Xucphra. Both of these companies agreed to control bacta prices, ensuring that the liquid and its associated devices were always sold for the highest profit. During the Galactic Civil War, the Emperor forged alliances with both Zaltin and Xucphra, then sent his stormtroopers to violently shut down smaller bacta suppliers, thus depriving the Alliance.

Although bacta was nearly impossible to acquire during the Emperor's reign, the Rebel Alliance did obtain a functional bacta tank and a small supply of the curative liquid for use at Echo Base on Hoth. After being attacked by a wampa and spending a night on the frozen surface of Hoth, Luke Skywalker would have surely died from his injuries if not for Echo Base's bacta tank. After the Battle of Endor, the New Republic initiated the so-called Bacta War in order to liberate the remaining bacta supply and spread it across the galaxy.

> **"How are you feeling, kid? You don't look so bad to me. In fact, you look strong enough to pull the ears off a gundark."**
> —*Han Solo*

❼ **Diagnostic Computer:** During his treatment, Luke's condition was monitored by medical droids, which constantly adjusted the bacta levels, tank temperature, and flow of antibiotics with the aid of the diagnostic computer.

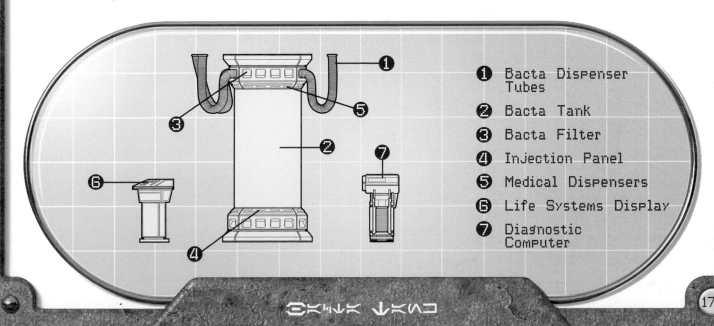

1. Bacta Dispenser Tubes
2. Bacta Tank
3. Bacta Filter
4. Injection Panel
5. Medical Dispensers
6. Life Systems Display
7. Diagnostic Computer

REMOTE

TECHNICAL READOUT

SIZE: 32 cm in diameter

OPTIMUM/MAXIMUM RANGES
(BLASTERS): 4 m/35 m

PRIMARY MANUFACTURER:
Industrial Automaton

AFFILIATION: Han Solo

Industrial Automaton Marksman–H Combat Remote

A remote is any small automaton, most often designed for use as a training tool, very basic sentry, or assassin. A typical remote, such as Industrial Automaton's Marksman-H combat remote, is a floating sphere with a rudimentary computer brain, short-range sensory array, low-grade deflector shields, and weak blasters.

At first glance, remotes appear to be tiny droids. Unlike droids, however, remotes can make no independent decisions. Instead, they rely on programmed instructions and a limited library of actions. The Marksman-H is designed to help sharpshooters hone their skills: for this purpose, the device is programmed to bob and weave while returning fire. During a training session, the shooter sets his or her blaster to emit light only, while the remote's weapons are set at stun. As the training sessions intensify, the remote begins to move more quickly and attack with more intense bursts of energy. In the most extreme cases, the remote's stun blasts can render the trainee unconscious. For such blaster practice, Han Solo kept a Marksman-H aboard *Millennium Falcon*. Luke Skywalker borrowed the remote to begin his training under Obi-Wan Kenobi's watchful eye. Similar training methods were used by Yoda and other Jedi Masters to tutor young Padawans at the Jedi Temple on Coruscant. Besting a remote with a lightsaber requires the Jedi trainee to deflect a preset number of blasts before closing for an attack.

A remote utilizes a miniaturized repulsorlift generator to float above the ground. Maneuverability is achieved through eight tiny thrusters. Remotes can travel up to twenty-five kilometers per hour, accelerate or decelerate in a split second, and make sharp turns or altitude adjustments. To the untrained, remotes appear to move erratically, but their flight patterns are actually well-timed evasive combat maneuvers.

The Marksman-H responds to a handheld signaler that emits high-pitched, coded bursts. A verbal emergency override code allows the user to shut down the training remote with a single word.

Remote technology has been expanded by the Empire to create dangerous "seekers." Like remotes, seekers are small and spherical devices. However, they possess a much greater degree of independence and are programmed specifically to hunt down and exterminate the Empire's enemies. The Arakyd Mark VII Inquisitor has a top speed of forty kilometers for overtaking fleeing targets. Its AA-1 verbobrain can comprehend fifty thousand languages, and an internal vocoder system allows the remote to imitate nearly any organic and droid language.

The seeker tracks prey relentlessly using a 360-degree sensor suite that incorporates visual scanners, electrobinoculars, directional audio sensors, heat sensors, infrared scopes, and even a genetic sampler for analyzing hair, blood, and skin in order to identify slain victims. Killing blows are delivered by a pair of blasters with the same energy output as a standard blaster rifle.

> "Look, going good against remotes is one thing. Going good against the living? That's something else."
>
> *Han Solo*

6   Emitter Nozzle: Remotes can be configured to emit stun bolts, blasts of compressed air, nonlethal gases, beams of light, and even shrieking audio attacks.

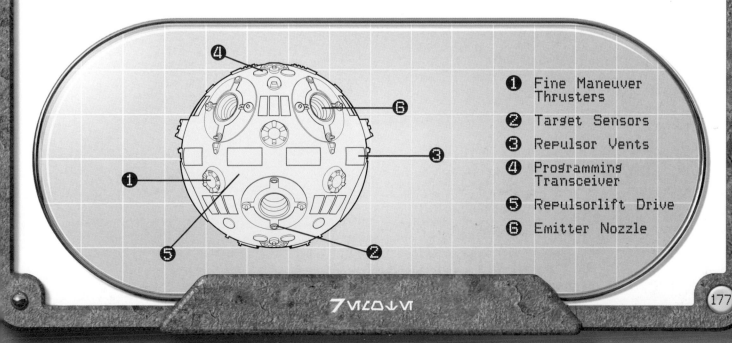

1. Fine Maneuver Thrusters
2. Target Sensors
3. Repulsor Vents
4. Programming Transceiver
5. Repulsorlift Drive
6. Emitter Nozzle

DATAPAD

TECHNICAL READOUT

WEIGHT: 0.5 KG

EFFECTIVE RANGE: Receives signals from up to 160 km

PRIMARY MANUFACTURER: MicroData

AFFILIATION: Tatooine Podrace spectators

MicroData Versafunction88 Datapad

The datapad may be one of the most undervalued devices in the galaxy. Nearly every New Republic citizen, from the Outer Rim to the Core Worlds, has access to a datapad. In fact, the appliances are so widely available that they are often taken for granted. Despite this, the datapad is a remarkable and versatile tool that has become a basic necessity for many beings on a wide range of planets.

Datapads are essentially personal computers small enough to be held in a human palm. A generic datapad serves as a portable workstation, with basic data collection, analysis, and storage capabilities. However, each datapad can host thousands of different programs, allowing it to double as a writing tool, calculator, slicing terminal, gaming device, map display, recording rod crystal reader, and hundreds of other gadgets. Data capture is achieved through input slots that can receive data cards, disks, and microdots. A recording rod allows capture of audio.

Datapads are designed to be easily reconfigured by users. While most datapads utilize touch-sensitive color screens for accessing and inputting data, some users prefer to attach keyboards or keypads to the devices. Datapads can also be loaded with voice-response or retinal motion tracking programs for completely hands-free use. Some models even include readout glasses similar to data goggles; these glasses scroll information across their transparent lenses, allowing the user to perform other duties while reviewing data.

One of the datapad's most important features is its ability to link with other appliances. Standard dataports allow a datapad to interface with droids, computer terminals, scanners and sensor arrays, other datapads, and holoprojectors. Special programs allow connections to any device with a computerized "brain," including vaporators, weapons emplacements, and many vehicles. Datapads programmed with a Galactic Universal Translator (GalUT) can even analyze unknown computer systems and develop new interface programs on the fly.

Other common features on a standard datapad include a built-in holoprojector that can produce holograms up to twenty centimeters tall or interactive holomaps. Miniaturized holo- and visual recorders can scan and store images, while audio and visual pickups, headphone ports, and comlinks allow users to tap into local comm networks. During Podraces on Tatooine, racing fans followed the progress of their favorite racers through datapads set to receive video feeds from remote cameras and recording balloons hovering over the track.

Users program datapads based on their primary use. Han Solo keeps a datapad aboard *Millennium Falcon* to aid him in repairs; the device contains schematics and manuals for virtually every starship component. Medical datapads boast databases filled with interactive physiological charts and treatment information for thousands of species, and Imperial interrogators often carried datapads loaded with dossiers on all known Rebel operatives.

> **"You don't realize how important a datapad is until you're stranded on Raxus Prime with nothing but your boots and a blaster."**
>
> —*Han Solo*

❻ Handgrips: The handgrips allow the datapad to be held horizontally or vertically, depending upon the orientation of the playback. On Tatooine, datapad handgrips are covered in leather or constructed from bone or bantha horn.

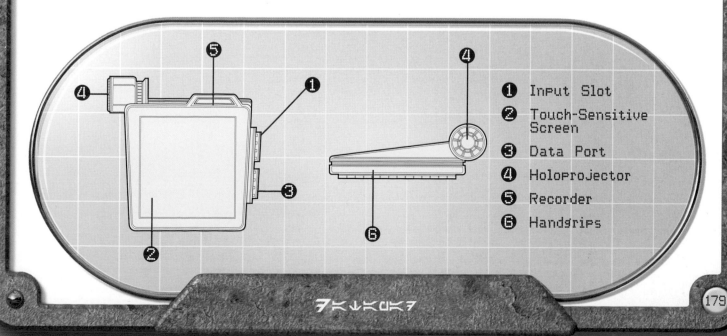

❶ Input Slot
❷ Touch-Sensitive Screen
❸ Data Port
❹ Holoprojector
❺ Recorder
❻ Handgrips

CYBORG UNIT

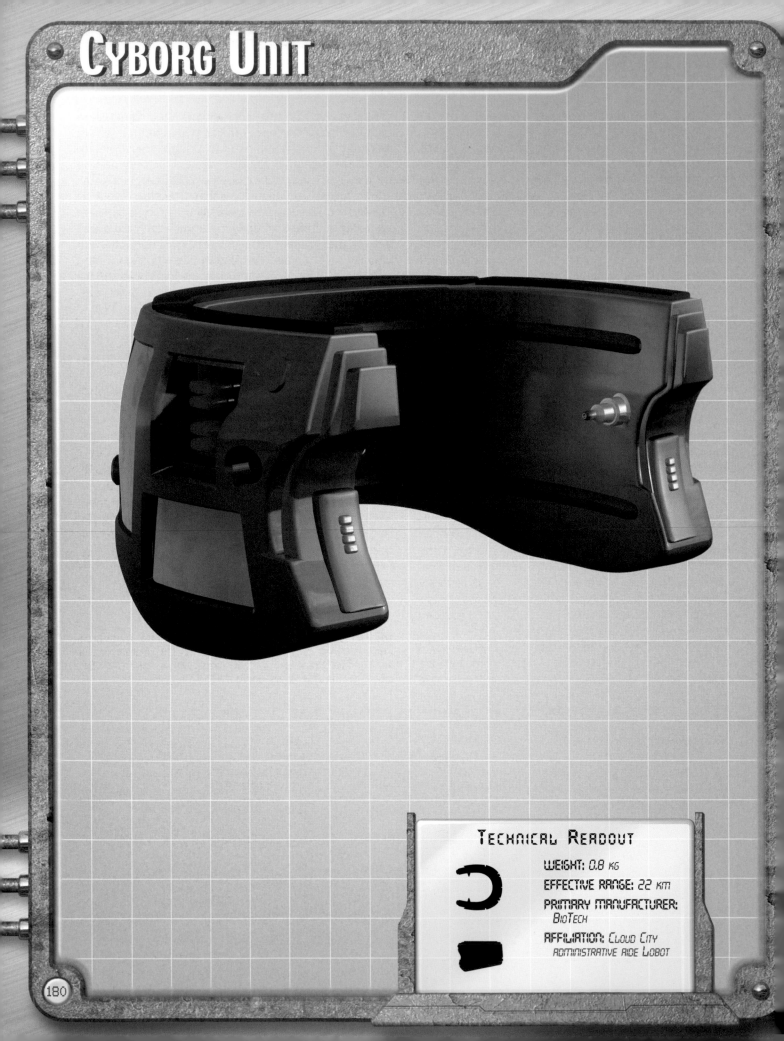

TECHNICAL READOUT

WEIGHT: 0.8 KG

EFFECTIVE RANGE: 22 KM

PRIMARY MANUFACTURER: BioTech

AFFILIATION: Cloud City Administrative Aide Lobot

BioTech Borg Construct Aj^6

Cybernetic technology represents the successful fusion of mechanical components with organic tissue, allowing surgeons to implant machinery directly into their subjects. Military uses of the technology are seemingly endless: aside from rebuilding grievously injured soldiers, cybernetic implants can provide a subject with eyes that serve as targeting scopes, powerful servos to increase strength and speed, and a host of other enhancements. At its most terrifying, however, a cybernetic implant can turn a victim into a computer-controlled slave or mechanical monstrosity carrying a number of deadly concealed weapons.

A handful of firms manufacture cybernetic implants for sale to military groups, medical facilities, and private buyers. Such devices are invariably very expensive and require difficult and costly surgical procedures to integrate. Undergoing cybernetic treatment is also very dangerous, especially if the implant affects the brain. Any mistake during such operations can cause permanent brain damage, coma, or death.

The BioTech Borg Construct Aj^6 is one of the most sophisticated cyborg units commercially available. Designed to allow users to interface with large computer networks, the Aj^6 is implanted against the skull. Once properly installed, the device sends nanothreads into the recipient's brain to form a link between the biocomputer unit and the newly created cyborg. Cloud City's administrative aide, the cyborg known as Lobot, relied on an Aj^6 unit to perform most of his duties.

The Aj^6 is remarkable because it actually improves the intelligence of its wearer. The device's cyborg computer increases logic and reasoning capabilities while

> ## "You think Lobot's mute, but he's just too busy talking to the central computer to bother speaking to us 'organics.' "
> —*Lando Calrissian*

providing access to a host of other functions. After receiving the implant, a cyborg can communicate directly with a central computer and mentally control computer systems. The cyborg can also analyze data at a rate roughly twenty times that of other computer operators.

The Aj^6's computer stores vast amounts of data, all of which can be accessed mentally by the cyborg. There are external ports for receiving "knowledge cartridges," devices that contain seemingly endless information on virtually any subject. This allows cyborgs to load and process the data needed for any situation or procedure. Lobot's cyborg unit allowed the administrator to control all of Cloud City's functions and systems, supervise the facility's Wing Guard, monitor comlink and subspace transmissions, and gather data from local scanners.

While Lobot personifies successful cybernetics use, he also reveals some of the technology's drawbacks. The Aj^6 and other similar devices are criticized for gradually stealing the recipient's personality and ability to express emotions. Essentially, Lobot and many other cyborgs begin thinking and acting like machines. Cybernetic psychosis is also an unfortunate side effect of brain-altering cyborg units. Victims of cybernetic psychosis lose control of their cyborg computers and eventually go completely insane.

⑦ Droid Interface Port: The droid interface port allows the cyborg to mentally communicate with, download data from, and alter the programming of nearly any droid.

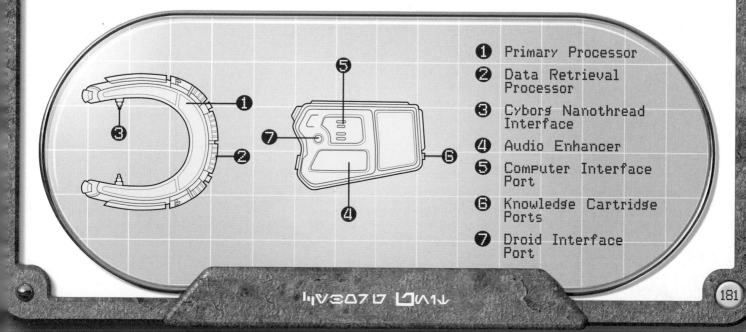

① Primary Processor
② Data Retrieval Processor
③ Cyborg Nanothread Interface
④ Audio Enhancer
⑤ Computer Interface Port
⑥ Knowledge Cartridge Ports
⑦ Droid Interface Port

PROSTHETICS

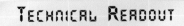

TECHNICAL READOUT

WEIGHT: 2.3 KG

COVERAGE: Anakin's forearm and hand

PRIMARY MANUFACTURER: Anakin Skywalker

AFFILIATION: Anakin Skywalker

Custom-Built Mechno-Arm

One of the most common forms of cybernetic implant, a prosthetic is a biomechanical device designed to replace a limb or organ. Prosthetics include everything from artificial hearts that merely mimic the functions of a normal heart to mechanical arms capable of dramatically increasing a cyborg's strength. Anakin Skywalker (who would later become Darth Vader) and his son, Luke, both received prosthetic replacements for limbs lost during lightsaber duels.

Based on the manufacturer, prosthetics can vary in their construction and functionality. Some replacement limbs are simple devices that, while they might appear authentic, possess only a limited range of motion. Others look cobbled together from random parts yet offer concealed weapons or other special features. But nearly all prosthetics must be connected to organic tissues via a synthenet neural interface. This interface is relatively simple for automated organs, such as a heart, which are not directly controlled by the cyborg and do not require any simulated nerve endings. Prosthetic limbs, however, require a much more complex neural interface that replicates a fully functioning nervous system; the synthenet interface must respond to the cyborg's commands and register pain to alert the cyborg when the limb suffers damage.

At the Battle of Geonosis, Anakin Skywalker engaged in a fierce duel with Count Dooku. During that conflict, Dooku severed Anakin's right arm at the elbow. As he recovered at the Jedi Temple, Anakin drew upon his extensive knowledge of droid construction to oversee the creation of his mechno-arm. The metal mechno-arm was actually quite advanced and featured electrostatic

fingertips that simulated a sense of touch. Data collected by the fingertips was transmitted through sensory impulse lines and into an interface module at the wrist. This module served as the junction between the arm's wiring and Anakin's organic nervous system. A small power cell near the thumb provided energy to the mechno-arm's servos and fingertip sensors.

Anakin covered his skeletal mechno-arm with a black glove, but most prosthetics are actually wrapped in realistic synthflesh. Synthflesh is nearly indistinguishable from organic tissue, and some prosthetic limbs can even simulate body warmth and perspiration to better conceal their true nature. Luke Skywalker's prosthetic hand is protected by a synthflesh coating.

Although prosthetics have been in existence for many thousands of years, their use was only widespread during times of great conflict. While fighting the Beast Wars of Onderon, the Jedi Cay Qel-Droma constructed his own prosthetic arm from salvaged XT-6 service droid components. The Mandalorian Wars, nearly four thousand years before the Battle of Yavin, led to many Mandalorians being fitted with prosthetic eyes, ears, and limbs to give them an edge in their battles against Old Republic forces. The Clone Wars proved to be a war of attrition, and the Republic sought to repair clones and Jedi with prosthetics whenever possible.

> "I don't know that Anakin ever missed his real arm. To him, the new one seemed so much better, so much more powerful . . ."
> —*Siri Tachi*

6 Motorized Knuckle: The motorized servos that form the knuckles on Anakin's mechno-hand provide him with crushing strength far beyond the human norm.

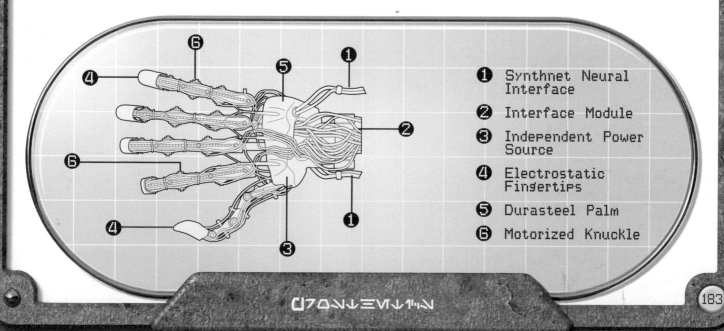

1. Synthnet Neural Interface
2. Interface Module
3. Independent Power Source
4. Electrostatic Fingertips
5. Durasteel Palm
6. Motorized Knuckle

CLONING TECHNOLOGIES

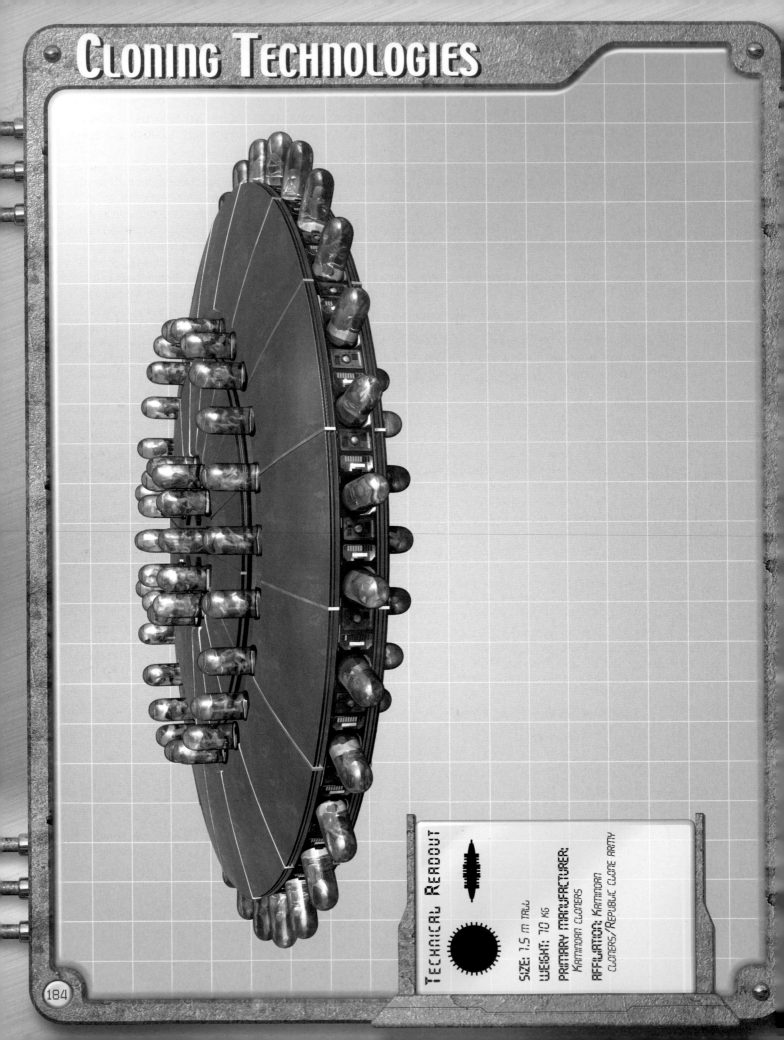

TECHNICAL READOUT

SIZE: 1.5 M TALL

WEIGHT: 70 KG

PRIMARY MANUFACTURER:
Kaminoan Cloners

AFFILIATION: Kaminoan
Cloners/Republic Clone Army

Kamino Cloning Chamber

The Old Republic was home to literally thousands of inhabited worlds, each populated by species with their own technologies, religions, moral codes, and ethical beliefs. While the Republic imposed laws to maintain order and prevent the abuse of science, on many worlds, especially along the Outer Rim, ethical lapses led to the creation of technologies that challenged the Republic's concept of morality. Among these questionable technologies is cloning, which led to major medical advances, and the Clone Wars.

Cloning—the creation of organic replicas—remains deeply controversial. What is not contested, however, is the skill of Kaminoan cloners. The lithe Kaminoans produced a massive clone army for the Old Republic. Each soldier was based on a genetic blueprint taken from the bounty hunter Jango Fett. Trained to serve as soldiers, these clones proved crucial in the war against Count Dooku's Confederacy of Independent Systems.

> ## "Clones can think creatively. You will find that they are immensely superior to droids."
> —*Kaminoan Prime Minister Lama Su*

On Kamino, the cloners first took genetic material and carefully modified its genetic code to accelerate growth and ensure obedience. Then the material was used to create artificial embryos within an Egg Lab. The embryos were then transferred to glass incubation wombs, or cloning chambers. The clones were nourished in a nutrient-rich bath until old enough to be removed and begin training. The growth acceleration modifications allowed a clone to reach adulthood in roughly ten years.

As clones matured, they endured rigorous physical and mental training to perfect their abilities. While taught to follow orders, clones were also encouraged to adapt to any situation. This allowed clones to think and act creatively in combat, which provided them with a considerable advantage over preprogrammed battle droids.

At the start of the Clone Wars, the Republic officially prohibited all nonmilitary cloning. The Empire continued to regulate the technology, although illegal cloning centers managed to appear in several locations across the galaxy. Imperial scientists themselves embarked on extensive cloning research using Spaarti cloning cylinders. Perhaps the fastest method for cloning, Spaarti cylinders are four-meter-tall tanks that grow clones within a protective gelatin, producing an adult clone within a matter of weeks. Spaarti clones are actually trained and educated during growth: a computer processing system linked directly to a clone's cerebral cortex feeds the clone a constant stream of useful information. Unfortunately, Spaarti cylinders create clones that suffer from "clone madness," a psychosis possibly caused by a disturbance in the Force or the accelerated growth cycle.

The Emperor established several hidden labs stocked with Spaarti cylinders. There, his most loyal scientists created clones of their leader. Even after the Battle of Endor, the Emperor continued to plague the New Republic through "reborn" clones. Grand Admiral Thrawn also used Spaarti cylinders to create clone soldiers for his own war against the New Republic.

❻ Fetal Clone: The fetal clones were actually larger and more resilient than normal human infants, allowing them to survive the accelerated growth that was part of the Kaminoan cloning process.

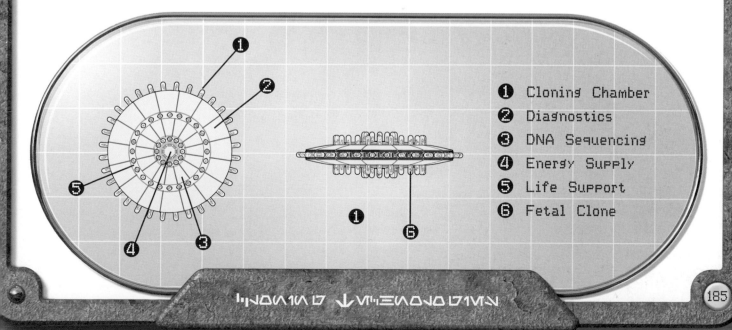

❶ Cloning Chamber
❷ Diagnostics
❸ DNA Sequencing
❹ Energy Supply
❺ Life Support
❻ Fetal Clone

ENTECHMENT RIG

SIZE: 2.3 m TALL

EFFECTIVE RANGE: Up to 3,000 km (with Jedi)

PRIMARY MANUFACTURER: Ssi-ruuvi ENGINEERS

AFFILIATION: Ssi-ruuvi

Ssi-ruuvi Entechment Rig

Like the invading Yuuzhan Vong, the aggressive Ssi-ruuk have introduced the galaxy to entirely new and disturbing technologies. A sentient, reptilian species, the Ssi-ruuk rely on a process known as entechment in order to produce energy for their equipment. Entechment is essentially the absorption of another sentient creature's life energy, which is then converted into practical energy that can be funneled into any number of devices.

Collecting entechment energy relies on first capturing suitable "suppliers." Humans are highly prized because they produce some of the largest quantities of energy. An abducted victim is strapped into an entechment chair and then fitted with a beltlike catchment rig. A Ssi-ruuvi droid injects a magnetic solution (magsol) directly into the prisoner's carotid artery. The magsol is selectively absorbed by the victim's nervous system, allowing Ssi-ruuvi technicians to tune the entechment rig to specific nerve clusters. The catchment device then emits a magnetic field designed to charge the magsol. This causes the victim's life energy to transfer from his or her nervous system into storage coils. Once the storage coils are charged, they can be placed in any Ssi-ruuvi technology, including battle droids, weapons, vehicles, and even starships. Unfortunately, the process is extremely painful and eventually results in death for the victim.

While humans provide the most entechment energy, converting that energy caused a number of problems for Ssi-ruuvi engineers. When a human is drained for entechment energy, an "echo" of the person's memory

> **"There's no way to describe the pain of having your very life force, the energy that sustains you, ripped from your body, nerve ending by nerve ending . . ."**
> *—Dev Sibwarra*

remains as part of the energy signature. The echo can actually develop a consciousness, but will quickly be driven insane. The energy provided by humans is difficult to sustain for more than a few days.

The Ssi-ruuk later discovered that a Force-sensitive individual could be used as an entechment conduit that would provide energy with a longer life span and without the troubling echo. In an attempt to tap into the potential of a Jedi, the Ssi-ruuk plotted to capture Luke Skywalker. They constructed a much more advanced entechment bed to hold the young Jedi. Among the bed's features were two tubes designed to puncture the prisoner's throat and force-feed him nutrients and magsol. The nutrient stream would theoretically keep a brainwashed Luke alive for days as he enteched other victims from a distance of several thousand kilometers. To keep Luke docile, the bed was equipped with an upper spine beamer that could numb a human body for more than two hours and an injector that pumped a Ssi-ruuvi mind-control drug into the captive. Fortunately, another Ssi-ruuvi captive named Dev Sibwarra resisted the Ssi-ruuvi mind control. He and Luke foiled the Ssi-ruuvi plot and escaped.

6 Intravenous Tube Connector: The entechment rig's IV tube is generally used to feed the victim a steady supply of mind-control drugs. While these drugs do not dull the pain of entechment, they do prevent the victim from resisting the procedure or formulating plans of escape.

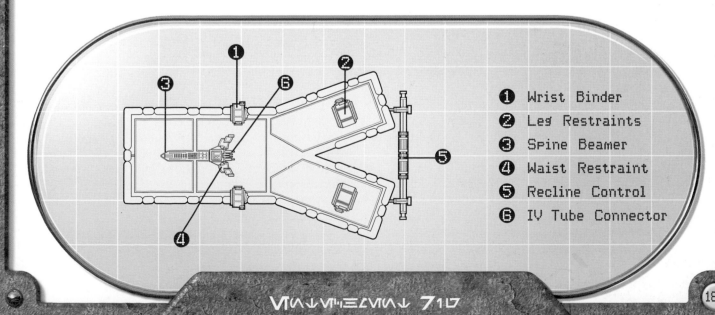

1. Wrist Binder
2. Leg Restraints
3. Spine Beamer
4. Waist Restraint
5. Recline Control
6. IV Tube Connector

ADDITIONAL EQUIPMENT

For nearly every task, the galaxy's inventors have developed some sort of effective tool. Below is a cross section of the wondrous technology devised for use *outside* of battlefields.

BEAMDRILL

A heavy mining tool that creates high-intensity pulses to smash through rock and other matter. Beamdrills, which can be calibrated for extreme precision, are primarily used to mine nova crystals and ore.

CHRONO

A device, usually worn on the wrist, that measures time. Chronos are frequently integrated into comlinks, life-support systems, and even weapons.

CONDENSER UNIT

A compact device that radiates a high level of heat while consuming minimal energy from a power pack or energy cell. Also known as warming units or thermal coils, condenser units are a standard component of many survival kits. They are used by explorers and scouts to cook food and provide warmth in hostile environments. Luke Skywalker wisely brought a condenser unit with him to Dagobah.

ELECTRORANGEFINDER

A computerized device that calculates distance between itself and a target. Electrorangefinders rarely exist as independent equipment, but are instead built into viewing tools, such as electrobinoculars, weapons, and targeting and fire-control systems aboard starships. Electrorangefinders can instantaneously determine distance (and in some cases trajectories) by projecting and receiving bursts of coherent light.

ELECTROTELESCOPE

A relatively primitive electro-optical device, once used on starships and other vessels for scanning the environment. Although stationary electrotelescopes have been largely replaced by modern sensor suites, portable versions of the device are popular because they offer greater power and resolution than standard electrobinoculars.

ENERGY CELL

A portable, rechargeable power cell. Energy cells are produced in vast quantities and variety for use in nearly every energy-dependent device, including tiny comlinks, handheld weapons, and sensor arrays aboard

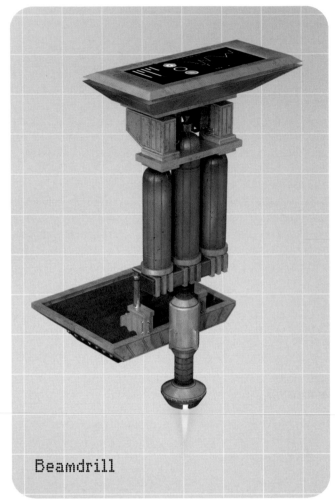

Beamdrill

capital ships. The most efficient energy cells rely on very complex circuitry to ensure a maximum energy output.

FARSEEIN

Primitive binoculars used by the Gungans, farseeins rely on oil magnifier lenses.

FUSION FURNACE

A portable power generator that produces both heat and light while recharging energy cells. Fusion furnaces are vital for recharging vehicles, droids, weapons, and even powered armor. Many small, energy-efficient domestic machines can be fitted with fusion furnaces, removing any need for power or energy cells.

GLOW ROD

A portable light. Glow rods are generally long, thin tubes that generate light using chemical phosphorescents.

Halo Lamp

A basic lighting unit. Larger than glow rods, halo lamps are typically installed aboard starships or vehicles.

Jedi Testing Screen

A handheld viewscreen used to evaluate an individual's Jedi potential. A Jedi testing screen lacks buttons and controls and can only be activated by the Force. During standard testing, the screen flashes hundreds of unconnected images across its surface, out of view of the student. If the individual correctly identifies a series of these images, this reveals a strong connection to the Force.

Liquid-Cable Launcher

A device that fires a special liquid that immediately solidifies into a tough yet lightweight and flexible cable. A standard component of Jedi field gear, a liquid-cable launcher can be easily carried on a Jedi's belt. The cables can be used as grappling hooks or swinglines.

Magwit's Mystifying Hoop

A bizarre teleportation device used by Magwit the Magician. The hoop actually consists of two separate teleporter frames. Magwit can walk through one hoop and emerge wherever the second hoop is located. The technology behind the mystifying hoop is still poorly understood.

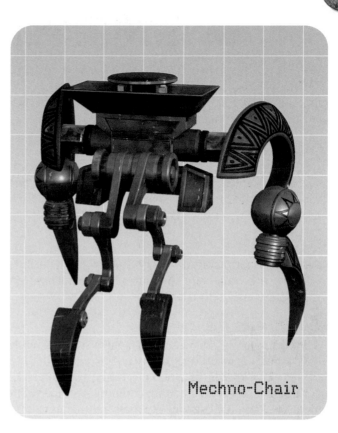
Mechno-Chair

Fusion Furnace

Map Reader

Any device that can project holographic maps. The Jedi used map readers in the Jedi Temple to create star map holograms.

Mechno-chair

A robotic throne that moves about on mechanized metal legs. Primarily used by Neimoidians prior to the Clone Wars, mechno-chairs are designed to carry high-ranking officials and can be controlled by a small touchpad located in an armrest. Handcrafted and expensive, mechno-chairs are a symbol of both grandeur and indulgence.

Power Chair

A floating chair often used by crippled or wounded individuals. Also known as a hoverchair or repulsor chair, a power chair relies on basic antigravity repulsorlift generators controlled by a panel in the armrest. Cliegg Lars, General Veers, and Princess Leia all used power chairs after being wounded.

Psychic Augmenter

A mind-control device that enhances the mental powers of the wearer. Unscrupulous villains have used psychic augmenters to control soldiers, creatures, and innocent civilians.

Quick-seal Splint

A common medical device designed to quickly and easily set a broken limb while out in the field. Shortly before the Boonta Eve Classic, Anakin Skywalker applied a quick-seal splint to the leg of an injured Tusken Raider the boy discovered on the edge of the Dune Sea.

Scan Grid

A device designed to analyze metals. Scan grids emit electrical charges to gather data from their subjects. Although never meant for use on organics, Darth Vader used a Cloud City scan grid to torture Han Solo.

Spineray

A multifunctional Yuuzhan Vong bioengineered creature that can interface with the nervous systems of most organisms. Useful in medical and postoperative analysis, tracer spinerays evaluate the condition of organic tissues and can determine an organism's physiological balance. A tracer spineray can also inflict pain, although this is more often the domain of the provoker spineray used to torture victims by targeting and inciting individual nerve endings.

Trace-breather Cartridge

A life-support device that provides small quantities of breathable gas over long periods of time. Trace-breather cartridges are not a complete substitute for a breathable atmosphere but are typically used in environments that are beginning to collapse.

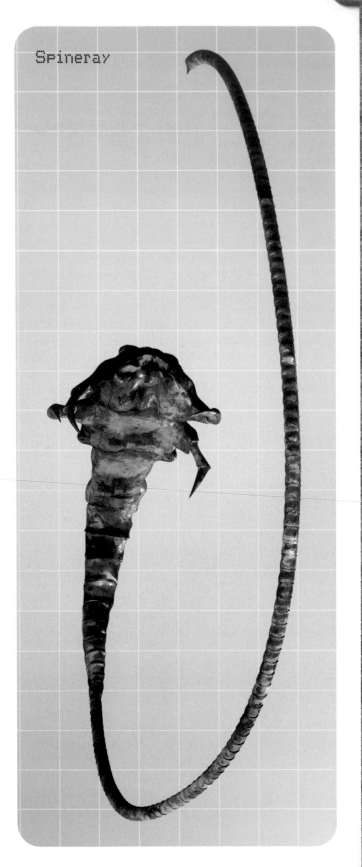

Spineray

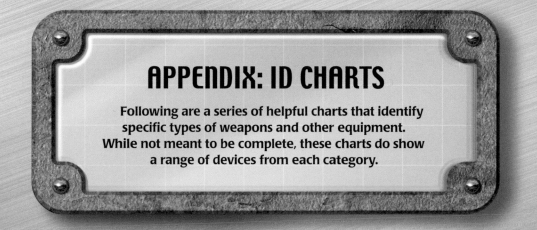

APPENDIX: ID CHARTS

Following are a series of helpful charts that identify specific types of weapons and other equipment. While not meant to be complete, these charts do show a range of devices from each category.

Blaster Pistol ID Chart

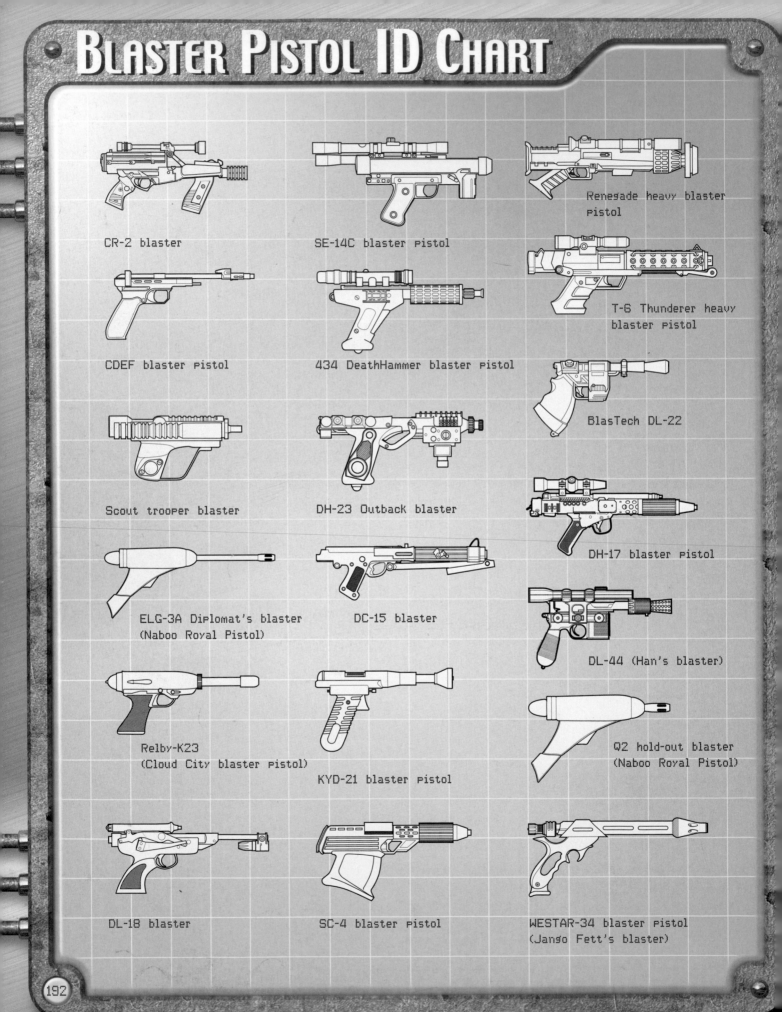

CR-2 blaster

SE-14C blaster pistol

Renegade heavy blaster pistol

CDEF blaster pistol

434 DeathHammer blaster pistol

T-6 Thunderer heavy blaster pistol

Scout trooper blaster

DH-23 Outback blaster

BlasTech DL-22

ELG-3A Diplomat's blaster (Naboo Royal Pistol)

DC-15 blaster

DH-17 blaster pistol

Relby-K23 (Cloud City blaster pistol)

KYD-21 blaster pistol

DL-44 (Han's blaster)

Q2 hold-out blaster (Naboo Royal Pistol)

DL-18 blaster

SC-4 blaster pistol

WESTAR-34 blaster pistol (Jango Fett's blaster)

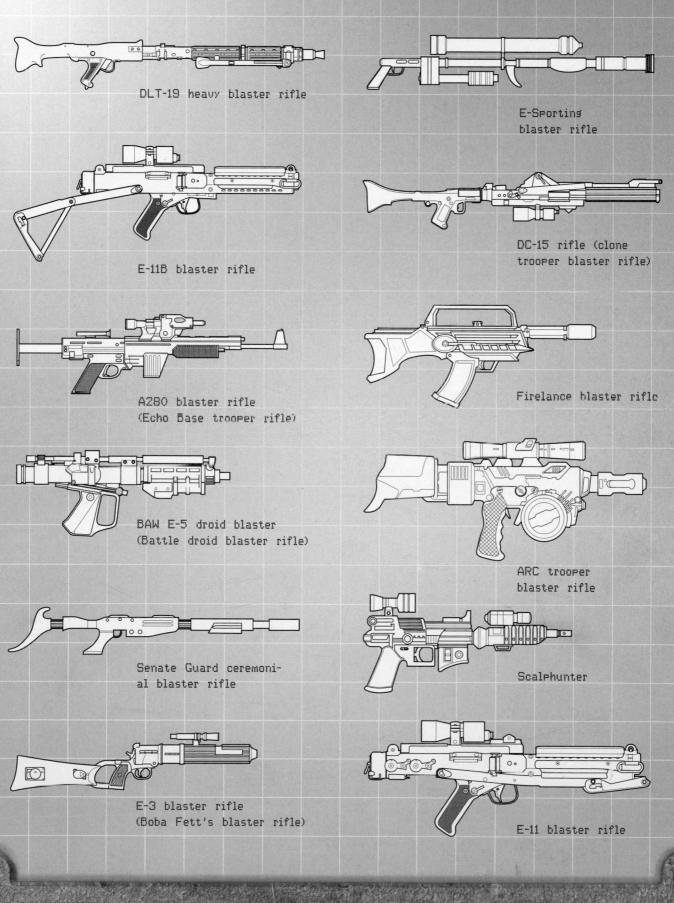

DLT-19 heavy blaster rifle

E-Sporting blaster rifle

E-11B blaster rifle

DC-15 rifle (clone trooper blaster rifle)

A280 blaster rifle (Echo Base trooper rifle)

Firelance blaster rifle

BAW E-5 droid blaster (Battle droid blaster rifle)

ARC trooper blaster rifle

Senate Guard ceremonial blaster rifle

Scalphunter

E-3 blaster rifle (Boba Fett's blaster rifle)

E-11 blaster rifle

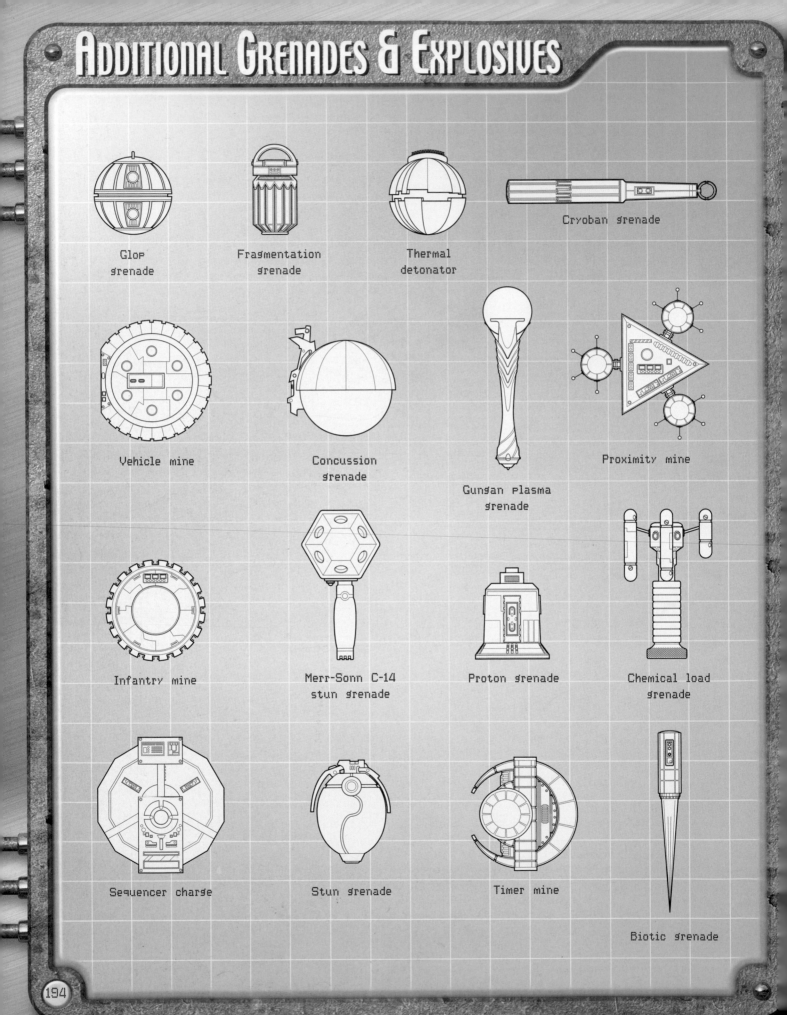

Glop grenade

Fragmentation grenade

Thermal detonator

Cryoban grenade

Vehicle mine

Concussion grenade

Gungan plasma grenade

Proximity mine

Infantry mine

Merr-Sonn C-14 stun grenade

Proton grenade

Chemical load grenade

Sequencer charge

Stun grenade

Timer mine

Biotic grenade

LIGHTSABERS

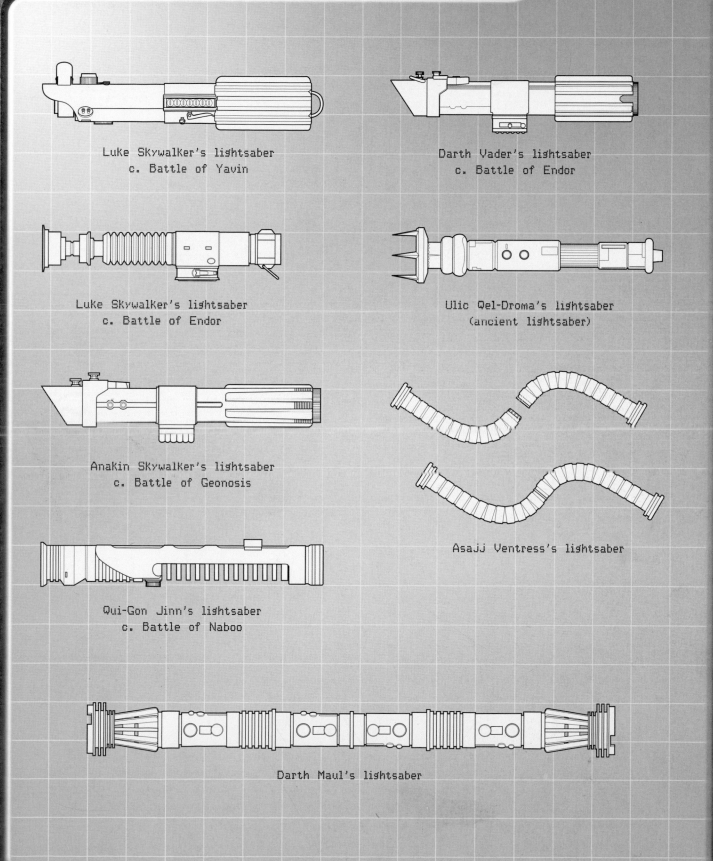

Luke Skywalker's lightsaber
c. Battle of Yavin

Darth Vader's lightsaber
c. Battle of Endor

Luke Skywalker's lightsaber
c. Battle of Endor

Ulic Qel-Droma's lightsaber
(ancient lightsaber)

Anakin Skywalker's lightsaber
c. Battle of Geonosis

Asajj Ventress's lightsaber

Qui-Gon Jinn's lightsaber
c. Battle of Naboo

Darth Maul's lightsaber

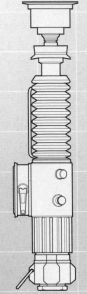

Obi-Wan Kenobi's
lightsaber
c. Battle of Yavin

Obi-Wan Kenobi's
lightsaber
c. Battle of Naboo

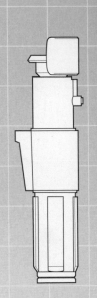

Yoda's
lightsaber

Count Dooku's
lightsaber

Corran Horn's
lightsaber

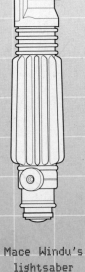

Mace Windu's
lightsaber

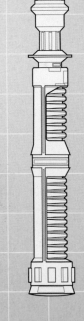

Kyle Katarn's
lightsaber

Exar Kun's
lightsaber

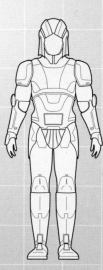

Sith trooper

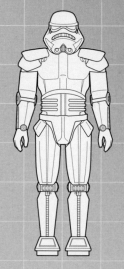

Snowtrooper

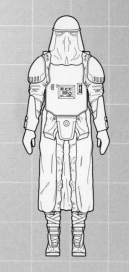

Spacetrooper

Swamp trooper

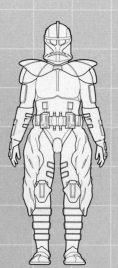

ARC trooper

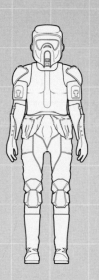

Scout
trooper

Shadow
trooper

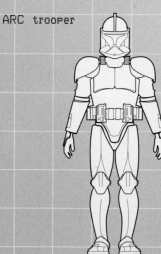

Clone trooper
c. Battle of Geonosis

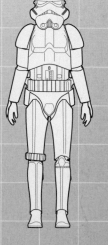

Stormtrooper

About the Author

W. Haden Blackman is the author of *The Field Guide to North American Monsters, The Field Guide to North American Hauntings,* and *Star Wars: The New Essential Guide to Vehicles and Vessels.* He has also worked extensively with the *Star Wars* universe on a variety of video game and comic book projects, including Dark Horse Comics' *Jango Fett: Open Seasons,* LucasArts' *Star Wars Galaxies: An Empire Divided,* and *The Ruins of Dantooine,* the first novel based on *Star Wars Galaxies.*

About the Illustrator

Ian Fullwood lives and works in Herefordshire, England, and has clients both at home and in the USA.
With more than fifteen years' experience in technical illustration and commercial art, he works with a range of clients, which include publishing and engineering companies. He produces a variety of work ranging from science fiction to product visualizing and animation.
Ian uses traditional drawing skills combined with computer programs—Illustrator, Photoshop, and Lightwave 3D—to produce technically demanding and visually exciting pieces of work. Visit *www.if3d.com* for more visual indigestion!